DIE BÄCKEREI

A tale of rare courage and resistance in Hitler's Germany
and a prologue to our 21st century stories

C H A R L E S
B I R M I N G H A M

Die Bäckerei

The Cider Circle Press—Laguna Beach, CA

ISBN: 978-1-66788-453-0
ISBN eBook: 978-1-66788-454-7

Die Bäckerei | Charles Birmingham

Available Formats: eBook | Paperback distribution

Editorial Services provided by Eagle Eye Editing and Upholstery Services, Laguna Beach, CA and

Martin Sauter, Ph.D., Berlin, Germany

DEDICATION

To the heroes of the German Resistance to
the Third Reich, who embodied 2 Corinthians 5:7,
We walk by faith, not by sight.

FOREWORD

However much the plays and the masks on the world's stage may change, it is always the same actors who appear. We sit together and talk and grow excited, and our eyes glitter and our voices grow shriller: just so did others sit and talk a thousand years ago: it was the same thing, and it was the same people: and it will be just so a thousand years hence. The contrivance which prevents us from perceiving this is time.

Arthur Schopenhauer
1788 - 1860

TABLE OF CONTENTS

CHOREG

VOLLKORNBROT

LEBKUCHEN

THE BREAD OF SORROWS

MANNA

CHOREG

I. VIA DOLOROSA - 1920

On a brilliantly sunny Easter Monday, the Captain of the King's 11th Hussars sat astride his charger on a Southern spur of the Tarsus mountains knee to knee with his counterpart, a Captain of the French Dragoons who stroked the withers of his skittish bay stallion. From their vantage point on the high ridge, the Captain of the 11th Hussars admired two enormous white eagles with wingspans as long as he was tall as they circled overhead blithely riding the wind before swooping precipitously toward the broad plain below.

He turned his attention back to the thousands of poor souls slithering toward him through a narrow valley pass from the direction of Marash to the Northwest. They reminded him of a serpent with shimmering scales that snaked as far as the eye could see toward the blue-gray contours of the Almonos Mountains in the Eastern haze.

It was bloody awful business, the Captain of the 11th Hussars mumbled to himself as he surveyed with binoculars the large coastal plain with its rich, loamy soil and patchwork of small farms and large fruit groves. Alas, the thrashing the French took in the siege of Marash, their likely withdrawal from the region altogether and ceaseless Kemalist incursions had yet again shattered Armenian aspirations for an autonomous homeland in the region.

It was 1920, and it had not been that long since measures were taken to repopulate Asia Minor with survivors of the Armenian Genocide of 1915 after the defeat of the Ottoman Empire in the Great War. More than 180,000 Armenian refugees, the majority of whom had originally come from this region, had been repatriated to their ancestral home.

But that was then, a period alight with hope. The Armenian population had been forced in recent weeks to turn heel yet again to face a long march and mortal danger in search of safe ground in the newly French-mandated State of Aleppo in Northern Syria, a fortnight's march to the East.

During the period of the first genocide in 1915, 1.5 million Armenians were systematically exterminated, most in caravans of starving men, women and children, many of whom marched naked or nearly so for days until they dropped dead in the searing heat. Those who stopped to rest were shot or bayoneted by Turkish gendarmes impatient with the brave and tenacious efforts of their prisoners to survive one more day.

Young Armenian men, many of them having served bravely in the Turkish Army in the Great War, were tied together in bundles of four, ten or twenty and were then riddled with rifle and machine gun fire by the Turkish *killing squads* or *butcher battalions,* as they were known. And to make matters worse if that were humanly possible, thousands of helpless women and children were placed on boats that were then taken to the middle of the Black Sea and capsized.

Jove, the Captain of the 11th Hussars cursed, there would be no damnable killings on his watch, even if the mission to hold the harassing Turks at bay was *at sixes and sevens. The bloody tossers*, he mumbled to no one in particular, *worse than the Huns*.

The job would fall to his own battalion deployed hastily to bolster two regiments of French Dragoons all in saddle and deprived of armored cars, air support, heavy artillery and even wireless transmitters. It was a finger in an unsteady dike, a cock-up like Marash, he fumed.

He lifted a gloved hand, eyes now focused on the horizon, and a young subaltern awkwardly pushed his horse forward through the ranks. The wind on the precipice whipped harshly about them throttling the spoken word, *Leftenant, it would appear that a number of our sheep have strayed, and a group now heads toward a stand of trees in the distance framed by a scrum of rocky hills. There, to the North-Northeast of our bearing.*

What is worse, I fear, there are visitors coming from the North, and the Captain of the 11th Hussars pointed to a cloud of dust on the far horizon moving steady toward the very same point.

That can mean only one thing. Dispatch two squadrons immediately to deter our Kemalist friends, he commanded.

The Captain of the 11th Hussars was no stranger to the misery writ large before him. At the Second Battle of Ypres in April 1915, his regiment along with the 2nd Dragoon Guards had conducted a bloody cavalry charge at the Huns capturing eight of their big guns at Néry. Later his squadron retraced its path, as was its custom, to collect their dead comrades or what little was left of them. At Sailly-Laurette, he himself had led a bayonet assault that took the Germans by surprise only to see his own brother shred by a machine gun moments before victory was assured.

The Captain of the 11th Hussars and his comrades endured all for *God, Country and Honor.* Yet the thread of anchorless souls that wound West to East before him was something altogether different. Its intrinsic perversion assaulted his sense of decency.

He had read English in Oriel College, Oxford as a younger man hoping his future lay in academia before joining the Great War, and the words of Shelley from *Prometheus Unbound* came to mind as he watched a people, a nation, yet again face its uncertain future –

No change, no pause, no hope!
Yet I endure

* * * * *

Hayk had feasted on uncertainty of late in the wake of the cowardly French retreat from Marash. The last 72 hours had been difficult for his father Asdadur and his betrothed Mina as well as his cousin Anya, just 13, who had lost her mother at birth and her father during the Great War.

They were near exhaustion when they took refuge in a large almond grove on the Cilician plain. It was as if the enormous column of men, women and children coming from Marash had slumped to its knees as one, leaving their British and French caretakers the task of regrouping the fractious elements of the column to shield them from marauding Turks.

The family luxuriated under a canopy of almond blossoms whose sweet bouquet ebbed and flowed with the breeze. With the intermittent breeze came sense memories of what it was like once to be human rather than livestock with numbered tags on their ears herded to places and experiences unknown and unwanted.

Hayk was barely 30 but looked decades older. He was a healer having been a medical student before the Great War in which he served in the Armenian Legion as a medical officer under the great British General Allenby in Palestine.

Hayk walked with a pronounced limp, a battlefield insult visited upon him at the battle of Meggado, where Armenian Legionnaires would find the enemy trenches filled with dead and dying Turks. Those who hung onto life proved to be the most unfortunate. The memory of the horrors visited on their Armenian countrymen in 1915 was so fresh in the minds of Hayk's comrades, the thirst for revenge so profound, there was no need for a medical officer because the wounded Turks were finished in their trenches.

Hayk earned a medal of valor at Meggado for repeatedly pulling his wounded comrades to safety from no man's land under heavy fire. It had been presented to him by Allenby himself.

Hayk's bravery in Palestine under Allenby would later earn him the role of medical staff officer under General Querette at the divisional headquarters of the French army in Adana. Querrette would throw Hayk head long into the task of organizing a response to the immediate medical needs of the 180,000 Armenians during their repatriation to the region.

And like his father, Asdadur, who had barely survived the genocide in 1915, Hayk would learn that great nationalist movements require a scapegoat against which their "greatness" could be falsely measured. In Hayk's time, it was the new Turkish Nationalist Movement that decimated Armenian hopes in Cilicia like a rapidly moving wildfire ignited in this instance by Mustafa Kemal Pasha known to his friends and enemies alike as simply Atatürk.

Was it the age-old enmity between Islam and Armenian Christians, the suspicions about Armenian allegiance to the Russian foe, or the resentment of local tribes to a community better educated and seemingly wealthier? Did it matter? At the rotting core of Atatürk's nationalism was anger concealed by a painted clown's face.

Hayk had been present in Marash just days before when the damnable Turkish police chief, Toğuz, had lit the powder keg with a single gunshot signaling the start of the current insurrection after a meeting with other Muslim leaders. When the small garrison of French soldiers there came under attack, Hayk and several members of the French Armenian Legion disguised themselves as Muslims to cross the battle lines seeking reinforcements from the French garrison in Adana.

He was as astonished as anyone when the leader of Querrette's relief column which rescued the beleaguered French garrison in Marash ordered the complete evacuation of the French military in the area. This was a dagger to the heart of Armenian independence that spurred roving Turkish mobs to throw kerosene-doused rags on Armenian homes and churches.

On that terrible day, Hayk worked round the clock to evacuate wounded Armenians who had gathered at the Catholic Cathedral in Marash. At one point, he led 300 of his countrymen to the tenuous refuge offered by the American relief workers in the hills nearby. There by happenstance he was reunited with his father and Mina for the first time since his return to Cilicia on Querrette's staff.

Their reunion was bittersweet and all too brief because Hayk returned immediately to Marash with his small group of Armenian legionnaires to retrieve more of his wounded countrymen who were still trapped in the Catholic Cathedral. On the outskirts of the ravaged city, the group encountered other legionnaires fleeing the city who told them to turn back. When the 2,000 Armenian civilians still sheltering in the Cathedral attempted to follow the last of the retreating French, they said, every single one of them had been cut down by Turkish rifle and machine gun fire.

All conventions of decency and morality had crumbled as the Turks and their Kurdish allies made life as miserable as possible for everyone including the American relief workers who tended to their Armenian neighbors. The hastily arranged mass exodus from Marash with the guarantee of safety from the additional British and French military units rushed to the area had been the only viable option.

Safe for the moment in the cool shade of the almond grove, Hayk and his family could rest. They had nothing but the clothes on their backs and a few possessions but against all logic they counted their blessings.

Asdadur, the patriarch of the family and proud father of a veritable war hero in Palestine, had been a notary in his professional life, which in that time was a position of stature that fell somewhere between a public official and a private lawyer. Asdadur had named his son after Hayk the Great, the legendary warrior and father of the Armenian nation who slew the wicked giant Bel to deliver his people from its tyranny. It was a noble, hopeful story that he wished would inspire his son and guide him at a time when the Turks had picked up the cudgel of Bel to wield yet again against his people.

Asdadur had also relished telling his young son stories of the First Crusade, claiming that his family could trace its line back to 1080 when the great king Ruben founded in the heart of the Cilician Taurus a small principality that he expanded into the Armenian Kingdom of Cilicia. This Christian kingdom, surrounded by Muslim states hostile to its existence, prospered for over 300 years.

In that glorious period, Armenians would fight shoulder to shoulder with the Crusaders and trade with the great commercial cities of Italy. Hayk had been recruited to the Armenian Legion with the promise that his people would one day return to the greatness that had once marked the Armenian Kingdom of Cilicia.

Soon after Hayk left for training in Egypt during the Great War, Asdadur was removed from his post as a magistrate in the Marash district, betrayed by the governor general of his province, who was a disciple of the *Young Turks* who preceded the Kemalists as the ruling power in the Ottoman Empire. Asdadur himself had hailed the Young Turks when they deposed the old and decadent Sultan Abdul Hamid with the promise of reforms *to make the Ottoman Empire great again*.

However, the Young Turks proved to be a ship adrift, a political force devoid of moral ballast seeking power for power's sake. For one contrived reason or another, the real energy that would fuel this movement's hold on power would come from the extermination of a common enemy, the Armenian population, through subterfuge and surprise.

Many in the political elite approved of the pogrom. Just as many were appalled by the tactics of their leaders but looked the other way to preserve their privileged lives.

Asdadur was conscripted soon after his dismissal as magistrate along with younger, non-Muslim soldiers who were transferred from combat units to provide logistical support in labor battalions. Transferring Armenian conscripts to passive, unarmed logistical units would set the wheels in motion for the horrors soon to follow. Asdadur was no fool and, amidst reports that entire units of these Armenian conscripts had simply vanished, he managed to escape to the hills first to fight with Armenian rebels supported by the Russians and then to help the American relief workers.

If Hayk, Mina and young Anya were emerging as the hope for the family's future, Asdadur stood as the guardian of its dignity. He would often muse about the age's old enmity between Christian Armenians and Islam and tell anyone willing to listen, *you cannot help but wonder if it is not our inheritance from Cain that some essential part of our souls was taken from us and, as a result, we are all subject to this lunacy of believing that whole races or nations are uniformly good or uniformly evil.*

For Asdadur, to be a refugee once again, cast off in the wilderness by those who could not control their impulse to destroy him and his people, was like being cut to the bone. It was an open wound that had been aggravated again and again over the years.

Asdadur was a man of faith who liked to say *the deeper the cut, the deeper one's faith*. Not all of his countrymen would agree with him, nor was it a particularly easy sell to Hayk and Mina. But it was in such faith that he found a sense of dignity for himself and his family. And it was such faith, he admonished, that separated one from becoming a soulless animal.

In the balmy shade of the almond grove, Hayk watched Anya dote on the aging Asdadur and thought to himself that she would make a fine physician. She was smart, brave and resolute. Her passion for helping others was unshakeable even in this time when their Kemalists tormentors would not think twice about raping, hanging or crucifying her.

She was tall for her age with short boyish hair that belied the fact that she was fast becoming a woman. It struck him that she was the earthly expression of her namesake, Anahid, the Armenian Goddess of wisdom, healing and, how fittingly at that moment, water. Hayk hoped her mythical lineage would count for something in their search for sustenance, and indeed it soon would.

Anya's relationship with her cousin Hayk was closer to one of brother-sister or father-daughter. She was a sponge that absorbed everything Hayk said and did. She tried to imitate his furrowed brow when solving a problem, his easy humor with those who needed encouragement and the way he deftly juggled humility and self confidence in difficult circumstances.

In the shade of the Almond grove now with the horrors of Marash behind them if not the threat of more to come from the Turks, it had been agreed that Hayk and Anya would set off to find sustenance in the jagged, rock strewn hills nearby. At the very least, there had to be a spring with fresh water, they hoped. So, Hayk and Anya trudged hand in hand toward the hills that were roughly a kilometer away and awash in the glare of an afternoon sun descending from its zenith toward the western horizon.

Nestled in these rocky hills was a large and ragged stand of trees. Hayk and Anya made it to the tree line without incident and, once they had invaded the shadowy world beyond, were surprised to find that the earth began to fall sharply away under their feet. They slipped and slid their way down to a small gorge concealed from above by fallen trees, brush and bramble.

They had come to a clearing of sorts when they heard the rustling of an unseen animal and then not one but many. Hayk grabbed Anya and pulled her away from the source of the rustling and positioned himself between Anya and the threat in such a way as they now stood back-to-back.

And in the beat of her now thumping heart, Anya found herself staring at two rangy, bearded men, Muslims she thought, who had emerged from the brush. One was holding what looked like an old flintlock pistol while the other threatened them with a raised scimitar, which he swirled above his head and theirs with the fluid motion of a warrior.

Hayk had not fared much better and was confronted by a larger group whose leader, a boy barely older than Anya, challenged him gruffly. Hayk explained their predicament and, after some hesitation and whispered consultation with his henchmen, the boy motioned to Hayk and Anya to follow them. Having little choice in the matter, Hayk and Anya did as told under the watchful gaze of ten pairs of suspicious eyes.

In short order, Hayk and Anya arrived with their entourage of surly young men at a large encampment hidden in a gorge about 25 meters below the level of the plain from whence they had just descended. On the outskirts of the camp, which was swarming with young and old, there were wooden lean-to's but, as they went deeper into the encampment, they found a more substantial network of tents.

At the farthest reach of the gorge on higher ground under a canopy of parasol pines there stood a handful of larger, more ornate tents. They reminded Hayk of the richly illustrated storybooks his father had given him depicting the Crusades and the magnificent encampments of the brave knights who fought in them.

Dôme épais, le jasmin, this place is Utopia, Hayk mused in wonderment, a beautiful respite from the horrors on the plain above them. Had it not been for the fact that they were the captives of a group of seemingly unfriendly Muslims, the sworn enemies of his kind, all would have been well.

Hayk suspected that this group was part of a larger contingent of semi-nomadic Muslims who worked the large fruit groves in the region. It struck him that it was a fairly relaxed and informal assemblage. The men generally wore simple white cotton shirts over their *Serwers*, the loose-fitting white pants worn by working class Muslims.

He found the informality of the relationships between the men and women especially surprising. Those women who had reached adolescence wore a simple *Hijab* along with a work-a-day *Salwar Kameez*. These were simple cotton trousers of white or tan like the men over which they wore a long tunic.

The boy deposited them brusquely in an area of the camp where the cooking was done and said, *sit. My name is Ahmad. My father will arrive to deal with you shortly*. Ahmad could not keep his eyes off Anya, who careened emotionally between anger and apprehension at the terrifying uncertainty of what would come next, tinged by curiosity at the attention paid to her by her young and handsome captor.

As Ahmad left, presumably to summon his father, several women of the encampment arrived with water and nourishment. Hayk and Anya were given a meat stew with lentils and spices accompanied by a stack of *Nan*, the Muslim flat bread, along with *Firni*, a sweet rice pudding to which almonds and apricots had been added. Hayk could not have imagined a meal at the Ritz in London nor even at the Topkapi Palace in Istanbul being any finer under the circumstances.

Soon thereafter, Ahmad's father arrived and greeted Hayk and Anya warmly with the traditional greeting reserved for those of the Mohammedan faith, *As-Salam-u-Alaikum* (Peace be unto you) and Hayk countered with a surprise of his own from his days tending to wounded Arabs in Palestine, *Wa-Alaikumussalam wa-Rahmatullah* (*May the peace, mercy, and blessings of Allah be upon you*).

Ahmad's father, both impressed and bemused by Hayk's knowing response, introduced himself as Al-Bari, although Hayk took it more as a title than a name as it meant *Maker of Order*. Al-Bari was a relatively young man with a groomed black beard.

Al-Bari had arrived with a much older man with a long, unkempt white beard whose attire suggested that he was an important elder. Al-Bari was dressed much like the other men in camp, but the older man wore an ornate *Bisht*, an ankle length robe of brown with an embroidered hem held in place at the waist by a green sash.

Hayk and Anya had risen from their meal out of respect for the arrival of the two leaders. Al-Bari smiled and said, in turn, *sit friends. Let us get to know one another better*. Hayk and Anya thanked Al-Bari and somewhat self-consciously sat again. The older man softly admonished both to continue with their meals.

Al-Bari did indeed introduce the older man as a dervish whom they called Baba and, at this point, Hayk finally came to the realization of just how lucky he and Anya had been. This was an encampment of Bektashi Muslims, a Sufi-Shi'ite sect, which like other Sufi's practiced a form of Islamic mysticism and Baba, it turned out, was the spiritual guide of an extended clan that did indeed work the farms and groves on the Cilician plain.

Like many Sufi sects, the Bektashi's were iconoclasts and one of their eccentricities was a lax adherence to Muslim laws and rituals. For example, women as well as men took part in ritual wine drinking and dancing during devotional ceremonies, thus the origin of the term *whirling dervish*. Some Bektashi's had even adapted such Christian practices as the ritual sharing of bread and the confession of sins.

Al-Bari began the conversation by saying, *we are simple people who work the Almond groves in Cilicia, you have nothing to fear from us. It is perhaps our greatest gift from God that we look inward, we call it 'zahir,' rather than outward for spiritual guidance. This has delivered us from the intolerance that strangles the hearts of so many of our brothers in Islam.*

Al-Bari quizzed Hayk about the current conditions above them on the plain and listened gravely as Hayk described the mass exodus from Marash. Al-Bari explained, *we toil in the nearby fields and have been forced to stay in hiding while the latest madness runs its course.*

After some time, the serving women arrived with an amber colored bottle of a liquid which Al-Bari called *Raki*, an alcoholic drink, usually flavored with anise seed, along with a small jug of spring water. Al-Bari directed the women to put a small amount of the liquid from the amber bottle into earthen cups into which Baba then somewhat ceremoniously poured a small amount of spring water. The cool spring water turned the liquid a milky-white color, similar to the louche of absinthe. He offered the drink to Hayk and a similar cup containing only water to Anya.

Please join us, Al-Bari said to Hayk raising his cup in a gesture that reminded Hayk of a priest raising a chalice. Noticing Anya staring at the Raki, the Baba said, *we call this drink 'aslan sütü' or in your way of speaking lion's milk, but it is not the kind of milk we give our young. It is instead sustenance for those of us with age who aspire to wisdom because Aslan the Lion is a symbol of strength in our language as it is in yours, so we call this drink, 'the milk of the strong.'*

Baba, as if to console Anya for her partial exclusion from this ritual, added, *you know, we Bektashi also admire good poetry, song and humor*. And indeed, the telling of jokes and humorous tales was an important part of the sect's culture and teachings. These stories frequently poked fun at conventional religious views by portraying the Bektashi dervish as blithely non-conformist.

The Baba persevered with Anya. *May I tell you one such tale,* he said. Anya smiled and said *of course, I would like that.* The Baba continued, *a Bektashi, one of us that is, was praying in the mosque. While those around him were praying 'May God grant me faith,' he muttered 'May God grant me plenty of wine.' The imam heard him and was terribly upset and asked him angrily why instead of asking for faith like everyone else, he was asking God for something sinful. The Bektashi replied, 'Well, everyone asks for what they don't have.'*

This drew a laugh from Anya and the group. Ahmad, who had hovered above the group, then tried his hand at it, also directing the story to Anya, *a Bektashi was a passenger in a rowing boat traveling from Eminönü to Üsküdar in the waters of Istanbul. When a storm blew up, the boatman tried to reassure him by saying 'Fear not—God is great!' The Bektashi replied, 'Yes, God is great, but the boat is small!'*

Again, the group laughed as one and Anya applauded the self-satisfied Ahmad, who had shown a less stern side of himself in delivering the joke almost as well as Baba. Al-Bari abruptly changed the subject, *it grows dark, and you should rest. We will wake you at midnight. Our tormentors will be fast asleep by then after a day of marauding. The moon will arrive one hour after midnight, and it will guide you back across the plain to your people.*

As Al-Bari and Baba made ready to leave, the elder who seemed to be deep in thought turned to Anya and held out his hands, *may I,* was all he said.

Any, not quite sure of what to do next, tentatively held her hands out to the Baba, which he took as he closed his eyes. The interlude felt like an eternity to Hayk but in truth it lasted barely a minute.

Baba opened his eyes to look at Anya with an expression that shimmered like a flame, at one moment grave, the next seemingly content with something visible only to his mind's eye. *Let me share an old verse with you that we Bektashi learn as we arrive of age,* he said. *It will help you in the years ahead, although its meaning may not be apparent to you at this very moment:*

Water that's poured inside will sink the boat.
While water underneath keeps it afloat.
That sealed jar in the stormy sea out there
Floats on the waves because it's full of air,
When your soul has the air of grace inside
You'll float above the world and there abide.

* * * * *

Hayk and Anya left at the appointed time weighed down by a large skin of water and a meal wrapped in cloth. Before ascending to the plain led by Ahmad, Al-Bari and Baba arrived to send them off with the appropriate Salaam's. Al-Bari added, addressing himself to Hayk, *I hope, friend, that we someday meet again on a plane where there are no strangers and therefore no tears.*

And with that Hayk and Anya were on the move. Ahmad deftly led them uphill in the faint moonlight through the series of blind turns and natural tunnels in the underbrush they had used on their descent.

As if to herald their arrival at the point on the plain where they had first entered the exotic world below, they could hear the call of an owl which Ahmad deftly answered with the rasping screech of a night hawk. Ahmad let Hayk and Anya know that there were riders in the area and that they would wait until the riders were well clear of the mouth of the gorge.

They waited – Hayk impatiently and Anya with her stoic strength and resolve. Ahmad finally gave them the go ahead and then disappeared into the brush as abruptly as he had appeared the day before.

Hayk and Anya emerged from the large rock formation onto the plain. He said a silent prayer of thanks that there was a waxing moon which lit the way toward the shimmering Almond blossoms of the cultivated grove of Almond trees some distance off where they would reunite with Mina and his father.

* * * * *

An imam was preaching about the evils of alcohol and asked, 'If you put a pail of water and a pail of Raki in front of a donkey, which one will he drink from?' A Bektashi in the congregation immediately answered. 'The water!' 'Indeed," said the imam, "and why is that?' 'Because he's an ass.'

Anya had just shared the last of her repertoire of Bektashi jokes with her grandfather and Mina to uproarious laughter. How much easier it was to appreciate humor on a full stomach!

Hayk and Anya's return to the Almond grove early that morning had been uneventful but for an encounter with a group of British Hussars commanded by an impressive captain who sat high and straight in the saddle and who expressed his displeasure at finding Hayk and Anya so far from the column.

Hayk managed to navigate the situation having by happenstance seen the glint of a service medal from the Palestine campaign worn by the burly sergeant major at the Captain's side. One dropped name led to another and the sergeant-major obligingly pulled his former comrade up on his mount as did the Captain with Anya, and the 11th Hussars supplied a rather fine escort indeed back to the Almond grove.

The British cavalrymen warned Hayk that he and his family needed to return to the column soon after sunrise for the modicum of safety it could provide. The column would be on the move by dawn the following day and with that the 11th Hussars saluted Hayk respectfully and rode off to continue their round-up of stray souls.

After their sumptuous breakfast feast, Anya's vivid account of the adventure among the Bektashi, and her rendition of Bektashi humor, a family council was held. The family had carried with them from Marash several large, exquisitely braided, and seasoned loaves of *Choreg*, the traditional Easter bread of the Armenian people.

It was said of Michelangelo, the great Renaissance painter and sculptor, that he could see the living form before he freed it from a block of marble. Mina, an artist in her own realm, could breathe life into the smooth and elastic dough to transform it into a loaf of *Choreg*.

In good times, which might be loosely defined as times when she and her Armenian countrymen were not directly under the Turkish gun, there would be a good-natured competition among Armenian families to create the most sublime loaves of this iconic, yeast laden bread as the celebration of Easter approached. Mina would rarely lose this competition.

The exquisite sculpture of her loaves, three braided ropes of dough representing the Trinity, filigreed with sesame seed, drew gasps of awe. The aroma of her loaves dominated by the potent and intoxicating perfume of *Mahleb*, the dried heart of a sour cherry pit, was legend in the community.

Mina's secret other than strict adherence to her mother's dictum, *do not be afraid of the dough*, was the ability to intertwine her will with the yeast itself. She seduced the yeast like a snake charmer with a cobra and bent the dough to her will as once Scheherazade had done with her Sultan, producing not a thing but a life force whose fragrance bound people to a community and a community to generations past and future.

Good flour and unadulterated wheat were in short supply in Cilicia because of Turkish embargoes. Some in the community were compelled to supplement their scarce supplies with ersatz ingredients like sawdust or worse.

Mina faced with the same challenges addressed them more creatively with a dough substantiated from whatever good wheat was available along with dried and ground almond blossoms, almond gum, almond seeds, cornflowers and the leaves of the black walnut. When one pondered the *je ne sais quoi* in the taste and texture of a new loaf, Mina would leave the answer a delicious mystery.

Then it should have come as no surprise that it was Mina who first broached the subject of a return to the Bektashi with three loaves of the family's precious *Choreg*, baked in the American camp just before they were forced to flee. Indeed, Mina had fled with only the clothes on her back and a silver locket given to her as a child by her mother so she could transport as many loaves of *Choreg* as she could carry.

Sides were drawn, arguments eloquently delivered, rhetorical points scored and dashed, but no démarche was achieved. It was Mina and Anya on one side of the argument and Asdadur and Hayk on the other, although in truth, Hayk was secretly on Mina's side and was of little real help to Asdadur.

Mina argued it was their obligation to return to the camp to thank the Bektashi with no less than three loaves to symbolize the Trinity. Asdadur forcefully countered, *there is danger all around us*, he said, *this must be the time to think about ourselves.*

Mina and Anya's urgent response rose sharply like a bouquet of angry pheasant cocked from its refuge. *These are people no better off than we who shared what little they had with total strangers, not to say Fakirs – beggars – and what is worse, unbelievers*, Mina said for both of them.

Asdadur and Hayk began to feel like two hapless swimmers being carried away from the shoreline by a moral riptide they could not overcome. Anya who had in her early youth been more likely than not to skip her catechism classes to run wild and free through the hills with the other children pushed still further, *in the book of Exodus, are we not reminded that when the Jews were lost and starving in the desert, God fed them with manna? The Bektashi broke bread with us, and we must repay them in kind. We were lost and starving, and they fed us.*

But Anya, dearest, it is too risky. Consider all that is going on around us, Asdadur countered.

My dearest Asdi, a term of endearment used by family and close friends with Asdadur, *if we are only to face tests that are easy and painless, then what kind of Christians will we become? Did our Lord die eating sweets in a warm bed?*

Anya had delivered the *coup de grace* compelling both for its vivid logic and its irrefutability. Asdadur and Hayk, vanquished, simply looked at each other throwing up their hands, although Hayk was secretly happy that in the end they had come around to Mina's point of view.

It was then the family decision was taken to have Hayk and Anya leave post-haste with the loaves of Choreg. Mina and Asdadur would wait to return to the column until Hayk and Anya returned from the hidden valley.

They set out in the late afternoon to leave enough sunlight to make it to the Bektashi camp before dusk. They would leave their tribute with the Bektashi and again use the light of the waxing moon to return to the Almond grove. The British were intent on mobilizing the fractious elements of the refugee column at dawn the next morning, so there was little time to spare.

No one seemed to notice two individuals wandering off seemingly to forage for food, two among many, but their destination was unique, a secret refuge, immune from intrusion, a Neverland full of magic. Anya felt as though she was floating on air at the prospect of seeing Ahmad again.

Hayk and Anya arrived without incident as they and their long shadows, birthed by the afternoon sun in its decline, disappeared into the brush at the top of the gorge. They stopped to survey the plain for several minutes to ensure they had not been followed by foe or friend. Satisfied they were for the moment alone, Hayk and Anya descended through the overgrowth, tentatively at first but with greater alacrity as the terrain grew steeper and familiar landmarks appeared – an ancient tree trunk at eternal rest on its side, a creeping juniper that looked like a large octopus with long, uneven tentacles.

They could see the clearing several meters ahead where they had first encountered Ahmad and his band, and it was at this point that both Hayk and Anya began to sense that something was amiss. For Anya, it was a young sapling off to her right that had very recently been snapped in two, the clear sap from the exposed pulp still dripping fresh. And there was the lush bramble to the left that had covered the ground like a thick blanket that was now trampled in some parts and missing altogether in others.

For Hayk, sense memories crept up on him and he felt a cold hand on his shoulder, a sensation that flowed icily to the nape of his neck making his hair stand on end. A knot in his stomach moved upwards to become a pounding in his chest.

The air had turned heavy and gray as they reached the small clearing where they had first encountered Ahmad, overwhelming the Spring perfume of this tangled but verdant garden. *Meggado! Fire and flesh!* Hayk's thoughts came in a jumble as the acrid smell of battle and the wicked incense of the vanquished reached them both.

An unseen force compelled Hayk and Anya onward. They followed the sloping terrain toward the Bektashi camp as the vile smoke trapped by the overgrowth in the glen thickened now with each step.

Two steps to the left to circumnavigate a boulder, a steeply sloping path to the right that tested their agility, and the lower branches of a spruce tree swept back by Anya at the edge of the next clearing revealed what could have been the threshold of Hell.

The sweet and savory stench of death carried by the dense black smoke swirling around them hit them full on like a crashing wave. Hayk put his hand on Anya's shoulder to keep her close, but she shrugged him off moving forward to inspect the ravaged Bektashi camp without apparent emotion.

To their right toward the cooking sheds, sagging awkwardly to one side was a large bundle. As Hayk and Anya moved toward it, it became apparent that bundled here were Bektashi men – four men wide and six deep, shoulder to shoulder, bound at the knees and chest. Asdadur, who had lived through the peak of the Turkish massacres of his countrymen years before, had described the technique to Hayk.

The perpetrators of this horror had tied the men together and marched them as one to this point in the encampment, a parade no doubt to be witnessed by their wives and children. It appeared that gunmen had been stationed on two sides at right angles to riddle the bundle of largely immobile men with rifle fire, enjoying the awkward dance of the dying and the cries of pain and horror of the helpless, until all the men had slumped, tilting the bundle to one side. Now, there was no sound, no movement, no one spared.

Directly ahead, Hayk and Anya were drawn to the encampment's well. Its cylindrical wall was haphazardly constructed of pieces of shale, and, on its rim, they saw two small legs flaring out of a water bucket.

Hayk stopped Anya from going closer and walked to the well's edge to confirm the bucket held the body of an infant that had been dropped head long into it. He looked over the rim into the 20-meter-deep well that had once provided spring water, fresh and clear, to find it filled halfway to the top with more corpses of infants and young children in a grotesque mélange of heads and legs, hands and feet.

Hayk wretched and braced himself against the rough stone of the well, but the die was cast. He and Anya were too stunned to do anything but explore the camp still further, their revulsion subjugated by surging adrenalin. They moved on, no longer feeling human but as vultures must feel, compelled by instinct to circle the dead and dying.

As they approached the back of the camp, what had been an exceptionally large tent off to the left was the principal source of the smoke. The remnants of the tent itself covered a large mound. The bodies of two women who had apparently sought to escape the tent by crawling out from under it lay dead where they had been shot by their tormentors. Hayk and Anya recoiled as one of the dead women twitched from head to toe and twitched again giving the impression that even in death she was still trying to crawl to safety.

This was where the women of the camp had been assembled and dispatched by setting the tent ablaze. Hayk would later learn that the Turks had taken the younger women of the camp to be sold or raped and then left to the beasts.

But it was not until they had reached the deepest point in the gorge bounded by the parasol pine trees that they reached the zenith of Kemalist depravity on that day in this place. These parasol pines, like most of their kind, had one main trunk from which other thick branches flared to the right and left creating a "Y" shaped pedestal to hold its green canopy aloft.

There, three across were Ahmad, Baba and Al-Bari each tied at the neck to the main trunk of one of the trees. Their arms were splayed along the main branches right and left so that they too formed a *Y*. Their hands and feet were nailed to the tree. Baba, who was the centerpiece of the grisly tableau had been crucified upside down, either a studied reference to Saint Peter or a testament simply to the extreme cruelty of the men who had done this.

The three were shirtless, and the Turks had carved the word *Kafir, Heretic,* on each of their chests. A crude sign written in blood on a plank of wood propped against one of the trees read İnanmayanlara Ölüm, *Death to the Unbelievers.*

Anya's knees buckled and she hit the ground hard, her tears flowing freely. She could not speak. She could barely breathe.

She gazed once more at the three crucified men. Hayk knew there was little they could do. He wanted to bury the Bektashi dead, but there were too many and to prioritize two or three would stand as an insult to the rest. The gorge itself must serve as their mausoleum.

It had grown dark, and they both sheltered in the halo of a small torch Hayk had commandeered from the cooking pavilion. He knew they had run out of time. He helped Anya to her feet and the two began to move unsteadily toward the path that would lead them back to the plain and out of Hell.

The climb might have taken hours or just a few minutes. Hayk and Anya were too numb to know. They were operating on instinct now. They fought the urge to think about what they had just seen, to drown in the suffocating pain that washed over them, because to have done otherwise would have been to forfeit their sanity.

Hayk and Anya left the cover of the hidden valley amongst its rocky, once sheltering hills, running, crouched close to the earth, the blood in their ears pounding, a full breath hard to capture. It was then that they heard the clash of hooves on the rocky ground as riders swept around the wooded ridge from the Northeast. Hayk's heart leapt.

The full moon was masked by ragged clouds concealing the identities of the riders, but their allegiance soon became clear. They spoke in the working-class patois of the *Chete*, bands of irregular Turkish and Kurd fighters that had played a central role in the fall of Marash.

There were shouts and curses from the opposite direction as more riders swarmed them joining the first riders on the scene to create a swirling, dusty barrier to Hayk and Anya's escape. One rider moved his horse in such a way as to let its rear flank knock Anya to the ground as she called to Hayk, pleading for help.

Then a rider slammed the back of Hayk's head with his stirrup. Hayk went to the ground dazed, trying desperately to hold on to his senses for Anya's sake. He caught a glimpse of her on her hands and knees looking for some opening in the scrum of men and horses.

As Hayk struggled to his feet, dirt and blood muddying his mouth, another rider hit him on the side of the face with the butt of a whip sending him to the ground again dazed and seeing stars. From the dark well into which his mind now descended, he heard a car or possibly a truck pull up as a man, perhaps the leader of this group, gave a command, *the girl will bring a fine price. Forget the Gavour (Infidel) cripple. Let the dog live with the loss of the girl until the end of his pitiful days.*

II. ALEPPO - 1938

You fool! That which you sow does not come to life unless it dies!

1 CORINTHIANS 15:36

The *Symoon* had arrived early to usher in the Christian celebration of Easter in the French Mandate of Aleppo. The heat of the bone dry desert wind had turned the brilliant sapphire blue of the morning sky gently hugging the earth into a pallid gray gauze that hung so high above the globe one could imagine the stars sitting just beyond.

Under this canopy thin and sere, three opposing sides watched as *Ondatra zibethicus* performed a pirouette in a small pond fed by fresh spring water on the rocky hilltop, one of eight surrounding the old city of Aleppo. The object of their interest would draw its last breath an instant later impaled on the end of a long, sharpened stick wielded by one of the two ragged boys watching with anticipation from the bank.

Because they were factory boys who worked in the sweatshops of Aleppo where shimmering bolts of silk cloth were made, they would not have known this animal as *Ondatra zibethicus* nor as its French derivation *le rat musqué* inasmuch as they were the expendable loose threads of the French Mandate of Aleppo to whom knowledge of a broader, better world was denied. They simply knew the once frolicking muskrat as dinner.

The two were a scrawny six and nine-year-old living lives of grey amidst richly textured cloth in blues and yellows, reds and creams, often adorned with gold and silver colored threads that made them shimmer in the light. The boys were the deadenders of the Silk Road which extended back to a distant time when cities such as Palmyra and Aleppo were critical stopping points on the route between China, India and the Mediterranean ports from which the textiles of Syria, prized by traders and travelers, were shipped to Imperial Rome.

The second of the three opposing sides was a group of three boys. Two were dressed in the knickers, crisp white shirts and bandanas of schoolboys from the French enclave in Aleppo. The third wore the same bandana except the white shirt was worn as a tunic over a chalwar, the loose fitting, ankle length trousers worn by Arabs and was the son of an officer in the Bedouin cavalry that fought alongside the French in the Levant. They were large and seemingly well-fed boys who by contrast to their pencil thin opponents diminished them still further.

They hid in a fold of the hill behind two ancient olive trees and used the fruit the trees had jettisoned to torment the two factory boys, who swatted away the olives thrown at them like mosquitos on a humid day all the while looking for the source of their torment. The schoolboys finally sounded the charge and swarmed the annoyed and bewildered factory boys throwing the nine-year-old into the pond and snatching the stick that still held the muskrat away from the younger boy.

An instant later the third of the three opposing sides engaged. Not amused by the cruel game the schoolboys were playing, a tall and lanky 13-year-old with a mane of disheveled, coal black hair collected a handful of the smooth, cream colored stones that covered his path to the ancient citadel of Aleppo and took the measure of the one he fingered in his right hand.

He had been carrying the daily delivery of bread arranged neatly in the bulging French army duffel bag to the German archeologists working at the citadel of Aleppo when he had come upon the *Battle of le rat musqué* and had placed his valuable cargo carefully against the large bolder that partially concealed his presence. Satisfied that the stone in hand would fly straight and true, he flung it at the largest of the three boys who screeched at the top of his lungs as the small stone found its mark hitting him squarely on the bridge of the nose and knocking him flat on his back.

The crying, screaming agony of the French schoolboy disoriented his two companions. It was barely a minute before the young Bedouin whose broad, square face made a perfect target, took a second stone dead-on cutting his lip and chipping one of his front teeth. Their unseen antagonist was playing for keeps.

The lanky 13-year-old rounded the bolder moving rapidly toward the vanquished schoolboys, arm raised with a third missile at the ready, as two of the schoolboys struggled to pick up the still blubbering first boy hit, who was licking blood from his upper lip, to make their retreat. The two factory boys, who had retrieved the muskrat in the confusion stood mesmerized by the ignominious defeat of their tormentors at the hands of a boy they did not know and who instead of a stone now threw a rounded loaf of bread at them.

The two factory boys brought three pursed fingers to their foreheads in a hasty *Salaam* and disappeared down the far side of the hill. The victorious 13-year-old, henceforth to be a marked man in the French Mandate of Aleppo, continued onward to the citadel with his daily delivery of bread to the German archeologists there.

* * * * *

The striking woman with Bedouin tattoos left conversation, comment, awe, admiration and revulsion in her wake among the denizens of the old city of Aleppo as she made her way first through the elegant stone arcade of the *Khan al-Shouneh* souq, the ancient, covered marketplace near the citadel that had been in continuous operation here since 1542. *Khan al-Shouneh* offered the traveler everything from dried fruit to exquisite Alepine art pieces. Shortly thereafter, she would pass through the *Souq Arslan Dada*, the bustling center of leather and textile trading in the old city at one of the main entrances to the walled old city from the north.

But as rich as these covered markets were with treasure, she barely gave any of it a second glance while the people milling around her could not help but linger on the exotic girl who strode past. It struck the basket maker, who routinely cheated his customers but was otherwise a good man and a good father to his children, that she was quite young and shy.

To the purveyor of dried fruit, nuts and all manner of spice, who was the best purveyor of such things in Aleppo but who was not a good man in any respect (but this is a story for another time), she was well beyond her prime. He saw a woman who was tall, shapely and aloof with a head of dark hair that was nearly shaved but for a thin carpet of bristle that gave her the other-worldly aura that bewitched the purveyor of dried fruit with an amalgam of fear and lust.

She wore the riding clothes of an aristocrat who was not of this place – a white shirt, khaki jodhpurs and riding boots that were caked in mud. Tucked into her belt was a sheath that concealed all but the ornate handle of a large dagger, a curved Bedouin Khanjar, capped by an ivory hilt in the shape of a lion's head.

More notable still were the tattoos – what appeared to be a cross in the customary Bedouin position on the chin as well as the Sufi symbol of a heart held aloft by wings on the back of her right hand. And at the hairline on the nape of her neck, there was what appeared to be a jar afloat on waves, a symbol whose meaning was known only to its bearer.

The striking woman with Bedouin tattoos was preceded by the major domo of one of the finest households in *Alepp*, the shortened form of Aleppo used by its natives, where she and her husband would be guests during their stay. The major domo, a nervous little man, moved at a fast clip changing directions in the Souq's like a frightened mouse in a maze while holding a conversation with himself the entire time.

She was followed at a respectful distance by *Pushpa*, her husband's manservant, in his customary royal blue fez, who reflexively placed his *pince-nez* on his nose to survey the treasures around them only to have it fall off a step later. This fast-moving procession eventually entered the winding alleys of the Christian quarter *Al-Jdayde,* where aristocratic mansions soared into the sky engulfing the procession in dark, stone canyons lit by a bright blue ribbon of sky.

The search today would not be for treasure but for provisions to fill the larder after the arduous journey in the truck convoy from *İskenderun*, Aleppo's main port on the Mediterranean. Her husband was a Bedouin who had exchanged the heat and grit of the Siwa Oasis and Great Sand Sea of Egypt to build an empire on another sea, and his shipping company now connected the Levant to all of the major ports of Europe. He had come to *Alepp* to personally supervise the transport of artifacts to Berlin from the newly excavated Temple of the Storm God at the ancient citadel that dominated the quarter of Aleppo known as the old city.

Her guide led their procession through twists and turns leading to other twists and turns and others still. At last, there was a high-pitched squeak as if someone had stepped on a mouse, but it was the triumphant major domo instead who had just set his sights on their destination – a bakery renowned for the best *Kebbeh Halab* in the region.

The major domo's mouth watered at the thought of the *Kebbeh Halab*, a baked or fried ball of bulgar wheat filled with lamb, goat or lean ground beef infused with mint, cinnamon, nutmeg, clove, and allspice. The exact permutations and combinations of ingredients were a day to day decision of the master of the bakery but in *Alepp* the best *Kebbeh* always came with a salted rice crust as it did here.

And then there were the sweets that filled every nook and cranny on the shelves of the baker's *Firdaus* (Islam's highest of seven heavens) on earth – the *mabrumeh, siwar es-sett, balloriyyeh*, all drenched in ghee butter and sugar and ladened with the pistachios for which this region was famous.

The major domo stopped short of the bakery door to caution his mistress that she should steel herself for the fact that this was an Armenian bakery and while the Armenians were deficient in most earthly respects, the heavenly beauty of what this bakery produced was sufficient recompense for doing business with unbelievers. Pushpa returned his *pince-nez* to his nose only to have it fall off seconds later as he looked down to study the gutter in embarrassment and apprehension of what might come next because he knew his mistress all too well.

The major domo was a narrow-minded Kurd from a narrow-minded family on the outskirts of Mosul and turned his nose up to sniff contemptuously each time he uttered the word *Armenian*. To

Pushpa's great relief, his mistress responded matter of factly, *we shall persevere, shall we not Pushpa?*

As the three entered the small shop, the heat and aroma of the crowded and insanely noisy bakery was as sensuous as taking one's first steps into the warm, lapping waves of *Byblos* or the *Ramlet al-Baida* or taking flight on the wings of a bird soaring skyward on a Herculean current of air.

The major domo prattled on about the delicacies on the shelves in front of them and in spite of his aversion to their hosts, struck up a conversation with the baker to solicit his recommendations for that day. The baker pointed to one counter with *Kocagormez*, meaning *husband doesn't see*, a dough-based dish whose name is based on the anecdotal tale of a woman who always prepares meat dishes when her husband is home but eats this simple dough herself to conserve the resources of the household.

Next, he nodded to the golden brown *Matnakash* off to the other side of the shop. This was a soft and puffy leavened bread, made of wheat flour and shaped into oval and round loaves. Its golden-brown crust was achieved by coating the surface of the loaves with sweetened tea essence before baking.

The major domo's exotic client awash in a surfeit of sensual delights had become fixated on just one, so much so that the major domo and Pushpa worried that their mistress might have succumbed to a sinking spell after her arduous journey. Just the opposite was true. Her heart was indeed soaring skyward, and she required a moment to calm herself and catch her breath.

Every piece of artwork, every artist, has a signature, and the provenance of what she saw before her on the counter was unmistakable. From the three thick braids of the Trinity to the small suggestion of a cross in the double notches at the end of each braid, she knew it must be true.

While her handlers watched her with concern, ready to spring to her aide if she buckled, the striking woman with Bedouin tattoos, who seemed to have turned to stone, knew in her heart of hearts that what she saw on the shelf before her was nothing less than Mina's Choreg.

* * * * *

Her eyes bored into the baker as Pushpa's mistress finally conjured a word or two for him starting slowly, *Peace be upon you, Sir. Your Choreg is a wonder to behold.* Pushpa understood what was about to come and watched with bemused detachment as the intensity in her eyes signaled this would be an interview like many he had seen before.

For his mistress had been trained as a physician in the finest medical school in Europe, the Friedrich Wilhelm University (after the war to be renamed the University of Berlin). He had seen her intellect cut through a problem like a sickle through ripe wheat to help the wretched of the City of the Dead in Cairo and in one damnable slum after another across Northern Africa.

It might be the misery of a child with symptoms of typhoid or a factory worker who had lost two fingers when his lathe blew up in his face and who had been cast off to fend for himself by the factory owner. To say his mistress was a relentless angel of mercy understated the point but overstated the term angel. She was instead a warrior, and no one stood in her way if there was a need she could address.

Pushpa's mistress continued, we *will have to take whatever number of loaves you still have available. May I say something to the artist behind this wondrous body of work. Would she have a minute or two to take away from her labors to tell me about this Choreg?*

The baker, who was indeed Armenian but spoke in a patois of French and Arabic hesitated, then responded in kind, *upon you peace, Madame, but the artist if you will is not a she, it is a he, a young man, a boy really. He is not here at the moment but will return from a delivery later this morning.*

A boy, she responded. *Tell me about him.*

Well, what can I tell you, Madame, the baker said as he shrugged his shoulders. *His name is Leo, and he has two pronounced talents... the wonders you see upon these shelves...and larceny. He is honest as the day is long with me and my clients but the rest of the time...well... so many stories.*

His art, as you say, is highly regarded, the baker continued, *as my clients have commented on the medicinal qualities of his workmanship.* The major domo smiled broadly and shook his head in agreement. *My business has prospered greatly thanks to this and to the intoxicating taste of his handiwork.*

Indeed, the medicinal qualities of the ersatz ingredients used by the boy, in particular, chicory root, had introduced much needed fiber into the diet of the baker's clients. And in so doing, the boy, Leo, had had lifted their spirits by flushing their enervated bowels.

His exotic client responded, *where can I find this multi-talented boy when he is not working here.*

He lives with his father, who is 'le medicin' at the hospital of le Croix-Rouge française to the east of the city. The Croix-Rouge française was the national Red Cross Society of France founded in 1864 and originally known as the *Société française de secours aux blessés militaires.*

It has been overrun with refugees since the recent earthquakes in our region and there are rumors of 'mort de chien' in the camps that have formed nearby, the baker said.

Leo is making a delivery to the German archaeologists at the citadel now, the baker added. *He will return later this afternoon for, how should I say it, his daily tête-à-tête with his beloved dough,* the baker said with a hint of irony.

The mention of *mort de chien* prompted a knowing glance from Pushpa to his mistress. It can rest peacefully in the warm water inside the hump of a camel for weeks but kill a human being mere hours after it is contracted. It was a disease of the poor and the weak, but in the day before antibiotics would kill rich and poor indiscriminately. Pushpa and his mistress had seen it before and, praise Allah, and they had not contracted cholera in spite of tending to those who would lose half their body weight in a day and fold like limp rags as a merciful death approached.

After appropriate Salaams, the striking woman with the Bedouin tattoos and Pushpa set out with some urgency for parts unknown as the major domo was dispatched to his master's house struggling like Atlas under his full body weight in baked goods.

* * * * *

Should Hitler strike east or should Mussolini or worse yet the Russians jump into the fray, the eyes of the World would turn to the strategic backwater of the Levant, in particular Syria. Here in its most important city to the bugle call of *Au Drapeau* at sunrise each morning rose a formidable French army under the command of the old warhorse Weygand.

The polyglot French expeditionary force headquartered in Aleppo brought under its wing Moroccans, ferocious Bedouin camel fighters, Algerians, Tunisians, Senegalese, Annamites, Madagascar's Malgaches, Lebanese, Syrians, Cherkess Cossacks and a large force of the French Foreign Legion. It was a beast bristling for a fight with tanks, planes and motorized guns waiting to be unleashed.

When the fighting came, and many thought it only a matter of time before it did, the ancient fortresses of Syria would crumble at the onset of aerial bombardment. Syria was not only the crossroads of trade where Asia, Africa and Europe met, it was a cauldron of blood that had boiled over through the ages from Abraham and King David who fought here to Pompey and Saladin, Lawrence of Arabia and Allenby.

The large, well trained French army was a force to be reckoned with if the bellicose Huns moved east. The fight would likely come without warning, and information on French troop strength, their commanders and the order of battle were closely guarded secrets.

The relative calm in the Levant at this moment in time belied a vicious battle that was being fought in the shadows. In Aleppo, facts and fragments of facts were exchanged as the coin of the realm among the proxies for the opposing sides.

Leo knew the envelope wrapped in oil cloth, which he had just retrieved from behind the camel pens on his way to the citadel, was contraband of some kind but its true purpose beyond its value to him was of little import. For months now, his arrangement with the German archeologists had been to operate sub-rosa as a courier moving such things back and forth when he was required to do so.

His contact among the archeologists was Richter, a nice young man who did not seem to get his hands dirty like the rest of them. He appeared to operate as a clerk of sorts and was always dressed crisply in a fine jacket and breeches. Under this fine jacket, Leo would occasionally catch a glimpse of a rather large handgun nestled in a shoulder holster.

As compensation for his exploits, Richter would amply compensate Leo in French francs and strong German beer. Leo had been drinking beer in varying quantities since the moment he could walk because his kidneys had not functioned well almost from birth. His father, who understood these things, had used barely a teaspoonful when Leo was a child, but it was enough to ensure the smooth operation of his kidneys at least for now.

As a boy approaching manhood, he required more to produce the same effect, but it worked without fail and one or two deep draughts of cool beer on a scorching Alepine day had its virtues beyond free-flowing kidneys. And thus, an alliance was formed – beer and boodle for a harmless detour to the camel pens from time to time.

The Germans had been a fixture at the citadel as long as Leo and for that matter most Alepines could remember. The kindly Herr Strasser, now the grizzled old Orientalist who was the *Besatzungsleiter* or chief of the current expedition, was just a boy fresh out of university back in 1912 when Sarre and his crew acquired the *Aleppo Room*. Herr Strasser would often share one of the large bottles of his prized bock beer with Leo, which he kept hidden in a cistern in the lowest and coolest reaches of the citadel, while extolling the beauty of the Aleppo Room, which could now be found in a Berlin museum.

Leo knew the details by memory. The Aleppo Room dated back to the early 17th century and had belonged to a Christian family, a minority in this great and tortured city, making the discovery all the more valuable. In time, it would take its place as the oldest surviving painted and paneled room from the original Ottoman Empire.

Its inlaid doors were ablaze with red, ochre and crimson. Painted on the wall panels were Jesus as a child, five images of the Virgin Mary, the Last Supper, Salome dancing before Herod and Abraham's sacrifice of Isaac – a scene familiar to Muslims, Jews and Christians alike. There were Islamic motifs, as well as wrestlers and dragons, a mythical Persian bird, tulips and hyacinths and the animals of the Creation.

As Leo put some distance between himself and the camel pens, he could not shake the thought of the factory boys at the pond. Democritus, a Greek scientist and philosopher, who is known as the father of the atom might have explained Leo's personality (and the atom) in the same way.

His explanation would begin with a stone. A stone cut in half gives two halves of the same stone. If the stone were to be continuously cut, at some point there would exist a piece of the stone small enough that it could no longer be cut. Indeed, the term "atom" comes from the Greek word for indivisible, which Democritus concluded must be the point at which a being or any form of matter cannot be divided any more.

In turn, the theory of the atom is first cousin to the principle of identity which tells us, *all that is, together forms the being*. In Leo's case, two forces fought for dominance of the indivisible Leo. On one hand, there was good borne of parents who arrived in Aleppo as refugees with nothing but a belief in themselves and the good of Mankind. On the other hand, there was anger, borne of the belief that Mankind was anything but good and that his parents suffered dearly for that fact.

From these competing forces issued a personality that was to some casual observers phlegmatic, even stoic. To all outward appearances, Leo's world contentedly revolved around Leo. And to most observers, it concealed the cunning that made him such a success in his more illicit activities in Aleppo.

Leo had watched his father's health deteriorate as he slaved in the hospital that killed his mother and would eventually kill him too.

His father, Hayk, often spoke of Leo's grandfather, Asdadur, whose faith in a better future guided the family. The young boy had faith in himself and that was that.

Once when Leo had fed a refugee mother and her two-year old, a small whisp of a girl whom she held tightly to her breast, Leo wondered what memories, what hopes were concealed behind their dark, vacant eyes. What must the child think of this new world into which she had been discarded?

Where did her mother find the strength to cope with that moment, that day, what lay ahead? Would they ever know a happy moment, he thought? Faith in the future be damned, he thought at the time.

When he had helped his father by carrying the cold, limp body of a young refugee boy who had been separated from a refugee camp on the outskirts of *Alepp* and run down by an army jeep, he saw not dignity just misery in the once proud hill tribes. The young boy seemed to be smiling as he lay in Leo's arms, and Leo wanted to know why. What had he looked forward to when he awoke that morning? What had he seen the moment he awoke from this life?

The patricians of Aleppo looked upon the refugees in disgust, but Mina had taught him the Bible, which said *but for the grace of God go I*. Except if it was God who wrote the Bible, how could anyone follow a God, Leo's searching adolescent mind wondered, who had created a world full of such misery.

Faith in the future be damned.

When Mina taught him as a young boy to affirm life by bringing his energy to the dough before him, she had spoken of this. *Our family is now relatively safe and secure*, she said, *but it was not always this way. Throughout history because history is cruel, not our Lord, we were all refugees at one time or another.*

Yet, Leo did not see the distinction. If history is cruel, so is God, he had concluded after coming to grips with the question. The thought of the factory boys only reinforced this view.

With the citadel in sight now, the delivery slung over his back and faintly smelling of camel dung, the thought of cold bock beer brought a spring in Leo's step. Leo had not noticed the stocky Bedouin boy who had seen mucking the camel pen during his visit. It was the boy's punishment for the cowardice that had given him a bloody upper lip and shattered his front tooth. The boy had thrown his pitchfork to the ground at the sight of Leo and run to his father, the Colonel of the Bedouin fighters in the Levant, with revenge in his heart.

* * * * *

They arrived at the sprawling refugee camp in the late afternoon as the dry winds of the *Symoon* retreated and a breeze that was fresh and sweet advanced from the East. The landscape surrounding the camp was what one would imagine the moon to be except here and there one would happen on a small stand of trees that through shear bravery and perseverance had flourished in such harsh conditions.

As they reached the rocky summit of the hill, they saw the hospital of the *Croix-Rouge française* sitting in a bowl about a quarter mile in diameter that looked like the caldera of an extinct volcano. To Pushpa and his mistress, who had seen many such hospitals, it seemed relatively well organized in spite of the long lines of patients seeking help.

They descended into the bowl and were challenged by French gendarmes almost immediately. When they explained their purpose for being there, they were allowed to pass in spite of the senior gendarme's discomfort with such an exotic woman replete with strange tattoos and a deadly Bedouin Khanjar at her hip.

Each step, each breath came harder for the woman with the Bedouin tattoos. It wasn't the exertion. It was an unseen hand from the past that tightened its grip on her windpipe. She pretended not to hear the ever-prescient Pushpa whisper in her ear, *I am always at your arm, Mistress.*

They entered the main tent of the hospital and were assaulted by the familiar scent of the living and dead. Pushpa politely asked for the *chef de medicin*, and a nun escorted them deeper into this den of hope and hopelessness.

And there he was. He was smaller than the image she had retained in a jar afloat on undulating waves. What had been salt and pepper hair was now fully gray, and he moved more awkwardly on the leg that had been battered at Meggado.

In spite of the physical insults time levels on us all, Hayk handled the bustling ward with his customary air of command and good grace. They found him in the triage unit, which required that he be firm in culling those with a chance for life from those who might be better served by a priest or Imam.

Her well-earned composure was a faithless friend at this moment. Sensing this, Pushpa closed ranks as they came up from behind Hayk, who sensing their presence turned toward them.

As-Salam-u-Alaikum, my cousin, my heart has come home. As-Salam-u-Alaikum, Anya said.

* * * * *

I was in a delirium between the conscious and unconscious worlds until the following dawn when they pulled me from the lorry into which the riders had thrown me like a sack of potatoes the night before. Dragging me by my hair, they quickly transferred me to a much larger truck that held other girls. I was still dazed but when I had a lucid moment, I thought of you, of Baba, Ahmad.

The boy had arrived minutes before and listened from the shadows of a tent lit by a single kerosene lamp. Pushpa replenished Hayk's glass of Raki to steel him for what was to come next as Anya continued.

The girls, most of them older than I, wept almost the entire time we were together. As I regained some semblance of my conscious self, I befriended a girl who called herself Mary-Tay. She was beautiful and a few years older than I. I thought to myself then that I would like to be so beautiful one day.

By mid-day, we reached a small freight station on the train line between Mersin and Adana, which seemed to be a collecting point for refugees, mostly younger women. There was also an area for mothers and their children, who congregated on the rocky ground in small clumps.

By happenstance, a gendarme shoved a bucket into my chest when I was standing in a line that went nowhere and told me to go to the small rivulet 1,000 paces away. I counted each and every one and returned with the water. Yet the water was not for the women and children but for the gendarmes.

The broad plain I had traversed held many small family groups and some of them huddled around the bodies of young children who had succumbed to hunger or thirst. Once I stopped to give water to a mother and her infant who cried faintly for the child did not have the strength to cry as you would expect an infant to cry.

Another gendarme saw this and rushed toward me in full stride hitting me in in my gut with the heel of his jackboot. As I tried to catch my breath and get back to my feet, I looked through the stars swirling in my head to see two people who seemed to be watching me from a nearby road.

It was unclear to me then whether they were sympathetic or simply took a morbid interest in my suffering like so many of the gendarmes. One appeared to be a large, handsome man with a regal bearing and another a smaller man with a funny blue hat.

The gendarmes continued to use me as their water boy while the older girls were auctioned off to groups of men who were milling about the freight shed seeking wives or slaves. I was spared because at that age I looked more like a boy than a girl.

The days passed and girls came and went. On one of my trips to the rivulet, the sound of hammering and the weeping of young women swirled in the fierce wind that whipped around us that day. It was so harsh that when it hit you squarely in the face, it was difficult to draw a breath.

I saw Mary-Tay again on my way back from the rivulet, my customary water bucket in hand, sitting in the field with another girl and I stopped to embrace her and to give both girls a drink of water. They were sun parched, scantily clothed and quivering, and I wondered why they had not already been auctioned.

As I stood to leave, a gendarme I had not seen approaching slammed the butt of his rifle into my gut knocking the wind out of me, putting me flat on my back. As I was struggling to get back to my feet, a now familiar experience for me, I saw the same two men again standing at the road in front of several large trucks. It had been a few days since I had first seen them.

And this is where, Cousin, as strange as it may sound, I have you to thank in part for having saved my life. It came naturally to me then, having watched you care for the sick, to do what I could to allay the suffering that swirled around me like the harsh wind on that plane. It had not gone unnoticed.

It was sometime later that day, I still cannot remember how much later because one did not try to mark time then because it only drove home the endless nature of one's misery, that the man in the blue Fez, he who sits next to you now, came to me and said, 'you are coming with us Ghazal,' an Arabic term of endearment that means what it sounds like – Gazelle.

He took me to his master's truck and shared water and a small meal of almonds and apricots with me watching me with concern, encouraging me to eat but not letting me do too much too quickly. Anya paused and looked at Pushpa with palpable affection.

Moments before his master returned to the truck the sound of many women crying in pain billowed like a storm. Those girls still in the camp, I learned later, had been taken as profit and were the property of the gendarmes or worse.

His master jumped into the cab and took the wheel, telling Pushpa that they must go before one of these scoundrels changes his mind. As our convoy turned on to the road and sped away, we could see on a small rise that had been hidden from view by the freight station a long line of large wooden crosses that ran parallel to the tracks.

There upon these crosses stripped of all clothing and dignity were a dozen Armenian girls nailed to them hand and foot. The girl closest to us, her head collapsed against her bare chest, her beautiful hair flowing to her knees, was Mary-Tay.

* * * * *

Are you married to this man, the master, as you call him, Hayk asked?

Anya did not answer with a yes or no and said, *his men call him Paladin. It was the name of the first ship in his fleet and a mark of respect for someone who had been a fierce Bedouin knight in his youth.*

His understanding of the world and its customs far exceeds the awareness of most of his countrymen. That is not to say he isn't Bedouin through and through. He has a wife in Beirut and several more near Cairo. His values are firmly rooted in the place of his birth.

After he and Pushpa rescued me from almost certain death, they took me first to Constantinople and eventually to his home in Beirut. We stopped at another train station as we approached Constantinople where bandits, a rebel band of Armenian Legionnaires in tattered uniforms, stopped a Constantinople-bound train looking for Armenian girls who had been kidnapped by the Ottomans.

They found more than they had bargained for in a rich Arab with his Armenian wife who had not been taken during the troubles that had afflicted you and me but instead during the horrors of 1915. 'Too late,' the woman told her would-be rescuers. She preferred to stay with her Turkish husband and their half-Armenian and half-Turkish children. Had Paladin and his men not arrived when they did, God knows what the Armenian Legionnaires might have done.

Paladin did not touch me then except with an encouraging hand on my shoulder and did not intimate anything more in our relationship than a genuine interest in the fledgling he had plucked from its shattered nest. He put me in school and had me tutored in German because this was the main language of his enterprise.

I reveled in his attention and would look forward to his return from his many travels. He brought something out in me that I never knew existed – an intelligence and strong sense of self. When I reached an age when young girls become young women and when young women are compelled to express that sense of self in their appearance, I adopted the ways of Bedouin women at least up to a point. I am sure that you have not missed that fact.

I excelled in all forms of learning and when Paladin realized my potential, he asked me to continue my studies in Germany, Berlin to be exact, and I stayed there for nearly seven years. My training as a physician at the university in Berlin and the Charité hospital was exceptional, as Paladin knew it would be.

This training included several visits to Alexandropol, the City of Orphans, which held at its peak nearly 31,000 Armenian orphans. Paladin encouraged these trips and, when I eventually returned to Beirut and his house, he sought to channel all I had learned in mind and heart into service to his own countrymen.

I had gained both knowledge and independence of will by the time of my return to Beirut and upon my return I went to him. I could not bear his children because of the Turkish boot but could finish what he started, my rebirth as a Bedouin woman.

* * * * *

It was approaching midnight and Pushpa had been dispatched to let Paladin know Anya was safe. It was just Anya, Hayk and Leo now and the conversation eventually turned to Asdadur and Mina.

Asdadur had survived the trek through the Almonos Mountains and once they had arrived in Aleppo seemed to gain strength with each passing day. More than anyone else other than Hayk, he was responsible for the creation and eventual expansion of health and social services working with the *Croix-Rouge française* for both the growing Armenian refugee population and for the seemingly endless influx of other refugees who were invariably in even worse shape than his own countrymen.

He lived another five years, Hayk said. *On a cool evening, it was in fact Christmas Eve, when the rain had passed and the air was crisp and fresh, Asdadur had demurred when ask to join us at midnight services. We looked in on him early Christmas morning to find that he had left us peacefully in the night.*

And Mina, Anya asked, as Hayk's attention seemed to wander off. She noticed the kerosene lamp flickering more brightly in the boy's moist, dark eyes.

Ah, well, two years ago, Mina accompanied local farmers to a village at the edge of the Syrian desert to our East to help two women with difficult pregnancies and to return here with them, if necessary, Hayk replied with such effort that he could have been rolling a boulder up a hill. *As you might imagine, she went with a full kit of bread, which seems to be the alpha and omega for us, is it not?* They met each other eye to eye to share the memory of a fateful conversation in an almond grove.

Mina was returning with one of the two women in a flatbed truck. They were rammed by a French army squad car. Everyone survived, but Mina came away with a bad, open fracture of the leg.

The time it took to get her back here was all the time needed for wound shock to take hold and no matter what we did upon her return with carbolic acid and everything else we could conjure to stem the tide, the fever would take her several days later.

One could hear a pin drop as Hayk sought another moment with his beloved Mina who lingered in his mind's eye. The silence was broken by an orderly who needed Hayk to attend to an emergency leaving Anya alone with Leo. Anya broke the ice.

When I look at you there in the shadows, Leo, I see Mina. You are as handsome as she was beautiful. Hers was a beauty of person and spirit.

She has also blessed you with her singular talent to nourish and lend a certain grace to the daily ebb and flow of life for those fortunate enough to partake of your handiwork. It is a gift not to be taken lightly.

You were one of us, Leo replied, his eyes fixed on the fearsome Khanjar at Anya's hip refusing to meet her gaze. *Why are you now one of them, one of our tormentors?*

You have heard our family's story, Anya said. *I would give anything never to have been separated from your father and my family. But like all refugees, I embraced a life that was foreign to me because I had no other choice.*

A Christian prophet once said, 'you must treat the alien as one of your own for you were aliens once in the land of Egypt.' Paladin gave me an opportunity to find the meaning in these words by helping those who are as vulnerable today as I was on that terrible night when I lost everything.

Leo who had still not taken his eyes off the Khanjar asked, *have you fought with the dagger?* Anya pulled it out of the sheath and handed it to him cradled in both hands, ivory hilt first.

Take it Leo. Feel its weight and balance. The figure at the hilt is Aslan the lion, Anya said. *It is a reminder that our strength lies in wisdom for this is what Aslan represents.*

To answer your question, Leo, before you ask again, I fight on my own terms and my own terrain, she said. *I fight to protect the people who are part of me now as I am part of them. The Bektashi who did not set me on this course but whose wisdom helps to illuminate my path have a riddle to describe how I feel,*

'I am the drop that contains the ocean. Its waves are amazing.
It is beautiful to be a sea hidden within an infinite drop.'

I fight to solve this riddle and to ensure that the meek do inherit the earth because with every generation of hardship, displacement and repression, they will grow stronger as those who despise them, those who turn a blind eye to their suffering, or wield their power and wealth to torment them, grow weaker.

This is how and why I fight, Leo.

* * * * *

Hayk and Anya stood on the hill overlooking the lights of the sprawling hospital where Anya and Pushpa had arrived the day before. Faint bands of red and blue hovered on the Eastern horizon signaling that dawn lay not far beyond. Leo had returned to the bakery crossing paths with Pushpa returning to retrieve his mistress.

He is a good boy, Anya said.

He is a lost boy, Hayk said. *I neglect him, I know, in favor of those I am bound to serve here. It has been good and bad for him because it has made him more resilient but has set him adrift with childhood to his rear and no clear path ahead to manhood.*

Apart from his genius with dough and the baker's oven, I am told he is quite the accomplished larcen, Anya said. It brought them both to laughter for the first time since their meeting.

I am told and often admonished for the fact that he is one of Aleppo's best. But the boy is a giant here in this hospital and the workers respect him. He does the work that people here do not want to do. He is brave and impetuous and is much like one of those young officers at Meggado who bravely threw themselves into the charge without a thought for their own safety only to be cut down seconds later.

Cousin, let's come back to Leo because you have given me the kernel of an idea, but how can I help you at this moment, Anya said. *We return to the port of İskenderun in a fortnight and then to Berlin with the artifacts from the citadel, but if I am needed here, I would gladly stay longer.*

Anya continued, *our work in Berlin on Cholera, particularly Koch's work in India on suppressing its spread, has opened new avenues for stopping this disease dead in its tracks. May I help you in this instance?*

It is dangerous, Anya. We isolate the problem in one spot only to have it flare up in another.

It is a common problem, Cousin. We have died and been reborn more than once, you and I, so we live on borrowed time. Let us continue to use it well.

Let me go with you to spend a few days in the camps that have been affected. You said it is isolated to two?

Yes, for now, Hayk said. *I would value the time with you and of course to spend it with such a distinguished physician as yourself,* Hayk said. They laughed again and in that unguarded moment each of them caught a fleeting glimpse of a clever 13-year-old girl, on one hand, and her hero, on the other, that fateful night when they were ripped apart in Cilicia.

And it was in that short and physically grueling interlude to stem the tide of cholera to the East of Aleppo that a plan was hatched for young Leo. Hayk wanted him out of Aleppo because the only path for him there led downward.

Anya would have Paladin add him to his crew, which would soon be off to Berlin. There would be many opportunities there for a young man with ambition and most particularly one who was a sorcerer with bread. Paladin would see to it that Leo was introduced to his friends in Berlin's large Arab and Armenian communities that prospered living and working together.

And so, it was agreed.

* * * * *

Allah, who is a merciful God, although it is debatable whether that means all the time or some of the time, had other plans. Two seemingly random events would turn Anya and Leo's departure from Aleppo upside down with deadly consequences.

The first comes to us compliments of the master of the first evening shift at the finest maker of all manner of Alepine silk. He had retired to the backroom to smoke leaving the older boys in charge of the younger boys with strict orders to beat them if they fell behind with the important order due to be shipped to Paris in the coming week.

This particular back room held shelf upon shelf of dyes and solvents in conditions that would horrify a fire marshal, but in that day alas, there was no such thing. The master of the first evening shift had long ago forsaken the pipe and had acquired the habit of smoking the cigarettes brought to Aleppo by the infidels who were damned to be sure but whose cigarettes he craved.

The first cigarette had relaxed him, making him drowsy. He had spent most of the previous night playing *Mancala,* the 7,000-year-old game that challenges players to move pieces from bin to bin on a special board.

Gambling in this way, that is obtaining undeserved money which makes Man forget his Creator, prevents him from performing prayers, leads him to laziness and causes enmity among people was *haram* or forbidden by Islam. But, as the master of the first evening shift dozed off with his second cigarette held limply between two fingers, he recalled contentedly how he had taken two months wages from the others who played.

The still burning cigarette fell to the floor and a spark flickered in the ash sending a small flame on its way down the length of a strip of tar to a bolt of cloth and then to another. Eventually the flame, now much larger, ravenously consumed the first wooden shelf it found, moving up to a tin of solvent that was leaking at its rusted corner and once amply nourished by its contents turned its attention to the rest of the workshop.

Allah the merciful God allowed the factory boys to flee like rats (along with the rats) from the inferno that followed. And He ensured that the master of the first evening shift would be forever pleased with his ill-gotten gains from the night before.

* * * * *

The second seemingly random event unfolded compliments of the Bedouin Colonel, who had been summoned by Weygand for maneuvers to assess the readiness of his corps, which would put the Bedouin Colonel in the field for at least the next week. Weygand could not be put off, so the Bedouin Colonel had to notify Richter that the back-up plan for the next exchange was in force.

In point of fact, it had been the Bedouin Colonel who was the source of many of the packets relayed to the Germans over the last 2 1/2 years. All in a good cause, he thought to himself, as he coveted his growing wealth secretly held for him on account in Beirut. As well as he lived now, better than most, he thought, it was no match for what was attainable through the generosity of the Huns.

The next and final satchel to be delivered to the archeologists at the citadel three days hence would be the crowning achievement of his treachery. It was the order of battle for a French response to a German attack on Syria along with plans for the further reinforcement of the garrison in the months ahead.

The back-up plan called for the Bedouin Colonel to send his best man disguised as a camel driver directly to the small courtyard where the archeological shipment was being assembled for the trip to *İskenderun* and then Berlin. The contraband would be carried in the saddle bag of a camel that would be tied to a post at the ornate *Salsabil* fountain that anchored the center of the courtyard. A few handpicked men would be hidden in the shadows of the *Riwaq*, the arcade surrounding the courtyard on three sides to ensure that the transaction was completed.

His man would leave the camel ostensibly to attend to business signaling the baker's boy dressed as a camel driver to casually sidle up to the animal when the moment was right and remove the saddle bag. Because of the value of this transfer, the Bedouin Colonel would have preferred a clandestine meeting with Richter himself, but it was not to be.

His man's second assignment was the baker's boy, who had served as the intermediary between the conspirators in the past. This was the boy who had also wreaked havoc on his son and, even had he not been his son's tormentor, was a loose end that need to be snipped off.

As to his own boy, he had given orders to the headmaster of the *Ecole Secondaire* to keep his nose to the grindstone on the day of the clandestine delivery and until the Bedouin Colonel had given the go ahead to send him home. He would have the satisfaction of presenting the baker's boy to his son later that day trussed like a pig with a large bullet hole in his skull.

But it would be a mischievous god on watch that day because the headmaster of the *Ecole Secondaire* contracted a case of food poisoning and could barely lift his head from the pillow or the pan. To confound matters still further, Richter decided that it would be prudent to replace the baker's boy with one of his own men as the other camel driver.

* * * * *

The best thing that could be said about the momentous day of the exchange three days hence, which was also to be the day of Leo's departure from Aleppo, is that it was *biblical* to say the least. To most Alepines, it was yet another plague visited on true believers by the unwelcomed presence of infidels.

The sky, black as coal smoke, had robbed Aleppo of its dawn that day and was pierced at regular intervals by fearsome lightning strikes. The rumbling of thunder in the storm clouds swirling around the old city followed the Alepines everywhere as they went about their daily business, occasionally seeking cover from short and intense squalls of heavy rain that hit them like shards of glass.

Their tribulations mounted as the morning progressed. Aleppo is equidistant from the Mediterranean to the West and the Euphrates River to the East. Heavier squalls propelled by waterspouts from the Euphrates bombarded the labyrinthine streets of the old city with an abundance of fish, frogs, toads and snakes that had been swept aloft by the storm and carried the 60 miles from the river.

At the same time, scores of large ravens, some two feet long with wing spans twice that length, were also carried unwillingly to Aleppo by ferocious winds. The city's resident crows, which had served Aleppo well by feeding largely on carrion, were driven away by their much larger and more aggressive cousins.

These black monsters whose iridescent feathers flashed hints of blue and purple feasted on the fish, frogs, toads and snakes that now formed a flopping, squirming carpet in the old city and when the opportunity presented itself also hunted the unsuspecting rats that had joined the feast and the unwitting poultry that freely ranged to and fro in the old city.

Amidst it all, Hayk and Leo approached the rendezvous with Anya at the Citadel from the *Bab Antakya,* one of the nine ancient gates punctuating the thick stone wall that runs for over three miles to surround the old city of Aleppo. From the gate, they were funneled into a series of long, narrow alleys connected by interlocking *Khans*, large two- or three-story courtyards characterized by beautiful façades and entrances with fortified wooden doors. The *Khans* accommodated craftsmen and merchants on the first rung and living spaces on those above.

Hayk and Leo eventually found themselves at the magnificent *al-Madina Souq*, a vast covered market that was home to raw silk from Iran, spices and dyes from India and local products such as fresh produce, wool, soap and ornate candles of all sizes and shapes. They arrived to the sound of gunfire as the merchants of the small marketplaces called *Caeserias* located in the large open square fronting the *Souq* fired rifles into the air to drive away the marauding ravens.

To add to the noise and confusion, factory boys set loose by the fire at the finest maker of all manner of Alepine silk, with nothing to do and nothing to lose, harassed the merchants by stealing what they could. Hayk put a hand on Leo's shoulder to steer clear of two of those boys who were being beaten senseless by a group of aggrieved merchants as they lay on their backs amidst the innumerable frogs and toads and fish and snakes that twitched and slithered on the worn travertine flagstones of the square.

Unbeknownst to Hayk and Leo, two factory boys who sat less than 20 yards away in the crenellations of an ancient wall that had once been part of the defenses of the old city took notice of them. A six and a nine-year-old recognized their champion still carrying the French army duffle bag that he had with him on the day of the *Battle of le rat musqué* in the nearby hills.

Yet in this instance, the duffle bag was not full of Leo's baked craftsmanship but of his few worldly possessions. It had taken less effort than Hayk had feared it would to convince the boy to return to Berlin with the Germans. Leo had known for some time that Aleppo was for him a long, slow death in a place not of his choosing. He was like his father in many ways and yearned to be more like him, but the fierce commitment that drove his father to serve his patients day in and day out eluded Leo.

He would miss his father but did not have the words to say so. So, Leo had taken the rather large cash hoard he had amassed from his larcenous endeavors outside of the bakery and divided it in two, leaving one half on his father's cot. Leo knew his father would understand what this meant in lieu of words.

As Hayk and Leo entered the *Souq* from which they would emerge on the other side in the shadow of the magnificent citadel of the old city, the factory boys noticed a scrum of schoolboys entering the old city at the *Bab Qinnasrin,* also heading toward the same open square in front of the *al-Madina Souq*. Their leader, the son of the Bedouin Colonel, had been tipped off that Leo could be found with the Germans at the citadel unbeknownst to his father and had appropriated his father's spare service revolver which was tucked into the red sash at his waist.

His adjutant, the first boy who had been wounded by Leo, wore a small cavalry saber strapped to his hip. The rest of their companions, six in all, were armed only with testosterone, which they wielded with varying degrees of ferocity.

The nine-year-old factory boy sitting in the crenellated wall sharpening his long and deadly stick jumped to his feet when he saw the new arrivals in the square before them and beckoned to his six-year-old companion who was in the next crenellation to do the same. The nine-year-old, intrigued and concerned by the invasion of a familiar foe, told his younger companion to assemble their compatriots post haste having noted that the schoolboys were armed and were marching toward the *Souq* barely 10 minutes behind Hayk and Leo.

* * * * *

Jacques Oublier, officer of the watch that day in Aleppo, had descended through the ranks of the French national gendarmerie with such steady and consistent progress that one could imagine his retrogression as having been sprung from a well-conceived plan. He had started his career in Paris, was transferred to Lyon, and from Lyon to Avignon. On a drunken rampage through Marseilles one night with his compatriots from Avignon, he was shanghaied to the *Gendarmerie Étrangère de France*, otherwise known as the French Foreign Legion, and whilst sobering up found himself in transit to the backwater of the French Mandate of Aleppo.

A messenger had arrived from Weygand's headquarters that morning ordering him in no uncertain terms to address the disgraceful situation in Aleppo without delay. Oublier was acutely aware that there were other postings even more hideous than Aleppo and sprang into action immediately.

He could do nothing about the apocalyptic weather conditions but could address the irruption of factory boys who currently terrorized the merchants of the old city. Oublier assembled a squad of his best men firstly to clean up the area around the *al-Madina Souq.* He had been given authorization from the highest levels of command to *shoot to kill* if it came to that.

* * * * *

Successive sheets of pummeling rain from the teeming black skies swamped the large open square leading directly to the fortified gate of the Citadel of Aleppo from the *al-Madina Souq* like a shroud. As Hayk and Leo emerged from the *Souq*, pausing momentarily to take their bearings in the arcade facing the Citadel, it struck Hayk that the awful scene before him must be how the Last Judgment would look. It would indeed be judgment day for some.

The vast fortified palace before them in the center of the old city of Aleppo was one of the oldest and largest castles in the world dating back to the middle of the 3rd millennium BC. It sits imperiously 160 feet above the old city on a massive elliptical base surrounded by a 72-foot deep and 98-foot wide moat built in the 12th century.

Hayk and Leo were already late for their rendezvous. Father and son had no choice but to leave the cover of the arcade and splash across the square in the unrelenting torrent to reach the arched bridge over a moat that would take them to the fortified gateway of the citadel beyond.

* * * * *

Preparations were all but complete at the center of the citadel complex, and there was a sense of urgency about moving out as quickly as possible. Strasser was determined not to wait for Richter's *Pferdescheiße, Horseshit,* to play itself out. The service road that the Germans had built to the rear of the citadel was in danger of being washed away by the rain.

The decision was taken that Strasser would leave while it was still possible with the eight trucks that held the treasures the Germans had expropriated from the citadel while the two remaining trucks with the logistical elements of the expedition would come when Richter gave the word. Strasser fretted for the boy. He was supposed to have come with him in the lead truck and now would have to take his chances with that fool Richter.

Anya had decided to stay behind to assist Hayk against Paladin's better judgment, but what had to be done had to be done. Pushpa would also stay and had been sent to reconnoiter for the missing father and son.

* * * * *

The command had been issued to the forward units to form a skirmish line to delay the enemy as much as possible in its steady progress toward the far side of the *Souq* and the citadel beyond. The six-year-old factory boy, now a battle-hardened veteran, adroitly chose the time and place of the ambush.

The Bedouin schoolboy and his French companions had to pass through a section of the *Souq* that was home to candle and soap makers, arrayed in long rows, soap makers lined up on one side of the main passageway and candlemakers on the other. As the lead element of the enemy force from the *Ecole Secondaire* entered the trap, a handful of factory boys on each side of the passageway snatched bulky wax candles and bricks of soap from the stalls, hurling them at the schoolboys before quickly disappearing into the shadows of the *Souq*.

And from behind the now angry and disoriented schoolboys came more missiles in squares and tubes, greens and creams, disorienting the enemy still further. This contingent of factory boys also melted into the background as per the plan after launching its volley.

What was left was a huddle of bewildered and screaming schoolboys who seemed to dance this way and that in the aisle searching for their tormentors and picking up the missiles that had been thrown at them to retaliate in kind. It had all happened so fast, that the merchants concluded that the schoolboys were the source of the mischief and destruction of their property. Fists flew as the students of the *Ecole Secondaire* learned a bloody lesson in cunning in the alley of the candle and soap makers of Aleppo.

* * * * *

True to form, *le Capitaine Oublier* was of little help to the candle and soap makers. His men floundered in their pursuit of the factory boys who were like a mirage – flesh and blood one moment barely feet away and then like hobgoblins vanishing into the shadows, cracks and crevices of the old city.

Oublier hit a bit of good luck when a message arrived from the sentries at the citadel that a large group of small boys was following a small group of large boys to the citadel and true to form had disappeared before reaching the Citadel's arched bridge to evaporate into the maze of underground passageways that ran below the moat. *We will trap them all at close quarters in the citadel,* Oublier proclaimed grandiloquently to his adjutant, slamming a meaty fist into the sweaty palm of a meaty hand.

* * * * *

It was still a matter of dispute some months later during the official inquiry as to who fired the first shot that fateful day. One implausible report had it that a bar of soap hit the Captain of the Guard squarely in the face, and it was then that the battle was joined.

As they had been trained to do by Oublier, the motley squad of gendarmes present that day when faced with a sensitive situation, close quarters and innocent bystanders, fired at everything. In the hail of bullets, they managed to put a bullet in the temple of the German agent who had just casually sauntered out to the camel to remove the saddle bag.

The German fell at the camel's feet still clutching the saddle bag as the animal shifted nervously on its tether but remained for the moment unscathed. A rumbling squall of rain nearly drowned out the sound of the next volley of gunfire that all but severed the right arm below the elbow of the French schoolboy with the cavalry saber, who was caught in the line of fire.

Hayk and Leo had arrived only minutes before the conflagration exploded and rendezvoused with Anya, who prompted Pushpa to take Leo's duffle bag to the trucks. They had taken cover in the large arcade of the semi-circular courtyard of white sandstone with the ornate *Salsabil* fountain at its center near the two remaining trucks idling just on the other side of the fountain from the nervous camel.

Father and son spent a moment together, unable to say what they wanted to say, and were rescued from having to say anything when the second volley of shots rang out. After a quick but heartfelt bear hug, Hayk helped to hoist Leo into the back of the truck from which Richter was now putting down covering fire.

Richter's objective was less about Leo's safety than it was about getting another agent to the camel, which against all odds, still remained unscathed. Anya noticed as she took cover that two groups of boys stood on opposing sides of the courtyard like a Greek Chorus.

A squall hit once more with a blinding downpour and when it passed there was a volley of stones, pieces of sandstone brick and, yes, large chunks of soap and wax, from one side of the courtyard to assail the *Ecole Secondaire* on the other, which was at barely half strength after the fiasco in the *Souq*. Leo also watched in amazement as the factory boys took this opportunity to advance as one to fire off yet another volley.

The confounding factor in a situation that did not need another one was the Bedouin Colonel's men. They too were on the scene and turned on Oublier and his men, who were themselves at half strength as many of them had called it a day by deserting under cover of the most recent downpour. Oublier went down with a wound to the shoulder but not before getting off several shots in the direction of the Bedouin Colonel's men and the factory boys.

Leo saw the six-year-old go down blood pouring from a head wound and jumped out of the cargo hold of the truck to drag him to cover where Hayk was already tending to the wounded *Ecole Secondaire* boy.

It looks worse than it really is, Hayk told Leo after examining the factory boy. *The bullet grazed him, and he will be fine, but I need to get him back to the hospital along with this other boy if we can ever get out of this hell hole.*

Leo sensed someone at his left shoulder and turned quickly ready to parry a blow, but it was the nine-year-old factory boy, a piece of sandstone in one hand and his now bloody killing stick in the other. Leo pulled a large leather pouch from his jacket pocket and stuck it in the nine-year-old's gut.

Go with my father and take your friends with you. Your friend here will live. Once my father has bandaged his wound, get the hell out of Aleppo, both of you. Go as far away from this place as you can. What you have in hand will make that possible, Leo bellowed above the din of more shots fired, men screaming in rage and the full-throated braying of the camel which had finally had enough.

You too, son, go now, Hayk shouted to Leo, barely concealing the pride he felt. Leo pursed three fingers to his forehead to give his father a hasty salaam and a sly smile before running to the trucks.

As Leo dodged the gunfire and a Bedouin who swung an empty revolver at his head, he noticed Pushpa for some inexplicable reason roll the dead German agent on his back and retrieve the saddle bag, which he tossed to Richter in the back of the truck. As Leo swerved to avoid a kick from the apoplectic camel, he collided with Anya who bellowed, *back to the truck, Leo, you fool. Now*!

They arrived at the truck together as the cacophony of rain squalls and gunshots waxed and waned in unison. Before Anya let him go, she took a firm grip of Leo's jacket and pulled him close until they were nose to nose, *our family has endured much and been given much because God turns us from one feeling to another and teaches us by means of opposites, so we will have two wings to fly—not just one. Never forget the example your family set for you, boy, or you will have me to answer to.*

Anya sensed someone rushing toward them from her rear. She turned quickly to see the Bedouin Colonel's son charging with the small cavalry saber held high and stepped between him and Leo as Richter hastily pulled Leo headlong into the back of the truck as it lurched forward to join the rest of the convoy.

VOLLKORNBROT

I. BERLIN 1942

Where one burns books, one will, in the end, burn people.

— *Heinrich Heine, 1821*

On Oderberger Strasse some called it *Mutter Nebel* – Mother Fog or the Merciful Fog. It had pushed into Berlin from the Baltic at sunset the evening before and one could if one tried catch the fecund scent of seaweed carried on the colliding eddies of mist.

It had frustrated the Tommies keeping them and their 4,000-pound blockbuster bombs at bay at least for one night. Although truth be told, the slums of the Wedding district of Berlin hidden now under *Mutter Nebel's* skirt, had been spared the full brunt of the sporadic bombing at least till now because the timid British flyers would typically drop their bombs in the Western reaches of the city before turning tail to run from the intense flak that greeted their nightly visits.

Nevertheless, the thunder of war that rattled one's teeth had drawn progressively closer, and it had been a hellish few days before *Mutter Nebel's* arrival. One errant bomb from a raid had mangled the above-ground U2 station at Eberswalder Strasse, a short walk from where the young minister now stood looking out at the fog from the small tenement apartment on the ground floor of Oderberger Strasse 61 to see his reflection staring back at him.

Dietrich fretted because he could do little to comfort the children. Driven to their basement shelters by the blaring air raid sirens for three nights running, they had emerged the day before on a sunny Easter morning so traumatized that they looked and acted more like their doddering grandparents than youngsters.

On this foggy Easter Monday morning, the dawn struggled to rise as the Lord had on the previous day. The faint light from the door lanterns that shone one after the other along Oderberger Strasse backlit the swirling paisley patterns of *Mutter Nebel's* wet embrace.

The young minister could make out faint forms moving this way and that in the fog as workers trudged home after 11-hour shifts crossing paths with their replacements, who hurried to catch up because those on the morning shift always seemed to run a few minutes late. Tardiness could get one reported to the Party and then there would be hell to pay.

It was also the time when the smells of a bustling wartime city fought for prominence – diesel fumes, sewage, grit from the rubble of Eberswalder Strasse station, wood fires and the body odor of hard-working men and women who bathed only when there was water to spare. The bathhouse at Oderberger Strasse 55 had been closed for nearly three weeks.

On top of this, old man Schultheiss had fired up the brewery just around the corner from the bathhouse now that the typhus scare had passed, and his men had returned to work. One could never have imagined that brewing something that tasted as good as the old man's beer could foul the air in such a way as to make it difficult to catch a breath.

Yet the gray tenement canyon of Oderberger Strasse in the Wedding was pierced that morning, as it was every morning, by a fragrance that evoked better times. Passers-by would linger for a moment at Oderberger Strasse 15 directly across from Dietrich's vantage point near an old exhaust fan that whined because of its bent blades to inhale the perfume of *Die Bäckerei* hopeful that if they took a deep enough breath, the sublime aroma of baking bread would stay with them all day.

* * * * *

The young minister let the shabby curtain at the front window of his small flat fall back into place and said a silent prayer of thanks to his Lord God for arranging the visit of *Mutter Nebel* when He had. The young boy slept on a small mattress in the corner and Dietrich would have to rouse him soon for their clandestine rendezvous with the proprietor of *Die Bäckerei* directly across Oderberger Strasse.

Mehdi, the baker, was an Arab who had managed to survive the harassment of the National Socialist Workers Party because he paid his dues to the Nazis in a timely manner and routinely slipped a thick wad of Reichsmarks to the gauleiter of the district. His was one of the few businesses in Wedding that could afford to do so.

According to Nazi racial laws, Mehdi was classified a "Hamite" after Ham, the son of Noah in the Old Testament. This term was adopted from 19th century racial science and used to classify natives of North Africa, the Horn of Africa, and the historical region of South Arabia.

Those classified as Hamitic were considered non-Aryan and subject to harassment, and Mehdi took every opportunity as he was padding the palms of local Nazi party officials loudly to profess his hatred of Jews – a Semite who was an ardent anti-Semite.

Mehdi was an odd duck, who defied Dietrich's attempts as a respected theologian to classify him in the academic constructs that he used to relate real life to a life in God, which made Mehdi's bravery in helping those he professed to hate all the more remarkable. Their meeting that morning would address the future of the boy in the young minister's temporary care, a Jew from Munich who had converted to the Church with his parents.

The boy was on the run from the Gestapo. His father, who had been a well-known judge in Munich and a close friend of Dietrich's, had been taken into "protective" custody by the Gestapo along with his wife. Protective custody ("Schutzhaft") was an insidious Nazi invention that prompted the young minister now to think of these two wonderful friends in the past tense.

The Gestapo were meticulous record keepers, and the missing boy was a loose end that they could not abide. There were informants everywhere and one slip-up would seal the boy's fate and for that matter his own.

Wedding was familiar territory to Dietrich Bonhoeffer. Soon after his ordination in 1931, Dietrich had preached at nearby *Zion-skirche* when he had been asked to take over a confirmation class of 50 rowdy boys in this notoriously tough neighborhood in Northern Berlin. They were 14- and 15-year-old hoodlums who had quite literally harassed poor old Reverend Fromm, the previous confirmation teacher, to death.

At first, the boys behaved like they were crazy, but his youth, athletic build, and kindly persistence helped the young minister slowly earn their respect. He had also visited their parents one by one, who allowed him into their squalid homes only because they felt they must. He remembered struggling to have a normal pastoral conversation with them amid their ghastly living conditions.

The young minister had also adopted an open-door policy at Oderberger Strasse 61, which was his residence at that time. This meant that his new charges could visit him unannounced at any time. And they did, especially when times were tough or tougher than usual.

It was also during this period that he first rented a nine-acre parcel of land in Biesenthal and built a primitive cabin that he would retreat to with students from the Charlottenburg Technical College where he was the chaplain and sometimes with the boys from Wedding. As before, he told the boys that they were welcome anytime.

The young minister considered it a gift from God that all but one of his boys was confirmed almost six months from the day that he took over their confirmation class. It had been a memorable Sunday in March 1933, the day of a national election when Nazi rowdies in their brown shirts and pill box hats rode around in the back of trucks with megaphones stirring things up in Wedding as in most of Berlin.

As he prepared to leave for the meeting across Oderberger Strasse, Dietrich chuckled as he reflected on that day when the roving brown shirts had made his boys look like cherubs by comparison.

* * * * *

The young boy was all but ready and when he let the boy go to the back courtyard to toilet, he found that a note had been slipped under the door. The Admiral would indeed join them at *Die Bäckerei* that morning under the cover of *Mutter Nebel*. He wanted to review the plans for Dietrich's latest assignment as he often did because he was an exquisitely, some might even say, excruciatingly detailed planner. As much as the young minister welcomed these meetings with the Admiral, the timing of his visit made a morning already fraught with danger complicated indeed.

Dietrich had always loved the poetry of John Donne and had read him voraciously during his ecumenical visits to Great Britain. He had a special affinity for the poem *No Man is an Island*, a sentiment that he found especially poignant because these days he felt like a man without any island at all.

His predicament owed much to the schism of the German Lutheran church into the *German Church*, on one hand, and the *Confessing Church*, on the other hand. The German Church, otherwise known as the *Reichskirche*, was now the official church of Germany and as such subscribed to the *Führer Principle*, which was aptly defined by Hitler's henchman Rudolf Hess when he said, *Hitler is Germany and Germany is Hitler. Whatever he does is necessary. Whatever he does is successful. Clearly the Führer has divine blessing.*

The *Führer Principle* required everyone in Nazi-controlled Germany to accept the notion that Hitler knew the solutions to all of Germany's problems and that whatever he said was right, insinuating Nazi control into every facet of daily life. And this same malignancy had spread to the Protestantism of the *Reichskirche* that now professed the unity of throne and altar thus legitimizing authority for authority's sake.

As a direct result, all Germans were required to use the formal salute of *Heil Hitler* when greeting one another, including children who were required to use the salute in all aspects of their lives, including school, where their schoolmasters followed – and obediently enforced – the rules. Students were also told that they were to report their parents and neighbors to the authorities if they saw them using the salute half-heartedly.

Good men, even Godly men, his fellow ministers and theologians, had succumbed to the idea that blind obedience to Hitler while unsavory at times was the salvation of Germany and the German church itself. Dietrich could not stomach the idea. It was a sad day for the church and for the German people.

His was a different path and, over time, he had been banned from preaching and for a period banned from Berlin altogether. He had embraced the *Confessing Church*, whose adherents while united in their principled opposition to the Führer Principle and Hitler himself, could not agree on what resistance truly meant and thus were impotent in mounting any concerted effort against the Nazis.

However, the young minister had finally come to his senses as he saw his beloved Germany being swept away by Hitler's river of blood. He did not want his tendency to be *spiritually minded*, to mean that he was in fact of no earthly good to his fellow countrymen.

To be an effete religious leader, who merely talked about God but refused to get his hands dirty in the real world in which God had put him for a purpose, was bad theology. And the young minister was the consummate theologian.

Through close friends, Dietrich finally found a way to get his hands dirty. But this decision was to alienate him from many in the Confessing Church because to all outward appearances he had acquiesced to the immorality of the status quo.

Dietrich had crossed the line from confession to resistance and become a double agent for Abwehr, Hitler's military intelligence organization, and would that morning receive his next assignment in the resistance from Abwehr's leader himself, a man Dietrich revered, Admiral Wilhelm Canaris.

* * * * *

Little Otto and Big Otto had made a mess of it. The ink used in making the counterfeit Reich bread ration cards had not cured properly and the entire batch, hundreds of them, had to be thrown into the furnace.

They were in the throes of deciding who would tell him. Had this been another gang leader, they would have been afraid for their lives. In this case, disappointing their own leader seemed like a fate worse than death.

A Fagin to their Artful Dodger and Charley Bates, their leader was not. He was equal parts, the *Bäckermeister*, because he was a magician with the basic staple that fed Wedding and the organizing force in their young lives, whom they followed without question because he seemed to be able to do anything, no matter how hard, without apparent effort.

Otto was in fact neither Big Otto's nor Little Otto's name. It seemed to fit them and had been perversely bestowed upon them by other members of the gang of 15-20 boys aged 8 to 18 who orbited *Die Bäckerei* and were in its employ from time to time.

They were the *Wolf Children* of Berlin, one of many packs of relatively young boys and girls who had been abandoned when their teachers fled Berlin and their parents were either sent to the front or indentured to one factory or another, disappearing from their daily lives for all practical purposes. Their common interest now was survival in an increasingly harsh and dangerous place.

These dark days in Berlin had not dampened their sense of humor, however, and the name Otto stuck to the two companions because they could not have been less alike. Big Otto was a strapping Nazi advertisement for young Aryan masculinity.

Little Otto, well he was something else altogether, and the gang had its suspicions but said nothing about them lest Little Otto disappear as so many like him had in the last few years. He was such a puny boy that someone might simply put him in a burlap bag and drop him in the Spree like an unwanted cat without it ever being noticed.

Big Otto was a born leader and talented conman and had become their leader's right-hand man. Little Otto possessed one exceptional talent that made him invaluable. He was a natural artist who could mimic in exquisite detail any official document of import. In recognition of his talents, he received a double ration of food and was forbidden from fighting and all forms of manual labor to preserve the hands through which his God given talent flowed.

The Ottos were foot soldiers in the battle to stay alive and out of the hands of the Nazi party, particularly the older boys in the pack, who might just as easily be shipped to the front or consigned to forced labor. They had become an extension of Mehdi and the *Bäckermeister*, who had emerged as two of the most effective players in Berlin's thriving black market.

Rationing had been introduced to Germany in 1939, shortly before the outbreak of the war. Initially it had applied to food but as the war drug on was expanded to clothing, shoes, leather, and soap.

One could subsist well enough on rations stamps but do little more. Color coded ration stamps were issued to all civilians and covered sugar, meat, fruit and nuts, eggs, dairy products, margarine, cooking oil, grains, bread, jam and fruit jellies.

By late 1941, when the war in the East began to tilt ever so slightly against Germany after its defeat within sight of the golden spires of the Kremlin, there were increasingly severe shortages in virtually everything and massive inflation in food prices. However, nearly anything was available on the black market for purchase or barter if the price were right.

Officially, selling and buying goods on the black market could result in a death sentence but local Nazi officials in Wedding were reliably corrupt and could be counted on to turn a blind eye in return for cash and goods for they had their own families to feed.

The Ottos sat in a large storeroom at the back of *Die Bäckerei* commiserating over their fate amidst sacks of flour and kaffee, real kaffee, the rarest of all commodities, stolen from the renowned Café Kranzler on *Unter den Linden* purportedly from Göring's private stash. There were also bins of *Blutwalnuss* – red walnuts – which the *Bäckermeister* would add to his baked goods to create something magical. Tucked in among the floor to ceiling crates and bags of every type were two printing presses and an impressive supply of inks and fluids that gave life to the printers.

The storeroom was a large hollow space hidden in the enclosed archway at the back of the *Mietskaserne* at Oderberger Strasse 15, a massive building, which dominated most of a city block. These ubiquitous block apartment buildings, which were integral to the personality of Berlin, were built in the late 1800's, the brainchild of James Hobrecht, who was considered by many the Hausmann of Berlin.

When constructed for wealthier tenants, the *Mietskaserne* had open archways front and back. Those for poor tenants had no second archway and thus no ventilation and were breeding grounds for disease as was true in this part of Wedding. The recent Typhus scare was no coincidence.

In any given *Mietskaserne*, wealthier tenants lived in exterior facing apartments and in the most exclusive *Mietskasernes*, their apartments faced West toward the prevailing winds. Despite their impoverished surroundings, many of these buildings were Neoclassical works of art.

This was indeed the case on Oderberger Strasse where access to *Die Bäckerei* from the street was through the shop's front door, which was set off by faux ionic columns and a decorative neoclassical pediment over the door. The shop stood several feet off center from the single archway at the front of the *Mietskaserne* with its huge and ornate wooden doors like the enormous wooden gates of a castle only without the drawbridge.

One could reach a small side entrance to *Die Bäckerei* from the storeroom through a long and dingy interior courtyard that led to the huge wooden doors at the front. It would be an especially long walk to the shop for Big Otto and Little Otto as the time of reckoning with Leo had come.

* * * * *

She pours another glass of schnapps hoping to wash the taste of him out of her mouth and to dull the senses so that the last three hours with her Gestapo handler, Joseph "Sepp" Lange would be soon forgotten or at least tucked into a tiny compartment in her psyche and ignored. She had more than a few of these compartments.

Sepp had good looks enough for a dozen men, the manners of a gentlemen and a sadistic streak that terrified her. Stella Goldschlag was his pawn, a way to play out his Aryan fantasy of submitting a helpless Jewess to sexual humiliation.

She was his prized *Greiferin*, his *grabber*, tasked with using her computerlike memory for names, dates, addresses and other useful minutiae to hunt down her fellow Jews hiding as non-Jews, the *Untergetauchten*, laughingly called the "U-Boats" by the hunters and hunted alike.

Stella and a small band of Jews like her were the tip of the spear for the Third Reich in consigning their fellow Jews to *Nacht and Nebel, night and fog*, as envisaged by the Final Solution, a plan to murder every Jew in the world, which Heydrich and Himmler had senior Nazis ratify at Wannsee just a few months before this sweaty rendezvous with Sepp Lange. The immediate objective was a to render Germany *Judenfrei, Jew Free*, because in the words of the Führer:

> *The Jews are undoubtedly a race but not human. They cannot be human in the sense of being an image of God, the Eternal...Jewry means the racial tuberculosis of a nation.*

Of the 160,000 Jews living in Berlin prior to the war, barely 40,000 remained in 1942. The lucky ones had emigrated. Thousands would be "resettled" in concentration camps while countless others would commit suicide or be murdered outright. By the end of the war, fewer than 5,000 Jews survived in Berlin.

Stella was probably the least political person in all of Germany and had no time for Hitler's rantings and ravings. *Vati*, her father, had been among the 100,000 Jews who fought bravely for the Fatherland in World War I and deserved everyone's respect she would complain to Sepp, who feigned sympathy.

But her acquiescence to the Gestapo was all in a good cause, she told herself. *Mutti* and *Vati* had escaped deportation and now lived a rather comfortable life just steps away in their tidy flat on *Sophien Strasse* thanks to her arrangement with Lange.

Moreover, Stella was tall, blonde and vivacious with a voracious appetite for life. It was not the rough, sweaty lovemaking with Sepp that she sought. That was a recent development and part of the job.

She simply wanted the life to which her handsome stipend entitled her and to avoid the scourge of wearing a yellow star on the fine clothes that she could now provide for herself. This was another privilege afforded a *Greiferin*. Hitler's Berlin was a fine place for a beautiful *Aryan* woman, by birth or by choice, who could afford the finer things.

And she had to admit to herself that she enjoyed the thrill of the hunt, the sense of achievement that came from a job well done. Stella excelled in combing Berlin for her fellow Jews and had become known by some as *Blonde Poison* by others as the *Blonde Ghost*. She was particularly adept at posing as a "U-boat" herself to trap her prey. Many were her former schoolmates from the segregated Jewish school to which *Mutti* and *Vati* had sent her as a young girl.

Sepp called her a survivor with contrived admiration. She detested the adulation from Sepp and his crude Gestapo companions and could not help but wonder in her unguarded moments whether she was indeed just a survivor, a loving daughter, a clever girl who simply loved life or the rottenest of rotten apples? She kept each of these possibilities in its own compartment.

How many had been captured thanks to her? Dozens by now, she thought. Other than Sepp, few could say because nearly all her potential accusers had been silenced in the extermination camps. Sepp would tell her, *send them to oblivion or face your own.*

Sepp had delivered another assignment during their small talk as they both lay on their backs in bed, their thoughts drifting upward with the smoke of their cigarettes to gently carom off the ornamental tin ceiling tiles above their heads.

The Führer is in a rage and wants to find this boy, the son of a Munich judge who had been his adversary at every step during the early days. We will double your stipend to 600 Reichsmarks, as well as the allotment of ration cards to your parents. We have reliable information that the boy has surfaced in Wedding. But please understand, the man at the top is watching, so failure will be dealt with harshly, Sepp said.

Reinhard Heydrich, his boss and the author of the *Final Solution*, had proclaimed that the boy and his kind were an open wound to the Fatherland whose infectious residue had to be stanched. His own failure would also be dealt with harshly so one way or the other, Sepp had to find a way to deliver the boy's head on a pike.

Stella simply responded by saying, *be a dear and pour me a bit of schnapps. You have nothing to worry about.*

* * * * *

The source of Sepp's intelligence on the fugitive boy had watched with pride on Easter Sunday morning as his two daughters pulled the silk ribbon from the large box. It looked like a dress box, but he and his girls knew that it would be something else, something quite special.

The Reverend Doctor Martin Sauter was a man on the make in the *Reichskirche*, and the garments that Klara and Karla removed from the box reflected his growing prominence. The first was a *chasuble*, a poncho like liturgical vestment worn by Lutheran ministers typically over a white Alb or cassock, which his youngest Karla now modeled with comic effect. The chasuble was dark green, embroidered along its cream-colored edges with a series of ornate crosses alternating with the image of the Reich's eagle.

The second vestment was a long stole in rich purple. Each side of the stole which would hang from the Reverend's neck and extend roughly to just below his hips displayed a scarlet cross set on top of a golden Reich's eagle, each symmetrically positioned on the right and the left about chest high.

It was a gift from Goebbels on the occasion of his appointment as vice chancellor of the *Reichskirche's* governing consistory. The good Reverend had achieved notable success of late as the man who had catalogued the dissenting ministers of Hitler's German Church, so they could be summarily drafted and sent to the front.

He was just the kind of man that Goebbels valued. He was malleable, easily swayed by flattery, shallow in intellect but clever with words, words quite often of little real import.

This had been Sauter's problem before the schism in the church. Most thought of him as a devout man with little potential. He was someone whom his superiors and colleagues thought would be better suited as the pastor of a small rural parish rather than a prominent posting in Berlin.

Sauter had aspired to become a theologian but had bumped up against the likes of Dietrich Bonhoeffer and Martin Niemöller in Berlin. Before the arrival of the National Socialists Workers Party, Sauter had been accepted for publication only twice. Both works were well crafted nonsense and critical reaction had, well, been highly critical.

His luck had changed with the advent of the Nazis. As the schism of the German Lutheran church approached, Goebbels plucked him from obscurity after a mutual friend introduced them over *kaffee und kuchen* at Café Kranzler and set him to the task of crafting the argument for the Party's stance on religion. Their invention was *Positive Christianity*, and the foundation for its manifesto had been a certain pleasing circular logic, a rhetorical specialty of Sauter's, that went something like this:

Christianity is National Socialism and National Socialism is the doing of God's will and God's will reveals itself in German blood. True Christianity is represented by the Party, and the German people are now called by the Party and especially the Führer to a real Christianity, as the Führer is the herald of a new revelation.

Truth be told, the author of this blubber, the Reverend Doctor Sauter himself, had not been impressed with the uncouth Hitler and his Nazi thugs at first. He and many in his social circle were appalled by Hitler's tactics but looked the other way because they saw him as a useful vehicle to achieve their desired ends. They believed they were in a unique position to look the other way for the time being because as Christians, well, all would be forgiven in the end.

But having scaled the moral bulwark of one's conscience in such a way, the fall from the other side is precipitously steep. Even Sauter knew it.

The growing power that he wielded in his weak hands and the occasional toast made in his honor at the opulent dinner parties thrown by Goebbels for his Nazi party colleagues were a narcotic that Sauter craved.

His effervescent faith as a young man, like the refreshingly sharp first breath of air on a bracingly cold day, had now become a knot in his stomach, an insomnia at 2:00 in the morning that had no other cause but this. But he had his wife and girls to look after and, well, all would be forgiven in the end.

This is why he had informed on Bonhoeffer to the authorities. His rival had secretly preached in Wedding on Palm Sunday, much to Sauter's personal annoyance and in defiance of the Party's general ban on Bonhoeffer's speaking and writing. Many of Sauter's regular parishioners had opted for Bonhoeffer over himself.

The good reverend did not know whether the troublemaker Bonhoeffer truly had the boy that the Gestapo sought, but he knew that he could make life miserable for his former brother in Christ and theological rival. And if by sheer luck he was right, there would be more ground to be gained on his march to the top.

11. THE CONSPIRATORS

Die Bäckerei was closed when Dietrich and the boy arrived as the rising sun turned the smoke-gray fog into a ball of cotton. The shop had been closed after the first batch of bread had been put out ostensibly for oven repairs, and a long line of patrons had been redirected to a door at the back of the *Mietskaserne's* long inner courtyard.

It was customary amidst the hardship in Berlin at this time for a bakery's patrons to bring a small handful of coal and a little water for the baker's use as full or partial payment for bread. Many of those in line bearing these gifts were small children.

Mehdi was nothing if not unconventional. For those patrons who were known to him, they would leave, depending upon the circumstances, not only with bread but a counterfeit ration coupon, a few Reichsmarks or even medicine, conveniently concealed in the paper with which the bread was loosely wrapped.

Mehdi had a good heart but there was also enlightened self-interest at play here. His beneficence created a network of loyal allies to counter the malignant and deadly network of Gestapo informants that infested Wedding.

She was in the shop just yesterday, and this is one new client I would just as soon not have, said Mehdi to the Young Minister as they sat at a small café-style table tucked into the front corner of the shop. The boy had been secreted to the back of the sprawling shop to be fed.

Looming over Dietrich and Mehdi on the wall above the table was a new and very large poster that read *Die Straßen Adolf Hitlers* that featured a larger than life Hitler with a broad smile and large shovel in hand as he personally broke ground for the Third Reich's new public autobahn system.

The small bell at the shop door jingled, and Dietrich heard in the Admiral's unmistakable baritone a note of exasperation, *truth be told, fleeting as its value may be these days, the truth is that work on the autobahn had begun long before Hitler's arrival but when one controls the instruments of mass communication, well, what does our beloved Herr Goebbels tell us, 'tell a lie once and it remains a lie but a lie told 1,000 times becomes the truth.' Morgen, Dietrich, Mehdi,* Admiral Canaris said warmly nodding to both.

Moment, Mehdi replied, and he was off to bring another kaffee to the table and fresh bread for the Admiral.

Dietrich to whom Admiral Canaris had addressed himself smiled as he hastily swallowed a large piece of Choreg, the traditional Easter bread of Armenia, of which he could not get enough, and replied in kind, *In John 8:32, the Lord says the truth will set you free, and it feels as though we are in a race through a dark valley where either truth or the hangman's noose will set us free.*

Canaris snorted as he took the cup of Kaffee from Mehdi. *I am sure this Easter bread is wonderful but I, my father and his father before him have had Vollkornbrot virtually every morning of our lives.* He had barely finished his sentence when Mehdi pulled a fresh loaf off the shelf and began cutting it at the table.

The German love affair with bread is eons long, and it should come as no surprise then that the word for the traditional evening meal in Germany is *Abendbrot – Evening Bread*. Germany was not unified until 1871 and the countless varieties of German bread, rolls and pastries sprung from the ingredients available to each of the 27 autonomous German speaking states and their smaller enclaves before their unification.

Canaris savored the dense, chewy richness of the Vollkornbrot baked with einkorn flour, a grain that had aged gracefully, staying little changed over its 10,000-year history, while every day wheat had been hybridized both purposefully and accidentally many times over. As far as Canaris was concerned, there was a certain *je ne sais quoi* about everything that Mehdi and the boy put out that made their baking more than the sum of its parts.

As he parsed with each bite the crunch of linseed, sunflower and sesame seeds that bejeweled the dense brown bread, sinking deeper into the spell it cast, he was transported to a time when Gods and Giants ruled. Canaris was an accomplished and learned man but like his countrymen, his German soul could not escape the grip of a primal, pagan tribalism, suppressed but not defeated by Christianity.

The Vollkornbrot drew him inexorably to the *Hearg*, high German for a grove, a dark place in which a mound of rough stones called a cairn served as an altar for the consecration of sacrifice, human and animal. It was a place evoked so richly in the mysticism of Richard Wagner's operas and in this moment, by the seductive earthiness of the Vollkornbrot he savored.

I rode with Heydrich this morning in the Tiergarten in spite of the fog, and it appears that there is a boy who has caused quite a stir and who appears to have been traced to Wedding. If either of you have him in tow, the noose of which you speak, Dietrich, is tightening and time is of the essence. Not waiting for a confession, Canaris added, *how can I help you.*

Reinhard Heydrich was Himmler's cadaverous deputy chief of the *Geheime Staatspolizei*, the secret state police otherwise known as the Gestapo. What seemed to most a constructive if not particularly warm professional relationship between Heydrich and Canaris belied the Gestapo's bitter rivalry with Abwehr.

It is worse than that, my dear Sirs, Mehdi jumped in. *As I told you earlier, the snake of a girl who hunts her own kind for Heydrich's Gestapo was in – here – in my shop yesterday morning. While a new client is always welcomed, she was not here for the Vollkornbrot or Choreg. She lingered at this very table for a time, looking at everyone up and down. Ibne-sharmouta, whore!*

Please forgive me, Sirs, Mehdi quickly added and went silent. Mehdi was an experienced operator with ice in his veins in the face of danger, so his heightened level of concern was not lost on his guests.

Dietrich, deep in thought, said a barely audible, *nothing to forgive.* Admiral Canaris said, as he looked adoringly at his Vollkornbrot, *if your visitor is who I think she is, she is quite capable and too calculating to fritter away her time without a trail to follow. We should be more concerned by the question of who put her onto the trail in the first place because it could threaten the whole of our small but productive collaboration.*

They sat in silence for a few minutes, breaking bread together. The Admiral slathering a rich marmalade on his Vollkornbrot while Dietrich still deep in thought picked at a piece of Choreg.

At the risk of offending you, my dear Sirs, there has been talk that the great roadbuilder might someday soon be buried under such a road. You are the most efficient race on earth. Why has this outcome not been achieved?

It was not Mehdi who asked this question as it seemed to come from nowhere. It was in fact a question from Mehdi's protégé, a boy with a mane of disheveled, coal black hair, delivered in mocking imitation of his mentor from behind the counter where he had gone unnoticed.

The protégé was a reluctant participant in political intrigue and was much more comfortable with the simple calculus of buying and selling on the black market, a realm where he was now at least the equal of his mentor. Fresh from his heart-to-heart with the Ottos, Leo was ready to put in his two cents here and pulled up a chair.

* * * * *

The three conspirators watched as the tall, lanky boy, barely 18, casually straddled a chair turned backwards to the table and slouched over its top rail. It had been five years since Pushpa had deposited Leo with Mehdi on the assumption that it would be a temporary arrangement. But Leo and Mehdi had formed a quick and strong bond borne of a common background, shared experiences and a larcenous *zeitgeist*.

Mehdi for his part was the product of the slums of *Ras al-Ayn*, then a part of the Ottoman Empire, where he spent his early childhood in a one room mud hut with 15 other people. His mother had gone to work as a domestic for the great Max Oppenheim, the German lawyer, diplomat and archeologist who was a member of the Oppenheim banking dynasty. Abandoning his career in diplomacy, Oppenheim discovered the site of *Tel Halaf* on the Anatolian plain near *Ras al-Ayn* in 1899 and conducted excavations there in 1911-13 and again in 1929.

Mehdi's mother, a beautiful woman of Chechen descent, went to work for Oppenheim at his villa near the *Tel Halaf* dig and they soon became lovers. Her third boy, Mehdi, became part of the bargain when Oppenheim discovered the boy's talent for mechanical engineering, which he used to the fullest extent possible at *Tel Halaf*.

Oppenheim's relationship with Mehdi's mother eventually ran its course, but he saw the potential in the boy and returned to Berlin with him in 1914. Chronically short on funds from galivanting around the Levant and from his investment in the *Tel Halaf* dig, Oppenheim eventually placed Mehdi with a distant cousin who owned a handful of bakeries in Berlin. Oppenheim's cousin succumbed to the Spanish flu pandemic in 1918 leaving Mehdi as his sole heir.

After liquidating all but the bakery in Wedding and the small building where Dietrich kept a flat, Mehdi set out on a path in life that included baking and the black market. He was much more successful in the latter than the former until the boy arrived with his superhuman powers to bend a lump of inert dough to his will and give it life. *Die Bäckerei* began to flourish. Clients came from across Berlin for the veritable works of art it produced.

It was not lost on Mehdi when he first met the boy after having his arm gently twisted by Pushpa that his roots were intertwined in tragedy with the boy's. During the Armenian Genocide, *Ras al-Ayn* was one of the major collecting points for deported Armenians. From 1915 on, 1.5 million Armenians were deported from all over the Ottoman Empire, many forced into death marches into the Syrian desert. Over 80,000 Armenians, mostly women and children, were slaughtered in desert death camps near *Ras al-Ayn*, a place that had become synonymous with Armenian suffering.

Mehdi could not get the boy to open up about his life before Berlin. He and Leo eventually learned through Mehdi's network that Leo's father, Hayk, had died 18 months after the boy's arrival in Berlin, buried by the aftershock of an earthquake while tending to his patients. The kindly Mehdi simply could not get the boy to open up even though it was clear that Hayk's death weighed heavily on Leo's heart.

In all other things, Mehdi and Leo were birds of a feather. They would talk constantly about their one abiding interest, the art of turning a deal to their advantage. A black market is created by the convergence of urgency and ingenuity, and they were its consummate arbitrageurs with a twist. The two often took razor thin margins to help feed their neighbors and relished cheating the wealthy and powerful when the opportunity presented itself.

Mehdi's kindness towards him was not lost on the taciturn boy. It wasn't an instinct that was foreign to Leo. He had been cut from the same mold as Hayk and was devoted to the wolfpack. Mehdi's humanity seemed to connect him in spirit to Hayk, Mina and Anya. Although, there had been no word from Anya since that fateful day when he left Aleppo. It was a loss that bothered him when he let it.

Boy, one can be as clever as one wants to be – you and I are just that. But I am here out of luck taking someone else's place in this good life that I live – you and I live, Mehdi had once told Leo.

My brothers and sisters and my dear mother were not so lucky. My brothers and sisters were beautiful children just as much as the scrubbed, blonde hair, blue eyed babies of our German clients.

One of my sisters sang beautifully, another brother was brave and forthright. They had talent, heart and ambition, but to the casual observer we were just a bunch of dirty, underfed animals living in squalid conditions and deemed deserving of those conditions because we didn't have the gumption to do anything about them.

Alas, as you and I both know, it is not a matter of gumption. It is a matter of what shell we are found under in the game of chance that dictates where and to whom we are born. And why am I here and not one of them? Pure dumb luck.

I am who I am in the way I treat others because I see my brothers and sisters in each and every one I meet, and I cannot let another human being be discarded like they were if it is in my power to prevent it. It is a debt to them that I will never stop repaying.

Mehdi in his kind way could even understand the brown shirts and the broader support for Hitler, at least up to a point. These people were in a way refugees themselves – battered by the extreme poverty and hunger that followed the end of the war in 1918, riven from their childhood dreams of a decent life. The revival of the 1920's had provided some modicum of prosperity and, with it, dignity only to be dashed by the collapse of the world economy in the late 1920's and early 1930's.

Hitler's rabid supporters fed on their anger, and anger leads people to do terrible things. *Remember Horst Wulff who lost his job at Schultheiss,* Mehdi once asked Leo? *He is one of them now. When your young child dies in bed next to you from pneumonia caused by malnutrition, you will follow the devil.*

On that fateful Easter Monday morning, an aloof and from all outward appearances eminently self-confident Leo took the measure of the group assembled at *Die Bäckerei*. The aristocratic Canaris, equally aloof, acknowledged his presence with a subtle but respectful nod. Canaris knew how important the clever boy was to Abwehr's clandestine efforts on multiple fronts because Mehdi, himself an Abwehr agent, gave Leo the most difficult assignments without a second thought.

Canaris had recruited Dietrich at the urging of Hans Dohnányi, one of his handpicked lieutenants in the Abwehr, who also happened to be Dietrich's brother-in-law. Almost from the moment that Canaris arrived on the job in 1935, Abwehr had secretly opposed and actively worked against the wishes of Hitler and his henchmen appearing to be the model of intelligence gathering efficiency. As such, it remained a bulwark of resistance in the ebb and flow of opposition to Hitler in the military and civil service.

Dohnányi had brought Dietrich into the fold to shield the outspoken minister from the increasing harassment of the Gestapo and from conscription with the claim that Bonhoeffer's numerous ecumenical contacts could be useful to Germany. Indeed, Abwehr hoped that Dietrich's British contacts, especially the influential Bishop George Bell, could pave the way to a fair peace after the conspirators in the German military had eliminated Hitler.

Time was of the essence for Germany. Hitler's river of blood had overrun its banks, making a rapprochement with the British less and less likely, so it was now or never if the conspirators were to make one more run at the British.

Time was not on Dietrich's side either, as the young minister had recently learned through Dohnányi that the Gestapo was watching both of them closely. Dohnányi's telephone had been tapped and his mail intercepted.

Leo acknowledged Dietrich respectfully, *Pastor Bonhoeffer, it has been a while. I hope that you are well and keeping your flock one step ahead of the Devil.*

Leo, it is a pleasure to see you again. This bread is wondrous, one of your best efforts yet. I am also grateful for your hospitality this morning more broadly speaking, Dietrich said with barely concealed irony.

Dietrich eyed the odd, gold crested dagger that he had occasionally seen hanging from the boy's belt. The Bedouin Khanjar had been a gift from Anya that she had concealed in Leo's rucksack on their last day together in Aleppo.

When challenged about the dagger by Dietrich when they first met, Leo would protest that it was nothing more than a baker's tool, good for cutting dough cleanly. To Dietrich it looked dangerous and deadly, not to say ungodly, if its purpose was not limited to dough.

Leo had been drawn into the young minister's orbit shortly after he arrived in Berlin, a troubled boy barely speaking *Löffelsprache*, the German equivalent of pig Latin, which he had picked up from the archaeologists in Aleppo. Mehdi had deposited the boy with Dietrich, who involved him with the other boys in his Wedding ministry and in his bucolic retreats at Biesenthal. Indeed, less than a year after his arrival in Berlin, Leo too was baptized.

Dietrich had been fascinated by the boy. There was a certain understated magnetism in Leo that drew other boys to his leadership. In fact, many members of the wolfpack that now operated from these premises had originally been members of Dietrich's youth groups. This was just as well from Dietrich's point of view because while he could help nourish their souls, Leo seemed better equipped to attend to their immediate physical wellbeing.

Leo challenged Dietrich, whose sturdy faith and logician's rigorous intellect failed in classifying the boy. He struggled to penetrate the hard shell to reach the soft core of Leo's personality, to understand his value system.

There was good in the boy but to Dietrich's way of thinking a feature of man's maturity is not only responsibility toward other people but an understanding that leadership derived its authority from God, the source of Goodness. Without this, Leo could not truly lead others to maturity.

This was the enigma of Leo from Dietrich's point of view as the boy seemed to skate across this foundational element of one's character without touching the surface of the ice. As Dietrich flashed back to his early days with Leo, he chuckled silently when he recalled the observation by Martin Luther that he had applied rightly or wrongly to Leo in the early days, *sometimes the curses of the godless sound better than the Hallelujahs of the pious.*

The heat of the ovens that had been opened after the first batch of the morning and the pressure of the moment closed in on the group seated under the larger-than-life poster of their nemesis. They were all accomplished men, men of action and principle, who had devoted themselves to answering Leo's semi-rhetorical question about the failure heretofore to eliminate the Führer.

With the fragmented and disorganized societal resistance to the Nazis as the backdrop, the conspiracy in the military and civil services to eliminate Hitler evoked the fable of the evil king Sisyphus whose eternal punishment in Hades was forever to roll a huge boulder up a hill only to have it roll down again as soon as he had brought it to the summit. Failed attempts by brave individuals taking matters into their own hands, bad timing and the incessant dithering of the generals would undercut any concerted effort to remove the Führer.

Some in the German elites saw through Hitler's populist, violent game from the start. Many conspirators in the ranks of the military and civil service who supported Hitler's nationalistic aims and helped to install him now saw him as a bloodthirsty, uncouth maniac. Yet the "high minded" Prussian aristocrats who dominated the German officer corps would shy away from any attack on the authority of the state. *Prussian field marshals do not mutiny*, they would say.

The generals had become increasingly disillusioned by the insanity of the Nazi regime as early as 1938 when Hitler moved aggressively to invade Austria, Poland and Czechoslovakia. Although, Ludwig Beck, the Wehrmacht Chief of Staff, was alone in resigning in protest. He had come to believe that Hitler could not be influenced to do the right thing and change his course and thus that both Hitler and the Nazis needed to be removed from government.

Canaris who would later join Beck as a leading member of the July 20 plot to assassinate Hitler, was a complicated figure. As master of backroom dealings in the Third Reich, he also maintained an open channel with British Intelligence during Operation Barbarossa, the German invasion of Russia, and intervened, often with Mehdi's assistance, to save victims of Nazi persecution, including Jews.

For example, he was instrumental in getting five-hundred Dutch Jews to safety barely a year before his Easter Monday meeting with Dietrich and Mehdi at *Die Bäckerei*. Many of the fugitives were given token training as Abwehr "agents" and then issued papers allowing them to leave Germany. These papers had by and large been printed in the back of Mehdi's shop.

Canaris also had been one of the first to raise the alarm in 1939 about the atrocities of the Nazis *Einsatzgruppen*, or killing squads, in the invasions of Poland and Czechoslovakia. It had been his hope that the sheer magnitude of this barbarity would convince top generals and eventually the German people of Hitler's criminality. Sadly, it had not.

The *Einsatzgruppen* comprised 3,000 SS stormtroopers, who entered Poland in the first days of the invasion in September 1939 to find and eliminate *enemies of the state*. By the following year, they had killed an estimated 60,000 of these internal enemies including prominent Jewish figures, priests, political leaders and anyone the Nazis considered a threat to their rule. Heydrich, then head of the security force within the SS, played a crucial role in coordinating the deadly work of the *Einsatzgruppen*.

The *Einsatzgruppen* should have come as no surprise to the Generals. Hitler told his Generals just before the war began, in August 1939, that they should *close their hearts to pity* and *act brutally*. When the brave Colonel-General Johannes Blaskowitz later complained about the Einsatzgruppen killings, Hitler reacted by saying that *one can't fight a war with Salvation Army methods* and accused Blaskowitz of having *childish attitudes*. Hitler immediately relieved him of his command.

Hitler's swift conquest of Poland and Czechoslovakia, and later France and the low countries, deflated the will of the German military to remove Hitler while creating a deep reservoir of popular support for his regime. It was hard to argue with the success of the German military even if that success would eventually destroy Germany.

The rout of the German army by the Russians sometime later, after they had come within sight of the golden spires of the Kremlin in December 1941, should have rallied the generals to overthrow the Führer but Hitler, the consummate survivor, threw the first punch cashiering the generals in the high command on the Eastern front, removing in the process General Brauchitsch, the linchpin of any likely coup, demoralizing the conspirators and making agreement on a plan action against Hitler all but impossible. Chance intervened once again when the Japanese entered the war on December 7, 1941, helping to prop up a teetering Hitler, although it also brought the Americans into the war assuring that Hitler would henceforth be fighting a war on two fronts.

And to make matters worse if that were possible, word had reached Canaris shortly before the Easter Monday meeting about a conference at Wannsee and Hitler's hellish vision for the fate of Jews in the Third Reich. It had been spearheaded by none other than Reinhard Heydrich.

Principled individuals looked into their hearts on that foggy Easter Monday in 1942 at Oderberger Strasse 15, like Beck and Blaskowitz, for a path to end this evil regime and the courage to take it.

* * * * *

The girl may be the least of our concerns, Leo said. *The SS, the Polizei and some of the most devoted informants among our neighbors have been swarming around the shop like fruit flies. A few of our boys are keeping an eye on this circus.*

Mehdi rolled his eyes looking at Leo, *remember that idiot Marcus Fischer who used to be a low-level bookkeeper at the brewery? He is now a fully-fledged Gestapo man complete with a new leather great coat and that wide-brimmed fedora that he pulls down over the sneer on his pasty face. He stopped by the shop yesterday, soon after the girl left. I don't think that he and the girl even know each other but their mutual interest in visiting us, I am sure, had nothing to do with baked goods. The fool left without buying anything. At least the girl made it look like she was interested in our bread.*

Have you inquired with your gauleiter, Mehdi, Canaris asked? *Can he be counted on for continued support?*

This has all happened so quickly, that I have not, sir, Mehdi replied. *I will, of course. My hunch is that he will not want to slay his golden calf, but even he must be feeling the heat.*

In the present climate, what are the options for moving our guest, Dietrich asked?

He is no longer in the shop and for the moment he has melted into the wolfpack. While our boys are clever, they are boys, and there are too many eyes and ears swarming around us to make this anything but a short-term accommodation, Leo replied.

Mehdi added, *we are reluctant to utilize our full network in this instance if in fact we have been compromised because we have too much ongoing activity in the pipeline that could be disrupted to the severe detriment of our friends and those they are currently helping.* Indeed, Mehdi's network was one of several in Germany serving as an underground railroad for Jews, political dissidents, deserters and others on the run. The network included everyday people, Lutherans and Catholics, Barons and green grocers, young and old, who hated the Nazis but could never hate their fellow Germans.

These networks were often vast and complex because it typically took at least ten committed souls and at times as many as 30 to save the life of one *illegal* in hiding. A fugitive from the Gestapo could never stay in one place for more than a few days, so new hideouts needed to be found. Others in the network provided food, while others still handled the falsification of documents and the petty bribery required to get lower-level officials who were not committed Nazis simply to look the other way at the right times, a discipline in which Mehdi and Leo excelled.

No one argued with Mehdi's instinct to leave well enough alone and all agreed that while the boy's days in Germany were most assuredly numbered, they would look elsewhere for inspiration to get him out of Berlin and out of Germany under the current circumstances. It was at that point that Dietrich interjected, *let us turn to another subject for the moment, which may bear on this predicament.* He got no argument as Mehdi refilled cups with the kaffee from Göring's ambrosian stash.

Admiral, Dietrich began, *my next mission is to Sweden to meet with Bishop Bell, as you well know because you gave it to me.* He looked at the others for effect and said, *Bishop Bell is a dear friend and has connections to the Churchill government. He is presently our best hope for a fair peace with the Allies if Germany can hold up her end of the bargain.*

No one present had any doubts about the price to be paid.

I have a special courier's pass compliments of Abwehr. It never occurred to me to ask, Dietrich said with mounting hope, *can we make the boy a stowaway?*

Before Canaris could respond, Leo asked, *why is this British Bishop in Sweden?* Canaris listened carefully, jumping ahead to the permutations and combinations of a tactical plan.

It is an ecumenical council at Sigtuna, about 50 kilometers north-west of Stockholm, Dietrich replied. *It will be attended by the Baltic consistories and presided over by his eminence Bishop Bell, who has been invited by Sweden, which is politically neutral, at least in a formal sense.*

Sweden's neutrality was debatable. It provided Finland with soldiers during the Winter War against the USSR in 1940 and was a major supplier of raw materials for Hitler's military.

Some Swedes volunteered for the Waffen SS and Sweden often failed to provide adequate asylum for refugees including Norwegian Jews who were nearly exterminated. However, the Swedish Lutheran Church would at times play an instrumental role in aiding the rescue of Jews from Nazi Germany leaving the world to wonder about the country's true loyalties.

This may be our last fleeting hope of a peace overture to Britain through an intermediary with real influence. If we are stopped before we arrive at the airfield by Heydrich's men looking for the boy, that will be the end of it for the boy and for our hopes with Bell, Canaris added.

Canaris and Dietrich were calm and focused working the same crossword puzzle together. Mehdi could do more than hold his breath.

Pastor Bonhoeffer, is this conference like the one that you took me to along with Lutz Schneider and the Lindner brothers some years back, Leo asked? *The place in Denmark? Remember? Is there a youth council in Sweden?*

Dietrich shot bolt upright. It would be unusual if there were not, but he really had not thought about the possibility.

Yes, Fanø. I recall now. Leo, good gracious, what do you have in mind, but Dietrich already knew the answer to this question, and the excitement of the moment made his face flush.

I think that you might consider taking three devout lads along with you, Leo replied. *I would join you and bring my best man Big Otto with me. His blonde hair and chiseled Aryan features will dazzle the most hardened Nazis.* No one present needed to ask who the third boy would be.

III. SIGTUNA, SWEDEN - MAY 1942

It would not be as easy, but the conspirators were on to something that might provide a way to hide the boy in plain sight. *Once we get him to the Abwehr airfield in Dahlem, he will be fine,* Canaris said. *There is no love lost between our men and Heydrich's ghouls. The Wehrmacht detachment there is quite loyal to us.*

Anticipating the Admiral's next statement, Leo chimed in, *so we need to find a way to get him there and…*The Admiral finished the thought…*and there will be SS border officers to reckon with upon your arrival in Stockholm. The Swedes allow them to operate freely.*

Well, about getting him to your base, we occasionally borrow a brewery truck from old man Schultheiss for our larger transactions, Mehdi said, raising his eyebrows at his liberal use of the term *borrow. And no one, not even the SS, would violate the sanctity of a tabernacle such as a beer truck,* Dietrich added with a wry smile.

Well, I would put nothing past the SS, Leo said. *We will put Big Otto in the front with the driver. He does a good job of presenting himself as cut from the same brown cloth as the SS, so if anyone can talk his way through it, it is Big Otto. I will be in the back with the boy,* Leo said.

As to our reception in Sweden? Dietrich raised his eyebrows buoyed by the contours of the plan taking shape. Canaris jumped in, *we will see to it that they have the right papers, but we must assume that they will call Heydrich before letting you through customs.*

I may have the solution to this problem, but it will take some time to arrange. I will start on it today, Mehdi interjected. Mehdi made eye contact with Canaris and there was a flash of recognition in the Admiral's eyes.

Can you be more specific, Dietrich asked?

A brave colleague may be willing to lend a hand, but it is best not to say more for now, a distracted Mehdi replied in such a way as to suggest he was already working on the plan.

* * * * *

He took a deep breath so those on the other end of the telephone line would not hear his voice quiver. In his mind's eye, he was for a fleeting moment the very personification of Joshua, son of Nun, a devoted student, a saintly man, and a brilliant military commander to whom the Lord said, *today I will begin to exalt you in the sight of all Israel, so they will know that I will be with you just as I was with Moses.*

The quivering passed, but he was drenched in sweat, which he attempted to mop up with the sleeve of his woolen blazer. We wanted desperately to rush to his wife and daughters to share the good news but told himself, *focus, Martin, focus. Ask good questions because they will expect you to look sharp.*

The *Lord* in the form of Goebbels, joined by Ludwig Müller, the senior most bishop of the *Reichskirche*, had called him at home without warning catching him off guard as he wrote a religiously tinted article for *Der Angrif*, a rude and aggressive mass circulation paper conceived by Goebbels that promoted antisemitism and support for Nazism.

My dear Reverend Sauter, we have approved the participation of Hanover, Hamburg and Berlin in Bishop Björkquist's synod at the Nordic Ecumenical Institute in May at Sigtuna. We want you to lead the delegation. Björkquist is a good friend of the Reichskirche, and we have asked him to greet you warmly.

Müller prattled on about the purpose and agenda of the synod but was cut off after a few minutes by an impatient Goebbels, *my dear man, we would also like you to treat our delegation as your flock and to keep an eye on them so that our lambs do not stray. Sweden today is such a complex stew of factions and interests, and only God knows how things will play out at the synod what with a British bishop in attendance. We will of course have our agents embedded in the flock but none with the access that you will have in your official role and by virtue of your standing in the Reichskirche,* Goebbels said.

I would be honored, your excellency, Sauter croaked, resisting the urge to spit up as the bile rose in his gullet. He took another deep breath wrestling with his nerves.

It goes without saying, Reverend Sauter, that you will shine on the world stage of ecumenical Christianity as the point of Joshua's spear for the Third Reich. And of course, if we can count on your full attention to the propriety of those representing us in the three delegations, well Reichbischof Müller and I see a bright future for you given the urgent near term need to fill the vacant post of bishop of the Prussian Union, Goebbels concluded with a flourish.

At that Sauter's bowels began to gurgle as his lunch liquified and the urgency of release built to its crescendo. Mercifully, Goebbels brought an end to the call as abruptly as it had begun but not before adding, *we are told that your colleague Bonhoeffer will attend in his nominal role as an agent of the Abwehr. He is an acquaintance of Bishop*

Bell's. We trust you will exercise all due discretion in keeping an eye on both and report to us any irregularities in Bonhoeffer's behavior. For that small service, your rewards will be manifold.

And with that the joyous and bilious Reverend Doctor Martin Sauter hurdled over a large ottoman near his desk, urgently seeking refuge in the nearest water closet.

* * * * *

Leo sat against the bulkhead of the Junker 52/3m the boxy, black-painted tin can that transported Abwehr agents to their clandestine assignments throughout Europe. Otto and the boy sat with him on a bench that ran along one side of the fuselage while Dietrich and an Abwehr security man sat on the opposite bench looking back at them. It was Leo's first flight, the first ever, and the intense vibrations and noise from the Junker's three engines did little to commend the experience. The pilots proudly proclaimed when they boarded that the Junker or *Tante Ju*, *Aunt Ju*, as they liked to call her, was the Führer's favorite type of aircraft. The Junker was also used as a troop transport and a bomber during the war.

That the Junker was renowned for its use by Hitler came as little consolation to Leo because like multitudes before him and after, he could not abide the loss of control, as the corrugated metal tube which held him captive hurdled toward Stockholm in the hands of two pilots who seemed to Leo to be far too relaxed under the circumstances.

Leo did not share Dietrich's strong belief that a better place awaited him in the afterlife and, judging from Dietrich's gray pallor on the other side of the fuselage, he might have been having second thoughts himself as they bounced along the top of a gray cloud deck. They hugged the thick gray clouds to avoid being detected by the enemy fighter planes that patrolled this same air space.

This particular Junker 52 was equipped with pontoons and they had taken off from the edge of a large lake near Dahlem that morning as the sun rose. They would, if all went as planned, land in the harbor of Stockholm by late afternoon following a refueling stop near Copenhagen.

They had left Berlin with a fighter escort to the German coastline, signifying the importance of this mission. How funny, Leo thought. If they had only known who they were protecting as he looked at the boy sitting between Big Otto and himself.

They had arrived at the Abwehr camp in Dahlem on the edge of a misty lake under the cover of darkness that morning. They were stopped as expected on the approach to the camp and half-heartedly searched by SS men, who were part of a detachment of home-sick cattlemen from *Staufen im Breisgau* in the rolling foothills of Southwest Germany bordering France and Switzerland.

This detachment of farmers would probably never qualify for the Reich's Eagle commendation for brains, and Otto was able to handle them easily with homespun charm and two cases of old man Schultheiss' Pilsner. Leo's last image of them was of the four eagerly dividing the two cases amongst themselves.

Had Leo been prone to thinking metaphorically, he might have found his confinement in a corrugated metal tube hurdling northward as reflective of a life's journey beyond his control since his abrupt departure from Aleppo, nearly five years before. Chaos propelled the world forward, and he was just along for the ride. Fortunately, Leo was not prone to thinking metaphorically.

Instead, he had brought with him from Aleppo a toughness, resilience and will to survive that had turned such chaos into Reichsmarks. He had amassed a small fortune in the process.

The part of him that held on to a little of Hayk and Mina compelled him to dote over the wolfpack and, against his better judgment, to help Dietrich with the boy. The hardnosed, more pragmatic Leo, however, asked himself what was he saving them for?

There would always be evil to replace evil. Of that Leo was sure. Hitler, who had replaced the genocidal monsters in the Ottoman Empire that had set his own life on its present course, would inevitably be replaced by something else, someone even worse perhaps.

And what of the other poor souls that used *Die Bäckerei* as a transit point? Germany wasn't the only place in Europe that hated Jews!

Dietrich would say that Good was inward looking, kind and gentle. But Leo knew that Evil was ruthless, strong and efficient. He harbored the fear that the brave but fragmented efforts of good people like Mehdi and Dietrich were admirable but simply no match for the forces that controlled Germany.

In times past, Anya would laughingly call him *Aslan*, the Lion, and in the same breath recite two lines of poetry, which were her favorite:

When your soul has the air of grace inside
You'll float above the world and there abide.

Boy, this will mean nothing to you now but, God willing, you will find its meaning in time, Anya would say. Leo was indeed still searching for the meaning in these words. Perhaps watching Mehdi and Dietrich in action would hold the key?

He had never asked Dietrich about these lines and wondered whether there was something in the Christian tradition that was comparable. It was hard to imagine floating above the chaos and danger that bore down on them now.

Later in the flight, as Leo and Big Otto stood watching the horizon over the shoulders of both pilots, a massive cloud bank appeared with no discernable top or bottom. They saw flashes of lightning in the roiling, apocalyptic mass of gray clouds that looked like a living thing, a grotesque chimera ready to devour them.

The pilots told the boys to go back, strap in and tell their companions to do the same. They could not go under, over or around the obstacle so they would plough through it.

There was a lull of several minutes during which Leo's hopes for a smooth transit through the cloud bank rose only to be dashed when rain showers hit. Heavy squalls slammed into the starboard side of the fuselage just as the pilot was making a sharp turn to the port side. All had gone dark inside the Junker 52 as clouds, as black as coal, enveloped them as they were thrown violently to port in the darkness.

Leo could barely make out Dietrich sitting on the starboard side of the fuselage straining against his harness without which he would have been thrown violently toward Leo and pulverized against his side of the cabin. The pilots fought to correct the attitude of the Junker but were buffeted again and again from squalls now bashing them on both sides of the aircraft. The whining of the struggling engines made it sound like the *Tante Ju* was writhing in her death throes.

The Junker finally straightened but was thrown straight up at the nose, rolling so sharply to the left that Leo could look through the window over Dietrich's shoulder and straight down to make out the white caps on the Baltic Sea visible through small slivers in the patchy clouds. The Abwehr agent and the boy vomited, while the others managed to maintain their composure, such as it was. A silent Dietrich sat with his eyes closed throughout the ordeal.

And then the Junker dropped abruptly, flaps and slats grinding into place. The ragged coastline of Denmark appeared in the distance as the *Tante Ju* dropped like a carnival ride to refuel at an airfield just south of Copenhagen.

* * * * *

Mercifully, the short hop from Copenhagen to Stockholm was uneventful and the pilots twice circled the beautiful city in its spectacular natural setting spread across hundreds of islands in an enormous lagoon as if they were giving a holiday tour. They made a point of flying low over the medieval cathedral of Stockholm called the *Storkyrkan* or *Great Church* tucked into Stockholm's old town, the *Gamla Stan*, steps from the royal palace.

While their passengers felt uncomfortably close to the ground as the Junker acrobatically banked this way and that, skirting Stockholm's rooftops, the pilots seemed to thoroughly enjoy the thrill ride. They treated their passengers to an exhilarating swirl of color as they soared atop the green tin roof of the cathedral, the yellow villas of the old city and the blue gray of its cobblestoned streets.

Once they alighted on the choppy waters of Stockholm harbor, it took nearly 30 minutes for *Tante Ju* to traverse the harbor to arrive at the foot of a long dock that t-boned into a broad quay fronting what appeared to be a series of warehouses. As they drew closer, Leo and Dietrich could make out a group of men on the quay milling about. Most seemed to be in uniform. Leo and Dietrich came to the same uncomfortable conclusion that even as they watched the men on the quay, these men were looking straight back at them.

They had been forewarned that this might happen – a greeting party of Swedish military police and the Gestapo. And they had also been told that they would be largely on their own to run this gauntlet on their way to the Archbishop's residence at *Sigtuna*.

They climbed a short ladder to reach the long dock bidding farewell to their happy-go-lucky pilots. Dietrich and Leo were weak at the knees to begin with after their harrowing flight and the gentle bobbing of the dock on the oil-laced gray wavelets did little to help them regain their equilibrium.

Dietrich, Big Otto and the Abwehr security man would take the lead while Leo hung back with the boy who was white as a sheet. Leo and Big Otto wore their game faces. Both experienced black marketeers, this was just another transaction to them. Leo had his Bedouin Khanjar in his rucksack just in case, but it would be of little use against the number of well-armed men bearing down on them.

The senior officer who approached them with his men was a bit of a dandy and looked like he had just stepped out of central casting for a well-kitted officer of the regiment. Behind him in standard issue SS costumes – fedoras and long leather great coats – were two rough looking men, who might have been dock workers at one time in their lives.

One appeared to be a Swede while the other spoke only German to his Swedish counterpart. Backing them up were a dozen heavily armed and seemingly unfriendly Swedish military policemen.

The leader of the group addressed Dietrich introducing himself as Överstelöjtnant Backlin. He held a rank that was roughly the equivalent of an Oberst in the German Wehrmacht or a full bird colonel in the American army.

We are guests of Bishop Manfred Björkquist, the Bishop of Stockholm and founder of the Nordic Ecumenical Institute and will attend his ecumenical meeting in Sigtuna. These boys have been hand-picked as emissaries of the Reich's German Lutheran Church to the youth synod,

Dietrich responded in turn. Dietrich conveniently overlooked the fact that he had been instrumental in the formation of the Reichskirche's rival, the Confessing Church.

Backlin listened with little apparent interest in what Dietrich had to say and commanded nonchalantly that the party turn over its papers to his adjutants who moved to the front and started leafing through them. The Gestapo agents shadowed the adjutants in this task.

Their paperwork was impressive, particularly the young boy's, all of it Little Otto's handiwork. His documents included his visa, membership card in the Hitler Youth – he was registered impressively as a *Hauptgefolgschaftsführer* or Captain of a unit of forty boys – his school identity card, and his imaginary parents' postal identification card. He even possessed a letter signed by Goebbels, which is to say by Little Otto, lauding an essay the boy had written about replacing Sunday mass in Catholic Churches with Saturday readings of *Mein Kampf*, a topic of some currency then among Nazi elites.

If Nazi Germany was nothing else, it was a regime built upon a mountain of paper.

The boy started quivering, at first a little, then a lot, as Backlin and the Gestapo examined the group more intently looking at each of them, then back to their respective documents and back to them again. It was then Leo smelled urine carried on the salt air that whipped around them now on the dock and saw a long stain on the leg of the boy's black suit.

Fortunately, Dietrich and Big Otto along with the Abwehr man formed an impressive phalanx whose bulk partially shielded the boy. Leo took the boy by the shoulder and whispered, *if there was ever a time for you to vomit, it is now*, and with that Leo took him by the shoulder and quickly walked him to the side of the long dock. The boy bent over the water while Leo wrapped his arm tightly around the boy's gut both to prime the pump and to keep him from falling in.

Needing no further encouragement, the terrified boy vomited impressively in all of its roiling, colorful glory, discharging undigested chunks of the *Medisterpolse*, the speckled Danish equivalent of German Bratwurst, which they all had devoured at lunch during their layover in Copenhagen. Big Otto had impressively downed three with Rugbrød, a poor cousin of Germany's Vollkornbrot. The boy's loud retching drew the attention of Backlin, and he pushed through Dietrich and Otto to confront Leo, still holding the boy's head over the water.

He is not a good flyer and did the same thing on the flight, Leo told Backlin, *we need to get him to the infirmary at Sigtuna*. The Gestapo agents had moved forward as well to take a closer look at the boy. As they did, the two pilots came up from the rear and said, *your next flight will be better, boy. The first is always the worst, especially with bad weather*.

This did not placate the Gestapo men who gave Backlin a wink and a nod. This was Backlin's cue, *the boy will come with us*, he said.

Dietrich protested loudly that the boy was in his charge and that these boys' parents, were all senior officials in the Party, who would be outraged at this treatment. Backlin waved a leather gloved hand somewhat theatrically as if he didn't care what the parents did or did not think, and the Gestapo men moved forward to grab the boy.

As Dietrich would say later, the blur of the next few minutes brought King David's Psalm 29 to life:

> *The voice of the Lord is over the waters;*
> *the God of glory thunders,*
> *the Lord thunders over the mighty waters.*

The voice of the Lord is powerful;
the voice of the Lord is majestic.

In this instance the thunder came from a formidable nun who was barreling down the dock toward them bellowing, a disembodied face and hands carried along by swirling black and white robes. *Move out of my way,* she commanded, as the ranks of the military police parted as the waters had for Moses and the people of Israel.

Leo, who kept himself between the Gestapo men and the boy, could not get a good look at her because of the commotion and because the small army of nuns and clergymen that followed her moved swiftly to round up Dietrich's group. She and the other nuns wore habits with an elaborate white coif and cowl that revealed little of their faces. It reminded Dietrich of the helmets worn by medieval knights in armor.

I am Sister Anna Maria, Deaconess of the Order of the Holy Paraclete, and I have been dispatched by his eminence, Bishop Manfred Björkquist, to collect our honored guests on his behalf. They are due in Sigtuna for an audience with his eminence this afternoon. What is the meaning of this delay, she demanded of no one in particular?

Backlin addressed her respectfully, *we are here at the request of our military high command to ensure that everything is in order with their paperwork. We have had difficulty of late with the infiltration of our fatherland by political and military provocateurs.*

The German SS man protested to his Swedish counterpart, and the Deaconess took one disdainful look at them and said, *and these two. We are neutral are we not? What is the reason for the harassment to which our guests are being subjected by the secret police?*

That shut Backlin up, who conscious of the fact that he was being dressed down in the presence of his men by a nun, sought to salvage the situation diplomatically. *You may take them, but concerns have been raised about our guests, and we shall pay a visit to his eminence later to speak with him.*

You do that, Deaconess Anna Maria shot back. *Now have your men stand aside,* she said. With a nod from Backlin, they did just that and Dietrich's entourage followed the Deaconess marching double-time to keep up with her flowing robes, which flapped like the wings of a large black bird under whose protection they would fly away, at least for now.

They arrived at a line of Volvo limousines that looked like small tanks and quickly piled into them as directed, Deaconess Anna Maria disappearing into the car in the lead. As they settled in, Dietrich closed his eyes and Leo saw his lips moving slightly and knew he was praying. After the episode on the dock, Leo was inclined to do the same to whomever or whatever had sent Sister Anna Maria.

* * * * *

They were an exquisite blue, he thought, as Bishop Manfred Björkquist gazed into Big Otto's eyes as he greeted the group from Berlin, upon its arrival in the gothic chapel of the Lutheran seminary at Sigtuna. In the infinite space beyond those brilliant blue orbs, Björkquist saw the future of Nordic youth intertwined with that of a Swedish Lutheran Church, a church that had in his view become feminized.

The field of sports had become the new missionary frontier for Björkquist and the Swedish Lutheran Church to bring young men back to church services because the Sabbath after all was the only day of the week available for both worship and sporting activity. In those twinkling blue gems, Björkquist saw himself in years past with other young men on the shores of Lake Mälaren exhibiting those robust, active, vibrant qualities he wanted to bring back to the Swedish Lutheran Church.

The intermezzo between Björkquist and Big Otto lasted barely a couple of minutes, but it seemed like longer and created an awkward moment for those waiting in the bishop's presence. Björkquist was too preoccupied to care.

The bishop of Stockholm was less enthralled, however, with seeing Dietrich again because during his previous trips to Sweden, Dietrich had spoken out against the *Volk* theology, which Björkquist shared with the *Reichskirche*. *Volk* embodied the idea of a church defined by racial identity and blood, which Dietrich saw as anti-Semitism in clerical robes.

Mercifully, the gregarious, larger than life personality of Bishop George Bell arrived at that moment to greet them warmly. What was not so obvious, was the arrival of the Reverend Doctor Martin Sauter minutes earlier, who watched the interlude with the good bishop and the three boys that Dietrich had in tow from the shadows of a side chapel. His suspicions would be duly noted in his report.

* * * * *

The three boys were sent packing to their rooms in the sprawling seminary, nestled in a deep pine forest that was perpetually blanketed in mist. It had once been a medieval monastery whose high, etched stones walls were better suited to a castle keep. The slender, erudite Bell, who was nearly 60 but looked 10 years younger, led Dietrich to a comfortable study for a joyous reunion, albeit one set in melancholy times.

Bell and Dietrich had first met in 1933 when Dietrich was in London for two years as a representative of the foreign churches to the World Ecumenical Council. They had become close friends, and over the years, Dietrich had frequently informed Bell about what was going on in Germany. Bell, in turn, had made this information known to the public in Europe and America through, for example, letters to major newspapers.

Bell's passion for building bridges between faiths was nurtured early in his career when he was a curate in the industrial slums of Leeds for three years. He had ministered to industrial workers there, a third of whom were Indians and Africans from outposts in the British Empire. He learned much in Leeds from the Methodists, whose connection between personal creed and social engagement set an example that he would endeavor to imprint on the Church of England.

Bell had become the most important international ally of the Confessing Church in Germany, publicly expressing the international church's worries over the beginnings of the Nazis' antisemitic campaign in Germany. Of the many perceived blessings Dietrich had derived from his relationship with Bell, none was more personally resonant than Bell's role in saving the life of Dietrich's friend and mentor, Pastor Martin Niemöller, after his imprisonment in Sachsenhausen in February 1938 and later in Dachau.

Bell had used his authority as a leader in the Ecumenical Movement to influence public opinion in Britain and the Nazi authorities in Berlin, branding Niemöller's plight as an example of the Nazi regime's persecution of the church. This forced Hitler to back off from Niemöller's planned execution in 1938.

Dietrich, I will of course do what is in my power, but we have been at this place before with expectations that have been set by your side and then dashed by inaction. And, when I say your side, My Son, I am talking about those in power. There is no question in my mind that there is not the slightest bit of daylight between what you and I desire. You are a man of action and for that I have always admired you, Bell said as their business began after they shared personal updates.

I will do what I can of course, Bell continued, *but the spilling of blood has created a strange alchemy in Britain. Firstly, let us say that the resistance of the public at large and those leading the war effort to your entreaties reflects a certain indifference to the terrible plight of European Jewry.*

Furthermore, their attitudes towards Germans in general are no less racially motivated. Germans are seen as innately evil or at the very least inclined to be so. There are intellectuals who would argue, I think wrongly, that this is the fruit of your historical and cultural heritage. If only they knew you and your like, my boy.

It is perhaps, Dietrich responded, *our inheritance from Cain that some essential part of our souls was taken from us and, as a result, we are all subject to this lunacy of believing that whole races or nations are uniformly good or uniformly evil.*

You will get no argument from me on that score, although this sentiment could open the door to a lively ontological debate, Bell said tongue in cheek. They both had a good laugh that devolved to sighs.

By the way, the weightiness of this conversation has made me quite thirsty, a thirst that is hardly amenable to quenching by this muddy Darjeeling tea that they have forced upon us. I have a lovely Knappogue Castle with me. The Irish do know their whiskey. Can I count on you to join me, Bell asked?

Of course, but only in moderation, Dietrich replied.

Of course, Bell said slyly.

* * * * *

You can call me Harry, Harry Barnes. The new arrival was young, blonde, almost cherubic-looking and, like Leo, he floated ambiguously between classification as a boy or young man. Harry had appeared at their room in the Sigtuna seminary without warning carrying a large rucksack.

He looked Swedish, which is to say he looked German, and he spoke good German with the air of a British aristocrat on holiday. *I shall be returning to Germany with you in the place of our young friend here,* Harry said looking at the boy. *Deaconess Anna Maria has big plans for you boy, so this shall be your last night with us, a matter that I think is cause for celebration. Don't we all?*

If you say so, Leo responded cautiously looking at Big Otto and the boy. *What did you have in mind?*

Do you know Akvavit? Rummaging through his rucksack he found a rather large bottle of clear liquid. Can we round up several glasses, Harry asked?

Akvavit or Aquavit is an 80-proof distilled spirit that has been produced in Scandinavia since the 15th century. It is distilled from grain and potatoes and is flavored with caraway and dill seeds along with a variety of herbs.

The requisite glasses found, Harry poured each of them a healthy portion, *it is customary that a snort of Akvavit be consumed immediately following the verse of a song for full effect – a "Snapsvisa," the Swedes call it,* he said. *One goes something like this,*

> *Here's the first*
> *Sing "hup fol-de-rol la la la la"*
> *Here's the first*
> *Sing "hup fol-de-rol la la"*
> *He who doesn't drink the first*

Shall never, ever quench his thirst
Here's the first!

Harry downed his full portion of Akvavit in one slug and ended with,

Sing "hup fol-de-rol la la"

At which point the other three boys did the same.

Sing "hup fol-de-rol la la"

All would have gone uneventfully that evening had Harry not known several more verses of the song, in this case called *Helan Går*, loosely translated as *Bottoms Up*. Each verse and its requisite shot of *The Water of Life* were transcendent for the boys, starting first with their utter and complete release from the fear and pressure of the past few days.

With the next toast came a sense that each of them could single-handedly set the world right because they, better than most, had the right answers to the problems that plagued it. Grand ideas came and went never to be remembered.

Soon, they began to like everyone – the Tommies who were bombing them in Berlin, the Polizei who continually harassed them and even the Gestapo men they had encountered on the dock. They just needed to be reasoned with, and they – the boys – knew how best to get it done.

And on and on it went with each verse as their consciousness expanded and their gross motor skills contracted to be followed in short order by the ebb of their fine motor skills. At first, their singing was well contained within the stone walls that separated their room from the hallway. A passerby might at worst have heard voices combined in some rhythmic chanting —something devotional perhaps.

As time passed, and the words to the song became raunchy at Harry's instigation, the muffled rhythmic chanting turned into bellowing and reverberated through the walls and down the stone hallway of the old seminary in both directions. It was at this point that the Reverend Doctor Martin Sauter, returning from his evening of Christian fellowship and duplicitous spying, deliberately passed by the boys' room.

At the same time, the boys finally succumbed to the siren song of the 80-proof Akvavit. Leo and Big Otto were blissfully unconscious. Harry, sitting on the floor propped against a bed, savored his last few sips, staring blankly ahead at the gray stone walls and back in time to cherished memories known only to him. The boy, whom no one realized could hold his liquor quite as well as he did, rose to his feet feebly starting from his hands and knees, like a newborn foal, to answer the call of nature.

Mistaking the main door to the room for the door to the communal water closet, the boy pushed the ornate wrought iron door handle downward and thrust the heavy wooden door outward into the seminary's hallway forcing the Reverend Doctor Martin Sauter, who was listening through cupped hands for some indication of what the boys were plotting, to scramble for a hiding place.

The dark hallway was lined with deep alcoves in which the patriarchs of the Swedish Lutheran Church were displayed in life size busts. Sauter barely made it to the cover of the imposing bust of Laurentius Petri Nericius, 1499-1573, the first Evangelical Lutheran Archbishop of Sweden and one of the country's main Lutheran reformers.

The boy, born a Jew and a convert to Roman Catholicism, was appropriately ecumenical in his choice of places to urinate. He did so with an elegant arc to the left of the pedestal upon which the bust of

Laurentius Petri Nericius was displayed, then to the right and once more to the left.

Sauter was trapped and his beloved Crocker and Jones brogues, a souvenir of his time spent in London, were doused in the used Akvavit that flowed in abundance as the unsteady boy relieved himself. It seemed like an eternity to Sauter before the boy was done and able to hitch up his pants to return to his room.

The good reverend, who felt he could never endure more for the Fatherland than he had at that moment, or so he thought then, emerged from his hiding place with malice in his heart and urine on his shoes and the pant legs of his brown herringbone suit. An Aramaic proverb came immediately to mind, *But God will cut off the head of his enemies and the hairy scalp of those who walk in their sins*.

As he tread uncomfortably through the puddles that surrounded the bust of the first Evangelical Lutheran Archbishop of Sweden, he promised himself that he would make that proverb a reality soon.

* * * * *

Harry and Big Otto had gone to breakfast while Leo stayed behind to walk through the escape plan with Dietrich that they hoped would get them back to Stockholm and the relative safety of *Tante Ju*. Dietrich blessed the plan, putting his faith in the ability of Leo and Harry to get the job done.

The two SS men had arrived at Sigtuna but kept a respectful distance from the activities of the synod. Nevertheless, they were a constant presence just beyond the front gate of the seminary and were stationed at their large black sedan.

The minister from Berlin whom Dietrich suspected of no-good continued to hover around the group like a pesky mosquito. Just the day before when Leo, Harry and Big Otto had arrived at the refectory with jackhammer headaches, hungover from Akvavit, he had joined them at their table and introduced himself as the Reich's emissary, the Reverend Doctor Martin Sauter. The boy had been whisked away that morning by two nuns, leaving Harry to return with the group to Berlin playing this part.

Harry had done a good job in assuming the boy's identity, taking his place at the over the three days of the youth synod. He was a natural conman, a trait that Leo and Big Otto admired. Sauter seemed none the wiser of the switch, but the good Reverend had asked way too many questions with an air of casual disinterest, and his duplicity was lost on none of them.

Had there been any doubt that he was a big shot in the *Reichskirche*, the gold cross nested in a red Reich's eagle which he wore as a lapel pin dispelled any doubt. Sauter's allegiances were reconfirmed the morning of their departure when Leo and Harry went to the west wing of the sprawling seminary to spy on the Gestapo men from the vantage point of a third-floor window.

In the faint light of the early morning drizzle that had swept in from Skarven Bay, they could make out Sauter deep in conversation with the two Gestapo men, and they could easily guess the nature of the topic. Leo, Dietrich and Harry had concluded that even if they were allowed to leave the grounds of the seminary, they would be arrested either on the way to Stockholm or when they arrived at the dock where *Tante Ju* was moored.

Leo and Harry had to improvise, and a plan took shape quickly. *Give me 20 minutes*, Harry said, *and then move fast if we are successful in getting them away from the car.*

Leo used the wet gloom to reposition himself near a utility shed at ground level about 50 feet from the black sedan, which was stationed in a thick stand of pine trees. Harry was true to his word, and two young and very pretty novices sprung from an old wooden door in the wall that was in fact the rear door of the kitchen, in a swirl of blue habits, white aprons and blonde curls, to invite the Gestapo men to breakfast.

It took a little bit of coaxing, but the young women overcame their resistance after one of their number volunteered to stay with the car. A cup of coffee and a hearty breakfast would arm them for the long day that lay ahead, the beguiled Gestapo men told themselves.

Once they had disappeared into the kitchen with their entourage of novices, Leo ran to the car as the young novice who had stayed behind kept an eye on the back door of the kitchen for him. Leo had just about completed his work when he heard a commotion at the kitchen door and hissing from his lookout. *Three would have to do*, he whispered to himself. He then frog crawled as fast as he could to the cover of a nearby Juniper hedge.

As Harry, Leo and Otto finished their breakfast later that morning, they could see Sauter with Bishop Björkquist feigning interest in what the bishop was saying as he snuck a glance now and then at the boys. Dietrich arrived to collect them and 30 minutes later they were piling their luggage into another large Volvo for the trip to the dock in Stockholm. Their driver was the Abwehr security man, and he was accompanied by a young cleric who had helped organize the synod and who would serve as their guide for the two-hour drive.

The car set off from the central courtyard of the seminary at Sigtuna after the Berlin delegation bade farewell to Björkquist who had come to see them off, while Sauter watched from an upper floor.

If all went as planned, Sauter mused, it would be a relatively short trip before the group got its due.

During their stay, they had sought an audience with Deaconess Anna Maria, whom they were told was on ecclesiastical business in Stockholm. Dietrich had tried again the morning of their departure to say goodbye to the elusive nun and was told that she was teaching and could not be disturbed.

The Gestapo men sat waiting in their car in the thick stand of pine trees and would let the Abwehr car leave as planned. They did not want to apprehend Dietrich and his companions within range of the seminary lest they receive another unanticipated visit from the Deaconess.

They would take a logging road straight to a crossroads 20 kilometers from the seminary and intercept the Abwehr car, which would be taking the long way around to the same point on the main road to Stockholm. If their quarry resisted in any way, their orders were to finish the job then and there.

If for some reason, they missed the intercept, Backlin and his men were waiting at the port of Stockholm. Backlin would not arrest Dietrich and the boys but would do nothing to intervene if the Gestapo men did.

In the rough and tumble world of the wolfpack in Berlin, turnabout is fair play. The common expression for it was *Wer Feuer frißt, scheißt Funken*. Translated literally, it means, *He who eats fire shits sparks*.

After giving the Abwehr car a five-minute head start, the Gestapo men roared off leaving the main road for the logging road, as planned, about a kilometer from the seminary. As they made the turn, the steering wheel began to wobble, and the car seemed to list to starboard.

Efforts to accelerate down the logging road led to more wobbling until the steering wheel was rendered incapable of turning the car one way or the other.

The angry Gestapo men jumped out of the car to see three flat tires. They had been had by an old trick, an area of specialization, in point of fact, of Wedding's wolfpack.

After some effort, they found on each of the three flat tires a thin but deep slit between the white wall and the wheel rim. Done properly, it would weaken the inner tube maintaining the appearance of a fully inflated tire until the car took to the road and the weakened inner tube burst proving that there were more uses for a Bedouin Khanjar than cutting dough.

Their only choice now was to backtrack on foot double time to the seminary to alert Backlin to detain the Abwehr group.

* * * * *

Dietrich and the boys arrived at the port of Stockholm around Noon, and Backlin slow-walked the review of their papers but did not otherwise try to detain them in the absence of the Gestapo. As far as Dietrich and the boys could tell, there had been no word from the two Gestapo agents.

There had in fact been an inconvenient malfunction of the seminary's new telephone system when the Gestapo men made it back to the seminary. Some might even have called it an act of divine intervention.

Once in the *Tante Ju*, Dietrich encouraged the pilots to expedite their flight preparations, and the ever-gregarious duo who had flown them over were happy to oblige. They too had had their fill of Sweden and longed for a return to the Fatherland.

The number three engine of the Junker 52 sputtered as they tried to start it. The *Tante Ju* could not take off without three functioning engines so the co-pilot jumped onto the starboard pontoon to take a look.

Backlin and his men watched from the quay. Dietrich and Leo saw him glance at his watch at the moment that his adjutant came running from one of the warehouses, which could only mean one thing. The Gestapo men had made contact! Backlin started to approach them with his men from the other end of the long dock.

Dietrich and the boys marked each passing second, matched each synchronous thud of approaching jack boots with the pounding of their hearts. As Backlin and his men approached the *Tante Ju*, Leo heard the pilot mumble *Scheiße*, before the number three engine popped and sputtered and finally settled into a smooth rhythm.

As the co-pilot jumped from the pontoon into the cockpit and strapped in, Dietrich shouted above the din, *it is now or never*. The pilots saw Backlin bearing down on the door of the airplane and, lest they spend another minute in Sweden, they quickly throttled-up, taking *Tante Ju* post haste to the middle of the bay where they would take flight.

It worked to their advantage that Gestapo or no Gestapo, the Swedish military police were not about to fire on a military airplane of the Third Reich. It seemed to take forever to get to the middle of the bay but once there the pilots took *Tante Ju* full throttle skyward for the return flight home.

As they settled in, Leo could see Dietrich in his customary pose, eyes closed and lips moving. Big Otto joined the pilots up front and Harry stretched out on the bench to take a nap. A thought seemed to jolt Harry upright, and he reached into his jacket for a crumpled piece of paper, which he handed to Leo, *from the Deaconess,* he said with a smirk.

The note read, *Well done, Aslan. If you are the man, I think you are, our paths will undoubtedly cross again. Yours. Sister Anya Maria.*

* * * * *

Bell was a man of his word but, in the end, the forces that had from time to time bedeviled the resistance in Germany worked against him with the British government.

Swimming upstream against the cynicism of Churchill's government to random German peace overtures, Bell sent a letter to Anthony Eden, the British foreign minister, within two weeks of his meeting with Dietrich in Sigtuna. He pressed Eden on the timeliness of the opportunity and his faith in Dietrich and his fellow conspirators to deliver on their promises.

Dietrich's loyal friend would pull out the stops and argue to Eden and to all who would listen that it was Churchill himself who paved the way for assistance to Dietrich and the co-conspirators when he said before the House of Commons in 1940 that Britain's policy was, *to wage war against a monstrous tyranny never surpassed in the dark and lamentable catalogue of human crimes*, and that his countrymen should strive for *victory at all costs*. Would it be right then to discourage or ignore those in Germany willing to risk their lives to achieve those same ends, Bell argued.

After an inconclusive meeting with Eden following the first letter, Bell would try again sending a 2nd letter to Eden less than a month later. Eden would write in response that the British Government had seen little evidence that the German people would rise-up against the tyranny of Hitler in the same way that the oppressed peoples of Eastern Europe had done. There would be little that the government could or would do until that time, not the least of which would be prematurely discussing what a fair peace might look like.

Bad timing would again deliver the *coup de grâce* to any hope for support from the British. At about the time Dietrich was traveling to Sigtuna, Churchill had signed a treaty of alliance with Joseph Stalin. London wished to avoid any action that would start this alliance off on the wrong foot by suggesting a lack of loyalty to its newest ally in the battle to crush Hitler.

In the elemental, often random, battle between good and evil, which provides the real energy in the universe, the man who would eventually coin the phrase, *Iron Curtain* would give it life.

IV. HIGH CLIMBERS AND DEEP SWIMMERS NEVER GROW OLD

— A German Proverb

It had once been a shimmering oasis among the gloomy tenement canyons of Wedding. On this balmy Spring day in Berlin, the sprawling beer garden should have been packed with a jolly, inebriated clientele.

Prater on *Kastanienallee* had been a labor of love for the Kalbo family backed by the Pfefferberg brewery since the mid-1800's when *Kastanienallee* lay on what were then the outskirts of the city. Over the years, it had become renowned as a beer garden, destination for day trippers, variety theatre, ballroom, garden and public gathering place under manicured winter lime trees whose bare branches would glow a bright red in the winter months.

It attracted a mixed clientele that included merchants and civil servants as well as maids, respectable families, workers and soldiers. The entertainment included musical comedies, burlesque shows and operettas, even pantomime and puppet shows.

Old man Schultheiss bought out the Pfefferberg family in the 1920's and later jettisoned the Kalbos in favor of new leaseholders whom he thought could grow with the times, and at that time, motion pictures had become all the rage.

Like many businesses of its kind, Prater's closed when Hitler made his push East starting the world war. The place was now as sad as it was empty, its disheveled equipment and furnishings rotting under the now rangy winter limes.

Old lady Kalbo, the great granddaughter of the original proprietors, owned a number of small apartment buildings in the area including the old St. Elizabeth's nursing home just behind the beer garden, where she rented apartments to tenants who could earn a few pfennigs with *Schlafbursche*, the practice of renting their beds to shift workers at Schultheiss while they were away at work. In many cases, an apartment would be occupied for the night by the day shift of the factory and during the day by the night shift. Such was life in Berlin at the time.

St. Elizabeth's had once been a thriving place representing the best care available to mostly young, physically and mentally disabled Berliners. That had changed a few years before when its population was decimated by *Aktion T4,* Hitler's euthanasia campaign.

At that terrible time, Frau Kalbo had returned from a short trip to her family farm in Pomerania just in time to pluck her niece, who suffered from a form of sclerosis, from St. Elizabeth's and the clutches of the Nazis. She had watched from her apartment window as the police and the buses from *The Charitable Society for Transportation of Sick Persons*, under the control of *Aktion T4*, arrived to remove 100 residents who had been designated as *genetically inferior*.

Those taken from St. Elizabeth's would join hundreds of thousands of other mentally and physically disabled Germans removed from hospitals and care homes from 1939-1945 to be *evaluated* and if deemed necessary administered a *Gnadentod*, a *merciful death,* is what they so cynically called it. In truth, these mentally and physically disabled Germans often became the subjects of gruesome medical experimentation and most were murdered outright.

Her niece now lived in the same apartment that she had vacated abruptly a few years earlier, doted over by her aunt and Little Otto, who viewed time spent with both of them as his own shimmering oasis in in the gloomy canyons of Wedding.

Old lady Kalbo had channeled her anger in a more positive direction by giving safe quarter in the various Kalbo properties to those who could not afford another place to stay and by allying herself with Mehdi to help *move product.* At the present time, this meant Harry Barnes, who had been spirited away by the wolfpack on his return to Berlin taking refuge in the apartment in St. Elizabeth's that the Ottos shared with several other boys.

There were informants among her boarders, so this would by necessity be a short-term arrangement. But she had done this before working with Mehdi and his boys, and she was known as a steady hand in the face of danger.

* * * * *

I was sworn to secrecy, boy. Your knowing she was there would have complicated matters. Your adventure in Sweden was a close enough call as it was, Mehdi said to a visibly angry Leo standing in the cluttered workspace behind the front counter of *Die Bäckerei* soon after his return to Wedding and Harry's transfer to the care of Frau Kalbo. Dietrich, who had just arrived to discuss the next steps for Harry, stood by and listened.

Leo was too stunned, or hurt, or angry, or all of the above, to say anything to Harry on the flight back to Berlin, and he had saved his venom for Mehdi. *Did you know about this, Dietrich,* Leo said.

No, son, and just as well. An unguarded reaction on your part or mine, one errant look at Deaconess Anna Maria might have been the end of it for us all, Dietrich replied.

We cannot always choose the field of battle in our war against the monster and his henchmen, Dietrich added, *Matthew said, 'Enter by the narrow gate. For the gate is wide and the way is easy that leads to destruction, and those who enter by it are many. For the gate is narrow and the way is hard that leads to life, and those who find it are few.'*

Leo let out a loud, exasperated groan, *you speak in damnable riddles like Anya,* he said. *We are risking our lives for what, pretty words?*

Leo caught himself at this point because he genuinely liked Dietrich and admired his bravery. *I am sorry, Sir,* he said sheepishly. *No offense taken, Leo,* Dietrich replied warmly.

Leo, Deaconess Anna Maria, Anya that is to say, is someone that I have been in contact with through Pushpa for years well before Pushpa brought you to me, Mehdi interjected. *Anya and Pushpa are agents for the British. Anya has led operations in Scandinavia, Poland, Egypt, and Hungary and quite successfully so, I might add. I am proud to say that I played no small part in her escapade in the land of the Pharaohs during my absence last year.*

When the final reckoning comes for the monsters we fight, no one will know what we have done, how clever you were in Sweden, how you felt about this and that and, I might add, how deftly I have assisted Anya in the past. Why? Because we will probably all be dead in the service of that outcome.

Yet we do what we are asked, and we do what we must. All of us, Mehdi said looking at Leo. *And this was true of Anya who risked her life helping us. The mission was to save the boy and to bring Harry back and success in that is all that mattered!*

Mehdi had made his point and Leo's anger in not having been included in the plan gave way to pride in Anya. Although Leo could not shake his unhappiness in not having spent even a minute with her during their three days in Sigtuna.

The three stood silent for what seemed like an eternity until Leo broke the ice, *and the plan for Harry?*

Dietrich hesitated for a moment and said, *Canaris has given the green light to a plan,* he said as he looked quizzically at Leo and Mehdi hoping the storm had passed, *and once again, you and the boys will be keys to its success.*

* * * * *

It had turned into an obsession, as ungodly as it might seem, but the Reverend Doctor Martin Sauter could not take his eyes off his Crocker and Jones brogues for more than five minutes at a time. The prominent yellow and, depending on the light, green stain along with the frayed leather on the toe of his right shoe could not be erased for long no matter how much he polished it. It was as if the boy answered the call of nature with a bladder full of battery acid.

He had made his report to Goebbels upon his return sparing no opprobrium for Dietrich albeit with scant evidence of any wrongdoing on the part of Dietrich and his boys other than the flattened tires of the Gestapo car. His lack of evidence was no obstacle, however, and he heaped one suspicion of Dietrich upon another in his debriefing with Goebbels.

Reverend Sauter, your suspicions are well founded, I am sure. The episode in Sweden is but a minor footnote in what is becoming a rather large and troubling file on Pastor Bonhoeffer, Goebbels said.

And it was soon after this meeting that Goebbels made a point of having Himmler introduce the Reverend Doctor Martin Sauter to Marcus Fischer, the former bookkeeper at the Schultheiss brewery and current Gestapo kingpin in Wedding, who would serve as his counterpart in escalating surveillance of the comings and goings of Bonhoeffer at *Die Bäckerei.*

Sauter had rejected an offer of additional help from the young Jewess who hunted her fellow Jews for the Gestapo because like his mentor Goebbels, he longed for a Berlin that was *Judenfrei.* In spite of the heavy blows dealt Berlin's Jews, Sauter like Goebbels fumed that the Jews who still remained were, as to be expected, an insolent and aggressive lot.

Fischer had his informants flood the area around *Die Bäckerei* in the hope of picking up a lead on the activities of the boys who operated like the tentacles of an octopus with Mehdi as its head. Leo and Mehdi noted the surge in street traffic and suspected its provenance.

Fischer also put intense pressure on the gauleiter of the district for information although up to this point, he had little to show for it. This was due in no small part to the ample *gratuities* the gauleiter was taking from Mehdi.

Their lucky break came when the girlfriend of a boarder at St. Elizabeth's told them about a cripple living there and her link to the boys in the wolfpack. *The boy who stays with her is one of Mehdi's and runs errands for the baker boy, Leo,* Fischer told Sauter. *We take the cripple, and the boy will be putty in our hands. He appears to wait on her hand and foot.*

Sauter wholeheartedly endorsed the plan. *What happens to the girl?*

We dangle her for a time until we round all of them up, especially the three boys, whom you encountered in Sweden. Once we extract confessions from the boys, and we will, Bonhoeffer and the rest of them will be done, including the girl. She will be dealt with mercifully as we do with all of her kind, Fischer snarled.

And the timetable for the plan, Sauter asked?

We have already put the plan into motion. The girl will be picked up tomorrow, said Fischer.

* * * * *

In the battle between good and evil that raged in Wedding's nine square kilometer microcosm, information was its most lethal weapon, as it was in most of Berlin. On one hand, its protagonists ranged from mere children who informed on family members who had been lackadaisical about giving the Hitler salute to one politically agnostic janitor of one upscale hairdresser on the Ku'damm who tipped the Gestapo off to its illegal Jewish clients for additional ration coupons.

On the other hand, there were those in Berlin who took genuine pride in the resurgence of Germany after the Great War but who never lost their innate sense of decency. Such was the case of the greengrocer on *Granseer Strasse*.

On the day before Frau Kalbo's apartments behind Prater were to become the field of battle between good and evil, the warmth of a glorious Spring day in Berlin signaled the coming of Summer. The greengrocer proudly displayed the abundant produce from his family farm on the Elbe about 30 kilometers from Berlin.

Berlin on a war footing and held tightly in the grasp of the Gestapo often felt like living in a vessel from which all oxygen had been bled. But on this particular day, the warm sun and a refreshing breeze were to the many passersby a sensuous evocation of joyful lives once lived.

As he attended to his clients, the greengrocer, Herr Knoebbel, overheard his wife speaking in hushed tones to Frau Dix, who rented a small apartment from them, little more than a glorified shed behind the greengrocer's shop. Frau Dix was a seamstress for the Staatsoper, who would take in whatever additional work she could find to make ends meet.

Both women were dyed in the wool Nazis, who had been seduced by the sexually charged magnetism of the young Hitler during his rise to power. Women viewed him as married to his mission, making him theoretically unattainable and thus an object of longing.

And so, it was for Frau Dix and Frau Knoebbel. In particular, Frau Knoebbel often talked about her desire to serve Hitler by becoming a concentration camp guard, which drove Herr Knoebbel to distraction.

Herr Knoebbel was a devout Catholic and a committed anti-Nazi. During the slow, often sputtering rise of Hitler years before, he would help the opposing Social Democrats put up their campaign signs while tearing down the vicious Nazi posters.

He, like many others in those years, eventually came around to the misguided idea that the only way to get rid of Hitler was to let him come to power so that he could demonstrate his incompetence. Like all Germans, Herr Knoebbel considered himself to be eminently rational, but Hitler's eventual seizure of absolute power in Germany defied all logic.

As he listened to the two women whose conversation alternated between hushed whispers and loud cackling, he wondered about why he had been attracted to Frau Knoebbel in the first place. Perhaps it was the passage of time, but he simply could not put his finger on it.

Frau Dix was a font of information because she saw the pasty-faced Gestapo agent Marcus Fischer from time to time. It would have been a vast overstatement to call it a love affair. If she loved anything, it was the ration coupons that he brought with him along with the bottle of expensive Stockvogler's schnapps straight from Vienna. Knoebbel had once heard Frau Dix say, *we are not Tristan and Isolde but after half a bottle of Stockvogler's, he is tolerable.*

Today the whispering was about a Gestapo raid planned for sunrise the next day at St. Elizabeth's that would lead to the capture of subversive boys wanted by the Reich. Fischer, she said, would lead the operation and he expected that blood would be spilled. Success would most certainly lead to a promotion for him.

Herr Knoebbel, who to all outward appearances had been consumed by putting out the white asparagus in his street side bins, as it was *Spargelzeit*, that is high season for asparagus, had taken note. *Meine schönes Damen*, he said to his wife and Frau Dix, *while things are slow, I am going to stretch my legs on this glorious day.*

* * * * *

While I speak the Kaiser's German and the King's English well enough, I am Polish by birthright – Henryk Hipolit – how is that for alliteration. Most kings of England by the name of Henry were called Harry, and ergo I am Harry. My father was Poland's military attaché to Her Majesty's government when your boy with the nasty mustache set the dogs on us. Leo and Big Otto had joined Harry at Frau Kalbo's the evening of the same idyllic Spring day to review the plan that would unfold the next day.

To return Harry's favor in Sweden, they brought with them a bottle of schnapps and absent glasses each took long drafts from the bottle. *Shouldn't do this I suppose before a big mission but bugger it, we could all be dead by this time tomorrow,* Harry said to laughter from Leo and Big Otto.

A tipsy but determined Leo pressed for more information on Harry's apparent relationship to Anya. Feeling no pain, Harry told the boys that he was Special Operations Executive, the British secret service and that he had worked for Anya once before. *She is beautiful, smart and deadly, so bloody deadly, if you get on her wrong side, lingering on the word 'beautiful' with a palpable sense of longing. Not many like her, actually not any like her that I know,* Harry said in response to Leo's probing about how he knew Anya.

Leo had never thought of Anya as beautiful in quite the way Harry did although *deadly*, was strangely enough something that Leo could grasp.

Is she involved in what you are planning when you return to Poland, Leo asked?

Don't know yet, Leo, Harry replied. *I hope so. If she is, I stand a fighting chance of getting through it in one piece. I know only the vague contours of what I am destined to do,* Harry said. *I will get my full brief in the field. I am no military man. I was a chemistry fellow at Oxford for Christ's sake. I just do what they tell me to do because I must.*

Harry was better at holding his liquor than Leo and Big Otto who finally passed out. As Harry took the last swig from the bottle, a waif of a young boy barged into the room, took a quick look at the inert forms of Leo and Big Otto, and said, *tell Leo when he wakes up that Siegfried and Brünnhilde are ready.*

* * * * *

The contours of the plan were simple, but its execution would be like running a gauntlet over a bed of hot coals. The last-minute addition of Frau Kalbo's niece to the escape plan would make it all the more challenging.

Yet challenging was the essence of life in Berlin at that time. Leo asserted operational control over the escapade to unfold that day as he reviewed the plan with Harry, the Ottos and several of his boys before sunrise. The residual schnapps in his system seemed to make the planet wobble as he reviewed each step in the plan.

The handoff is planned for noon at the Polnische Extravaganz at KaDeWe, Leo began. He passed around the flyers for the *Polnische Extravaganz*, a weeklong special event that would put on sale the rich trove of luxury items taken from Jews and political elites in Warsaw and its environs. It would be opening day for the sale and a huge crowd, albeit of staunch Nazi sympathizers, would be on hand making it easier at least in theory to hide the exchange in plain sight.

KaDeWe, otherwise known as *Kaufhaus Des Westens* at Wittenbergplatz, was established in 1907 by a Jewish businessman and was the largest department store in continental Europe, serving tens of thousands of customers each day. In 1927, KaDeWe was purchased by a Jewish family enterprise and was later boycotted by the Nazis, who finally seized the store in 1933.

Our contacts will leave promptly at 13:00 hours for their return to Poland and will not wait, Leo said. Polish resistance fighters who had infiltrated the shipping company involved in the transport of these stolen goods would see to Harry's extraction from Berlin and injection into the Polish field of battle.

Frau Maas, most of you know her, will be there to take the girl. She will be wearing a red beret with a white feather so that we can easily spot her in the crowd. She will be near the door of the Extravaganz, he added.

What would not be so easy would be the trip to the rendezvous point on Wittenbergplatz about three kilometers as the crow flies to the Southwest from their current position in Wedding. They would have to walk for at least two reasons.

First, a bombing raid earlier that week had taken the U2 out of commission at Stadmitte in central Berlin, and there were no practical alternatives for using the U-Bahn/S-Bahn system to reach Wittenbergplatz. Worse, where trains and trams were running, the Wehrmacht had intensified patrols searching for illegals as well as young men avoiding military service.

They would run the gauntlet on foot starting out toward the Charité, the main hospital in Berlin, to their West with the girl in a wheelchair. This would give them greater mobility and a cover story if challenged by SS patrols.

They would then angle South toward the Tiergarten and Wittenbergplatz beyond. Before the war, the 520-acre Tiergarten was Berlin's most popular inner-city park but was now a patchwork quilt of anti-aircraft defenses, fields producing agricultural products and oddities like a landing strip down the main boulevard connecting the Western reaches of the city to the Brandenburg Gate.

It will get more complicated between Charité *and the Tiergarten. There will be slave labor crews farming, clearing rubble and building defenses in the Tiergarten. We need to stay to the east of all of that and slip around the Southeast corner of the park to get across the Landwehr canal at Schillerstrasse. From there the worst will be behind us,* Leo added.

A seven-year-old girl with a loaf of bread under her arm arrived at that moment with a message from Mehdi. *Leo, Mehdi says that they are coming. Thank you!* And the little girl left as abruptly as she had arrived skipping from the room.

Let's wrap up. Those of you who will take care of things here, raise your hands? Good. Those of you doing reconnaissance for the trip? OK, Leo barked with an air of command.

Those with us, he asked? Big and Little Otto raised their hands along with Harry and two older boys, burly twins who would assist Little Otto with the final exchange.

Good luck and let's get the hell away from this place, Leo said, as the boys piled out of the room.

* * * * *

They were hungry and when they were hungry, they were angry to the point of being uncontrollable. The two stood about 30 muscular inches at the shoulder, each weighing about 100 pounds. Their glistening black coats and thickly muscled hindquarters with rust markings rippled with imposing strength.

They had endured the night without food and by the predawn hours had largely destroyed everything in the small apartment in which they were confined. Their noble lineage dated back to the Roman empire when ancient Roman drover dogs, dependable and rugged mastiffs with great intelligence and guarding instincts, drove huge herds of cattle in support of Roman legions traveling in large numbers across Europe.

It is said that they could be loyal, loving and even playful. But Siegfried and Brünnhilde reflected the personality of their owner and trainer Frau Schultheiss, who was none of the above.

God forbid an interloper on the grounds of the Schultheiss villa should encounter the two Rottweilers after dark. Even old man Schultheiss was afraid of them, and the massive beasts seemed capable of taking orders only from Frau Schultheiss and Little Otto, who took care of them for Frau Schultheiss and whom they considered one of their own.

Although at this moment they were having second thoughts about Little Otto, as it was he who had left them alone in the room the evening before without so much as a bone to gnaw. They were hungry, very hungry, and angry, very angry.

* * * * *

Fischer and two *Bulls*, plain clothes detectives from the *Alex*, the headquarters of the *Kripo* short for *Kriminalpolizei* at Alexander Platz, watched the girl's apartment at the West end of St. Elizabeth's. There was a door to the apartment accessible directly from the outside. They had been stationed there since midnight.

The Bulls took occasional Gestapo assignments for extra beer tokens and the opportunity to rough up a few Jews or anyone else unfortunate enough to fall into their hands. More often than not, the victims of their tender mercies had valuables, which they confiscated and split with Fischer leaving just enough tribute for Fischer to pocket or share with his superiors.

Waiting at the telephone at his home on Kufurstenstrasse 7, the Reverend Doctor Martin Sauter was like a child waiting for the arrival of Father Christmas. They would get the girl soon and then the baker's house of cards would crumble giving them the fugitive boys and exposing the treachery of Bonhoeffer and his friends. He played and replayed in his head the gratifying moment when he would inform Goebbels.

* * * * *

In the gloom of the predawn, a dark swath of sky with a ragged gray crown stood in relief against the faint purple light of sunrise to the East. The ominous mass of clouds moved steadily toward them carrying the smell of the Spree and torrential rain, which it would unleash on a wakening Berlin.

Sepp Lange and his team observed a stream of boys emerging from the east end of St. Elizabeth's while Fischer and the Bulls waited to make their move at the opposite end of the building. Sepp knew that Fischer was there but let him pursue his fool's errand. There was more at stake here than a few hoodlums who had offended a sniveling churchman.

Lange had been given orders to ignore Sauter and Fischer and to focus on the third boy who returned from Sweden, whom the Gestapo wanted to identify. When the Gestapo checked the identity, which he had provided in Sweden, they found no trace of the boy or his parents in Berlin.

The first group of boys to emerge from St. Elizabeth's dissolved instantly into the night. The group that followed close on their heels seemed to circle around the back of the building and a third group, bigger, older boys pushing a wheelchair, kept to the shadows behind Prater moving in the direction of Eberswalder Strasse.

Sepp and his team would follow this group. Apart from who they were, the even more intriguing question was where they might be headed and why. He sensed that the prize waiting at the end of their clandestine journey, wherever it took them, would be bigger than a few hoodlums who would soon find themselves fighting for the Fatherland in a *Strafbataillon* or *penal battalion* on the eastern front.

His people had been watching them over the last few days. It was a lucky break. A young boy was overheard boasting to his friends about the important boy that they were hiding. He had learned it from another boy, who knew a bigger boy who was part of the group. They were going somewhere important, but the young boy couldn't remember where exactly.

Sepp and his prized Greiferin stood in the shadows together as his men began to follow their quarry at a safe distance. It had been she who had happened on the small boy as he bragged to a friend in close orbit to *Die Bäckerei*. It struck her then that the *important* boy whom everyone had been frantically trying to find might just be trying to make a last, desperate bid to escape Berlin.

Let's see if we can find out more about where they are headed, Sepp whispered to Stella. They moved cautiously forward toward the end of the building which had disgorged the boys in search of clues.

* * * * *

The malevolent downpour that muffled the rumbling thunder felt like falling gravel as it side swiped St. Elizabeth's and blinded anyone unlucky enough to get caught in it. It was deafening, drenching, but a scramble of voices manage to penetrate the crashing rain.

They could have been very close or very far, because the intense downpour played tricks on you. Someone shouted, then came a gunshot, then a shrill, a primal scream of fear followed, another gunshot, someone or something howling in pain, then again, caterwauling rage that was not quite human, and yet another shriek of pain, this time human.

Fischer had unleashed the hounds of hell. After kicking in the door to the girl's apartment, two powerful projectiles, two heavily muscled buzz saws, hit them with no warning and no mercy. One Bull was down and missing the flesh from the right side of his face. Siegfried stood over him trying to decide what he would do next. He was angry, very angry.

His companion, Brünnhilde, had removed the gun from the other Bull's hand along with three of his fingers. The Bull cried like a baby as Brünnhilde chewed on one of those fingers.

Fischer knew in an instant that he had been had when he and the Bulls charged through the door of the girl's room to find only the Rottweilers. He was so dumbfounded that he shot himself in the foot as he stumbled backwards trying to make a run for it.

Siegfried cast his eyes on his love Brünnhilde as his fabled namesake had once done eons before, and she returned his frenzied gaze. They heard Fischer's agonized cursing in the drumming rain just beyond the doorway and knew what they must do.

* * * * *

It was a muggy, overcast morning in which one could escape the rain for one block only to be pummeled by a rogue Spring shower the next. Here and there one could hear cars splashing through puddles and see steam chasing glimmers of sunshine as it rose from the pavement.

All had gone as planned at least as far as the Charité in spite of two interludes in which large black sedans crept slowly along the street to observe their movements. The group nonchalantly waved and moved on toward the hospital, pushing the girl in the wheelchair, phony smiles glued to their faces, hearts racing.

Leo had sent the younger, faster boys ahead like cavalry scouts to reconnoiter and report back at intervals on the obstacles that lay in their path. The boys could blend into the landscape like chameleons because they mattered to no one.

As Leo and the group approached the Tiergarten from the Northeast, a scout reached them to say that there was a large SS patrol ahead. Worse still, it was the dreaded *Kettenhunde* patrol with dogs that combed the streets for deserters, and they were stopping and they were roughing up the men and boys they found.

Harry, we will be forced to stay to the Northern side of the park for a time unless we want to risk a run for it dead ahead. We must turn South sooner rather than later as time is not on our side but not here, I think, Leo said as they took cover in a stand of Linden trees about 100 yards from the charred hulk of the Reichstag.

You know this territory better than I and that's an understatement, my friend, Harry replied. *If we do get caught, I am not going down without a fight. Run for it when the fireworks begin,* Harry added as he pulled his field jacket aside to display the large handgun tucked into his pants.

Another scout joined them at that moment panting, face a scarlet red from exertion, *Leo, the SS patrol is heading straight toward us from the South as if they know we are here. We only have a few minutes!*

* * * * *

Scheiße. Verflucht, Scheiße. Sepp repeated these epithets rhythmically as if he were meditating and they were his mantra.

He and his own scouts had seen the same thing taking shape. The boys they pursued would be intercepted in the park by the SS patrols before they could reach *KaDeWe*, which is where the detritus in the boys' hideout suggested they were headed. What this all had to do with the *Polnische Extravaganz* was a mystery, but one Sepp was determined to solve before the day was done if the SS patrols didn't ruin the opportunity.

Get a call to headquarters and get these patrols turned eastward and away from the Tiergarten, Sepp ordered at the top of his lungs.

* * * * *

Leo and his entourage moved as swiftly as they could pushing the girl in the wheelchair along the Northern perimeter of the park toward the immense hulk of the Zoo flak tower. He knew that if they didn't turn South soon, they would be in the thick of it with the garrison posted there.

The flak tower looming ahead was a monstrous structure 13 stories high and 70x70 meters square with walls that were eight meters thick. The roof of the facility had four, twin mounted 12.8 cm FlaK 40 guns that together could fire 96 rounds a minute at the high flying Allied bombers. It was the largest of three enormous flak tower complexes in Berlin with an 85-bed hospital on its third floor and the capacity to house 15,000 people. It could store so much food and ammunition that its military garrison believed it could hold out for a year, if necessary, regardless of what happened to the rest of Berlin.

The boys happened upon a pathway that descended steeply away to the South from their position on the service road that formed the Northern border of the Tiergarten toward a culvert about 50 yards away. In that instant, they heard Big Otto utter, *Ich idiot*! Just a heartbeat behind was Little Otto with, *ausgezeichnet!* Leo quizzed them, *so what is so excellent?*

The culvert there below us parallels a bridal path and cuts under another. It will take us to the Freiarchenbrucke under cover, which gets us most of the way to the bottom of the park, Big Otto replied. The *Freiarchenbrucke* was a scenic bridge in the middle of the Tiergarten that had the reputation as a "lover's lane," because of its beauty and seclusion in the urban forest primeval surrounding it.

How do you know this, Otto? It was Little Otto who answered, *he meets a girl here sometimes, a student from Charlottenburg,* eliciting a pained expression from the other Otto who at the same time could barely stifle the glimmer of a smile.

You dog, you, Harry said laughing as he slapped Big Otto on the back. *And what of our other guest, Otto, not addressing the question to either one,* Leo asked. *Can we get her through the culvert?*

We can and we must, Harry interrupted, with a reassuring smile on his face that was more reassuring than his quick calibration of what it would take move the girl through the culvert. *Little Otto and I will carry the girl as if she is on a stretcher using her blanket. Won't be comfortable, but she seems to be a tough little thing. And Otto,* Harry said, looking at Big Otto, *you take charge of the wheelchair. Any questions? Right then, Leo? Lead on.*

Leo and Harry's eyes met for an instant, signaling their mutual assessment of the rapidly dwindling odds of reaching their destination in time, but they knew there would be no going back.

* * * * *

The culvert was essentially a large pipe encased in concrete to direct runoff when the numerous small bodies of water in the area overflowed their banks. Fortunately, it was dry as a bone in spite of the rain showers in the area. The group disappeared into the culvert's Northern opening one by one with Leo taking the lead and the bulky twins bringing up the rear.

Leo forbade talking. They had just enough room to crawl on their hands and knees, but there was far too little space to carry anyone. Harry and Little Otto improvised seating the girl on the blanket with Harry on his knees awkwardly dragging it for several feet before being forced to stop and rest. Little Otto's job was to make sure that she did not slide off the back of the blanket.

It was a frustratingly slow process. What would come of Harry if the Polish truckers left without him, Leo thought? Could they make up time once they got out of the Tiergarten if they did at all? More worrisome still, were the SS patrols looking for something or somebody in particular and had their plan been compromised in some way?

They were close to the end of the first stretch of culvert when they saw the silhouette of someone sitting in the culvert several feet ahead backlit by the daylight streaming in from the opening just beyond. As they approached, the figure, that of a man, it did not move and simply sat there with its back resting against one side of the pipe, staring at the opposite side of the pipe.

Leo waved so abruptly to the group to stop that the girl squeaked when she rolled forward into Harry. It was then that the figure turned toward them. Leo could make out in the dim light that he was holding a finger to his lips.

Leo moved forward not knowing what to expect and, as he drew closer, he saw the telltale white and gray stripes of a slave laborer. *Who are you and what are you doing here*, Leo demanded?

My name is Huber, Arnold Huber, he whispered and held up a hand rolling his five preternaturally long fingers in an eccentric way and then pointing to the open end of the tunnel behind him. *They are coming*, he mouthed without making a sound.

Unhappily, *they* were armed SS trainees on a morning march, scores of them fervently singing a song that Leo had heard before about how Jewish blood would spurt around their knives. The chorus of voices and the pounding of so many jackboots reverberated through the pipe as disembodied marching legs passed just beyond the opening of the culvert.

When they had passed, Huber said, *it should be pretty clear what I am doing here, why are you and your companions crawling around in a sewer?* Leo hesitated, wary of giving too much information, *we have a rendezvous at Wittenbergplatz and wanted to avoid the SS. How long have you been here?*

How long? I would estimate about an hour based on 11 parades such as the one that you just saw that seem to come roughly every five minutes. I am, was, a prisoner at Sachsenhausen for political rather than ethnic reasons, but that is of course a distinction without a difference.

My group and I distribute anti-Nazi leaflets, while indulging ourselves in a bit of vandalism here and there —that is to of Nazi interests of course. I was part of a construction brigade from Sachsenhausen that has been working in the park since dawn, and a politically agnostic guard, a policeman, was willing to look the other way for 500 marks. The truck will be well on its way to Tempelhof before my absence is known.

Sachsenhausen was a Nazi KZ, short for *Konzentrationslager*, the German term for a concentration camp, just outside of Berlin in Oranienburg and was used from 1936 to the end of the Third Reich in May 1945. The camp held mainly political prisoners who were subjected to forced labor. There was also a gas chamber and a medical experimentation area. Prisoners were treated harshly, fed sparingly and murdered indiscriminately.

Can I ask you a favor, Huber said, without waiting for permission, *my sister Marta works at KaDeWe. She works the Épernay exhibit, the one that serves the stolen French champagne. It is on the Erdgeschoss (ground floor) right at the door on the West side of the building facing the U-Bahn station. Tell her I am OK.*

I need clothing as you can see if I have any hope of leaving this place, Huber added.

Leo responded, *I will send one of my group back to our friends who can find something for you because we may not have time to visit your sister. It will take a few hours because the Tiergarten is crawling with SS today, but you will have your clothing.*

It was then that they heard it – the syncopated rhythm of marching jackboots approaching. *When they pass, you will have five minutes to make it to the other side of the path and into the next culvert that leads directly to the Freiarchenbrucke,* Huber said. Leo turned back quickly to the group, retracing his tracks and gave the assignment of clothing for Huber to one of the twins. Leo brought the group forward toward Huber ready to make their move when the parade passed.

As the sound of jackboots receded, Leo carefully peered around the edge of the culvert opening. There was nothing to the left and nothing to the right. He waved the group forward while waiting at the mouth of the culvert to make sure that they all had made it across the narrow road to cover.

Once accomplished, Leo popped his head back into the darkness, *good luck, Huber*, he said. *God bless you*, was all he got in reply.

* * * * *

They had finally made it across the Landwehr Canal, which put them within a kilometer of their destination but well behind schedule. Before leaving the cover of the Tiergarten, Harry and Big Otto had exchanged their grimy field jackets for smart looking blazers that had been given to them by Frau Kalbo. Little Otto, did much the same thing, donning a loden waistcoat over leather lederhosen, which made him look like a Bavarian cupie doll. They would not be the most fashionable guests among the Nazi super luminaries at the *Polnische Extravaganz,* but they would be less likely to stick out like a sore thumb from the well-heeled crowd.

After zigging and zagging from one gloomy street lined with commercial buildings to another, they turned on to Bayreuther Strasse, and there it stood dead ahead, *KaDeWe*, in all of its luminescent commercial glory, gleaming under rays of golden sunshine that slashed through the leaden clouds over Wittenbergplatz.

The huge edifice reminded Leo of the fable that Mehdi liked to tell of the *Lorelei*, a large rock at a narrows on the Rhine that produces an echo and of its mythical source, a beautiful maiden who threw herself into the Rhine at that very spot in despair over a faithless lover. She was then transformed into a siren who lured fishermen to their destruction for all eternity. Leo could not help but wonder whether such a thing waited for them just ahead.

The group had to maneuver around and through a street fair on Wittenbergplatz and perhaps the hardest part of the journey was passing a stand selling beer and bratwurst without stopping when the collective growling of their stomachs could be heard above the din of the crowd. The layout of the fair funneled them to the side door of *KaDeWe* that coincidentally would bring them directly to Huber's sister.

It was at that moment that an internal alarm sounded for both Leo and Harry. It was an instinct that something was not right as it had become vaguely apparent in the random mass of revelers and bobbing heads that movement to their left and their right tracked their own movements.

A false smile broadly beaming, Leo turned to Harry, *you see what I see. Right? If we get to the door and inside, we have a fighting chance.* They would have no way of knowing that Sepp and his Gestapo detachment were all too happy to have them do just that.

Leo and his companions, including the young girl in the wheelchair were greeted as they entered the store by the babel of the roiling crowd and the sound of champagne corks exploding from the bottles arrayed in abundance on the countertop dead ahead. The *Polnische Extravaganz* was at least a football pitch away on the opposite side of the massive store.

It was glorious pandemonium amidst glistening glass counters overflowing with goods —champagne, fine watches, jewelry, men's furnishings and all manner of merchandise. The spoils of war were in abundance in Berlin at least for now.

Like an animal being stalked, Leo was operating on instinct and adrenalin now and without thinking he went straight to the Épernay counter, found Marta and beckoned her to come over. *Your brother sends his best. He is OK and free and will contact you soon, but we need your help now*, he said as he nervously glanced back at the Gestapo men entering the store.

We must get to the Polnische Extravaganz, Leo added. Marta momentarily confused but delighted by the news of her brother looked at the group, the crippled girl, then at the squad of rough looking men entering the store and knew what she must do.

Who is coming with me, she said briskly. Harry, Little Otto and the girl moved forward in unison. Marta promptly put on a red and orange vest and picked up a gong that she banged loudly as she left the counter, cutting a swath through the milling crowd toward the red and white banner of the *Polnische Extravaganz* on the other side of the Erdgeschoss.

This is not a drill. Make way, Marta bellowed. *We have a report of a fire. Make way, comrades. Heil Hitler*, she shouted using her pointed arm as the tip of a spear to clear the crowd in front of her. Some of the confused shoppers got out of the way as others attempted to return the Hitler salute while being jostled in the stampede to clear a path for Marta.

Other fire wardens from nearby counters followed suit sounding the alarm with loud, shrill whistles, joining Marta to propel the phalanx of shoppers and retail employees still further forward cutting a broad swath toward the *Polnische Extravaganz.* Leo could see from the Épernay counter, however, that at least two Gestapo men following in her wake were gaining ground on Harry and the girl.

Inspiration struck and Leo first told the remaining twin to run toward the Southern end of the store and shatter as many glass countertops as he could on the way before taking the last available door and getting out. This would draw the uniformed police, who were also milling about in the crowd, away from the Épernay counter.

When the boy had gone, Leo jumped up on the Épernay counter followed in turn by Big Otto. After a brief commiseration on the right words, they started singing the Horst Wessel song, at first tentatively, and then with more gusto as the words fell into their proper place. At the same time, Leo followed by Big Otto started throwing champagne bottles, some empty and some not, as far as they could across the grand surface of the department store.

The song had been named in honor of Horst Ludwig Wessel, a Nazi activist who was made a posthumous hero of the Nazi movement following his violent death in 1930. He wrote the lyrics to the song *Die Fahne hoch* or *Raise High the Flag,* commonly known as Horst-Wessel-Lied, which had become the Nazi Party anthem.

Die Straße frei den braunen Bataillonen.
Die Straße frei dem Sturmabteilungsmann!
Es schau'n aufs Hakenkreuz voll Hoffnung schon
Millionen. Der Tag für Freiheit und für Brot bricht an!
Clear the streets for the brown battalions,
Clear the streets for the storm division!
Millions are looking upon the swastika full of hope,
he day of freedom and of bread dawns!

The effect on those assembled at KaDeWe was as magical as it was chaotic. The flying bottles and sounds of shattering countertops produced a roar from the crowd. There was shrieking from shocked and confused women along with angry protests from their men that soon gave way to a growing chorus of patrons picking up the thread of the Horst Wessel song.

The swelling chorus ignited a patriotic hysteria in the crowd that Leo and Big Otto egged on, still standing on the countertop, opening champagne bottles, gulping some of their contents, pouring some on the heads of those below them, and throwing what was left into the crowd.

More importantly, the wake behind Marta, Little Otto, Harry and the girl abruptly closed ranks as the surging crowd, the curious and those who wanted to join in the Horst Wessel, reversed course sweeping the helpless Gestapo agents back toward the Épernay counter. This gave Marta and her charges just enough time to evaporate into the *Polnische Extravaganz.*

Two companions at the Épernay counter, who would change the trajectory of Leo's life, watched with awe as the episode unfolded before them while they casually sipped champagne in the champagne mist surrounding the counter. One was the formidable anti-Nazi, Countess Maria von Maltzan, and the other her close friend, the proprietor of the popular Café Alois at Wittenbergplatz 3, just around the corner from KaDeWe. He was Alois Hitler, the Führer's brother.

Alois said to no one in particular as he looked up at Leo, *I must get to know that boy.*

LEBKUCHEN

I. THE INNER FRONT - BERLIN JUNE 1942

...the black dog follows you and hangs/
close on your flying skirts with hungry fangs

– HORACE C. 65 BC TO 8 BC

It was a black dog day for the young mother, who had just left her four-year-old daughter with her granny, Oma Helena, as she set off on a balmy June evening to join her comrades. There was much to do that evening and deadlines to meet, and Erika was the glue that held the operation together – equal parts scribe and task master.

It was pure torture each time she left Saskia with her granny – the impulse to break down in tears and the gnawing pain in her stomach were ever present. She told herself that someday Saskia would understand —that everyone would understand the choices she had made, choices that had to be made.

She had married the handsome aristocrat and sculptor Graf Cay–Hugo von Brockdorff in 1937 and soon thereafter they had been blessed with Saskia. She prayed each morning as she rose and each night as she lay down to rest that Cay, who was fighting in the East, possessed the *soldier's luck* so the three of them could look ahead to a good life together someday.

It was at a costume party at the Academy of the Arts in Berlin in 1938 where she and Cay first met the actor, Wilhelm Schürmann, and from that a discussion circle evolved attended by the writer and journalist Adam Kuckoff and his equally erudite partner

Greta, Janna, the beautiful dancer, and Herr Schauer, the distinguished and argumentative architect. In those days *club talk* had been the hallmark of the resistance. Critical voices that crossed religious, political and class boundaries criticized Hitler's policies in small groups.

But the knot in her stomach that was now a constant in her life had become more pronounced with the advent of Hans Coppi and his friends, dyed in the wool communists, who had given the group a sharper edge pushing, nudging, even demanding more persistent action that would draw them into the growing web of conspiratorial networks in the sprawling city.

Erika was a simple girl from Pomerania who had come to Berlin at the age of 18 trained as a housekeeper. She had also modeled then and hoped that more of this glamorous work lay in her future.

She prided herself on having become a woman of the world in spite of her simple origins. She had gone on to train as an office worker and excelled in shorthand and typing. A single woman in a man's world needed to excel at all things, she believed, and it was this inner drive that made her indispensable to the group.

The knot in her stomach was of a distinctly German origin. The conspiratorial Erika was before all German to the core and wrestled with her disavowal of the conformity and compliance that now characterized most Germans in Berlin and for that matter the rest of the country.

Most opponents of the madman's regime had been ruthlessly suppressed and psychologically crushed by the mass show trials of the peoples' courts and the brutality of the concentration camps. Men, strong and accomplished men, returned from places like Sachsenhausen and Oranienburg faint shadows of their former selves.

Her small group was defined by its willingness to run the risk of discovery and arrest for the sake of human dignity and a constitutional state. Their efforts had started with leaflets and graffiti and tonight they would publish the latest edition of their communiqué, *The Inner Front*. This time it would be an open letter to Berliners about the atrocities in the East.

Yet leaflets and graffiti had evolved to something much more dangerous. Hans Coppi had managed to convince her to hide a radio transmitter in her third floor flat in Kreuzberg. This was espionage pure and simple. One's heart might succeed in justifying such a move but not one's common sense.

Would Saskia, she fretted, ever understand the seemingly unpatriotic choices that she had made to challenge the regime's claim to the future? Or if the 1,000 year Reich prevailed in spite of her best efforts, would Saskia view her as an enemy of the state and, torn between a daughter's natural love for her mother and fealty to the Reich, despise her for all time as would Saskia's daughter and her children thereafter?

As hard as it was to contemplate such an outcome her distinct advantage in wrestling with her conscience was that she was of solid German stock and as such was not prone to dwell on the maudlin. She had a job to do, principles to uphold, and her ambivalent German soul could not escape recognition of what they were.

* * * * *

Napoleon is famously quoted as saying, *I would rather have a general who is lucky than one who is good.* Napoleon might have found such a general in Leo had history been painted with different strokes.

Leo and Big Otto had languished overnight and for the better part of a day after their performance on the countertop of the Épernay exhibit at *KaDeWe* in a dirty cell at the Alex, Berlin's main police station in Alexander Platz. In this, they had been exceedingly lucky.

They had been detained by the *Bulls*, that is to say the Berlin police, who quelled the chaos on the *Erdgeschoss* of the sprawling department store before the Gestapo had time to regroup. The stench of the holding cells in the Alex and the amused opprobrium of the detectives who questioned them was much to be preferred to a cell at Prinz-Albrecht Strasse 8, where the Gestapo practiced a less genteel form of interrogation that could rearrange one's skeleture in pursuit of the truth or the particular answer the Gestapo was after. Worse still, being taken into custody at Prinz-Albrecht Strasse 8 was often a one-way trip.

Inspiration had turned to self-doubt for Leo as time passed at the Alex and he scolded himself for his impetuousness at *KaDeWe*. He had seen Little Otto in the crowd as he was being arrested with Big Otto and had been given the high sign that all was well with Harry and the girl. A victory, yes, but one where he ultimately had lost control of the situation.

He would also learn in due course that Marta had come out smelling like a rose because Harry and Little Otto had the presence of mind to start a fire in a storeroom near the *Polnische Extravaganz* to provide a suitable cover story. Indeed, Marta would receive a commendation and small sum of money from the store for her timely efforts in fire suppression.

The leader of the Gestapo squad that had pursued them had pressured the Bulls to turn the two boys over to him. It was a heated argument won in the end by the commandant in charge of the local police unit. Oddly, he had done so after consulting a well-dressed man at the Épernay counter, whose hair was matted with champagne, and who appeared to know the commandant well.

Their false identities had initially given them cover, but Leo was sure it would not last. It was Little Otto's handiwork of course – two military ID's bought on the black market from a deserter who dealt in the identification papers of his dead comrades. There was little that could not be bought or sold on the black market in Berlin at that time.

Little Otto had simply substituted photos of Leo and Big Otto in the appropriate spot in the stolen military paybooks. However, official seals were especially difficult to counterfeit, but Little Otto had worked his magic using a newly shelled hardboiled egg. With that egg, he could pick up the official seal that covered the original photo on the document by rolling the soft and porous egg over the seal to lift it from atop the original photo. Then he skillfully rolled the hardboiled egg back over the counterfeit photo to reapply the official seal to the document.

The hope had been that the counterfeit documents would at least get them past a cursory review if they were stopped on the street for any reason on the way to their rendezvous at *KaDeWe*. They were just two soldiers, or so the story would go, home on medical leave from the 4th Panzer army, which at that moment was somewhere on the Northern approaches to Stalingrad. Leo knew, however, any concerted effort to check their papers would do them in.

The boys' second stroke of luck soon became apparent when one of the Bulls, who had questioned them, complained that the Wehrmacht had rejected their request for identity verification because it was too busy with something called *Operation Blue.* Germans would soon come to know Operation Blue as the offensive that would pit over one million German soldiers against an equal number of Soviets at Stalingrad, a hellish battle that would turn the tide against Germany in the East.

As dusk approached on the second day of their detainment, they were released into the custody of the man whom Leo had seen talking to the commandant of the police at *KaDeWe.* He was dark haired with a neatly trimmed mustache, well dressed and polite with an easy smile that seemed at times to communicate he was enjoying Leo and Big Otto's predicament.

Gentlemen, you will come with me as you have been released into my custody. I have a small bierstube not far from here, and it would honor me if you would be my guests for a bite to eat.

By the way, my name is Alois Hitler and, yes, the other Hitler is my brother, but we are two peas from very different pods. And you are? Well, let's get to who you two really are over a meal. I suspect that you can use one. Please come with me.

And with that gentle but firm command, Leo and Big Otto followed Alois out of the Alex into the fresh summer evening and a waiting car amidst the hustle and bustle of crowds in Alexanderplatz returning from and going to work in the early evening hours at one of Berlin's major transport hubs.

Alois and Adolf were in fact half-brothers born to the same rage-filled and incestuous father, Alois, Sr. The two boys never got along as youngsters and rarely communicated during their lives.

Alois, the younger, was a draft dodger and suspected bigamist, who eventually became a legitimate businessman opening Café Alois on Wittenbergplatz. His half-brother never frequented the café, but it was rumored that the seed money for the new café flowed through the accounts of the *NSDAP* – that is to say the Nazi Party.

Upon arriving at Café Alois, Leo's first impression was that of an immense cavern that the sun had never penetrated. A small *bierstube* it was not. The vaulted ceilings and rich wood paneling were festooned with hundreds if not thousands of Teutonic tchotchke's along with what could easily have been the world's largest collection of ornate beer steins.

It could have been a cozy way station on the road to the seventh ring of Hell as it was instantly apparent that they were awash in a sea of undulating swastikas worn by Nazi elites rubbing elbows with a raucous herd of grubby stormtroopers. It was one big, convivial party as long you were Aryan.

Café Alois was particularly popular with stormtroopers and, after giving a bear hug to a fat stormtrooper whose mottled face was as red as his Nazi arm band, Alois made a beeline to the back of the establishment where a piano was the centerpiece of a more refined amphitheater where café tables with white linen tablecloths replaced the long oak tables and benches that served the porcine clientele at the front of the house. *I want to introduce you to someone*, Alois told the boys.

At the piano, they were introduced to a nattily attired piano player whose name was Charley. He was tall, rail thin and handsome with dark features. *Charley and I have been together since my days in the nightclub business in England*, Alois said. *Charley please meet my friends, who are....*

Leo and Big Otto, Leo replied after a moment's hesitation. *So, not Hans Schröder from Köln and Franz Streibl from Frankfurt an der Oder!? Imagine that.* Leo's mordacious soul half enjoyed being skewered as deftly as Alois had just done.

Gentlemen my pleasure, Charley replied. *I look forward to meeting Little Otto one day if there is one.*

It was the rigidity of his head and shoulders, his slightly off target gaze that tipped Leo off to the fact that Charley was blind. Sensing this, Charley preempted the question, *Gentlemen, I have been nearly blind since I was a child, and the gods tease me by only letting me see the contours of an object without being able to enjoy its full beauty.*

Charley, Alois interrupted, *would you be so kind as to take our new friends to my apartment and find them clean shirts and please show them where they can freshen up. It will help their appetites and mine to leave the scent along with the memory of the Alex behind.*

* * * * *

The stein of strong Czech Budvar had done its work. Leo and Big Otto, the former in a shirt that was too large for him and the latter in one so tight it bulged at the seams, felt their cares float away with each sip.

Charley was on the piano playing for the tony Nazi clientele at tables arranged around the piano in a semi-circle with two tiers. Against the backdrop of Charley's sly rendition of Gershwin's kaleidoscopic and for many of Alois's Nazi patrons *degenerate* jazz harmonies in "An American in Paris," Leo and Big Otto inhaled a large plate of *Masurischer Wildpfeffer*, the house specialty which was a dish of wild boar and stag, bacon and mushrooms served with potato dumpling, stewed cabbage and cranberries.

As Alois attended to a guest, Big Otto said, *I don't know what his angle is, but he sure can cook, or someone can. I suspect that we are about to find out,* Leo replied.

And they were. *My dear boys, the Gestapo have no illusions about who you are, and I would make haste to let your friends at the bakery know if they don't already. The word is that you have ties to anarchists and after your tour de force at KaDeWe, I can see that you have a certain talent for insurrection,* Alois said.

We had too much to drink and behaved stupidly, Leo replied. *You are too clever for that I think,* Alois said. *Remember, I was at the counter and saw the situation evolve. I trust that you were ultimately successful.*

Leo did not respond. What was there to say? *What do you want,* he finally asked Alois?

I am told you bake well, Alois said. Big Otto jumped in, *he's the best. You should come to the bakery.*

Or perhaps the bakery can come to me, Alois replied.

I have commitments there, Leo hastened to add. Alois did not respond to this.

Well, we have the overhang of your admirers at the Gestapo to address. At least for the time being. If you were to walk out on to Wittenbergplatz at this very moment, I suspect that you would be picked up instantly, so you would do well to stay here for at least a few days and demonstrate your handiwork, while I address your future.

How will you do that, Leo asked?

Alois responded by saying matter of factly, *Himmler is a dear friend whom I expect to see him tomorrow night. He always comes for tomorrow's Wurstplatte when he can. Alas, my friend, the failed chicken farmer, cannot stand the sight of fowl, so we ply his voracious appetite with wurst. I will have a talk with him to settle the matter at least temporarily.*

So, we pay our debts with baked goods, Leo asked facetiously, because he knew that there was much more to the bargain. *Charley will fill you in on the details of a proposal that would be to the benefit of us both. I have a few people to greet, so please excuse me as I do, and eat up!*

* * * * *

Ingrid knew that she had made a mistake, a terrible mistake. She had let her pride and stubborn streak make things worse for herself and her mother. And, in Nazi Germany, that was really saying something if you were Jewish.

She had tempted fate before but never with her mother as she had tonight. *Damn me, Damnation*, she said to herself as she waited for her mother to collect from their small bedroom the bag that they always kept packed for an occasion they hoped would not come. They would have to spend the night in the woods near their flat in Pankow and hope that they could make it to the relative safety of Otto's workshop under the cover of the morning rush hour.

They had a fighting chance because Ingrid and her mother had the bone structure and light features exalted by the master race, so they could easily blend into the crowd. For the strong-willed young woman barely thirty, her secret weapon though was her unshakable sense that she belonged.

To be German was her birthright, and no one could say otherwise. She would never surrender to their oppression, no matter the number of insults heaped upon Jews by the Nazis. We are all good and loyal Germans, she told herself, time and time again.

It had been nearly 10 years since Hitler had gained power and pushed through the Enabling Act that gave him dictatorial powers. Barely a week after that, he had turned his anti-Semitic raving into action, and the boycott of all Jewish businesses took hold in Germany.

It was then that her father, targeted by the Nazis, fled for England. He was a wealthy merchant, who had become a leader in the progressive social democrats. A local policeman, god bless him, had tipped them off with barely an hour to spare that an SS squad was detached to bring him in.

What a long way they had come since her privileged childhood in the upscale enclave of Gruenwald where Gentile and Jew lived in relative harmony in stately homes on beautiful, wooded lots. She longed for their beautiful red brick house set back from the road and shielded from view by a row of cultivated cypress trees.

They had been forced to sell their home for a prayer and song in 1934 to an up and coming member of the Nazi party. In effect, the Nazis had confiscated it. Their dear friend, Otto Weidt, had been able to arrange the tiny flat in Pankow for them with a kindly Catholic woman.

Ingrid's young life had been one of cultural abundance in a large family of aunts, uncles and cousins who valued ideas, literature, concerts and plays. She was an intelligent girl, who had set her sights on a university education and a career in medicine. However, by the time she reached the age of 19 in 1933, Jews had been denied a university education.

It was less than a year ago, September 1941, when all Jews older than six years of age had been ordered to wear the Star of David embroidered with the word *Jude* over their hearts. Her heart, indeed every fiber of her being, had rebelled against the idea of turning such an illustrious symbol into a badge of dishonor.

Then in January 1942, they had been ordered to surrender their winter coats, warm clothing and blankets which were then shipped to German troops on the Russian front. Shortly thereafter, all Jewish households were required to post Stars of David on their front doors.

And the storm of insults had intensified still further. In June 1942, it had been barely six weeks since Jews had been ordered not to use public transportation, to circulate only in their immediate districts and to surrender their electrical appliances including cameras, typewriters, bicycles and radios.

What is worse, they were also told they were no longer permitted to buy milk, eggs, fish, cheese, spirits and bread. Their kindly landlord now shared her meager pantry with them.

But Ingrid was tough and resilient and to this list she now added prideful and stupid. She had purchased opera tickets when she had her hair done earlier that day on a window-shopping excursion to the *Kufurstendamm*. She had not worn the star. This was an illegal act that would be harshly punished if she were discovered, but it was her form of silent protest.

Their tickets were for a performance of Beethoven's *Fidelio* at the Staatsoper that evening, and she and her mother did their best with what little they had to dress elegantly. No yellow stars this evening. Ingrid's mother had gone along with the plan because she trusted Ingrid's judgment implicitly.

It had been a beautiful performance. And those around them were none the wiser to who they were or what they were other than two elegant German women enjoying an evening out.

They stayed put in their seats during the first intermission out of an abundance of caution but at the second intermission decided to risk stretching their legs to get a bit of fresh air. As they were heading toward the main doors, a beautifully dressed young woman, glass of champagne in hand, approached them and addressed herself to Ingrid whispering, *hello, my name is Stella, Stella Goldschlag. Weren't we together at the Jewish school in Grunewald some years back?*

Ingrid feigning ignorance tightened the grip on her mother's arm as they casually strolled out into the night air. They kept walking, never turning to look back, until they had reached Pankow.

And now with all their worldly possessions in two bags, they left their flat for the last time. To the sound of barking dogs and dishes clattering behind open kitchen widows, a disconsolate daughter helped her mother navigate the rough ground into the dark woods and a darker future.

* * * * *

The Reverend Doctor Martin Sauter felt like a man caught in the jaws of a vise that was being tightened by diminutive gargoyles. He was reminded of the illuminated Medieval manuscripts in which lost souls were tormented and dragged to hell by such demons.

Tightening from one side was his patron, Joseph Goebbels, the Reichsminister of Propaganda, who was disappointed and embarrassed by the failure of the Gestapo mission that Himmler had somewhat reluctantly delegated to him. Sauter's information had been faulty, and as a result three of his agents were dead, including Fischer who had quite literally been torn to pieces by Rottweilers.

Turning the screw on the other side of the vise, was the head of the SS himself, Heinrich Himmler, who was still grappling with mixed emotions weeks after the assassination in Czechoslovakia of his protégé, Reinhard Heydrich. Himmler had felt a genuine fondness for the *man with the iron heart,* as Hitler had so aptly described Heydrich at his funeral.

Himmler and Heydrich had formed a partnership of sorts, a ruthless and successful one indeed for the Nazi cause. It was not, however, without its ambiguities. Their knowledge of each other's strengths and weaknesses was as intimate as that of partners in a marriage in which a relationship runs hot and cold, as in this marriage with Heydrich posing a theoretical if not immediate risk to Himmler's favored status with the Führer.

For that very reason, he had replaced Heydrich immediately after the funeral with the weak drunkard Kaltenbrunner, who was present in Himmler's study that evening reeking of alcohol and cheap cologne as was his wont. So too were Goebbels and Sauter.

While Goebbels was consumed by self-pity, Himmler was seething and distant. Sauter's well-rehearsed rationalizations ricocheted off Himmler like bird shot off a Tiger tank.

I had dinner with Alois last night and the boys who caused a stir at KaDeWe are in his custody and just as well for now, Himmler said. *This bäckerei in Wedding is the hub of a spider web of conspiracies that go beyond a couple of young anarchists who will soon find themselves in a penal battalion on the Russian Steppe being eaten alive by the mosquitos or the Russians.*

What Himmler failed to disclose was his personal financial interest in the designs that Alois had on Leo's skills. Alois was among other things a smuggler of fine jewels from the vanquished countries of the Reich to be set in fine jewelry for sale to German elites or sold for foreign currency in Berlin. Himmler did not seem particularly concerned that these jewels were sold in Switzerland to Jews.

Himmler imagined a day when all in the 1,000-year Reich would live in peace having dominated the world, and he would be one of its wealthiest patriarchs thanks to this enterprise. Himmler was also adept at hedging his bets and used the same pipeline to maintain an open channel with counterparts in Switzerland who could be exploited to negotiate the end of the war if the tide turned against Germany.

So, what action do you recommend, Herr Reichsmarshall, the obsequious Goebbels asked?

Within the radius of this web surrounding these two boys, we will expose the gang of ruffians they utilize, this annoying fellow Bonhoeffer and, we think, Canaris and his golden boys, Himmler said.

Sir, if I may ask, Sauter said interrupting Himmler's train of thought, *why not round the lot of them up now? Nip it in the bud as it were?*

Himmler did not acknowledge Sauter or the question but answered it anyway addressing no one in particular. *There is, we believe, more to this than meets the eye. It is not simply the mystery of what those we have identified are planning but the plans of those we have not identified. Our working theory here is that to shred one web is to ultimately shred many.*

And the plan, Goebbels asked as he leaned forward like an enrapt child in the presence of a master storyteller?

Kaltenbrunner, Himmler addressed himself to his new Gestapo chief, *the Reverend here will make every effort to infiltrate Bonhoeffer's social circle. You and I have discussed targets and timelines, and you will brief the Reverend on our expectations immediately after we are done here.*

Without waiting for a response, Himmler continued, *we will let the boys now in the care of Alois return in due course to the bäckerei and that, we believe, will stir the pot. They will undoubtedly be in contact with Bonhoeffer and whether that also means others in the Abwehr, time will tell.*

And for the first time that evening, Himmler turned to Sauter, leaning forward to address him directly, *Sauter, we are greatly in need of chaplains for our soldiers in the East. Whether you serve the Fatherland here or serve it there will be up to you and dependent on your getting it right this time.*

* * * * *

It had been three days, and Leo and Big Otto had yet to escape their velvet chains although they had managed to get word of their predicament to Mehdi. In return, Mehdi sent word by Little Otto that Leo should be cautious about his newfound friends, whom he knew by reputation, and that henceforth Little Otto would serve as their principal channel of communication until matters had been resolved with Alois.

Leo had been put to work in the kitchen as the house baker and soon established his credentials with the chef and his staff by producing a treasure trove of bread and rolls as varied as the tchotchke's on the sprawling café's walls, while Big Otto went to work as an apprentice to the barkeep. He also bussed the long oak tables and was rapidly acquiring a following among the depraved stormtroopers who infested the front of the house.

Charley finally took Leo aside, *as formidable as your baking skills are, Leo, allow me to get down to business on your new assignment with us. While Alois is fair and views this as a temporary arrangement, you may find that it is sufficiently lucrative to maintain your interest for some time to come,* he said.

They were sitting at a café table near the piano sipping *Budvars* after Leo had put out the daily order of baked goods. They were alone in the darkened amphitheater to the back of the cavernous *bierstube* during the morning lull before the birds of prey began descending on them for lunch.

For some time now, Charley continued, *Alois has had a small enterprise that buys and sells precious stones on the open market. Inas-*

much as the spoils of war are stolen by those in power the moment they are seized, we have opted for greener pastures and do our trading from time to time in Switzerland. In most cases, the stones are generally set in jewelry and sold to our upscale patrons. In other cases, we trade a few stones in Switzerland for others or for Swiss francs.

Leo was intrigued. *Tell me more,* he said. *It would seem to me that something this illegal would have powerful investors behind it, investors well placed in the Reich?*

Well said, my boy, Charley responded. *On one hand, it may be viewed by some as unseemly on so many different levels, not the least of which is that our counterpart in Switzerland is a Jew – a fine fellow nonetheless, I might add. Beyond that, a man of the world such as yourself would require no primer on the myriad ways our little enterprise is fraught with risk. On the other hand, yes, we do indeed have sponsorship – one very highly placed investor, who suffers no fools and therein lies the rub.*

So, we think you are a fine candidate, Charley was interrupted by Leo completing his thought, *to be your front man for these transactions traveling, I assume, to Switzerland with a suitcase full of jewels? Reichsmarks?* Charley was beaming and said, *Alois's confidence in you is well placed, my boy.*

So why me? What happened to the man or woman who has been the go between until now, Leo asked?

Charley hesitated, suspended between the full truth and the impulse to sugar coat it. *Well, your predecessor was quite skilled at the game, but fell into the arms of a beautiful courtesan who was the tip of the spear for a gang of Roma thugs. After a raucous night of athletic rumpy-pumpy that tested the patience of the hotel guests in adjoining rooms, he awoke well pleased with himself until he discovered that his lover and 50,000 Reichsmarks in precious stones had alighted from their love nest.*

And, Leo asked?

And, all might have been forgiven, in point of fact, had he not lost his nerve and made a run for it. Our investor has many tentacles that reach far and wide, and it was not long before he found the poor man. The last that Alois heard was he was in the KZ at Mauthausen carrying heavy boulders in its stone quarry.

But I know nothing about gems, fine jewels, Leo replied. *Alois is convinced after your bravura performance at KaDeWe that you have the nerve and the savvy to do well in this venture. It is I who arranges the transfer and for obvious reasons it is Alois who is the final authority on what we buy or sell. The rest I can teach you, most importantly how one smuggles fine gems and currency across the border to and from Switzerland because while we have a powerful patron, to do so is distinctly illegal and you will be largely on your own at the border crossings,* Charley responded.

And when will that be, Leo asked. *In a week's time, Leo once we go over the details of the itinerary, procedure and of course your remuneration,* Charley replied.

Charley continued, *the exchange typically happens in the lovely town of Schaffhausen just across the Swiss border. You will be provided with fine accommodations in one of the town's best inns. For your own good, we simply ask that you avoid young women whilst there.*

It was at that moment that the two conspirators sensed a third presence and there looming over them was a figure who at first glance looked vaguely familiar to Leo. Leo looked up to see a ghostly figure with hollow eyes and sunken cheeks as dark and deep as the craters of the moon. His next impression was of clothing that was too large for the bony frame on which it loosely hung. Charley had also sensed the presence of the man and listened with anticipation.

It's Huber, the figure said, *Arnold Huber*. It was the man from the culvert in the Tiergarten, Marta's brother.

11. THEY CAN ACCUSE ME OF A LOT, BUT NOT OF ONE THING

It was at that same moment that Little Otto also arrived for his daily *powwow* with Leo and not coincidentally for lunch. Little Otto had anything but a *little* appetite and shared a passion for bratwurst with another diminutive gnome, Heinrich Himmler.

Charley politely excused himself and left the three to themselves. Leo ordered the bratwurst special for both Little Otto and Huber as it was that day of the week. After inhaling an impressively phallic *Bregenwurst* from Lower Saxony, which seemed to bring tears to his eyes, a shaky Huber said, *Leo, I have a favor to ask.*

Please, was all Leo said in reply. He was grateful to Huber but more so to his sister for effectively saving his life and the lives of those with him at KaDeWe.

I am part of a group to which I was introduced by Marta. We are active in educating our fellow citizens about the lunacy of the current regime and the evil that it has visited on Germany and its neighbors. We are sincere in the hope that there is still time to bring our countrymen to their senses before Germany is destroyed from within and to find a new way of governing ourselves whether it is a democratic republic, monarchy, or a proletariat paradise. Anything would be better than this.

It was Little Otto who responded first, whispering, *take a look around you at the clientele, Herr Huber, the jackboots and arm bands. It would be better if we had this conversation somewhere else or if you could make it seem that we were three companions casually talking about the horse races at Hoppegarten.*

Leo sat in silence satisfied that Little Otto had said what needed to be said.

I am sorry, Huber said, feigning a broad smile, which he struggled for the next hour to maintain.

I would like you to meet someone, who is spearheading our effort to publish a piece that is an open letter to our countrymen about the atrocities on the eastern front, Huber said. *It is a subject that, it is fair to say, put me in the KZ at Sachsenhausen, which led to your finding me in a culvert in the Tiergarten.*

I remember you from the Tiergarten, Little Otto replied. *So, you were there on the eastern front?*

I am – was – a cinematographer and was assigned to a propaganda unit that followed an Einsatzgruppen, or in other words, a mobile killing unit, in the East. We found ourselves in a god forsaken part of the Ukraine at a place called Bila Tserkva. Over a period of two days, virtually the entire adult Jewish population of Bila Tserkva was shot. All that remained were the children and a few of the women, who were confined in the town's school to await execution.

Members of a nearby Wehrmacht unit were so disturbed by the crying of the children and infants at the school that they asked their chaplains what they could do. Two of their chaplains visited the school and were appalled by the condition of the frightened, hungry children.

Joined by two other chaplains of the 295th Division, they were finally able to persuade the local Wehrmacht commander to postpone the executions and order the army to address the immediate physical needs of those in the school. My colleagues and I could be spectators to this horror no longer and helped feed the children.

However, the local commander was overruled by Field Marshall von Reichenau and the next day we found ourselves filming the result. We arrived in a wooded area to find that the Wehrmacht had already dug a long shallow grave. The executions were to be conducted by our allies in the area, the Ukrainian Einsatzkommandos, who stood around trembling as they awaited the children's arrival.

The children were eventually brought along in a tractor and upon arrival lined up along the top of the grave and shot so that they fell into it. The Ukrainians did not aim at any particular part of the body and many children were hit four or five times before they died.

The wailing was indescribable. Until my dying day, I will remember a small, fair-haired girl who had taken me by the hand the day before after I fed her, who was among those shot.

I protested our filming, but we were forced to do so, nonetheless. Had it not been for the intercession of the chaplains, I might also have been shot on the spot. As it was, I was sent back to Berlin later to be summoned by the 'Peoples Court' and the rest you know.

While the broad smile was gone, to Huber's credit he had managed to maintain his composure. The raucous crowd in the front of the house barely noticed the three of them at the café table behind the piano.

So, how can we help, Huber, Leo asked.

Through a friend of a friend, Marta learned of your association with Mehdi and that you might have access to printing supplies on the black market. Ours were destroyed in a fire in Rudow. So, I would like you to meet with the young woman whose good sense holds our fractious group together and around whom our efforts to produce our open letter revolve. She will have more knowledge of our needs, Huber replied.

A meeting was set for early the following Sunday morning at Café Alois. Leo was noncommittal with Huber but asked Little Otto after Huber had left to look at what they could spare in ink and stencils and to join him for Sunday's meeting.

* * * * *

It would have been the beginning of a glorious day had Hedwig Porschütz not been so exhausted. A crisp breeze off the nearby Spree competed with the warm morning sunlight to beguile commuters on Rosenthaler Strasse just around the corner from the bustling Hackescher Markt. There were smiles on everyone's faces but, apart from the weather, Hedwig was of the mind that there was really very little to smile about in Berlin in these times.

It had been one of those nights. She was hiding the Bergman twins for Otto and the three of them had taken refuge for most of the night in the stairwell at the end of the hallway to her apartment in a sprawling *Mietskaserne* in the slums of the *Scheunenviertal,* a short walk from Otto's workshop. This was by design because her apartment was on occasion occupied by prostitutes and by agreement Hedwig and her charges could not return to her quarters until the prostitutes had dispatched their clients.

What had not been foreseen was a police raid and this was why she felt so damned tired. The police had chosen last night to raid the building to look for black marketeers. More power to them if that were all they were after, she thought, but it had forced Hedwig and the twins to move several times to stay one step ahead of the raid.

As bad as things were at times, Otto always managed to make things better, and Hedwig looked forward to seeing him as she approached the entrance to his shop. It was his soft voice and his sense of humor when he teased her that lifted her spirits along with a playful cuff to the jaw.

Otto Weidt, who was approaching 60, owned a workshop in Berlin for the blind and deaf. He had grown up in modest circumstances, attended elementary and high school and, like his father, had become a paperhanger. Soon after the Weidt family moved to Berlin he became involved in anarchist and pacifist circles of the German working-class movement.

With his own eyesight failing, he learned the business of brush making and broom binding. In 1936, Otto established a workshop to manufacture brooms and brushes in his cellar apartment in Berlin-Kreuzberg and later moved to his current location in the backyard of Rosenthaler Strasse 39 in Berlin-Mitte. His largest customer was the Wehrmacht, and he cleverly managed to have his business classified as vital to the war effort.

Over 30 blind and deaf Jews were employed at his shop between the years of 1941 and 1943. For a long while, he was able to operate under the protection of the Wehrmacht but when the Gestapo began to arrest and deport his Jewish employees, he fought to secure their safety by falsifying documents, bribing officers and hiding them in the back of his shop or with friends.

Hedwig was his righthand *man*, so to speak, and at most times his *left and right hand man,* in his perilous enterprise. Her ingenuity served their mutual objectives well. Goods she bought on the black market would be given to the persecuted Jews in Otto's orbit and used to bribe Gestapo officers. She was also exceedingly clever in hiding fugitives from the Gestapo.

Hedwig had been literally dragging her feet that morning as she often did when she was tired and her toe hit the edge of a flagstone in the sidewalk hurling her to the pavement. As she hit the ground hard, she saw them. It was Otto's friend, Ingrid, and her mother, and they had just reached the pedestrian island in the middle of Rosenthaler Strasse between opposing trolley tracks directly across from Otto's shop.

A split second later, two men pounced like great cats on their unsuspecting prey. As Hedwig struggled to her knees, she could see Ingrid protesting and frantically attempting to convince the two men, Gestapo agents most likely, that she and her mother were good, law-abiding Germans. Neither wore the obligatory yellow Star of David, an offense that would be punished harshly.

Ingrid kept her body between the men and her mother until they were both gripped roughly by their arms and pushed back across the street away from the workshop. As they reached the opposite side of the street, one of the Gestapo agents nodded to an attractive young woman who smiled, nodding her approval in reply.

Hedwig had to see Otto right away because she knew that time was of the essence. It was more likely than not that Ingrid and her mother would be taken to a nearby building on Grosse Hamburger Strasse that had once been a home for elderly Jews but, since the deportations started in 1941, had served as a collecting point for Jews about to be deported.

Past deportations had been accomplished through a formal process housed in the *Reichsvereinigung*, the Association of Jews of the Reich, where all Jews were required to register. In one of the many perversions of the Third Reich, this organization was compelled to administer all anti-Jewish decrees including deportations.

Those Jews selected for deportation were always notified in advance and ordered to report to Grosse Hamburger Strasse or other collecting points. Those who did not report were seized by the Gestapo and forcibly deposited at these collecting stations. Once the requisite number of Jews had been assembled, usually 1,000 people, they were taken in trucks to railroad yards where they were then crammed into freight cars for the journey East.

Hedwig hoped that Ingrid and her mother would be lucky enough, although good luck hardly seemed to apply to any of this, that they had missed the most recent *shipment* East and that there might be a way that she and Otto could extract them from the collecting point before the next. This had been done before on rare occasions and if there was a way to do it now, Otto would know how.

Out of breadth with a bruised wrist and a scraped knee wet from bleeding, Hedwig found Otto at the shop's loading dock and frantically told him the story between huge gulps of air. Otto listened to all she had to say calmly and said, *it is Friday and typically the trucks leave today. I am not optimistic. I will send someone to check on their status.*

I will also call my Wehrmacht counterpart, but he is proving less and less helpful as the Gestapo asserts itself, Otto continued. *Two of Mehdi's boys, the twins, are here to help me get today's shipment onto the truck. I will send one to Mehdi right away to see if there is something that our resourceful friend can do.*

* * * * *

After the meeting with Himmler, Kaltenbrunner called on none other than his cousin, Sepp Lange, to join him and the Reverend Sauter in the campaign against the denizens of *Die Bäckerei* overlooking for the moment Lange's failure to capture the third boy at KaDeWe. Sepp, who detested the sniveling Sauter, resisted the invitation pointing to his many successes with his band *Griefer* and *Greiferinnen*, particularly his prized asset, Stella Goldschlag.

Kaltenbrunner needed someone he could trust to run the operation and would not take *No* for an answer. He assured his cousin that the new expense account that came with the job would be several times the size of the account currently at his disposal, money he could use at his complete discretion.

Kaltenbrunner also wanted Stella Goldschlag as part of the team. She was clever whereas Sepp was diligent and reliably brutal. The success of the operation he envisioned might require both their talents.

Sauter, from Kaltenbrunner's point of view, was more of a hindrance than a help. It was Himmler's wish to involve him, however, and he would make the good Reverend Sepp's problem henceforth.

And, so it was that *Belial* and his fallen angels gathered for dinner at Max and Moritz on Oranien Strasse in Kreuzberg, named for the dark German fairy tale in which it is written of two terrible boys, Max and Moritz, who

...instead of early turning, their young minds to useful learning,

often leered with horrid features, at their lessons and their teachers.

Max and Moritz were notorious for their cruel practical jokes of which the seventh and last would be their comeuppance. Hiding out in the granary of a local farmer by the name of Mecke, they slit some of his grain sacks. Carrying away one of the sacks, the farmer immediately noticed the problem and found Max and Moritz, putting them in the same sack. He tied it up and took it to his brother's wood mill where the boys were ground to bits and devoured by the miller's ducks. Later, as the fable goes, no one expressed regret.

It was fitting then that Kaltenbrunner and Lange harbored a certain sentimental attachment to this turn-of-the-century, Art

Nouveau beer hall because, during the ascendancy of the Nazi party a decade earlier, their *SA Home* sat next door. From these local offices or, more aptly, clubhouses for the criminally insane, the Nazi brown shirts expanded their claims to territory in Berlin neighborhoods using violence and terror to ensure that the Nazi regime would be established quickly and efficiently.

During their salad days, Max and Moritz, that is to say Kaltenbrunner and Lange, along with their fellow Nazi stormtroopers became the *Masters of the Streets*. Operating from their SA Home, the two cousins shot three workers in *Neukölln* and *Stieglitz*, stabbed a Marxist auto mechanic in the same district, fired at a political opponent in *Siemensstadt*, beat up three communists in *Bäkepark* and punched a 60 year old Jewish grandmother of 12 on the *Ku'damn*. And this was all in just one day's work in the summer of 1932.

Kaltenbrunner and Lange had already polished off a bottle of *Prinz von Hessen* Riesling and were ordering another when Sauter and Stella arrived. Kaltenbrunner ordered the waiter to bring two more glasses and a third bottle of the expensive white wine.

The cagey Stella nursed her Riesling while marveling at the velocity with which Kaltenbrunner consumed his. She knew that her on-again, off-again, lover, Sepp, enjoyed a drink as much as anyone, but even he was having some difficulty keeping pace with his boss.

Sauter was in a funk, abandoned by Goebbels to work with people he viewed as ruffians. Adding to his distress, the place was hot and noisy, and he had not been able to eat a bite that day because of his anxiety about this meeting, leaving him dizzy and disoriented.

He could feel the cold sweat forming on his upper lip, at the top of his eyebrows and along the contours of his hairline. He had assiduously avoided eye contact with the harlot sitting across the table from him.

But as the queasy delirium he had been fighting tightened its grip on him, he could not avoid looking at Stella's ample chest which seemed to swell in size before his eyes and move across the table toward him.

Sauter, are you OK? We are ordering dinner, Kaltenbrunner barked above the din of the crowd. Mercifully, the command brought Sauter back to the world of the living. *Focus, Martin, focus*, he said to himself.

Kaltenbrunner's brain chemistry, not to say, his liver might have been of great interest to medical science for at least two reasons. Not surprisingly, he became more belligerent with each successive glass of Riesling. This no doubt served him well in his Max and Moritz days knocking heads among political opponents in Berlin as a rising star in the SA.

Of more interest to science perhaps was that the alcohol also seemed to integrate his thinking, connecting his frayed circuitry, so as time passed, Kaltenbrunner demonstrated an increasingly nimble mind for tactics and strategy, a talent that one would not have foreseen as he guzzled wine like a late model Mercedes roadster guzzled gasoline. The only one of his dinner companions who rivaled Kaltenbrunner's mental agility at that moment and who was often one step ahead of his thinking was the clever Stella.

So, Doctor Sauter, your role is to insinuate yourself into those circles of the elite, the military and civil service establishment, who are aiding and abetting Bonhoeffer and others. Where do you stand with that, Kaltenbrunner asked as if he were a drill sergeant addressing a common soldier? Sauter noticed for the first time that the broad shouldered, six-foot, four-inch Kaltenbrunner in full uniform but for his crush cap loomed over his dinner guests like *Fafner*, the giant in *der Ring des Nibelungen*.

One of my flock is the major domo in the house of one Hanna Solf, who is the widow of Doctor Wilhelm Solf, Sauter replied. *He served as Imperial Colonial Secretary before the outbreak of World War I and ambassador to Japan under the Weimar Republic. Dr Solf died in 1936.*

His widow is a political moderate as was her husband and according to my source a committed anti-Nazi, Sauter continued with a tilt of his pinched nose upward as if he had smelled something disagreeable. *My parishioner's dilemma was whether to inform the authorities about this perceived lack of loyalty on the part of Frau Solf, so he came to me.*

My thought as a layman in the protocols of the secret police was to have him do nothing for the moment but keep me informed of the comings and goings there. Apparently, there are occasional teas or Kaffeeklatschen where the guests, some quite well placed in our government, offer opinions and ideas that my parishioner finds most distressing.

It would be well, Kaltenbrunner responded, *if you could find a way to join these social gatherings. If that is not possible, I may have an alternative.*

My prominent role in the Reichskirche may prove an obstacle where this is concerned. Yet, I will explore the possibility, Sauter replied.

No pat on the back for Sauter, but Kaltenbrunner was satisfied for the moment. Turning next to Stella, he barked, *and*?

As Sepp and I agreed the other day, I have been keeping an eye on the comings and goings at Café Alois. We will also be stopping in for dinner with greater frequency than before, she said.

The tall, lanky boy is the baker at Café Alois. His name as we know is Leo. The small boy seems to be Leo's messenger to the man called Mehdi, the proprietor of Die Bäckerei in Wedding. We know him for his black-market activities but have, perhaps, overlooked undertakings that pose more of a threat to our Fatherland, Stella added.

This drew a sneer from Kaltenbrunner as if to say, *this is not your Fatherland*. Stella ignored the slight if she noticed it at all and continued, *we have also seen a man called Arnold Huber who is a fugitive from Sachsenhausen, visit Café Alois. We observed him at a table with Leo and the runt. My suggestion is that we let Huber remain a fugitive for now so as not to forewarn the conspirators that they are under surveillance.*

It is a mystery to me why Himmler tolerates this business between Alois and those boys from KaDeWe, but for now we cannot make a move unless it is fully justified, but I sense that you think justification is only a matter of time, Kaltenbrunner asked?

Something is going on, so we watch and wait, Stella concluded for the Gestapo chief who was warming to Stella's cunning. *She is after all a Jew*, he told himself.

For their part, Kaltenbrunner and Lange would follow the final thread of the investigation to wherever it led by tapping the phones of the top lieutenants of Wilhelm Canaris the head of Abwehr. The fact that one of them was Bonhoeffer's brother-in-law, Hans Dohnányi, made the opportunity all the more interesting.

Kaltenbrunner knew they were onto something, but what was it? He compared the moment to hunting wild boar in the primeval forests of the Carpathian Mountains as a younger man. Hunter and hunted knew the other was there, one was as deadly as the other, but the boar was the cleverer of the two in concealing its movements.

It took courage and cunning to corner the hidden beast and more than one hunter had lost his life trying. But the beast was there, it was big and it was dangerous and, if it made one false move, he would kill it.

* * * * *

They had been unceremoniously thrown into a room no larger than five square meters and were alone at first. More Jews kept coming and by dusk on the day they were seized, they numbered 14 in the small room. The saving grace of their new quarters was a barred window that let in fresh air along with the raucous banter of the guards playing soccer outside in the old Jewish cemetery at the rear of the heavy stone building.

The cemetery was overgrown, many of the headstones lay on their sides, and there were spots where the guard dogs had dug up a grave and gnawed through the simple wooden coffins. It upset Ingrid to know that some of the most prominent Jews in the history of Berlin were being defiled on this sacred ground.

Ingrid wanted to cry, to scold the guards about the terrible things that they were doing to their fellow Germans, good Germans who had done just as much for the Fatherland as anyone. She knew that she could do neither because her sole focus had to be on getting her mother away from this awful place before they were sent East.

Ingrid's mother had found that one of their fellow detainees was an old friend from childhood. Her name was Ruth, and she had been her oldest sister's best friend. Ingrid's mother had looked up to Ruth as a child. Ruth was frail now but the glow of kindness that was ever present in Ruth as a beautiful young girl had not diminished with age. Ingrid's mother was spending much of her time now doting over the wellbeing of her childhood hero.

They were fed twice a day and allowed to exercise by walking up and down the long hallways where they would encounter other groups, all Jews apart from a few SS jailers. Ingrid had used these intervals to appeal to the sensibilities of the guards in a fruitless effort to gain the release of her mother and Ruth to the care of friends. *Keep me if you must, they are no threat*, Ingrid argued.

Word had been passed from one captive to the other that they would be leaving in just three days' time, sometime on Tuesday afternoon. Ingrid had overheard a guard on the telephone confirming the arrangements.

She had also overheard the destination —Auschwitz-Birkenau. Her heart sank because Ingrid knew enough to know that if this were true, the next two days would be their last spent in the city of their birth.

* * * * *

Dazzling was the first word that came to mind as Dietrich shook hands with Erika von Brockdorff when introduced to her by Leo. Dietrich had not been invited to this meeting, which was ostensibly about printing supplies, but the urgency of the situation with Ingrid and her mother had compelled him to see Leo before it was too late to do anything for the mother and daughter.

It was early Sunday morning, and a balmy breeze swept through the lazy shadows on Berlin's nearly deserted streets. Little Otto was in attendance as well as Erika's four-year-old daughter, Saskia, the spitting image of her mother. Rounding out the group was Charley, who was mildly exasperated at Leo's cavalier use of Café Alois as his personal clubhouse.

Erika dominated the room. She was taller than everyone but Charley while Saskia and Little Otto might have been mistaken for twins.

Erika looked like she had stepped out of a propaganda newsreel for Aryan purity. She was blonde, broad shouldered, rosy cheeked and when her sharp-eyed gaze hit Dietrich and Leo, they felt the balance of power in the room tilt in her direction. Erika wore a bright red bandana tied around her neck so that she could have easily been mistaken for a member of the *Bund Deutscher Mädchen*, the girls wing of the Hitler Youth.

Leo put out the kaffee and a platter of freshly baked *Lebkuchen*. It was Alois's birthday. Charley had put Leo up to making a batch of *Lebkuchen* telling him, *it is a delicacy typically reserved for the celebration of Christmas, as you know Leo, but Alois insists on having it be served on his birthday.*

Lebkuchen, a dense brown bread, is a magical transmutation of honey, spices and nuts with roots that go back to 14th century Germany when it was created by Catholic monks and baked in monastery kitchens. Those clever monks had not only created an exceptionally delicious treat but found an additional use for their communion wafers. They increased the diameter of the wafers and used them as the base for this sticky gingerbread-like dough.

The name of this exalted sweet bread is derived from *Leb-Honig*, the early German word for the solid crystallized honey taken from the hive that could not be used for much besides baking. The ancient Egyptians, Greeks and Romans believed that honey, the only sweetener widely available to them, was a gift of the deities and had magical and healing powers. Honey cakes were even worn as a talisman in battle or as protection against evil spirits.

On this balmy Sunday morning in Berlin, Leo had conjured up a version of this ancient delicacy inspired by other delicacies of like *mabrumeh, siwar es-sett, balloriyyeh* from the days of his apprenticeship in the winding alleyways of Aleppo, sweets that were typically drenched in ghee butter and sugar and ladened with pistachios.

Young Saskia was entranced by Leo's magic. Each 10-centimeter square of *Lebkuchen* was adorned by a star of pistachio rays emanating from a dried ginger nucleus, and a delighted Saskia devoured them, a square in each hand, until Erika reigned her in.

Charley, who decided that the less he knew about what was going on among those assembled at *Café Leo* the better, eventually led the sticky-fingered Saskia to the piano. For the next few minutes, the group was regaled with an on again, off again duet of *Backe, backe Kuchen, der Bäcker hat gerufen*, the German children's equivalent of *Pat-a-Cake*.

Thank you for seeing me, Erika began. *I hope that Arnold was correct in his belief that you can be of help to us. He speaks highly of you.*

How do we know that this is on the level, Leo asked a little more sternly than he had intended, looking Erika squarely in the eyes, *who else knows about this meeting in this group of yours?*

Erika's first reaction was who is this boy to be so snappish? Erika, whose bare neck was beginning to match the scarlet of her kerchief, returned Leo's gaze with the intensity of brass knuckles being raked across the bridge of the nose.

To allay your concerns, no one knows except for Arnold, Erika replied. *I have put my trust and as such my life in the hands of those in my group who include several influential people at the highest levels of the military and civil service and more than a few common people like myself. You can trust them and me.*

Without taking a breath, Erika continued, dripping with sarcasm, well, *I would be a craven, despicable agent of the Gestapo to use a four-year-old child to infiltrate your group, your operation, your beer hall, whatever it is you do. Why would you be such a great catch anyhow?* The brass knuckles had landed squarely yet again.

Erika added without a hint of irony in her voice, *my greatest wish for my daughter is that she lives one day in a world where she can be an open, honest and straight person. Those of us who need what you can supply try our best to be just that and to educate our fellow countrymen with our pamphlets about the great lie that will drive us all to ruin. With any luck, we may plant a seed that will prevent that from happening.*

Arnold has made you aware, I believe, of what we hope to convey with your help if we are able to print the next issue of 'The Inner Front.' If I am wasting your time and mine by this visit, please let me know.

At this point, Saskia, who must have been listening, left the piano and rushed to her mother, protectively putting her little arms around her mother's neck, *Mama, ich hab' dich soooo lieb, I love you so much,* she said. Saskia then turned to Leo and scowled as if to reprimand him for not feeling the same way.

Under Saskia's critical gaze, Leo asked his next question more tactfully, *what about Saskia's father. Is he part of this?*

My husband is fighting in the East and his parents take care of Saskia for me when I am at work, which is at the Reich Office for Labor Protection. It is my fervent hope that my, how should I say it, leisure activities escape detection and that Cay, my husband, returns home in one piece, and we can be together again as a family.

Though if I should be detained or worse, fate can't be that hard on Saskia that it robs her of her father too. Worry and guilt are demons that sit atop each of my shoulders, but I ignore them as best I can because I have faith, I must have faith, that the risks I am taking will ensure a better future for my daughter.

Dazzling, Dietrich thought to himself once more. This was an observation less about Erika's imposing physical beauty than it was her strength. Here before him sat a living, breathing specimen of everything he preached about faith and resistance. Hers was the torment of a martyr who, having made the solitary decision to act, led a life that was one, endless night in Gethsemane. *If I were only this brave*, he thought to himself.

Leo's caution crumbled. Beyond the wall that he had erected between himself and Erika, he saw another warrior, Anya, and truth was the sword they both wielded.

The transaction itself took barely a minute or two. They would deliver stencils suitable for an old Garmisch-Partenkirchen Model 1 printer and enough solvent and ink to last Erika for the foreseeable future with the promise of more. Little Otto was to handle the delivery to Erika's flat on the following Thursday evening when Leo would be on his way to Switzerland.

After showing mother and daughter out, Charley discretely left Leo, Little Otto and Dietrich alone, although not before he wondered, given the procession of visitors to see Leo in recent days, who was in truth captor and captive in the equation between Alois and the remarkable boy.

You like her, don't you, Little Otto asked studying Leo?

I do, a seemingly distracted Leo replied, *but not in the way you think, at least I don't think so. She is a breath of fresh air*, Leo added. *I like her optimism and faith in the future. You can't find a lot of that now, can you? She reminds me of others who were once in my life and it connects me to them and makes me feel like I can be more than I am now.*

Scheisse, Leo added growling, as he reacted instantaneously to what he viewed as excessive philosophizing. *I have been spending too much time with…!* Leo caught himself just in time because the object of the jab, the person with whom he had been spending too much time, a bemused Dietrich, was sitting across the table from them.

Little Otto said, *I have not had such people in my life except for you and Mehdi. We are lucky to have people like that in our lives. I think that it is a lot like Father Christmas, the beautiful chocolate ones in the window of Rausch at the Gendarmenmarkt. I may never be able to buy one, and they are too hard to steal, but it makes me feel good just to know they are there.*

Leo and Dietrich looked at Little Otto with newfound respect for his flair for the philosophical.

Dietrich had also experienced something approaching Little Otto's rapture as he observed Leo with Erika and Saskia. He saw that something had happened in this encounter with mother and child that fanned a flame in Leo. He could see it radiating brightly in Leo's eyes.

Little Otto left shortly thereafter to arrange for the delivery to Erika, and Dietrich got down to business about the predicament facing Ingrid and her mother. *We have been blessed that the two women missed the trucks to the railyard by a hair's breadth. For all practical purposes, we have tomorrow to get this done whatever "this" is because they will be taken away the day after,* Dietrich said.

Dietrich added, *there may be one possibility. Leo, do you remember Frederick Raffler? You must. You and he were fast friends at Biesenthal if I remember correctly.*

Yes, Leo said. *I like him. He has done some work for Mehdi, but I have not seen him since the start of the war. I wondered if he had volunteered or been drafted.*

In point of fact, Dietrich replied, *he joined the SS and is a guard at the Jewish collecting station on Grosse Hamburger Strasse.*

That is hard for me to believe, Dietrich. Freddie was one of the good ones. I thought that he would end up in a seminary if you had anything to do with it.

He was a devout young man, yes. His parents were also devout Catholics – same God as mine but different mountain tops from which to view Him, Dietrich replied with the wry smile of one who enjoyed his own humor.

He now has a wife and young child, and such a responsibility will change one's perspective on what's up and what's down. Apparently, the job pays well.

So, we go talk to him, correct, Leo asked?

My thought as well. I am told he will be there tomorrow, which will be our last chance to set this right, Dietrich replied.

So, we get them out, what happens then, Leo asked? *We will get them to Mehdi's,* Dietrich said, *and beyond that we have some thinking to do, because they must leave Berlin right away. Their absence won't escape notice by the Gestapo for long. Leo, can you escape your gilded cage here long enough to come with me?*

I will talk to the people here because I cannot say no to you, Dietrich, and can never envision a situation in which I would unless you asked me to consider the seminary myself, Leo said.

Never say never, Leo, Dietrich responded with a chuckle. *Meet me in front of Otto Weidt's shop at 10:00 tomorrow morning.*

* * * * *

Charley expressed his concerns about Leo's field trip to Grosse Hamburger Strasse, particularly because Leo's inaugural trip to Switzerland on behalf of Alois was only a few days away. In the end, he relented because whatever Leo needed to do seemed to be a matter of some urgency to him.

Leo met Dietrich at the appointed time and place, and they did the barely 10-minute walk to Grosse Hamburger Strasse from Weidt's workshop. As they passed by the old Jewish cemetery, they reviewed the plan, which they agreed was not much of plan at all. It all boiled down to what Freddie would or could do for them.

Freddie was exceedingly happy to see them. They spent the first few minutes catching up on old times. Dietrich, who was at that time thinking about his own engagement to be married, was eager to know more about Freddie's wife and child.

Dietrich asked if they could take a stroll around the cemetery, which served as the exercise yard for the Gestapo guards. Dietrich quickly got down to business with Freddie while no one was around. If Freddie was self-conscious about his role with the SS, it was not apparent to either Dietrich or Leo.

As they walked the perimeter of the cemetery, Freddie listened carefully to their pleas. He knew the two women in question and had in fact helped Ingrid's mother by making extra rations available to them.

So, say I can do something. What happens to them then? It will be only a matter of time before they are caught again. They are on the list, Freddie said, as they walked the perimeter of the yard. Dietrich noted that at the farthest point of the cemetery from the building, at the apex of a ragged isosceles triangle formed by the cemetery, there was a wooden door hidden in the wall that was chained shut.

Dietrich responded by saying, *we have a plan*. This was in fact a white lie, but Dietrich was hopeful that this would build confidence in their reluctant ally.

Leo asked Freddie, *how do we do this without it costing you your job?*

If this were only about my job, I wouldn't hesitate to help. Remember, I have a wife and child now, Freddie replied. The fact that Freddie had not said *No* at that point gave Dietrich and Leo some glimmer of hope.

On they walked. Dietrich and Leo, sensing something approaching acquiescence in Freddie, were reluctant to say more. Freddie, known in his youth as a man of few words, eventually resurfaced from his internal deliberations and said, *return at 22:00 hours sharp.* Freddie then shook their hands and returned to his post.

Leo decided to spend the balance of his day free from Alois and Charley catching up with Mehdi even though he still risked being detained by the Gestapo goons who loitered near the café. Little Otto, the aspiring restaurateur, had stepped in to pick up the slack in his absence.

At Grosse Hamburger Strasse, Freddie examined the mountain of paperwork that usually accompanied a deportation. It was especially heavy this time as they had a full house and that was saying something given the number of people they could cram into the sprawling building.

He sequestered himself in the administrative office after the change of shift that usually accompanied the lunch hour. They were short staffed and getting everyone fed was usually chaos amplified by the slovenly work of a staff that really did not care if anyone was fed.

The deportation orders for Ingrid and her mother were easy enough to find and destroy. The thornier problem was how to erase their names from the manifest of Jews who were to be loaded on to the trucks the next day.

Raffler, why aren't you done with the paperwork, the assistant commandant of the unit bellowed as he barged into the office. A startled Freddie jumped to his feet and in the same motion gave the Hitler salute to his sergeant, *Heil Hitler, Oberwachmeister! I have taken it upon myself to straighten this mess out, Oberwachmeister!*

Placated, his senior officer bid him *carry on* and left him to his work. Once Freddie brought his pounding heart under control, he decided that the only way to get the manifest right was to completely redo the typed page of the list on which the names of Ruth and her mother appeared. He could not simply cross them off the list because that would be far too obvious. He could, however, replace their names with the names of others on the long list, making the duplications look like a simple administrative error.

The risks in what he was doing gnawed at him. It was less about what would happen to himself. He could take that. He had a wife and daughter and therein lay the dilemma. What might happen to them if he was caught was too distressing to contemplate. He must simply get it right, he vowed.

He owed Dietrich and if he were just clever enough, no one would know the difference. And besides, what is the loss of one old woman and her daughter to the war effort?

* * * * *

It was a night tailor-made for fugitives, Dietrich thought to himself. It was not quite dark at this time during a Berlin summer, but a grimy haze of factory smoke and mist had descended on Berlin adding to the gloom of the waning day.

The swirling, granular brume formed a bright sphere around the glowing streetlamps that were lit or would be until there was a report of British bombers approaching from the West. It reminded Dietrich of a Christmas scene in a snow globe after it had been shaken the grimy snow afloat.

Freddie met Dietrich and Leo at a small gate in the chain link fence across from the end of the building nearest the cemetery. Freddie was all business, *they are waiting just inside that door,* Freddie said nodding to the end of the building, *and I will bring them out in a minute. We must do this quickly. There is more Gestapo activity here tonight than I had anticipated. It is as if you are expected! Once I give them to you, walk to the rear of the cemetery as if it was a casual stroll and a harmless conversation. Stay in the shadows close to the wall. The gate that you saw earlier today will be unlocked.*

Understood, Dietrich said.

Then let's get on with it, Freddie replied.

* * * * *

The kind young man, although *kind* and *SS* were two terms that Ingrid could never imagine being used in the same sentence, had patiently helped Ingrid's mother navigate the stairs to the basement of the building. He first brought them to the pantry as if to have them assist with the clean-up of the evening meal and then to a broom closet near the back door of the building that opened out onto the cemetery.

You will not be coming back, was all he had said when he plucked them from the room where they had been detained for the last three days. Ingrid worried about her mother who was confused and torn between her attachment to her daughter and her concern for Ruth, whom they had left behind.

Ingrid's first thought was they were being taken somewhere to be shot, but she ruled that out. She and her mother were simply not important enough for their captors to go to that kind of trouble.

Following the SS man to the basement, Ingrid remembered a childhood friend, a Christian girl, who described one's last moments on earth as entering a tunnel full of vibrant colors with an overwhelmingly bright light at the end of the tunnel that pulled one toward the ecstasy of one's first moment with God. In the basement hallway on Grosse Hamburger Strasse awash with dingy brown light and the aroma of an inedible goulash, Ingrid saw only a dim gray light at its far end. If these were their last moments on earth, it was clear to Ingrid that her friend had her colors all wrong.

As they finally exited the back of the building, two men with concerned smiles on their faces appeared in the copper-tinted haze. The older of the two simply said, *God bless you, Freddie*. He gently took a hold of Ingrid's arm, *please come with us*, he said. The younger man took her mother's hand.

But her mother would not budge when they started toward the back of the cemetery. *Where are we going and must we leave Ruth behind*, she asked?

Madam, it would be our pleasure to have you and your daughter as our guests for the next few days. Please, time is of the essence, the older of the two men said. Ingrid saw Freddie and the younger man glance nervously at the back door of the building, as did she following their lead.

After turning to meet her mother's gaze, Ingrid sensed that her mother had finally grasped what was happening and the gravity of their situation.

Mother, please, we must hurry and go with these kind gentlemen, Ingrid said. *My darling child,* her mother replied, cupping Ingrid's hands between her own as she had always done when she had something important to discuss with Ingrid as a young girl, *I would ask your understanding because I would like to return with this kind young man*, nodding to Freddie, *to be at Ruth's side.*

Mother, Ingrid started to protest, but her heaving chest got the better of her. On the tips of her toes, Ingrid's mother kissed her on the forehead and said, *it will be a difficult journey tomorrow for Ruth, and I cannot let her do it without my help. Please tell your father when you see him, and I know that one day soon you will, I have found a purpose in the last few days that brings me great joy, one nearly as rich as the time spent loving you and him.*

Carry that strength you wear so smartly and your mother's love with you always, my dearest. And with that, Ingrid's mother turned away, took Freddie's hand and returned to Ruth.

* * * * *

Hedwig Porschütz had seen and heard it all, or so she thought. Sometimes, the little things, *sie waren verrückt,* were the *real doozies.*

Otto's latest request was insane. And she knew Otto was anything but insane.

Hedwig would in time distinguish herself as one of the bravest and most effective champions of the persecuted in Nazi Germany – relocating, feeding and where possible exfiltrating them from a land obsessed with their annihilation.

I would like you to find a blue suede Schliersee jacket with staghorn buttons for a woman. For a woman roughly Ingrid's size. And I need it Wednesday, that is to say, tomorrow, my dear Hedwig, Otto had told her.

Hedwig did not dare ask whether the blue suede *Schliersee* jacket with staghorn buttons was indeed for Ingrid. She hoped that it was and that it meant Ingrid and her mother had been freed. Ingrid trusted that Otto would let her know if she needed to know.

The traditional Bavarian *Schliersee* jacket is typically a brown-green, double-breasted wool blazer with rounded lapels, patch pockets and a banded collar that is itself usually a dark green. It was almost always adorned with buttons made from deer antlers.

Hedwig was sure that the buttons would not be a problem. They could be found in many shops that sold notions and sewing supplies. But the jacket, a woman's jacket, well that was another matter.

It was still early morning when she spoke with Otto during the quiet lull after the flood of factory workers in the area had started their morning shifts and the night shift had straggled home. At this time in the morning, office workers had begun to scurry to their jobs in the concrete canyons of Berlin like mice in a maze.

Hedwig would start her search at KaDeWe when it opened in a few hours. One could find anything there. She had also begun to put a mental list together of other shops that traded in Bavarian clothing.

It was the wrong time of year for this type of jacket, she thought. The harvest and Oktoberfest were when the Bavarian troglodytes from whose muck Hitler was spawned paraded their garish ornamental costumes around Berlin. *Aber*, blue suede?!

Yet Hedwig would persevere and succeed somehow. She lived a life undaunted by its complications.

* * * * *

The young couple might have passed without notice had it not been for their matching *Schliersee* jackets. As they approached Track 2 where they would board the express train to Zurich that evening, they struck casual passersby in the dimly lit train station as a garish flash of blue that attracted shards of available light like magnets attract metal filings.

Anhalter Bahnhof, Berlin's gateway to all points South, was undoubtedly its most important railway station given the sheer number of people who passed through its cavernous booking hall, lavishly decorated with zinc sculptures. Its splendor belied its sinister function as a cog in the machinery of the Third Reich. It was one of three train stations currently in use to deport Jews from Berlin.

Of the 55,000 Jews eventually deported from Berlin in the period from 1941-1945, 9,600 would pass through Anhalter Bahnhof, in groups of 50 to 100 at a time. In contrast to deportations from the other train stations that used freight wagons, here Jews were taken away in ordinary passenger coaches which were coupled to regular trains departing according to a normal timetable. Men, women and children were sent first to *Theresienstadt,* a waystation in Nazi-occupied Czechoslovakia, and from there to the extermination camps.

It was grim irony then that Ingrid accompanied by Leo, both resplendent in their iridescent blue livery, should seek her freedom in Switzerland from the very same station. The train to Zurich was one of the few to run reliably and without meaningful harassment from Allied air forces because of the complicated web of relationships in which Switzerland, the Third Reich and the countries allied against the Third Reich were simultaneously bound.

Hitler's relationship with Switzerland was not unlike that with Sweden – equal parts prickly and ambiguous. The Führer was heard to say on more than one occasion, *Switzerland possesses the most disgusting and miserable people and political system. The Swiss are the mortal enemies of the new Germany.*

Das Kleine Stachelschwein or *the little porcupine* as Switzerland was known in Nazi jargon, was technically neutral. This did not stop Hitler from developing and nearly unleashing *Operation Tannenbaum* to invade Switzerland with a force of 500,000 German and Italian troops, an operation that was forestalled by none other than Wilhelm

Canaris who supplied false intelligence to discourage Hitler from pursuing the plan.

Like most porcupines, Switzerland was not without its defenses against predators. It had assembled a formidable army of 800,000, many citizen soldiers. While it was assumed that the Germans could take the Swiss flatlands and cities, many believed, including Hitler's military, that it would have been far too costly in terms of manpower and materials to conquer the *Fortress Alps* from which the Swiss could continue to harass the invading force.

More importantly, while Hitler was crazy, he was not so crazy as to attack his own banker. The Swiss helped transform most of Germany's gold into highly marketable Swiss Francs. As a result, Germany was able to keep its financial connections to the rest of the world intact, for example, using Swiss Francs to buy strategic raw materials from countries like Spain and Portugal.

To confound the historical record still further, this historically tolerant country, which was the preferred destination of French Huguenots fleeing the aftermath of Louis XIV's persecution 300 years earlier, rejected nearly 25,000 refugees fleeing Nazi persecution at the heavily guarded border between the Reich and Switzerland during the war. A Swiss government representative blithely opined, *our little lifeboat is full.*

Yet, by the end of the war, over 50,000 refugees had in fact reached safe haven in the Swiss Alps. This was the official number of refugees who remained in the country. However, another 60,000 refugees were permitted to cross the border to move on to Spain and other destinations. Many were Jews.

For Ingrid, the ambiguity of what lay ahead was preferable to the certainty of what was to come if the Gestapo caught up with her. The indignity of their cheap Bavarian costumes notwithstanding, which she thought made the two of them look like the cheap ceramic figurines sold in flea markets, she was exceedingly grateful to the two kind and, each in his own way, quirky heroes to whom she had been introduced in the cemetery at Grosse Hamburger Strasse.

They had managed somehow to soften the blow of losing her mother. The earnest Lutheran minister had spoken of her mother's bravery. The pride Ingrid felt at his heartfelt and inspirational words overcame her pain at least momentarily. And the handsome young man with unruly hair along with his band of lost boys doted over her every need like solicitous older brothers.

Ingrid was both humbled and uplifted at the same time if that were humanly possible by the risks that her champions were taking to save an insignificant human being like herself. In the overall scheme of things would she ever be missed? But then did her mother's bravery with Ruth not count for something with an act that lent grace to her remaining time on earth and new meaning to the entirety of Ingrid's life?

The blue *Schliersee* jacket worn by Leo was in fact the uniform of his new enterprise. It would identify him to his counterparts when he arrived at Shaffhausen and alert certain officers of the Third Reich that its wearer was not to be trifled with at the Swiss border.

Ingrid was another problem altogether. She was traveling with Leo without the knowledge of either Charley or Alois. They had to improvise by having the young woman dress in much the same fashion as Leo with the hope that her approximation of a blue *Schliersee* jacket would secure her safe passage across the border in his company.

Leo would then take her to an address in Zurich that Dietrich had given him and continue on to Shaffhausen. The nearly matching outfits were a gamble but with the Gestapo closing in on them, their options were few and dwindling.

Hedwig had indeed come through for Otto and Ingrid. It had been pure dumb luck that the Führer to celebrate his conquest of France was hosting performances of Delibe's *Lakmé* by the Paris Opera company at the Deutsche Oper in Berlin that week.

Hedwig had happened onto a display at KaDeWe depicting a scene from the opera in which two British army officers stationed in India during the British Raj, Frédéric and Gérald, encounter in the dark forest under a dome of jasmine the beautiful Lakmé, the daughter of the high priest Nilakantha, where and when Lakmé and Gérald promptly fall in love.

A British artillery officer of the Raj like Gérald would routinely be kitted in a bright blue double-breasted jacket of wool and cotton with brass buttons and a banded collar of scarlet, the color of the Tudor Rose. That costume was on display at KaDeWe in a tableau depicting the opera. Hedwig noticed that whoever sang the role of Gérald must have been quite small in stature.

As Hedwig had learned through practice, if one is doing something wrong in a place where one should not be in the first place, do it with conviction. In most cases, those around you will consider the behavior quite normal.

And thus, the diminutive mannequin of the love struck Gérald would be found the next morning head down in a trash bin in a third-floor storeroom of KaDeWe. His jacket newly emblazoned with staghorn buttons would depart at 23:00 the next day on the Berlin-Zurich Express.

* * * * *

Little Otto, the budding poet-philosopher, admired in the waning evening light the nearly full moon that followed him down the street playing peekaboo through gaps in the trees above. He wondered if Leo and Ingrid were looking at the same moon at this very same moment.

While Big Otto shadowed Leo and Ingrid on their journey to Anhalter Bahnhof, Little Otto and the twins took care of the delivery of printing supplies to Erika von Brockdorff. She lived in an attractive cul-de-sac lined by red brick townhouses nestling under a lush stand of ancient pin oaks.

Little Otto and his companions pushed a coal wagon with a false top that gave the appearance of a full load of coal. The printing supplies, just enough to help Erika handle the next edition of *The Inner Front,* were neatly concealed in the hidden compartment below the tray carrying the thin layer of coal.

Erika was waiting for them at the basement door near the coal chute, where Little Otto and the twins sent the supplies wrapped in burlap down the chute. It was a relatively simple matter after the contraband had been offloaded to the basement to carry it up the four flights of stairs to Erika's third story flat.

Little Otto was disappointed to find that Saskia was not there to greet them. However, the lovestruck boys later agreed that being with Erika however briefly was worth the trip because she looked like a famous actress from the movies and was, they agreed, prettier many times over than either Zarah Leander or Käthe von Nagy and, after some earnest debate, prettier than the two combined.

From the point of view of the smitten boys, who lived in a two room flat with five other boys, Erika's apartment, though simple, was as elegant as she was beautiful. The boys lingered, soaking up each moment with Erika, but to Little Otto's credit, he ignored his aching heart to roust the boys from their reverie and finalize the list for the next delivery.

As the boys bid Erika farewell, they moved reluctantly toward the door. On the way, one of the twins stepped on the edge of a white sheet draped over a prominent piece of furniture. It slid to the floor revealing a contraption that appeared to be a radio transmitter sitting atop a desk. The standup microphone and headphones could have been associated with nothing else.

As the boys were leaving, two men arrived. One was tall and haggard. He was limping slightly and seemed to be fearful of his own shadow. Taking one look at the exposed radio and the boys, he fled immediately to the bedroom. His companion, short and surly with closely cropped black hair reacted instantly, *Erika, I asked you, no, I told you not to bring them here.*

Hans, they are the nice young men who have supplied the materials that we need to produce 'The Inner Front.' Where else would I have them go?

An exercise for intellectuals that no one will read, thank you, he huffed.

And, stopping in mid-sentence, Hans rushed to throw the sheet over the exposed radio. He turned toward the boys and exploded, *I take it that you are done here?*

Hans, out of my way please. I will show my friends to the door. Get a grip on yourself, Erika said.

They left by the basement door where Erika thanked the boys, playfully mussing Little Otto's hair. Her casual display of affection, that of a big sister to a little brother, was the most sensuous moment of Little Otto's young life, so much so that his knees began to wobble.

As the twins vaulted up the cellar steps to the street trailed by Little Otto, unsteady and laboring under the weight of a full heart, two agents of the Gestapo sipped Pilsners in a small bierstube across the way and took notes.

* * * * *

Leo, by nature cool and calculating, was not liking the whole thing. The damned jacket that he had been made to wear grabbed him in the shoulders and the gut, making it difficult to get a full breath. Adding to his discomfort, his skills in holding a normal conversation with a woman like Ingrid were quite limited.

Ingrid, sensing this, took the lead and Leo fell into step. To his credit, she thought, Leo was sweet and honest like the horse that she once had as a child. It was not her horse but a friend's and her parents had worked out an arrangement so that for all practical purposes, it became hers for the time she was able to use it. They could not speak to each other, Ingrid and the horse that is, but she could always sense what the dappled colt was thinking.

She knew that Leo was worried and on guard, and she wondered if she could ever measure up to the expectations of those who might depend on her one day quite as well as Leo and his friends had done for her. Hadn't they defined the job of being a good parent with their meticulous planning for what lay ahead for her, at least in the short run? And hadn't this made crystal clear how badly she had failed at the job of being a good daughter?

In the monotonous lull before the train moved out, as the white noise of people boarding and searching for their seats washed over them, Leo and Ingrid began to relax. At least a little. They had been seated in first class, and Ingrid wondered if any refugee had ever lived so well.

She admired the beautiful upholstery of their seats studying the apple trees, vaguely portrayed by tightly stitched patterns of red, green and white silk threads. There was even a framed painting on the wall signed by Ernst Ludwig Kirchner from *Die Brücke* (The Bridge) school of German expressionist artists. If this trip amounted to nothing else, she would consider herself fortunate to have enjoyed their plush, artistically appointed accommodations.

Leo and Ingrid shared the first-class cabin with two young women who introduced themselves as students at the University of Zurich who had been in Berlin for a wedding. The four sat in a sizeable parlor car of their own from which each couple could retire to a separate, private sleeper compartments.

Their posh surroundings notwithstanding, a frisson of suspicion tinged by fear crackled in the air around the chance traveling companions like static electricity. It was wartime, and the cost of long-distance train travel had grown beyond the reach of most people. Leo surmised, not without some justification, that 90% of those onboard were Gestapo or their lackeys chasing the 10% who had done something so objectionable to the Reich as to merit being hunted by the other 90%.

It would be a good eight hours to the border and safe ground, so who were the hunters and their fellow hunted among them, Leo wondered? And what threat if any did these young women represent?

About 20 minutes into the journey, a chime sounded repeatedly in the hallway of their train car floating toward them from one direction and fading away in the other. They were being summoned to dinner in the club car. Charley had tutored Leo on the vicissitudes of train travel since it was only the second time in his life that he had traveled by train. Leo's initiation in train travel was as a young boy with Pushpa on the Istanbul to Berlin run.

The dining car was paneled in a polished dark wood of some kind and the floor was covered with well-worn oriental rugs. Ingrid and Leo were directed to deep easy chairs at a table glistening with fine china and crystal to which sharply dressed waiters brought soup, Sauerbraten, boiled potatoes, canned fruit and coffee.

The restaurant car, like their compartment, had been blacked out by painting the outside of the windows black. So, Ingrid and Leo would not see stations coming or going the entire night.

Ingrid ordered a glass of sherry. It was not Akvavit, Leo thought, but it would do. He joined her, as did the two young women dining with them, who introduced themselves as Tomi and Jani, pronounced *Yani.*

They were strikingly attractive young women. Tomi, the brunette, was tall and broad-shouldered, who they learned over dinner had competed in the pole vault and javelin for the Swiss in the 1932 Olympics. Jani, the radiant blonde, who struck one as a young girl at first glance, was slender in build and seemed better suited to the 100-yard dash.

It became apparent to Leo that there was also a subtle muscularity to the personalities of the young women, whom a relaxed Ingrid was now chatting up. Something told Leo that they might be more than guileless schoolgirls, an impression that was reinforced by the quick and clever ways they were sizing up their surroundings and fellow guests in the dining car from across the dinner table.

It was nothing obvious unless one delved in the black market. There was the instantaneous flash of recognition from the corner of Tomi's eye at one point and at another a casual glance from Jani toward the far end of the dining car behind him while pretending to look at his water glass.

Toward the end of the meal as the coffee came out, Leo felt Ingrid step on his foot, which made him flinch. Taking a ragged breath, she said, *I wonder if we are in the mountains yet*, which was their agreed signal if something was wrong.

Ingrid pressed even harder on Leo's foot as an attractive young woman walked by their table. As she did, Stella smiled at Ingrid as would a Cheshire cat to a country mouse. She seemed to deliberately brush the table and her perfume hung in the air over the four dinner companions as they finished their coffee.

None of this had been lost on the two young women. One stared at her lipstick in the opaque black window. The other followed the attractive young woman to the far end of the dining car where she joined a male friend for dinner.

The young woman who had just passed their table and the fashionable young woman from the opera, who had sent Ingrid and her mother fleeing barely a week before, were one and the same. In a private moment after dinner, they agreed that there was little doubt that Stella and her dinner companion were there for one thing and one thing only.

Ingrid retired later to the adjacent sleeping compartment to close her eyes for a spell as had Tomi. Leo tried to occupy himself with a book that Dietrich had loaned him called, *The Book of the Martyrs*. He enjoyed the adventures of the brave men and women, not much older than he, who had endured the unthinkable in the early days of Christianity. He was always somewhat disappointed, however, to find that all of them had died a grisly death that might have been avoided had they done a better job playing the angles that were so obvious to him and, by doing so, turn the tables on their tormentors.

You know, Leo, you would make more headway on your book if you sneaked a peek at me less often. His companion in the parlor car, Jani, the younger of the two women hit him with a sassy smile as she toyed with her long blonde braid.

Leo blushed scarlet. She quickly added, *oh, I didn't think of it in that way although in another time and place, who knows?*

Who were the people who seemed to upset you two? You have been watchful since the moment we first met, like a mountain hawk, Leo. Yes, you have been 'hawk-eyed' as my father would say.

Leo said nothing. Needing no encouragement, his companion added, *my friend and I mean you no harm, so worry less about us than the real problem that seems to have overtaken you.*

Leo's companion fired another sassy smile at her reflection in the opaque window of the parlor car and said no more.

* * * * *

Leo briefly dozed off in his seat in the parlor car after Ingrid's return. He woke to the sensation of the train slowing and the acrid odor of grease and metal burning as the brakes were applied.

He looked at his watch. They could not be anywhere near Zurich. Basel and the German border might be more like it but were it Basel, there should have been an announcement. Reflexively, he touched the handle of the *Khanjar* concealed under his jacket as reassurance that he had some means of self-defense if it came to that.

The self-possessed young women watched him and Ingrid closely. While their bags were still in the overhead, they had collected their gear in the cabin and seemed poised to disembark.

A commotion came from the direction of the dining car to Leo and Ingrid's rear, and Leo sprung to the door of the parlor car to take a look. A man, the dinner partner of the woman who had approached them at dinner, was moving toward them. Sepp Lange wore a leather trench coat, standard issue for the Gestapo but no hat. His hands were in his pockets, an ominous signal that he might be carrying a handgun. To his rear at the far end of the car, Leo saw Stella and another man.

Lange barked at Leo to return to the compartment. Leo stood his ground between Lange and the door of the compartment. Ingrid stayed seated but the two young women wedged their way past Leo at the door to get a look at the oncoming Gestapo man.

Leo considered his next move. They were obviously coming for him and Ingrid and would take them from the train. He could probably bring the first man down with the *Khanjar*, but then what?

Halt! Stehen bleiben!, came from the other end of their train car, bellowed in the form of a command not a request. It was directed at Lange.

There, approaching the compartment wearing a fawn Macintosh trench coat, broad brimmed hat in hand dripping wet with the rain that tapped the outside of the train car, was a man with silver hair and the demeanor of a university professor. He was followed by two formidable thugs in uniform. Lange stopped dead in his tracks.

When Jani and Tomi heard the second man's voice, they hastily pulled their luggage from the overhead rack and wedged their way past Leo to arrive in the narrow hallway of the train car. *Meine Engel,* my angels, was the next thing the man said with an aristocratic lilt reminiscent of crystal tapped by a spoon. The two young women made a beeline toward the men in uniform who now stood immediately behind their leader.

Jani took the man in the trench coat by the arm, while Lange stood in place unsure of what was unfolding. The intense conversation between Jani and the man in the Macintosh took several minutes.

He finally capitulated to the young woman but only reluctantly. He moved toward the compartment door and Lange sought to block his path. He showed the man in the Macintosh his handheld Gestapo medallion and introduced himself as a senior officer in the Reich's *Sicherheitsdienst*.

The man and woman in this car must come with us. There is a warrant for their arrest for acts of subversion against the people of the Reich, Lange intoned.

And I am Brigadier Roger Masson of Swiss Military Intelligence, and you will be so kind as to stand back while I assess the situation, the man in Macintosh told Lange, who briefly contemplated pushing past Masson into the compartment until he took another look at the unfriendly men in uniform behind Masson.

My men will keep you entertained here while I am inside, Masson said suavely as the force of his personality made Lange flinch and step back to let Masson enter the compartment.

Addressing himself to Leo, he said, m*y friends with whom you have traveled here speak well of you but why does your secret police want you so badly? Can you enlighten me? We do not have all night to sort this out.*

I am traveling on business to Shaffhausen, and my sister accompanies me, Leo responded nodding toward Ingrid. *Papers, please*, Masson commanded, cocking his head to the side in a gesture of bemused skepticism.

The papers did their job admirably. Ingrid's were some of Little Otto's finest work.

Masson huffed glancing at Ingrid and then Leo and said, *let us be frank with one another. You might turn out to be the crown prince of Austria, but the unfriendly people outside would like nothing better than to take you away under arrest. My friends, your recent travel companions, have advocated for your safe passage, but I....*

Before he could end his sentence, Ingrid blurted, *I am Jewish, and this kind young man was helping me escape my tormentors. Give me to the Gestapo, please, but take him with you. He bears no blame, none, he is a simple businessman.*

Masson seemed to snort in the way that one does when he is telling himself, *I thought so*. He turned and looked at Leo; they were eye to eye barely inches from each other. Leo said not a thing.

Masson then happened to glance toward *The Book of the Martyrs* still on Leo's side table and moved to retrieve it. *This is your reading material, young man?* Not waiting for a response from Leo, he began to leaf through the book as if he were looking for contraband and found the inscription on the inside front cover,

Dietrich --

To my cherished brother-in-law. God willing, we will not follow in their footsteps or at least not soon.

H

Hans von Dohnányi
12 Februar 1939

The man in the trench coat slammed the book shut and stuck it in Leo's gut. *Collect your things,* he said, *you two are coming with me. And that means now.*

*****

The three emerged into the narrow hallway of the first-class car and Lange, now seeing red, moved toward them. Stella remained at the far end of the car in the direction of the dining car, but the second Gestapo agent had moved closer, splitting the difference between Lange and Stella. The young women and the two Swiss policemen converged on the door of the compartment from the opposing end of the car.

I must remind you that the border treaty between our two countries requires that if a train is at the border, deference will be provided to the German authorities, Lange was not pulling his punches any longer!

Thank you, it is a treaty to be valued, by all means. However, this train currently straddles the border, which is roughly demarcated by the dining car. We are currently to the South of the dining car and hence to the border between our two great nations, Masson said with measured antipathy.

You are now standing on Swiss soil and have no jurisdiction here. These two, whoever they may be, will be taken into custody under the authority of the 'Schweizerische Eidgenossenschaft,' the Swiss Confederation. We do not tolerate anarchists and will most certainly contact German authorities if warranted when we confirm their identities.

So, please return to the Reich, which is just on the other side of the dining car with our thanks for bringing this matter to our attention, Masson said.

Lange's face glowed red like an overripe tomato about to explode. He took one look at Leo and Ingrid, *if looks could kill*, and one final look at Brigadier Masson and returned to the dining car.

Masson and his men moved Leo and Ingrid from the train to automobiles quickly and efficiently. They put Leo and Ingrid into one car and after Masson huddled with the young women for several minutes, Jani approached Leo and Ingrid's car. Like a big sister, Ingrid whispered to Leo, *I think she would like to speak to you.*

They met at the boot of the car in the heavy drizzle, rain drops turning to rivulets on their young faces. *This is a Walther PPK, 9 mm,* Jani said matter of factly, as she slapped the pistol into Leo's hands. *You may need this more than I do at the moment, Herr Businessman. It might help keep you alive long enough for Tomi and me to see you again. We live in Zurich when we are not otherwise engaged by the Monsieur Masson.* Jani slipped a piece of paper into the patch pocket of Leo's *Schliersee* jacket. *We are easy to find when we want to be.*

Leo wrestling with a lump in his throat the size of a loaf of Choreg, replied simply, *I would like that,* and the two went their separate ways.

* * * * *

Ingrid and Leo did not see Masson again that night or more aptly that morning because a red-gray band on the horizon spoke of a coming dawn as they pulled away from the railroad siding. One of Masson's police officers drove them the rest of the way to Zurich, barely two hours from Basel.

When Leo and Ingrid arrived at the appointed address in Zurich, they were greeted warmly by a young husband and wife. They offered Leo and Ingrid breakfast, but Leo chose not to stay. The longer he did, he knew, the harder it would be for him to go. And besides, he had 60,000 Reichsmarks in small gold ingots burning a hole in his satchel, and he could not let Charley down.

As he stood on the front step of Ingrid's new refuge, Ingrid gave him a farewell kiss on the cheek and said, *thank you, Leo, my knight in shining armor,* as she took the measure of Leo who looked like a luminescent stuffed goose in his *Schliersee* jacket. *Stay brave but, more importantly, stay lucky.*

Both laughed, a much-needed release of the tension that had been building for days. Leo responded by giving her a note from Dietrich, which she read later,

Ingrid,

In our tradition, which is not that much different from yours, inasmuch as Moses parted the Red Sea for us both, it is said 'We walk by faith not by sight.' This is a truth that your mother knew all too well. She walks with you now.

I have been privileged to be your friend.

Dietrich

* * * * *

It was a running joke in Berlin as it was elsewhere that people begin after a time to look like their dogs. Frau Zott, who worked in the exotic mammals section of the *Naturkundemuseum*, where she artfully stuffed the carcasses of new arrivals, did not look like her dog because she did not have one. However, her eyebrows which ran continuously from east to west across her forehead and her demonstrably convex lips made her resemble a platypus, and few who labored at the Museum of Natural History had overlooked that fact.

Frau Zott was generally well regarded for her taxidermological skills but otherwise was feared to the point of loathing for her role in the NSDAP, that is to say the Nazi Party. Had she simply gone about her business like everyone else, worn her arm band, and *Heiled* when the spirit moved, few would have given her a second thought.

However, Frau Zott had installed herself as the arbiter of Nazi fealty and the sufficiency thereof among the museum's employees. For example, if someone failed to deliver the Nazi salute when circumstances called for it or saluted with a perceived lack of ardor, she reported it to the museum's political officials.

She also collected Party subscriptions and sold emblems for the Winter Relief Fund, a purely passive aggressive exercise on her part, to raise from her fellow workers, funds that could be used to support German troops in the far-flung battles being waged by the Third Reich. Here too, she had established herself as the arbiter of how much her cash-strapped colleagues should give and would *pish, pish* or *tutt, tutt* if someone dared offer less than their fair share, as she measured it.

There had even been talk, centered in the Cervidae unit of the Artiodactyla division of the museum that it might be arranged for her simply to disappear one day on her rounds in the vast and sprawling complex of the museum. But the two principal conspirators had been arrested, turned in by a third, who was in fact a Gestapo informant. This underscored for any potential conspirator the peril in discerning friend from foe in the darkness of daily life in Nazi Germany.

In truth, Frau Zott had been apolitical most of her life. At first, she did not care much for the brown shirts and their tactics but enjoyed the bravura of their leader as he rose to power albeit in fits and starts in those early days. She had no time for the Jews and the Bolsheviks, so if Hitler could clean that up, he had her full support.

Most importantly, she wanted to be on the winning side and, at least at that moment in time, Hitler epitomized the term. So, for her two Reichsmark, the smart money was on the Nazi Party and her fellow countrymen needed to do as they were told. Many of her misguided countrymen had it in their skulls, she reckoned, that thinking would do them some good. But now, as far as Frau Zott was concerned, they should let the Führer do the thinking for them.

Her sister, also Frau Zott, was of the same mind. They lived together on a tranquil *cul de sac* at the end of a row of neo-renaissance, red brick townhouses nestled under a canopy of rangy pin oaks. Back in the day each of these magnificent townhouses had been inhabited by a wealthy family, the *beau monde* of Berlin, but today they accommodated three apartments – a trinity – one each on the first, second and third floors.

From their large bay window on the first floor at the apex of the *cul de sac* that looked like the bridge of an ocean liner pointed aft rather than fore, they were able to monitor the comings and goings of their neighbors and when necessary, inform the authorities when it struck them that something was amiss. Frau Zott, that is to say the sister of the *platypussian* Frau Zott, who as luck would have it did not share these features, worked at night filing patient records at the Charité and by day devoted her efforts to steering her neighbors on the righteous course charted by the Third Reich as the *Blockwart* (Block Warden).

Like the museum, the Zotts did what they could to fill the Party's coffers and to send reports to the Party on the behavior of her impecunious neighbors. For example, she had just the other day caught wind that the local plumber, the perpetually disheveled Herr Kleb, had demanded cooking fat from Frau Prall to replace a leaky pipe. It was a punishable offence to demand fat in exchange for goods and services, and punishment came swiftly thanks to Frau Zott.

And then there was the young von Brockdorff. The Frau's Zott were taken with the dashing young Graf, who was a junior officer risking his life for the Third Reich somewhere in the East. He was such a feast for the eyes!

Erika, however, was an enigma to them. She was equally attractive, yes, with an air of sophistication that seemed a bit snooty to the Zotts given her origins as a simple country girl. They also found it irksome that Erika never hung out her flag nor was ever willing to dig deeper for a few more pfennigs when they made their local rounds for the Winter Relief Fund. After all, her handsome man would surely be a beneficiary.

The daughter, well they could barely tolerate the girl. Her laughter was bloodcurdling, the *platypussian* Frau Zott liked to say.

And if that were not enough, the von Brockdorff flat was the focal point of a constant procession of people coming and going that upset the equilibrium that the Zotts sought to curate on their quiet street. Many of them looked quite upstanding, indeed, one was a military officer of some rank judging from the ornaments arrayed on his chest and lapels. They often came and left with parcels, which the Zotts assumed at first had something to do with Erika's work at the Reich Ministry of Labor Protection, but they had made a mental note to verify this assumption.

The tipping point that turned questions into suspicions was one early morning when Frau Zott was returning from her shift at the Charité and saw the two men hugging the shadows to reach Erika's flat, which stood at roughly a 45-degree angle to her bay window in the *cul de sac*.

She knew one of them, the one with closely cropped, wiry hair, narrowly set eyes, the eyes of a criminal to be sure, and a swarthy complexion. Frau Zott had bumped into him recently on the stairway as he was leaving Erika's third floor flat and she was arriving to give Erika a small flag and picture book that she hoped would spark Saskia's interest in joining the BDM, the League of German Girls, one day.

The other man she had not seen before. His height and limp gave her goosebumps because his silhouette reminded her of the grotesque fiend from *The Student of Prague*, the terribly scary silent movie that she and her sister had seen as young girls. It was a costume piece about a young man at the university who sold himself to the devil. One day his reflection came stalking out of the mirror on its own and went about committing dreadful crimes so that everyone in the neighborhood believed it was the young man.

Frau Zott arrived home unsettled. Was it guilt by association with a scary old movie or the fact that they were lurking in the shadows on the way to the flat of the less than patriotic Frau von Brockdorff?

Upon reflection, the Zotts agreed that this was a matter for the authorities. If they were wrong, a good talking to from the Gestapo would do Erika some good anyway.

The Zotts were amply rewarded for their efforts by the Gestapo with an extra month's worth of ration cards. The Zotts knew that playing for the winning side had its temporal as well as spiritual benefits!

* * * * *

Compared to his adventure at the Swiss border, the rest of the trip was *duck soup*, an English expression that Charley seemed quite fond of. Leo had acquitted himself well with his counterparts in Switzerland and even hit it off with their leader Emil Rauschenberg, a Sephardic Jew with a cheeky sense of humor and larcenous world view, that made Leo feel very much at home. He struck Leo as a younger, less serious Mehdi.

Indeed, things went so well that Leo and Emil were able to cut a side deal in which Leo would smuggle Swiss Francs to a group associated with the Swedish Lutheran Church in Berlin, which at that time was doing a thriving but dangerous business "buying" captured Jews from willing Gestapo agents. The Swedes then either housed the Jews in secret locations or when possible, smuggled them out of the country.

In exchange for his services, Emil would give Leo a gem, usually an uncut sapphire or emerald, which he told Leo to sock away for the future. Emil would say, *in their present state, they are like a beautiful girl who doesn't know she is beautiful. With the proper attention from a gemsmith, they will dazzle the eye of the beholder.*

In total, Leo would make five trips to Switzerland for Alois and Charley in quick succession, and each time he would receive marketable jewels or Swiss francs for Himmler, cash for the Swedes, an uncut stone for himself, and an ample commission from Himmler via Alois. Leo had never met someone as cavalierly generous as Emil, who explained it once by saying, *your tradition and ours tells us, whoever is kind to the poor lends to the Lord, a skill of which my people have some knowledge. I simply trust that the Lord will reward us accordingly.*

Upon his return from the first trip and his adventure with Ingrid, Leo arranged at Little Otto's strenuous urging to meet with Erika. His mission as Little Otto saw it was to sort out what was going on with the *slimy bastard* that Little Otto had met at Erika's flat and the illicit radio set, which meant a death sentence to be sure if Erika was caught.

Leo and Erika met at a small bistro in a shady corner of Savigny Platz whose proprietor was Big Otto's uncle. Erika felt that a meeting at her flat might be too risky. She could not walk more than half a block these days without bumping into one of the Zotts, and tension seemed to roil their small street like a cyclonic burst of wind that bent the uppermost branches of the sheltering pin oaks as a thunderstorm approached.

Big Otto's uncle doted over them and served a delicious Wienerschnitzel that was a half size bigger than the plate. This was a mystery solved for Leo as Charley had been complaining all afternoon about an order of veal that had not arrived from the butcher, an order that had apparently been intercepted by Big Otto.

The conviviality of the setting and the food made for a different meeting this time between Erika and Leo. There might even have been lessons learned over dinner on a train to Switzerland, a new *savoir faire,* that Leo applied to his rendezvous with Erika.

They talked about their backgrounds, Graf and Saskia for her part, Hayk, Mina and Anya for his. Erika's warmth and intelligence had managed to pry open that place in Leo where he guarded his most valuable memories. That evening with Erika would be the first time he had ever had an intelligent conversation with anyone about his past. He had never taken it this far even with Mehdi or Dietrich.

Leo did finally come to the point, *let's put aside Little Otto's dislike for the man who growled at him and the twins that night. The greater concern is the radio set, which will buy you a one-way ticket to Plötzensee and the guillotine.*

My arrangement with Hans is temporary and serves an important purpose, at least in my mind. We are able to work with his contacts in Russia to identify German soldiers who are still alive in their prison camps. It has been generally understood that our prisoners are executed immediately upon capture, which apparently is not the case. We are able to identify individuals and to inform their families here that there is hope for the eventual return of their loved ones, Erika said.

But this is not the radio set's only use, I suspect, Leo said, the concern evident in his voice.

Believe me Leo, I have no death wish, but should Plötzensee be my fate, I do not think I will have died in vain, she continued.

Not in vain? Leo responded with a look of disbelief and with a hint of exasperation, *but what about Saskia?*

Hans, Little Otto's nemesis, once told me that no one could risk more than his life. In that, I believe he is wrong. It might take a mother to understand this, but I cannot risk condemning Saskia to a future in a Nazi-ruled world, Erika said.

When the hubbub of my day is behind me in those few moments before I fall to sleep, I take refuge in the same place each and every night. That place is my daughter's future, and I am there with her in a way that is as real as you and I sitting here now.

Each time I am there with her, she thanks me and, at first, I did not know what she was thanking me for. And then one night it became clear, she was thanking me for fighting back to ensure a future without the Nazis and Hitler and the whole ugly lot of them.

But, Leo said before Erika cut him off.

But, I am not so egotistical as to think I am some hero. I might fail in the end. Our entire movement might fail in the end. If I dwell on my odds, it is a pretty lonely feeling. There is no camaraderie in a world full of failures.

You say you are Christian, Leo, or your family was. The Christ who died on the cross was to all outward appearances a lonely failure. I have faith that the future I imagine for my daughter is as real as his own idea of salvation.

As Erika spoke, Leo was transported to another night years before on the outskirts of Aleppo and a similar conversation with another driven warrior, who told him,

I fight to solve this riddle and to ensure that the meek do inherit the earth because with every generation of hardship, displacement and repression, they will grow stronger, as those who despise them, those who

turn a blind eye to their suffering, or wield their power and wealth to torment them, grow weaker.

This is how and why I fight, Leo.

* * * * *

The evening ended with the perversely funny suggestion by Erika that they both should try to stay alive at least long enough to meet again for dinner. Big Otto's doting uncle had ended the evening by serving them a fresh blackberry strudel baked of the finest flour expropriated by the Reich from the French in the Auvergne enriched with dried almond flowers.

It had in fact been baked that morning at Café Alois by Leo himself, unbeknownst to Big Otto's uncle. Leo made a mental note to tell Big Otto that he should be more careful about filching from Café Alois because Charley was on the hunt for the thief and it would not go well for him if he was caught.

* * * * *

Mildred Harnack had just left and, as usual, was brave and reassuring about the perilous road they traveled together, arm in arm, for the group. Erika and Mildred had grown close and while they admired the utopian ideals of Mildred's husband, Arvid, they were people of action before all.

Mildred, who had gained some notoriety in literary circles for translating Irving Stone's masterpiece about Van Gogh, *Lust for Life* into German, liked to repeat a line from the book whenever she and Erika found themselves in the doldrums after considering the risks they were taking. She would say, *you cannot be (the) good all the time; sometimes it is necessary to get angry.* It was this idea that energized them as the linchpins of a clandestine enterprise to educate the German public about the atrocities perpetrated by the Third Reich.

The Gestapo would eventually come to call the group the *Rote Kapelle* (Red Orchestra). At first, the designation *Rote Kapelle* was a cryptonym used by the counter-espionage unit of the SS to classify a group, the *Orchestra* within which resistance radio operators were referred to as *Pianists*, their transmitters as *Pianos*, and their supervisors as *Conductors*.

Eventually, *Rote Kapelle* came to be used interchangeably by the Gestapo as a collective term to identify a loose network of resistance circles, connected through personal contacts, that united hundreds of opponents of the Nazi regime. However, neither Mildred nor Erika would ever associate themselves with that name.

The name was also to became convenient propaganda fodder for the Gestapo to portray the group as a cabal of Bolshevik agents and sympathizers thus the word *Rote*. Indeed, the Rote Kapelle was neither directed by the Soviet Union nor by a unified chain of command of any stripe. The Rote Kapelle's loose network of groups and individuals, often operating independently, would eventually number about 400 members.

One of its many circles of friendship and discourse centered around Harro Schulze-Boysen and the aforementioned Arvid Harnack. Schulze-Boysen was a left-wing German publicist before, and a high-ranking Luftwaffe officer during, World War II. Soviet intelligence agents had developed a close working relationship with Schulze-Boysen over the years, and the plans for Operation Barbarossa, the Axis invasion of Russia, were among the fruits of their labor.

Arvid Harnack was a German jurist and Marxist economist, who had studied economics at the University of Wisconsin in Madison in the 1920's where he married the literary historian Mildred Fish. He founded the "Scientific Working Community for the Study of the Soviet Planned Economy" or ARPLAN in 1931, which he hoped would build a free and socially-just Germany and serve as a spiritual and economic bridge between East and West.

From 1935, Harnack tried to camouflage his activities by becoming a member of the Nazi Party working in a senior role in the Reich Ministry of Economics. Like Schulze-Boysen, he had occasional contact with Soviet agents.

Arvid and his American wife Mildred led a group of friends including Erika that printed and distributed illegal leaflets, posters and stickers hoping to incite civil disobedience; helped Jews and opposition figures escape the Nazi regime; and documented its crimes through such means as the publication of the *Inner Front*. Its members, which for the most part were unaware of Schulze-Boysen's and Harnack's espionage, included the German politician and former Minister of Culture, Adolf Grimme, the industrialist and entrepreneur, Leo Skrzypczynski, and the journalist Adam Kuckhoff and his wife Greta, who introduced Erika to the group.

At first, these activities were an annoyance to the Gestapo, which was working a long list of more immediate threats to the state and were anathema to the punctilious Goebbels. They were like the elusive, whining, biting mosquito that could not be killed nor ever go away. Finally, Goebbels put his foot down. As far as he was concerned, if the German people were to be misled by anyone, there would only be one person leading that charge.

* * * * *

On his unflinchingly intense visage, the badge of a true believer, sat round horned rimmed glasses and a caterpillar mustache. The bookish former Bavarian police officer enjoyed the adventures of Hercule Poirot and consciously or unconsciously had cultivated a physical resemblance to his hero.

SS-Obersturmbannführer Friedrich Panzinger led the *Sonderkommando Rote Kapelle*, a small independent Gestapo unit whose remit was to discover and arrest members of the Red Orchestra in Germany, Belgium, France, Netherlands, Switzerland and Italy. He sat across from Himmler and Kaltenbrunner giving his report in the capacious cab of Himmler's limousine, which seemed to stretch for half a city block.

Panzinger husbanded his breath carefully because Kaltenbrunner wreaked of alcohol to such a degree that it was nearly suffocating in closed quarters. How did Himmler tolerate it, Panzinger wondered? If one lit a match, he was sure they would all go up in flames.

Kaltenbrunner, the hunter, like Himmler was absorbed in Panzinger's report. Both believed that with sufficient patience, their quarry would eventually make a fatal mistake or luck might simply abandon them altogether. One needed to be vigilant, however, to capture the moment when it was possible to close in for the kill. Panzinger's progress with the *Rote Kapelle* was the apotheosis of this principle.

Let's set aside the fate of the boy for now. He is a small fish in a big pond, and we can make an example of him later. Frankly, we see no connection between him and the Soviets, Panzinger continued after being interrupted in his report by the flammable Kaltenbrunner.

It has now been over a year since we began to intercept the radio transmissions of Soviet intelligence and are just now putting the pieces together. Indeed, the radio transmission that first exposed the Soviets was intercepted at 3:58 am on 26 June 1941 at our intercept station in Zele-

nogradsk. Until then, we were unaware that there was a Soviet network operating in Germany and the occupied territories, he continued.

So where does this put us now, an impatient and ungracious, Himmler said through a coughing fit.

We have made several arrests of suspected Soviet agents in Paris and Brussels from whom we have received scant help, Panzinger continued unflustered. *The breakthrough came in July of this year when our man decrypted an additional 200 messages from the original trove. This yielded three addresses in Berlin.*

We are running down these leads and have already connected these addresses to at least one highly placed government official and to several known communist sympathizers, who have been under careful watch, one of whom did cross paths with the small boy in question. We also believe that one, possibly two, sophisticated radio transmitters are presently in operation in Berlin.

What do you need from us, Kaltenbrunner asked?

When the time is right and that time will come soon, I will need a strike force of your best. My men are spread across the occupied territories where they are presently cutting off the tentacles of one very large monster.

III. UNTERNEHMEN SIEBEN

As the Kübelwagen, an ugly tublike military vehicle produced by Volkswagen, ferried them back into Berlin from the Abwehr airfield where their adventure in Sweden had been launched earlier that summer, Dietrich and Leo compared notes on the unusual meeting that had just concluded with Admiral Canaris and his right hand in all things subversive to the Third Reich, Generalmajor Hans Oster. Canaris had insisted on meeting at the secure Abwehr base near Dahlem secreted in the conifer forests of Brandenburg where the River Havel meets a large lake called the *Schwielowsee.*

Canaris and Oster had arrived in uniform. Oster who bore a notable resemblance to his mentor Canaris stood ramrod straight, a military man through and through. Joining their group was Hans von Dohnányi, Dietrich's brother-in-law and another of Canaris' principled acolytes in the conspiracy to remove Hitler from power.

Like his brother-in-law, the bespectacled Dohnányi, today in civvies, was taciturn and cerebral, preferring to let Canaris and Oster take the lead but was, when called upon, incisive and witty, a charming sense of humor that always reached its zenith during gatherings of the Bonhoeffer clan. Canaris and his guests sat at an outdoor table near the communications hut of the Abwehr airfield enjoying the fresh breeze off the lake on the warm summer afternoon.

Oster called the meeting to order with a *Zum Wohl, bottoms up*, that struck Dietrich more as a crisp military command than a convivial salutation among friends as the group clinked their large glass steins of pilsner. Oster then turned his attention to Leo, *your exploits far and wide, young man, are to say the least impressive. We still on occasion get a rather nasty inquiry from our Swedish brethren demanding a status report on our efforts to find you!*

Dietrich chuckled, Hans smiled, and Leo braced himself for what he suspected would come next. The price to be paid for the pilsner! A bemused Oster and Canaris studied Leo closely.

Add to that your exploits at the Swiss border and in Zurich, and you are proving yourself a rather interesting fellow indeed, Oster added. Leo, notorious for keeping his own counsel, deadpanned when he heard Switzerland mentioned. He knew he was sitting across from two of Germany's greatest spies but was intrigued by how and from whom they knew anything about his activities in Switzerland.

Leo, we have a proposition for you. It was Canaris this time.

I will let General Oster and Major Dohnányi fill you in on operational details. I would simply say, you have proven something to me, young man, and to the others. Whether it is bravery or luck or resourcefulness, or some amalgam of the three, there is a certain, as the French would say, 'je ne sais quoi,' about you that would make you a formidable asset to any spy service and the perfect solution to our immediate problem.

With an arched eyebrow and shrug of the shoulders, Leo shot a quick look at Dietrich who if he had some knowledge of what was to come, was playing it close to the vest. Leo said, *I won't ask how you know about Switzerland, not yet at least. And I have never been good at taking orders, so the military might do just as well without me.*

Switching gears, Leo now addressed himself respectfully to Canaris, *what do you have in mind, sir?*

Oster took the lead, *Leo, there are people, upstanding citizens of the Reich, who require safe passage from Germany to Switzerland. And lest I sugar coat the problem, they are Jews. We call the operation 'Unternehmen Sieben,' but we shall refer to it in present company simply as U-7.*

We have met with some resistance from our cousins the Swiss and would like you to join Dietrich and Hans on an upcoming mission to sort things out. Hans shall try to conclude our negotiations with the Swiss government, Dietrich will attempt to find allies in the Swiss church who can pressure the government to allow our friends to cross the border safely and you if you would be willing to step in would be tasked with enlisting the aid of Herr Rauschenberg in Zurich.

Time is not on our side as we have removed these friends of ours from the deportation list, and questions will be raised, Oster added. Indeed, the animus between the Gestapo and Abwehr had intensified since Heydrich's death, and Himmler was looking for any opportunity to discredit Canaris and take control of all military intelligence.

Leo was more impressed than surprised that he had been connected to Emil. *And what role does he play in this,* Leo asked?

Oster responded by saying, *we need someone who will shepherd our flock once they have made it across the border and coordinate the disposition of funds there to support a reasonable standard of living. We have known of his activities for some time now but of the five of us, you are the only one to have a working relationship with Herr Rauschenberg.*

How many friends are we talking about, Leo asked?

Seven at least but possibly in the end upwards of thirteen or fourteen, Oster replied.

In case you haven't noticed, it is not easy to get across the border these days thanks to your boss, Leo said. Oster and Canaris sat back and started to relax. Leo was beginning to engage as they had hoped he would.

The plan is to make them agents of Abwehr with the ostensible mission of infiltrating Jewish communities elsewhere to convince their brethren that things are not quite as bad as they appear to be here in the Reich. They will have training and documents to establish their bona fides as our agents.

Dietrich interjected, *Hans has taken the lead in putting their documents together but to minimize bureaucratic interference, we would ask your assistance in recruiting Little Otto to complete the work.*

So, let's say all of this falls into place, do they simply walk across the border, Leo asked cheekily?

Hans stepped in to take this question, *this is also where you come in. There are many in the apparatus of the Third Reich who are antagonistic to the aims of the Abwehr, not the least of which is the ultimate patron of your Swiss enterprise, Himmler.* Himmler's involvement with Alois was not news to Leo as, unbeknownst to Alois, Charley had let him in on Himmler's involvement to impress on Leo the high price he would pay for failure.

The precise choreography of their departure here and arrival there has yet to be plotted, Hans replied. *However, we are seriously considering taking a page from your book as to how this might be approached.*

My book, Leo asked incredulously?

I believe that you have made the acquaintance of one Roger Masson, who happened to arrive fortuitously as your fate and the Zurich Express straddled the border on your first trip to Switzerland, Hans continued. *To refresh your memory still further, he leads Swiss Military*

Intelligence, which is inclined at least for the moment to be helpful to our cause.

Leo's memory needed no refreshing and leapt quickly from Masson to linger on Jani and Tomi.

Roger mentioned you as a possible chaperone for our debutantes with whom he could work, Oster added.

Oster pointed to his watch and Hans quickly wrapped up, *we will have an opportunity soon to discuss operational details for that phase of U-7. For now, let me review plans for our next trip to coincide, Leo, with your excursion this week to see Rauschenberg.*

Later, as Leo and Dietrich made their way back to Berlin in the hold of the noisy and uncomfortable Kübelwagen, they tried looking ahead each in his own fashion at whether they were equal to the perilous mission that lay ahead. Leo snidely prodded his good friend by saying, *Dietrich, why me? Why is it that you continue to involve me of all people in escapades like this?*

Dietrich, preoccupied with worry as he often was about the danger to which missions like this might be subjecting his family and friends, hesitated but gave no ground on the answer, *look inside yourself, Leo, and you may see as we do the gifts that God has given you. We will not let them go to waste nor should you.*

* * * * *

Leo and Dohnányi arrived first at the small bistro in the shabby splendor of the Niederdorf, Zurich's old town. The bistro was tucked away in a dark alley fifteen minutes from Zurich's main train station, perfect Leo thought for people plotting something that they should not be.

It was a decidedly Bohemian place where grungy men and their exotic women sipped their drinks standing in clumps, one nearby clump admiring a mural by Emmy Hemmings, a founder of the Dada art movement in Zurich. The mural read, *Dada is the best lily-milk soap in the world.* Leo hadn't a clue about its meaning but appreciated it for that reason alone.

Both Dohnányi and Leo had completed their assignments in Switzerland, and the amiable and relaxed Dohnányi deftly managed to engage Leo so in a relaxed conversation while they were waiting for Dietrich. It was only the second time they had ever spent time with each other.

The conversation finally came around to Dietrich. *He is one of a kind*, Hans said. *He gives me strength in the belief that our cause, whose linchpin may be an assassination of a head of state, is not a craven act of degeneracy at a time when our brothers are giving their lives in war for the Fatherland.*

It seems to me that it bothers him despite his strong convictions, Leo said. *Almost as much as it bothers him that I do not seem to him to have any convictions.*

Hans laughed and said, *I was privileged to witness the last public sermon that Dietrich was allowed by the Nazis to give in Berlin. It was 1932. His words did not mean much to me then, but God knows they do now. It was something to the effect of 'the blood of martyrs might once again be demanded, but this blood, if we really have the courage and loyalty to shed it, will not be innocent, shining like that of the first witnesses for the faith. On our blood lies heavy guilt, the guilt of the unprofitable servant who is cast into outer darkness.'*

Leo had been around Dietrich long enough to sense what he was driving at, *for me, I am motivated primarily by rewards. I am a merce-*

nary, Leo said. *If Dietrich feels he has an obligation, no geld, no pat on the back is required. And if the good and the bad of it are a bit foggy, he will take his chances that he can work it out with God. I suppose that is what Faith is to him.*

Hans had no chance to reply as Dietrich, who had been mingling with the locals briefly to admire the Dada mural joined them at the table. The discussion promptly turned to U-7.

For starters, Dietrich uncharacteristically downed in one draught the contents of a stein of pilsner and when he caught his breath said, *Barth has put a good word in for us but I dare say with little real enthusiasm. I am puzzled and troubled by this. My belief is that he simply did not want to get my hopes up for a dramatic breakthrough.*

Karl Barth, one of the great theologians of the 20th century, now lived in Basel since his expulsion from Germany in 1935 after refusing to sign the Oath of Loyalty to Adolf Hitler. Barth, along with Dietrich was one of the founders of the Confessing Church. He was also largely responsible for the Barmen Declaration rejecting the influence of Nazism on German Christianity by arguing that the Church's allegiance to the God of Jesus Christ compelled it to resist the influence of other lords, such as the German Führer. He had even mailed this declaration to Hitler personally.

Perhaps, he had some influence because my conversation with the Swiss yesterday was easier than it had up to then, Hans said. *However, our pecunious Teutonic cousins who have no compunctions about laundering Nazi gold into millions of Swiss francs, are concerned about how we will pay for it, that is to say ensure the financial independence of our 'agents' and their families. In short, the Swiss have raised the price of admission.*

By how much, Dietrich asked?

By a healthy multiple that is problematic. We are already funding this operation through Abwehr accounts to a degree that is increasingly conspicuous. Not everyone at headquarters is aligned with our thinking, so I must consult with Oster and the Admiral. We cannot let it stop us dead in our tracks but, Hans did not complete the sentence momentarily rehearsing in his mind's eye how to approach this subject with his superiors.

There is, however, a ray of sunshine in all of this, Hans said picking up the thread of the conversation once more. *Masson walked me out and we can count on help from Lucy*, Hans added.

Lucy, Leo asked?

Let's say that Roger has access to an extensive network of resources that he will put at our disposal, Hans replied.

In fact, the spy ring codenamed *Lucy* was a highly effective anti-Nazi espionage operation headquartered in Switzerland. Working principally with the British and Russians, its major accomplishments were to deliver details of *Operation Barbarossa*, Germany's planned invasion of the Soviet Union; high grade military intelligence about *Case Blue*, the German operations against Stalingrad and the Caucasus; as well as Germany's plans for *Operation Zitadelle*, a planned summer offensive that ended in a crippling defeat of the German army at the Battle of Kursk. Its victory at Kursk would give the Red Army the initiative on the eastern front for the remainder of the war.

In due time, Hans and Dietrich turned to Leo. *We hope you had better luck than we did, Leo,* Dietrich said with more than a hint of self-deprecation.

Well, Emil will act as, what did you call it the other day, our safe harbor for the operation. He has extensive financial connections in Zurich and for that matter throughout Europe. He will also provide a bank relationship so that you do not have to rely solely on Abwehr accounts, Leo said.

Something gnawed at Leo as Hans and Dietrich briefly turned to planning a birthday celebration for Christel, sister to Dietrich and wife to Hans. Leo ran his fingers around the grooved shape of a heart that had been carved into the rustic wooden table where they sat as he worked through the variables of the problem. Inside the heart was the inscription – *Christoph et Suki.* He hoped that their romance was happier than this sad, back alley place where it was memorialized, which now smelled of spilt beer, cabbage and body odor.

It bothered Leo that there were too many people involved in this affair and accordingly too many ways to slip-up. Mehdi would often cancel a big black-market operation and say, *it isn't tight, it just isn't tight,* meaning too much was out of their control. Hans seemed to know what he was doing, but there were still too many loose ends here. *It just was not tight*, Leo said to himself, which made it all the more dangerous.

To add to Leo's dilemma, he knew where to find the money that the conspirators needed for U-7, which was likely to make matters worse rather than better.

Dada is the best lily-milk soap in the world.

* * * * *

Bratwurst night at Café Alois and Himmler cursed Kaltenbrunner for going AWOL from the dinner meeting he had arranged with him and the insufferable accountant, Toeppen and his legal man Herzlieb. Himmler's bodyguards had reported that Kaltenbrunner was on one of his benders. Thus, is the price of obsequience, Himmler mused, placated for the moment by the tiny pearls of animal fat bubbling up from the Bratwurst he had just impaled with his fork.

Herzlieb was bearable, but Himmler had an immediate aversion to Toeppen, the *Oberintendent* responsible for Abwehr finances, and for that matter detested all accountants since his days as a failed chicken farmer. The bean counters always managed to find a problem you didn't know you had and to explain it in a way you didn't understand. *Die Scheißköpfe* had been anything but helpful in saving his failing business.

Toeppen and Herzlieb were, however, both loyal and fanatical Nazis. This alone would not have earned them a seat at the table with Himmler on such an august occasion as Bratwurst night. It was instead the growing body of evidence that they were piecing together on Canaris and Oster that might soon be actionable against them in Himmler's quest to control the entirety of German military intelligence.

Toeppen, in particular, hated Oster, who continuously belittled him while playing fast and loose with Abwehr funds often establishing new accounts outside of Germany ostensibly to fund espionage operations. Toeppen saw a more sinister motivation and, in the end, he would be proven correct because there were accounts under Oster's control that were intended to underwrite the ongoing conspiracy to kill Hitler.

For his part, Herzlieb harbored the same intense animus for Dohnányi, who constantly reversed his legal work often with the encouragement of Canaris. It was simply not proper, he thought, the reckless use of Abwehr funds without detailed accountability to a higher authority. Herzlieb also had not perceived in Dohnányi the same joy and commitment that he himself felt in serving the Führer.

Then there was that fellow Schmidhuber, Toeppen added, as Himmler listened patiently, warm potato salad caressing his palate. Schmidhuber and the preacher Bonhoeffer had free reign on recent operations in Rome and to make matters worse there was a strange new account in Portugal established seemingly without brief.

And there was the anomaly that had precipitated the evening's less than convivial dinner with Himmler. There were substantial sums of money placed in Swiss accounts for a group of agents whose identities and mission were unclear and thus unsanctioned by the chain of command.

Himmler had some inkling of what this might be, having given tacit approval for a small propaganda operation that Canaris had undertaken with a handful of Jews who had converted to the church, although that did little to redeem them in his eyes. A Jew was a Jew was a Jew. Yet, why so much money, Himmler mused?

Taking Kaltenbrunner's place at the table was Gestapo Commissioner Franz Sonderegger, a former Bull from the *Alex* in Berlin. He had the ascetic physique and demeanor of a monk and, as Himmler savored each crunch of peppercorn in a large mouthful of sauerkraut, he watched Sonderegger inhale his email like a monk who had just been released from a prolonged vow of abstinence.

This was OK with Himmler and to be preferred to agents who drank themselves blind or cavorted with Jewish whores. Himmler turned to Sonderegger and said, *what do we do?*

Your Excellency, Sonderegger replied, *there is a trail of breadcrumbs here, yes, but Canaris and Oster are formidable adversaries. Allow me to work with Herren Toeppen and Herzlieb to construct a case that will be unassailable.* Himmler made a mental note to use the strange man for future investigative work.

Himmler nodded as he slathered onion butter on the freshly baked *Bauernbrot,* farmer's bread, to Himmler the highlight of the evening's meal but for the fat-speckled Bratwurst. Cuisine aside, it had been a good day as days go, he thought.

There was Sonderegger and his breadcrumbs that might in time form the pattern of financial crimes bordering on treason in the case of Abwehr. And there was Panzinger of the *Sonderkommando Rote Kapelle*, who was leaving Café Alois as Himmler arrived. In their passing conversation, Panzinger reported that he had the strike force he required and was ready to destroy the conspirators in the *Rote Kapelle* along with their elicit radio transmitters.

And finally, there was Kaltenbrunner's man Lange and the progress he was making to expose the odd connection between those in the orbit of *Die Bäckerei and* the seditious Bonhoeffer, the unlikeliest of military intelligence agents.

It is the small things that prove lethal, thought Himmler now in a state of rapture as he cleaned his plate of the last crumb. Would it be a snapping branch or the rustling of leaves in the overgrowth that would draw the patient hunter to its prey?

* * * * *

Unternehmen 7 started propitiously despite the fact that the number of Abwehr agents and family members had doubled from seven to fourteen. The complexity of an already intricate operation had not simply doubled. It had grown geometrically.

The team scrambled to rethink escape routes, plans and finances. Undaunted by all of it was Little Otto, who produced some of his finest work, often ahead of schedule, under intense pressure.

More importantly to the future of the 14 in Canaris's care, Leo had been successful in exploiting Emil's one weakness, which was had he not been a Jew he might have been quite an acceptable Christian saint. The pouch of cut jewels that he had given Leo after Leo had put the problem of the new Swiss demand for money before him would sustain the refugees for a period far into the future. Leo vowed to repay this debt someday.

An amazed and humbled Oster accepted the jewels from Leo and gave them to a first cousin, Walter Jauch, the founder of Jauch & Hübener, which was at the beginning of the Second World War the largest insurance broker in continental Europe and the precursor of today's German branch of Aon Corporation. Jauch, in turn, created a credit equivalent to the value of the jewels in the firm's accounts in Switzerland.

From the end of August to late September 1942, the conspirators made their moves. Two of the refugees-cum-agents accompanied Dietrich on an Abwehr mission to Rome melting into the ether on a walk around the Vatican in the company of two female guides, ending up several days later in Zurich to pave the way for the others.

Leo was able to move eight additional refugees on the Zurich express, a family of three and a family of five, in two successive trips ostensibly for Alois and Charley. The second had been unplanned, but Leo was able to convince Charley who, in turn, convinced Himmler that the second trip was warranted by an unusually beautiful addition to Emil's inventory whose provenance was the Medici treasury in Florence. In fact, they were rather ordinary stones reinvigorated by a clever goldsmith in Turin.

During both trips, the transfer ran like the proverbial Swiss watch. Masson arrived as the Zurich express straddled the border to "arrest," certain suspected enemies of the state.

Things had gone so smoothly for the conspirators that Leo hoped against hope his earlier apprehension about the sloppy state of planning was unwarranted.

And then their luck changed.

* * * * *

They had assembled at Oderberger Strasse 61 in the same flat where Dietrich had hidden the young boy they eventually smuggled into Sweden. In most of Berlin, it was a crystal-clear night with twinkling stars that typically attracted British bombers to the city like flies to honey. Yet tonight they did not come.

Wedding itself was another story. That crystal-clear night had been fouled by an especially potent discharge from Old Man Schultheiss's brewery. It had collected in a dome that flumped over Wedding as if held in place by an invisible bell jar. It made the eyes water and the nose run and amplified the misery of the disconsolate group that filled the small flat to its brim.

It was the last family to make the leap to freedom in Switzerland under the auspices of U-7, and they had gummed up the works. Herr Kindler had been a successful lawyer before the Nazis revoked the licenses of Jewish lawyers in 1939. He had managed to eke out a living representing his Jewish countrymen on issues related to the Nuremberg laws and other anti-Semitic legislation and had through dumb luck managed to hold onto their spacious flat on Mommsen Strasse, an elegant tree lined street near the Ku'damm.

The Kindlers were close to the Dohnányi's. Herr Kindler had studied law with Hans, and Christel Dohnányi had been the preceptor for their *shotgun conversion* to Christianity.

The Kindler's, their sullen teenage son and bright teenage daughter who at times inserted herself into the conversation, were joined by Dietrich, Hans Dohnányi and Leo. Their escape to Switzerland now hung in the balance.

What was I supposed to do? The Gestapo man and your Abwehr agent would not let go of the question of what my role is with Abwehr and the financial arrangements that have been made. I told them I knew nothing about the finances as I am not a financial person and just take my orders as they come. But they were persistent and not easily satisfied, Herr Kindler said.

It had been a mission launched by Toeppen and Herzlieb. In time, they would send their own agents to interview some of the 14. Happily, most had safely dispersed in Switzerland.

The offshoot of this visit was that the Kindlers had failed to appear at the designated rendezvous at the Kaiser-Wilhelm-Gedächtnis-Kirche at the foot of the Ku'damm earlier that day. *After that visit, I could not put my family at greater risk. Perhaps some other accommodation short of leaving Berlin could be found,* Kindler asked?

Why if Papa is part of you now did one of your own behave in such a menacing way, chimed in the daughter for good measure.

Richard, Dohnányi responded, *I am afraid we are beyond accommodation at this point. That visit should be a wake-up call to you.* Looking at Kindler's daughter, Hans patiently addressed her question, *the Abwehr is a large organization and while many of us revere Admiral Canaris and all he stands for, there are numerous others who insanely revere the Führer.*

Dietrich added, *Herr Kindler, we cannot force you to go. Stay if you must but do not let fear burden your decision. Otherwise, you and your family will be rewarded by the Fatherland with four one-way tickets East.*

Sir, it was Leo's turn to chime in, *I have done this trip twice already. I can't say that it has become routine, but we have help from the Swiss that minimizes the risk. The sum total of the unknowns involved in the trip pale in comparison to the terrible certainty of what will happen to you if you stay.*

And on it went. Finally, the family huddled in a whispered tête-à-tête. From Leo's vantage point, it appeared that the women were making their best case to leave while Herr Kindler and his son, who seemed constantly on the verge of tears, resisted.

* * * * *

The steward handed Leo a small envelope containing a note, which read, *the bar in five minutes.* The Kindler women had prevailed upon their men that escape was their only true option, and they were sitting with Leo in a cramped first-class compartment on the Zurich Express. They were three hours into the trip and despite the late hour, no one in the family could relax enough to avail themselves of the adjoining sleeper compartment. Leo had not even been able to convince them to go to dinner.

Dietrich had offered to accompany Leo given the nettlesome attitude of their flock, but Leo demurred. *I would easily sacrifice the lot of them for you if push came to shove with the Gestapo, Dietrich, so let us avoid that possibility*, Leo replied.

The trip thus far had been uneventful. The blocking and tackling of getting the family situated on the train was by now second nature to Leo despite the tension crackling around his charges like electricity from a frayed wire. The only unusual thing to happen was an unscheduled stop at a railroad siding a couple of hours North of the border. The steward had explained they were waiting to allow an oncoming freight train to pass.

It had given Leo an excuse to stretch his legs and survey those with whom they shared the first-class car. There was one other family, two Catholic clerics and two decidedly unclerical passengers, whose surliness as he passed the open door of their compartment said all that needed to be said. The reek of alcohol from this compartment nearly made him gag as he casually sauntered past the open door.

Leo took his leave of the Kindlers later after receiving the note and strolled casually to the wood paneled club car and its ornate bar. There in civvies stood one of Masson's two goons, a term that Leo applied affectionately as he was happy that this particular goon was on his side.

As he arrived at the bar, his companion greeted him as an old friend and bought him a drink. The message was clear. Act naturally because we are being watched.

A small envelope peeked out from below an ashtray and Leo's companion tapped it casually as he babbled on. They continued the conversation for roughly 20 minutes, ordering another drink, and laying it on thick for all to see – just two mildly inebriated friends, cares melting away with each sip, having a good time.

Leo eventually palmed the envelope and returned to the car. The note read, *Change in plan. SS Stormtroopers waiting at the border. Train goes on with exchange in Zurich.*

So, it was clear that they were anything but home free, a fact that he dared not share with the family except to tell them, *you have a bit more time to rest if you wish. We do not get off until Zurich.*

* * * * *

The train rolled through its customary border stop to a chorus of whistles and warnings from a bullhorn wielding SS officer backed by bristling with guns. No shots were fired because the SS squad was caught completely off guard.

At the same time, Leo stood at his compartment door braced for the two men in the nearby compartment to make a move, hand on the Bedouin Khanjar under his jacket. No one came.

What could they do to them anyway on Swiss soil without any back-up, he thought. Then, the hair bristled on the back of his neck as it occurred to him that they could simply shoot the bunch of them.

The transfer went as planned just outside Hauptbahnhof Zurich, the main train station in central Zurich. Truth be told, Leo was happy to see the last of the Kindlers as the sullen family hurried off with two plain clothes Swiss military intelligence agents. His only thanks had come with an awkward quick kiss on the cheek from Fräulein Kindler.

Leo discretely followed the group from a distance as he knew Hans and Dietrich would want to know that they were out of harm's way. He had already picked up the fake Medici jewels on a prior trip, so there would be no meeting with Emil this time around. He would simply nap on the train station bench and await tomorrow morning's express to Berlin after a visit to Niederdorf to mingle with its grungy men and their exotic women.

They had walked barely five minutes from the train station and arrived at a dark square at the center of which stood a white granite obelisk, which served as a dim beacon absorbing light from the ivory fog that tumbled into the square from the *Limmat* river whose icy waters united Zurich with a crystalline thread.

From a side street to his left, about 50 feet ahead, a man appeared. He was tall with broad shoulders and closely cropped blonde hair, a military cut. Damned if it wasn't one of the two surly looking men in first class on the Zurich Express. SS no doubt.

He was closing in on the Swiss agents and the Kindlers, who were unaware of his presence. Leo saw the man's handgun held at arm's length close to his side as he hugged the shadows. This was not going to end well, Leo thought to himself.

The SS man's quarry was midway between the obelisk and a street perhaps nothing more than an alley at the far edge of the square. He, up to this point, partially concealed by the obelisk, broke cover and picked up his pace.

It was now or never, Leo thought, and he emerged from the shadows to the SS man's right trailing him now by about 25 feet. The hunter focused on stalking his prey had himself become the quarry. Leo closed the distance with him at full speed as yet undetected.

It was clear that the SS man was going to intercept the Swiss agent and his charges just as they entered the alleyway. Leo broke into a run and before the SS man realized what was happening, Leo hit him full bore in the lower back bringing the man to his knees and then to the ground.

Leo landed hard on the man's back and it knocked the breath of both of them, but the sight of the large handgun in his adversary's right hand was all Leo needed to get over it. The SS man managed to hold on to the butt of the handgun with his right hand, despite the impact of the tackle, and was struggling to get a finger around the trigger. His left arm was pinioned under his body, but he was trying to use it to gain enough leverage to throw Leo off his back.

Leo lunged forward and sent his elbow into his adversary's gun-side shoulder blade. Hell, this guy is a brick, all muscle, Leo thought, and worse was gaining control of the gun. The man bucked again and was nearly successful in hoisting Leo off and rolling out from under him.

Then the spiked heel of a woman's shoe came down hard on the SS man's right hand, creating a bony pulp where the big knuckle of his trigger finger had been. A grunt, a soft metallic clang, a muffled pop and the smell of a firecracker followed in rapid succession. The Gestapo man's torso seemed to flop under Leo's weight and then lie still.

Leo looked up to see Jani, in a trench coat and a fedora drawn down over her beautiful face. She had just put a large hole in the SS man's head using a gun with a silencer, a hole that was already oozing an ugly red-gray goop.

Up we go, Business Man. Are you OK, she asked with more than casual interest? *We are done here and must go!*

Leo scrambled to his feet bruised and battered but in much better shape than his adversary.

I was told they had sent you, she said. *Have you someplace to go tonight?*

No, he replied, still trying to catch his breath.

No? Come back to my place. It is not far. Tomi and I would enjoy your company.

Even in the gloom, Jani's eyes sparkled under her fedora, a Cheshire cat who had found her country mouse.

I trust that you can handle it, mon cher, the cat said grinning. *Handle what,* said the mouse.

Jani laughed, a throaty, sustained purr. *Oh, Tomi will be so pleased to see you,* she intoned.

So, you two live together then, Leo asked as they quickly moved toward the far edge of the square? *Tomi and I do everything together,* Jani said, as she wrapped her arm in his and they disappeared post-haste into the gloom.

* * * * *

Jani and Tomi parted reluctantly from Leo the next morning. Call it beginner's luck or natural talent, but Leo managed with the fervent encouragement of Jani and Tomi to make every minute of their time together count. Having reached the Hautbahnhof Zurich where Leo would board the train for his return to Berlin, the three young warriors embraced, hearts full and hopes cresting for the prospect of *Unternehmen 8.*

* * * * *

Mildred and Erika were numbered among the privileged class in Berlin, who had telephones in their flats, Mildred because Arvid was a senior official in the Reich Ministry of Economics and Erika because she worked for a highly placed official in the Reich Ministry of Labor Protection, whose director would have been lost without her. Erika should have been flattered, but she viewed the telephone as a leash that kept her at her patron's beck and call.

Mildred and Erika rarely used the telephone for a casual conversation with each other because they assumed that someone was always listening. When they did talk, their conversations were short and usually coded – the time and date of a meeting, a rendezvous point, all established while trading a recipe or commenting on the weather.

The telephone call Erika dreaded most came two weeks earlier, heralded by a ferocious thunderstorm that rattled the windows of her flat. It had been Mildred and started, *hello dear. My Uncle Edgar has given me tickets for the opera, would you care to join me? There are two.*

Translated, this meant that Harold and Libertas Schulze-Boysen —Uncle Edgar —had been arrested and that all in the orbit of the Schulze-Boysens and Harnacks should take the necessary steps to save themselves. *Save, myself,* Erika thought. *I am the mother of a four-year-old girl. She must be my only concern now.*

Less than a week following Mildred's call, she and Arvid were themselves arrested by the Gestapo. Hans had come by to tell Erika and move the radio set to the boiler room. He took it apart and put the pieces in the furnace but did not light the furnace because it would be like sending a smoke signal to the enemy, he told Erika. One could only pray that the radio set would not be found. Hans then left in a hurry and that is the last Erika ever saw of him.

That was a week ago. Today, on a mid-September day with a refreshing hint of autumn in the air, Erika met Saskia and her grandmother, Oma Helena, with whom Saskia was living temporarily at the playground near Parisier Platz and the Brandenburger Tor. Erika warned her mother-in-law that she may fall on hard times and to shield Saskia from anything that she might hear. Erika gave Saskia's grandmother a small box of family mementos for safekeeping and a sizeable sum of money that she said, albeit somewhat disingenuously, she would replenish when they saw each other next.

Erika picked Saskia up from the swing set and hugged her tightly and gave her delighted daughter a playful peck on the nose but did not linger in case she was being followed. Her own arrest would be one thing, but Saskia used as a pawn would be unbearable.

Later that morning, she tried to walk by the Kuckhoff's, but there was a police guard at both ends of the short city block where they lived. The erudite and elegant Adam and Greta must have suffered the same fate as the Harnacks and Schulze-Boysens, she lamented.

Then the thought occurred to her that she had one detour to make before returning home, one more person to warn. The U-Bahn was operating, and she made good time to Wedding and *Die Bäckerei.*

Little Otto had spoken of Mehdi, and there he was in the flesh. Erika asked if it were possible to see Little Otto, but Mehdi told her he was nowhere to be found.

Mehdi sensing a problem pulled Erika aside. *I am Erika von Brockdorff*, she said.

Yes, I know who you are. Is everything OK, Mehdi asked?

Everything is not OK. Please tell Little Otto to stay away. It is not safe for him to visit me again, she said calmly.

How can we help you, Mehdi asked in reply? *It is too late for that, thank you*, Erika responded. She had no place to run, nor did she intend to run.

That evening, in the dim light of a small art deco desk lamp that was more decorative than useful, she toyed with the large telescope atop a tripod at their bay window as she did almost every night because it reminded her of Graf, whom she adored. Erika hoped that he would be proud of her or if not proud try to understand the choices that a mother and proud German had to make for Saskia and her family's future.

As she studied the waxing gibbous, the paper-thin slice of moon that foretold the coming of a full moon, there was a knock at the door or more aptly banging. She paused to take the measure of herself in the mirror, corrected her posture and walked calmy to the door.

Her confidence fled for an instant, her stomach clenching at the thought of Saskia, *sleep tight, mein Liebling. Her confidence* restored, she opened the door.

Am I addressing Erika von Brockdorff formerly Erika Schönfeldt? It was a puggy man with a horned rim eyeglasses and caterpillar mustache along with a jumble of hats and heads milling behind him.

Erika nodded and replied with the wisp of a cheeky smile, *and you are?*

I am Obersturmbann-führer Friedrich Panzinger of the Gestapo. You will kindly step aside.

* * * * *

Leo was fortunate to have made it to Anhalter Bahnhof upon his return from a memorable night in Zurich, arriving just as a horrific wall of sound and light ground through Berlin moving the detritus of human beings and what had once been their worldly possessions steadily Eastward with the prevailing wind. Train crews often abandoned a train altogether when bombing approached.

It was as if British flyers, the *Tommies,* were dead set on finding him personally, Leo imagined. He had seen one of the first bomb craters in Berlin on a delivery to Spandau some time back and the sight of it gave you a sinking feeling about what a single bomb could do to you personally. Old man Kramp who had lost a leg and three fingers at Verdun in the last war liked to say when he came by the shop, *this war is a lot like the last one, meine freunde, except the holes are bigger.*

By 1942 the Allied policy of bombing only those targets of direct military significance had gradually given way to *Area Bombing.* This was large-scale bombing of German cities to destroy housing and civilian infrastructure.

Although killing German civilians was never the aim, it was clear that such an approach as area bombing would cause large-scale civilian casualties. With the technology available at the time, the precision bombing of military targets was possible only by daylight albeit with unacceptably high losses of British aircraft. Bombing by night led to far fewer British losses but was more indiscriminate due to the vagaries of nocturnal navigation and targeting.

Truth be told, Berlin actually had fared rather well in relative terms up to and including most of 1942 because the RAF's first priority was attacking U-boat ports as part of Britain›s effort to win the Battle of the Atlantic. However, area bombing of German cities would arrive in full force in 1943 leading to massive losses of life and property in Berlin.

An RAF commander is quoted as saying, *the Nazis entered this war under the rather childish delusion that they were going to bomb everyone else, and nobody was going to bomb them…they sowed the wind, and now they are going to reap the whirlwind.*

As agreed, Dietrich met Leo in the main concourse of the train station under a zinc statue of Zeus that was so anatomically explicit that it seemed to be competing with the statue of David to establish the hegemony of Teutonic over Italianate manhood. Mehdi had *borrowed* the Schultheiss Brewery truck and waited outside with Big Otto.

They quickly brought Leo up to date on Erika's encounter with Mehdi and the fact that Little Otto had gone missing. The twins had told Mehdi that Little Otto had set out earlier that day after an encounter with that fellow Hans who told him to stay away from Erika's flat because he said, *the game was over*. Hans and his wife Hilde were themselves fleeing Berlin.

The twins could not persuade Little Otto to wait for your return, Leo, Mehdi said. *He was apparently obsessed with finding the radio transmitter and smuggling it out in the coal cart with the false bottom that they had used to smuggle printing supplies into her flat. Little Otto managed to hitch a ride in Herr Kruger's milk truck with his coal cart in tow.*

Leo was stunned that so much, so much that was bad, had happened while he was away. What was he thinking to have not had a Plan B for Erika! Now Little Otto had taken it into his own hands to save her.

We must find them, Leo said. The hollowness of what he had just said rang in his ears. He knew he had let the two of them down.

We will, Mehdi replied. *We are picking up the twins and one or two others at Frau Kalbo's and are going straight away to Frau von Brockdorff's.*

They could now see the two classical granite statues that framed the near portal of an oncoming bridge over the Spree, which would put them within 10 minutes of Frau Kalbo's. Fittingly, they were the ill-fated lovers Hero and Leander – one who drowned trying to reach his love by swimming to the opposite side of the Hellespont on a stormy night, the other who later drowned herself to join him in eternity.

Of his manifold virtues in life, Mehdi did not count driving skills among them. The mechanics of the process were never a problem. The fact that he had to share the road with others, well.

It might have been the tension of the moment that enveloped those in the truck, the cacophony of explosions that drew closer or the man-made lightning unleashed by the fire and fury consuming their countrymen because Mehdi did not see the military convoy bearing down on them from the portal of the bridge until it was too late.

He saw the troop carrier just as the driver of the troop carrier saw him. Both swerved but the rear of the troop carrier fishtailed into the rear bumper of the Schultheiss truck sending it spinning like a top.

The truck hit the curb and went airborne flipping a full 360 degrees and landing on its side with a bang that no one heard in the din of the nearby bombing. The truck ground its way down a long grass and gravel incline coming to rest against a retaining wall above a small canal that led to the Spree.

* * * * *

Earlier that day, Canaris had taken a short detour on his way to Paris for a briefing from senior Abwehr agents landing at a small airfield near Épernay, France in champagne country. Épernay lies in the rolling green plains of the Aisne-Marne where the Germans came within 34 miles of Paris in 1918 but were stopped at the Marne River in a bloodbath for both sides.

From there a car took him to the nearby village of Hautvillers high atop a wind-swept hill with a commanding view of the vineyard laced countryside. The meeting would take place in a small but elegant country house across the cobbled country lane from the ancient Benedictine abbey of Hautvillers where the monk Dom Pérignon discovered the champagne wine-making process in the 18th century.

The owner of the house had been the executive officer in Canaris's first U-boat command during World War I, and they both had been awarded the Iron Cross First Class for their exploits. Wisely, Max, who remained a dear friend, had left the military to throw in his lot with Moët & Chandon to help create the first batch of what was to become their Dom Pérignon brand of champagne.

With time to kill before the meeting, Canaris walked over to visit Dom Pérignon's tomb in the chancel of the Saint-Sindulphe abbey church. He would toast the great man later with his very own invention because Max ever the gracious host had left a bottle on the table in the *salle a manger* of a 1936 Dom, the first year it would be sold under that name, along with two cut crystal flutes as his contribution, he said in his welcoming note, to the war effort.

A side trip like this was not unheard of but required an issue of grave concern and a counterpart with the gravitas to make it worth his while. In this instance, the matter at hand could determine the survival of the Fatherland and for that matter his own.

He watched his counterpart in today's meeting emerge from the abbey church to arrive punctually as she always did. Had she been inside the church all along and seen him pay homage to the Dom?

To one like himself, who created enigmas and solved them, she remained one. Although since the beginning of the war when they first met, a few things had come into focus. She was an agent who did not appear to serve one master. He had made her an Abwehr agent as a matter of convenience, but she also had close ties to MI5 and to the Americans. The latter would figure prominently into today's discussion.

Canaris knew her as Mary-Tay, and he had seen the young woman evolve over the years. She was smart, tough and ruthless. This much he knew from her operational track record, one few could match.

They began their meeting by first sharing a glass of the Dom Perignon along with pleasantries, which gave him a few minutes to renew his study of the young agent. She had let her hair grow since their last meeting in Cairo from something that had looked quite masculine then to what was now long, raven black hair, parted in the middle, falling sumptuously onto her shoulders. Her dark eyes drew him into a mysterious place to which one could easily and willingly be drawn, a beautiful Gorgon with an unshakeable grip on one's attention.

She must be using makeup of some kind, he surmised, because the cross in the customary Bedouin position on the chin had disappeared. The Sufi symbol of a heart held aloft by wings on the back of her right hand was still partially visible beneath her heavy green sweater.

Her persona reminded him of Hedy Lamarr, whom he had known as Hedy Kiesler during her early rise to fame in Austria and later the United States. Hedy had the most incredible personal sophistication and command of the peculiarly European art of being womanly. She knew what men wanted in a beautiful woman and gave it to them naturally and without artifice.

As Canaris poured a second glass for them both, he studied the sandy brown liquid in his glass and remarked, *Bonaparte is always good for a crisp observation about someone or something when one needs one and said about this lovely concoction, 'In victory, you deserve champagne. In defeat, you need it.' So, what does the future hold for us, Mary-Tay?*

Anya took the reins of the conversation, *Admiral, Donovan feels that there is still an opening but one that shrinks with each passing day.*

Canaris interjected politely, *please give my regards to 'Wild Bill' whom I am sure continues to live up to his name.*

I shall, Anya replied. The two were talking about *Wild Bill* Donovan who in 1942 had taken over the OSS, the forerunner of the CIA. Anya and Canaris had both worked together long enough to dispense with the spy craft of code names for key figures like Donovan.

Sir, Anya pressed on, *Donovan knows that you and your comrades have put your lives on the line to end your collective nightmare by means of a coup d'etat, but there will be no direct support for this action. This is per Donovan and with great reluctance on his part.*

Then Mary-Tay, what is possible? Canaris asked his question with a hint of disappointment?

Donovan asked me to convey that there are still those around the U.S. president who are open to your peace feelers and want to find a middle ground, something short of total and unconditional surrender. However, he is hampered by the absence of any notable progress toward your objectives. When can he expect you to move against the target?

Soon is all I can say at the moment. Please emphasize to Donovan that countless lives will be saved on both sides by a negotiated peace between Germany and the United States, and no one in Berlin expects to be treated with kid gloves once that has been accomplished, Canaris continued.

Canaris pressed his case. *You know, my dear friend, the students of history will not need to trouble their heads after this war, as they did after the last, to determine who was guilty of starting it. The case is different, however, when we consider guilt for prolonging the war. I believe that the other side will disarm us of the last weapon with which we can end it if 'Unconditional surrender' is what we are left with. No, our generals will not swallow that.*

I would ask for some affirmative signal soon from Donovan because it will add much needed fuel to the fire that we have ignited to end this thing once and for all, Canaris added. *These are generals and other senior officers, good men by and large, yes, but they are human, and it is simple human nature to want allies in a dangerous fight.*

Eventually, Anya and Canaris came to the realization that they had arrived at an impasse – *action begets action*. And for Canaris, at least, this applied equally to both sides.

Their conversation turned as it usually did to *the boy*, as Canaris liked to call him. *He never ceases to surprise. And this is especially true since you saw him last in Stockholm. Indeed, I may have to stop referring to his as a boy. He deserves more than that,* Canaris volunteered without prompting.

I am pleased to hear that, Anya replied. *He comes from good stock, parents who were heroes in their own right.*

I have no doubt of that, Canaris said warmly. *There are people, friends and enemies alike, who underestimate your cousin, whom he constantly proves wrong. He is brave, yes. But he is dangerous, and I mean that in the best possible sense, because he is unpredictable. I am pleased that he is on our side – at least I think he is on our side,* Canaris added with a wry smile.

They parted as they had greeted each other earlier in the day with an embrace in the French style, a light kiss to both cheeks. Anya said with a look of concern, *please take care of yourself, Admiral.*

Canaris harrumphed and replied, *thank you, Mary-Tay, but please do not worry about me. I am an incurable optimist. And as far as those fellows on the wrong end of the equation are concerned, I think I know how to get along with them.*

* * * * *

A capricious *Mutter Nebel* had left Berlin in the lurch arriving in the early morning hours only after the Tommies had pummeled the city with its bombs, a harbinger of even worse things to come in the months ahead. The four comrades stumbled back to *Die Bäckerei* in the damp, gritty haze left by their unseen tormentors gaining confidence with each new air raid.

The accident had hobbled them all in one way or the other but miraculously all had survived thanks in large part to the Schultheiss truck, which was built like a tank and now lay abandoned on its side above the canal. Leo and Big Otto carried Mehdi, who seemed to have gotten the worst of it, holding him up under each shoulder. The three labored forward, stumbling each time they arrived at a new curb. Dietrich led the way.

They were so exhausted that given the choice they might willingly have embraced their eternal rest by walking under a falling bomb. Barely in command of their senses, their ears rang so loudly that when they spoke, the echoing of their jumbled words was painful.

Dietrich was the first to see it as they approached *Die Bäckerei*, which had sustained minor damage to its façade but was still intact. The source of light was a bit of a mystery at first. It did not come from the streetlight whose lamp was shattered but from the small lantern over the shop door that had been blown from the pediment and lay askew on the sidewalk still attached to its wiring. It looked like the glowing head of a coiled serpent as it cast its beam upwards into the damp white haze.

There above and before them on the horizontal strut of the darkened streetlight was a massive Goshawk, an enormous predatory raptor that they knew well. It nested in the Tiergarten but would make its regular rounds to search for small vermin, which were in abundance in Wedding.

It seemed larger than life projecting from the white haze in all of its regal splendor staring ahead diffident of their approach. Two feet from crown to talon, a barrel chest of white with a pattern of black chevrons, the Goshawk finally acknowledged their arrival by flaring its wings, which were twice as long as it was tall.

It was as if the Goshawk was trying to warn them. Was there a hint of sympathy in the predatory glare of its yellow eyes?

Then Dietrich saw the vague form over which the Goshawk stood vigil. At first, it seemed to be only a long, dark smudge in the hazy light. Had someone hung a cat from the streetlight, he wondered?

As the rest of the group closed ranks with Dietrich, they saw two feet, each with a single gunshot wound in its center. Then one hand and a second appeared in the gloom, both with the same type of wound, vile stigmata sanctioned by the Scribes and Pharisees of the Reich.

The torso, taut with the rigor of the newly dead, swung toward them out of the haze, twisting in a cold gust of wind. *Cut him down, cut him down, Big Otto screamed.*

And they did, draping the small body over Leo's outstretched arms on this concrete Golgotha. A Pieta, not of Carrara marble, but of real flesh and blood like the original.

Beneath the unrelenting gaze of the raptor, they knelt in prayer around the valiant poet-philosopher vanquished in battle but not in life. Little Otto was at rest in the embrace of his family.

THE BREAD OF SORROWS

I. BLESSED ARE THE PEACEMAKERS

He bakes bread and other goodies for us in the morning, makes our coffee, even runs to the market for provisions. I must confess that we loved having him around at first, but I fear it is time to throw our little bird out of the nest.

What faint light there was afloat in the upscale amphitheater of flickering candles, white tablecloths and fine china at the rear of Café Alois rushed to the beautiful young woman to bask in her warm glow. The rowdy Nazi thugs in the front of the house, holding their breath as one when she walked in, had been ensnared in Parsifal's enchanted garden of alluring young women by the arrival of their Queen.

Jani sipped champagne with casual grace as she continued to report about Leo to a concerned audience of Alois and Charley. Leo had taken refuge with Jani and Tomi a month earlier, soon after Little Otto's death.

At first, he would go out drinking and more often than not pick a fight. We stopped going with him after a time and finally laid down the law because we could not stomach that handsome face of his coming home so black and blue. Leo is clever and fearless, but it would appear that no one ever taught him how to use his fists, Jani laughed. The grin of the Cheshire cat had now been replaced with tenderness.

Emil came to me to see what he could do, and we agreed that I should come to see you. He wanted to come himself but, even more perilous than placing a telephone call to you about this matter as we know Uncle Adolf is always listening, would be for a Jew to tempt fate by traveling to Berlin. Alois nervously surveyed his guests at adjoining tables behind the mask of a gracious host to ensure that they were not overheard.

Wise choice, Alois said. *What can we do*? Charley added, *I would also say that our patron who thinks very highly of Leo has a job for him and is impatient about getting started.*

Well, my patron is no less impatient with this situation and has work for me as well, Jani replied. *Emil and I will speak again with Leo and make it clear that it is time to rejoin the struggle. As Emil likes to say, all of us in the fight put on the 'Shirt of Nessus,' and it is alas that time again for brave Leo.*

I need two things from you, Jani said with an air of command. *In the first place, I must see Big Otto, whom we will need to escort Leo back to Berlin. I understand he is in your employ. In the second place, much as we will miss him, I need you to keep Leo here once we get him here.*

* * * * *

As Jani, Alois and Charley plotted Leo's return, the patron of whom Charley spoke sat in the dark in his sumptuous office on the top floor of Prinz-Albrecht-Strasse 9 in his favorite leather easy chair, a gift from his father. He sat next to a roaring fire sipping Calvados alone with his thoughts.

It was just past midnight and the roaring fire danced across his blue-grey eyes and turned Heinrich Himmler's unhealthy pale complexion into the ruddy hue of a fearsome Teutonic warrior seized by the blood lust of battle.

Out of uniform he might have impressed one as a bookish elementary school teacher but as 1942 waned, Himmler was at the height of his power. As Reichsführer-SS, he commanded the Führer's personal bodyguard, the *Schutzstaffe* or *SS* and its paramilitary wing the Waffen-SS, now Himmler's personal army of nearly one million men. He also controlled the dreaded state secret police, the *Geheime Staatspolizei*, otherwise known as the Gestapo.

His father had been a professor of classics, who had instilled in his son a reverence for his Teutonic heritage and a quiet refinement that belied a fanaticism that would carve his name into history as its greatest mass murderer. The Final Solution had been Heydrich's inspiration, but the execution of the plan was Himmler's triumph ensuring the extermination of millions in the name of racial purity.

A fanatic yes, but on this night, it was the pragmatist in him that ruled his thoughts. Himmler revered Hitler and had thrown himself headlong into achieving the Führer's objectives since the early days of the National Socialist German Workers' Party —the Nazi Party, supreme among them the perpetuation of the *Master Race.*

But as the Reich's once invincible armies were being battered in the East, Himmler knew it was time for decisive action to find a negotiated solution. No system of terror, even one as effective as his own in staining politics with crime, was equipped to hold the tottering Third Reich upright for much longer.

Himmler poured another two fingers of Calvados and in the flickering light admired the rich caramel coloring of the thick apple brandy, stolen by the crateload from Normandy. At the same time, he admired his faintly contemptuous smile and two rows of perfect white teeth in the reflection of the heavy crystal tumbler.

Hitler had promised much and delivered much, but his efforts to come to a negotiated agreement with the Allies on his terms had fallen on deaf ears. For all his gifts, Hitler operated by instinct and if he listened to advice from anyone it was simply to find validation for his own impulses. Hitler's ideas had become increasingly far-fetched as the conflict drug on, and he was forced eventually to give up on a political and diplomatic solution.

It would be a fight to the last man he proclaimed now as he harangued anyone and everyone within earshot. It was bad enough that tens of thousands of his countrymen would perish as a result of such hubris, Himmler mused, but so would Himmler's own dreams of leading Germany to a brighter future as the dominant force in continental Europe.

Himmler did listen to others. It was a skill that he had honed as a young man on the make during the Nazi party's ascendancy to power. A prime example of this was the *Freundeskres-RFSS*, or Circle of Friends of the Reichsführer-SS, which had formed toward the end of the Weimar Republic. Its purpose was to forge closer ties between the industrial elites and the emerging Nazi Party to influence its mercurial leader to the extent possible through Himmler's intermediation.

They were insistent now that Himmler act decisively to put a straightforward plan in front of the Allies before all was lost, one that was more earthbound than those proposed by Hitler. Hitler's proposal, a five-point plan, had offered guarantees that the British Empire would remain intact but that the continental supremacy of Germany would not be called into question; left the future of French, Belgian and Dutch colonies to discussion and negotiation; preserved the Polish State under terms to be negotiated; and, last but certainly not least, held that Czechoslovakia belonged to Germany. Additionally, the Anschluss, the betrothal of Austria to its kissing cousin Germany, would also remain intact.

The plan had been rejected of course, several times in fact. There had been a slim hope that it might hold sway in the dark days after the fall of Poland and France when the Allies were on the run. But, by the time of this cold early December morning in 1942, the tables had been turned thanks to the bloodbath in Central Russia and the entry of the Americans into the war.

The Reichsführer-SS scribbled a diagram in his diary outlining a strategy that had evolved from discussions with the *Freundeskres*. He had begun to test the waters with the British through intermediaries in Sweden and Portugal, as yet to no avail.

He would now do the same with the Americans because surely, they were as concerned with the threat of a Bolshevist Europe as was he. He also surmised that it would put pressure on the British to be more responsive to his inquiries.

The *Freundeskres* had proposed an acceptable candidate as the emissary to the Americans, a young man who had already come to Himmler's attention. He was a young, German nobleman with a Swedish mother, who had acquitted himself well in work in counterespionage with the Gestapo.

And then there was the boy. Himmler's contact with the Americans ran through the intermediary in Zurich from whom he bought and sold his fine gems. The boy was devilishly clever, more so than all of the Gestapo agents combined who had tried to stop him. Himmler needed that level of cunning for this mission and, moreover, the Jew trusted the boy, which might hasten a meeting with the American Dulles or perhaps Donovan himself in Switzerland.

Using the boy would also create a trap door through which Himmler might gain additional insight into the ongoing efforts of men in the military high command and foreign office to find a separate peace with the Allies, which apparently did not include him. He had been tolerant of these efforts until now with the hope that he could eventually co-opt one such overture if it proved successful.

And should his plan not work and for that matter even if it should, the nettlesome boy would be expendable and dealt with once and for all at a time and in a manner of his own choosing.

* * * * *

Come again?

The 'Shirt of Nessus,' Leo. It is a myth about the son of the Greek god of all gods, Zeus, whose name was Heracles. The story goes like this. Fearing that Heracles had taken a new lover, his wife gives him a shirt, actually a sleeveless tunic like those you see on the statues of ancient Greeks, which had been stained with the blood of the evil centaur Nessus slain by Heracles. Emil lectured Leo and Big Otto as they waited for the express from Zurich to Berlin in a café across from the train station over hot chocolates fortified by an ample ration of the Akvavit that Big Otto had fortuitously spotted on the shelf behind the counter.

Heracles's wife had been tricked by the dying Nessus into believing it would serve as a potion to ensure her husband's faithfulness. In fact, it had been dipped in the venom of a Hydra, a gigantic sea snake. When Heracles puts on the shirt, the Hydra's venom began to cook him alive, and to escape this unbearable pain he built a funeral pyre and threw himself onto it.

Sounds a little bit like our lot under present circumstances on a continent ruled by Nazis, Emil continued with a sarcastic grimace. *In other words, it is a source of misfortune from which there is no escape or, better put, it is a fight only for the crazy and brave.*

Leo laughed but reluctantly. It hurt to laugh.

Leo, we have lost people we love. Little Otto may have been the first for you, but I fear he will not be the last. Strength against the Hydra's venom is the only thing that will see us through.

As the Akvavit numbed his tongue and focused his mind, Leo remembered the last few moments alone with Harry, the young British MI6 agent, before they set out from Frau Kalbo's for KaDeWe. Harry had given Leo a bear hug, and because he delighted in quoting poetry and singing drinking songs, shared a verse of poetry from one of his favorite poets. He told Leo then that it was more positive than it sounded and always seemed to get him over a hurdle when he needed a good kick in the arse.

No change, no pause, no hope!
Yet I endure

It ain't them bloody good looks of yours, Leo, that will win the day. It's grit, old chap, borne of righteous anger that must keep us going until brother Adolf's head is on a pike, Harry had told him.

Leo had seen flashes of this righteous anger in Jani and Tomi, who operated at the tip of the spear for Swiss intelligence. He would never forget how Jani had dispatched the Gestapo agent with a single shot to the head.

He had seen the same anger in Erika and Anya and finally understood it for what it was. He had even seen unexpected flashes of it in the kind and godly Dietrich Bonhoeffer, a man who he now relied on as a mentor.

That same righteous anger had cost Little Otto his life.

Leo was fumbling his way through a fog of revulsion and self-recrimination wandering alone in his private no man's land. It was his carelessness that had cost Little Otto his life and Erika her freedom of that, he was sure. His feckless behavior was of use to no one and dangerous to everyone who relied upon him.

This pretty much summed it up at this moment in his sorry life, Shirt of Nessus, or no Shirt of Nessus, he thought. Worse yet, he had run away into the arms of Jani and Tomi when things got rough. Coward!

Like Heracles, he knew he would rather die than live this way. But first, he would avenge Little Otto and thought he knew how.

* * * * *

Marushka warmed her hands on the steaming pot of tea to ward off the chill from the icy curtains of fog that concealed one city block from the next in Zurich that morning. My God, she marveled, Ursula her vivacious friend and fortune teller had been right again!

Marushka, known in fashionable circles in Berlin as the Countess Maria von Maltzan, was hardly superstitious and before all an eminently rational woman of science. She had received a doctorate in natural sciences in 1933 from the University of Munich and was now within a few months of earning a degree in veterinary medicine. In fact, she had been in Zurich for the week to attend a symposium on animal husbandry and was waiting for the Zurich-Berlin Express.

Ursula, her Hungarian friend and fortune teller, had once told her to check her bank account balance and indeed Marushka had found errors. She was being cheated, and it had been going on for quite some time. On another occasion, she had warned Marushka to beware of something ominous that would happen at 3 o'clock although what that something was, and on which day at 3 o'clock, were not apparent at first.

And then Ursula's prophecy revealed itself. It was a visit from the Gestapo, and Marushka had barely enough time to hide her Jewish lover, Hans, in the large and hollow sofa in her flat before the two Gestapo agents barged into her apartment and accused her of harboring Jews.

She could still remember the encounter in excruciating detail. The ample dandruff on the lapel of the older Gestapo agent, the gray hair prematurely painting the temples of the much younger man. She would also never forget the attractive, fashionably dressed young woman she had seen at the end of her block directing the men to her apartment as she was returning from an errand.

Despite her protests touting her family name and its solid Nazi pedigree, the Gestapo agents spent the better part of an hour searching her apartment and finally turned their attention to the oversized couch in the middle of the small flat. *How do I know someone isn't in there,* the older agent demanded.

You are welcome to look, Marushka replied, blood pounding in her head as she tried to maintain her composure. The older man pulled aside the cushions and tried to pry open the top of what appeared to be a man-sized compartment. When it would not budge, he said, *please open it up.*

I have only had this couch for two weeks, and I don't believe it opens, Marushka replied.

I don't believe you, the older man said. *Someone could easily be hiding in there.*

Enough, Marushka shouted! *I'm tired of this. I have work to do. You think there is someone in the couch, there is one way you can find out! You have a gun, don't you? Take your gun and shoot through the couch but understand one thing. You will pay for the fabric and whatever else is required to repair it.*

She shivered and it was not from the cold in Zurich but from the thought of what she had done. Had it been inspiration or madness? *Go on! Shoot! And then get out! I haven't got all day*, she said to the two flustered Gestapo men. They glared at her as she glared back at them.

Ach, I still don't believe you, the older man growled! Then both Gestapo agents abruptly stormed out of the flat.

And if that were not enough for one day, there was a knock at the back door of the flat minutes later as Marushka sat at the kitchen table, holding her head in her hands, trying to regain her composure. A young Jewish girl had arrived seeking a counterfeit residence permit. *Go away*, Marushka said more abruptly than she had wished. *The Gestapo has just been here*. The terrified girl fled instantly.

Marushka had all but forgotten Hans, who a half hour later undid the latch that held the compartment in the couch shut from the inside. He too was shaking from the encounter with the Gestapo and the thought of what might have happened to him had the Gestapo man called Marushka's bluff and fired his gun into the couch.

The truth of the matter was that the visit from the Gestapo had been long overdue. She had been active since the early days of the Nazi party in underground efforts to save political prisoners and Jews, something she had been able to manage quite nicely at first because as a countess from an old and respected family that supported the Nazis, she was well known in Nazi social circles and kept a high profile there to divert attention from her clandestine activities.

Yet now she worried that her success would prove her downfall if she did not make some adjustments to her approach. As she was drawn deeper into these underground efforts in concert with the Swedish

Lutheran Church in Berlin, more and more Jews sought her help. Now she was the one who needed help.

At first it had been one or two Jews in any given week. Now it could be 10 times that many. Some she would hide in her flat for a day or two before finding another hiding place for them. But the numbers had become overwhelming. There would be no let up now from the Gestapo. They would most certainly be back, and it could prove deadly for those she was trying to save and for herself.

Ursula's most recent note spoke of help from an unexpected quarter on her trip to Zurich. Again, cryptic but she had come to trust her friend's second sight.

And here in the *Bahnhofscafe* was the proof of Ursula's powers. Directly in Marushka's line of sight were three men huddled over a bottle of Akvavit. Two of them were the remarkable boys from KaDeWe who had given her and Alois a champagne shower and the thrill of watching their derring-do.

She remembered that Alois had taken the boys under his wing. She also recalled how clever the boys were in deflecting attention from the two individuals they were trying to protect from the Gestapo.

The help of which Ursula had written was there for the taking. Marushka had no intention of wasting the opportunity.

* * * * *

You owe me that much considering how much champagne you two poured on my head at KaDeWe!

Marushka had lured her quarry to her private first class compartment with the promise of sandwiches of some non-descript wurst and two bottles of excellent Riesling, which she had coerced from the steward responsible for first class. The dining car was now closed for lack of provisions and would remain so for the balance of the war.

Well, how do I put this. I think it was because my mother was such an unjust person and treated me so unjustly that I have such a strong feeling of justice. When I was 13, my father called me to his deathbed to say, 'you know your mother does not like you. Try to be polite and do what you should do.'

So why, Leo was interrupted before he could complete his thought.

My father adored me and I him, she continued. *Our family's estate, and I say this not to boast, is 18,000 acres in Silesia, and I was the youngest of eight children. My father built orphanages and old age homes for the peasants living in our province and once when I was a young girl made me use my savings to help rebuild my former nanny's house which had burned to the ground.*

My mother, well, that's another story altogether. My delivery took 27 hours and since all the other children had been born in three or four hours, she was forever angry with me.

She hated Jews and told me never to marry one. Mother was a Nazi through and through as are my siblings today. As a schoolgirl, I read 'Mein Kampf' and was thoroughly appalled by it and from that moment despised Hitler and all he stood for. At this point, Marushka finally came up for breath.

So, what does all of this have to do with us, Leo finally managed to ask, as he discretely discarded the iridescent brown and green mass that posed as wurst and proceeded to wash down the soggy bread with its few embedded radishes with a gulp of Riesling.

Alois and Charley, whom I see on occasion at the café, are impressed with you both, as was I with your tour de force on the countertop.

Although truth be told, Leo, Charley worries that given the company you keep, you are a cat well along through its nine lives, Marushka replied.

Leo chuckled, *and that doesn't include the company to whom he has introduced me himself.*

I can only imagine, she groaned.

Well as to the what and the why in my case, she added. *I am a proud German and as such am disgusted with my fellow countrymen, who have been cowed by the puny Austrian who seems incapable of speaking our language correctly. But when people live in terror as many now do, they simply cannot use their brains.*

I will make it plain. I have been providing help to political dissidents and Jews for some years now. It is complicated and dangerous work and my proficiency with it is likely to be my undoing.

These poor people, the Jews I mean, no dammit I should say our fellow Germans, are far more numerous in this day than one imagines. Despite all that hobbling midget Goebbels and others are doing to rid the Fatherland of Jews, many still wander about. In the daytime, they might go to the Zoo or anywhere they can blend in and at night dissolve into the woods or sleep in shops or increasingly at my place.

At this, Leo took a few seconds to ensure that no one was listening at the door. Big Otto for his part nervously surveyed the cabin for any sign of a listening device.

Leo and Big Otto weighed whether Marushka was indeed genuine or a devilishly clever Gestapo agent. They were intrigued by Marushka's rather blunt overture and surprised that their exploits at KaDeWe had lived on to this day. They were at the same time wary of their newfound acquaintance and her motives, but Marushka assuaged their concerns by leaving nothing unsaid.

Therein lies the rub, gentlemen, Marushka said ploughing on. *I have been in tough spots in my life but have mostly pulled through because I can think. So, I need allies, partners who can not only think but who are clever and brave. If your KaDeWe escapade proved anything, you are all of the above.*

So, places to hide, food to eat, documents to keep them one step ahead of the Gestapo, no doubt, Leo replied. Marushka beamed like a proud parent.

Leo could never, would never, let go of his desire to seek vengeance for Little Otto's death. Yet, here was perhaps another way to achieve something that Little Otto, the budding philosopher, might have wanted. It was to measure the value of one's own life by weighing the value of the lives one saves.

I am the drop that contains the ocean. Its waves are amazing.
It is beautiful to be a sea hidden within an infinite drop.

Leo thought back to that night long ago in Aleppo, when Anya shared this idea with him and gave him his first glimpse into what made his cousin tick. Marushka like Anya was a warrior who fought to solve this very same riddle.

An impatient Marushka finally broke Leo's reverie, *you know, you two, as well as anyone, I am putting you in a tough spot. There is nothing in it but danger, day in and day out.*

Despite the endless turmoil swirling around him, so much of what Leo had done to date in his young life had fallen into place easily like a finely machined gear falls into its sprocket. Now something was eating at him.

He was stranded on one island as those he admired like Anya and Erika, Dietrich and Mehdi were heroically engaged on another. Had it taken Little Otto's own heroic death to open his eyes? And now there was this stubborn woman, who would not be cowed by the bastards on Wilhelm Strasse and who was not going to take *No* for an answer from him.

It had been a source of endless aggravation to Leo that Anya and Dietrich seemed to speak only in damnable riddles, but the full force of something that Dietrich had written on the flyleaf of *The Book of the Martyrs* finally began to make some sense. It read, *when I was a child, I talked like a child and I thought like a child and reasoned like a child. When I became a man, I put away childish things.*

I think that we prefer tough situations over going to bed with a bad conscience, Leo said after a long silence. A relieved Big Otto met Leo's gaze with a knowing smile and playfully elbowed the *Old Leo* in the ribs.

Excellent! Marushka leaned into them. *We start tonight.*

* * * * *

As the trip back to Berlin with Marushka drew to a close, Leo stood on the small, open platform between train cars as the Berlin Express slowed to a crawl making its way through a series of train yards to Anhalter Bahnhof. It crept past an S-Bahn platform with people milling around an old movie poster that read, *Theresienstadt: The Adlon of the Ghettoes.* The Adlon was the most luxurious hotel in Berlin and Theresienstadt was the notorious concentration camp that was frequently the first stop for deported Jews on their journeys to extermination.

Leo had been away for barely a month but returning to Berlin was much like visiting the ruins of an ancient civilization. As he lurched back and forth each time the train slowed down and sped up, he surveyed a landscape of gray upon gray – gray mist, the rundown buildings with broken windows that always seemed to line train tracks and the now ubiquitous rubble that lay next to scorched holes in the ground that had once been homes or places of work.

Had it been this bad when he left, he mused? Rubble and ruin had now become as much a part of the personality of Berlin as green parks and boisterous beer halls. It was hardly the romanticized rubble of a once wondrous Rome in recline but instead that of a civilization slowly and methodically being pulverized under increasingly adept Allied bombing runs.

By design, there had been no elaborate farewells as he and Big Otto left Marushka at Anhalter Bahnhof. A rendezvous had been set for that night shortly before midnight.

Leo's first thought was to reunite with Mehdi to make sure he was OK and to ask his forgiveness as once did the Prodigal Son ask forgiveness of his father. He hoped Mehdi could provide an update on Erika as well, along with a plan to save her if that were humanly possible.

He then needed to talk to Charley, who had helped engineer his return to Berlin in the first place. Leo had been freed from his velvet shackles at Café Alois, but Charley had sent word that he urgently needed to see Leo. Leo knew this could mean only one thing.

* * * * *

The procession followed the contours of the Serpentine, the curving, snake-like lake in Hyde Park, London. For all intents and purposes, Hyde Park in 1943 was a military installation peppered with bivouacked troops, tanks and artillery pieces along with the occasional bomb crater, which in most cases was being filled with debris created by the Blitz in West London.

The procession was led by two men. One was a tall cerebral looking man with round, horn rimmed glasses and wavy blonde-red hair, who stooped to listen intently to the second, a squat, much older man who was wearing a brimmed sailor's hat along with an ill-fitting pea coat that seemed one size too small for him. He was chewing a cigar and looked like a British bulldog. In point of fact, he was the topmost among them.

His nervous security detail followed at a respectful distance never losing sight of its charge. The bulldog was fuming and without thinking flung the butt of the cigar he had been chewing into the Serpentine, which glanced off one of a group of Egyptian geese gliding languidly toward shore. He instantly regretted having done so as it was his last cigar.

God save us, man, our project is at sixes and sevens thanks to the Americans, the bulldog said.

Sir, the Americans are not the problem, at least not at the moment. Tiresias, a most able undercover operative in Berlin, as you know, is close to Himmler's thinking on the matter and advises that Himmler grows impatient with the slow nature of our response to his entreaties to parties in our Swedish and Portuguese consulates. It would appear that the Americans will take the meeting in or near Zurich unaware of its full import, the taller man replied.

Ah, our blind Tiresias to whom Athena has bestowed the gifts of prophecy and long life! May both gifts prevail against the perils to which we subject you daily, my friend, the bulldog said to no one in particular.

The taller of the two companions was Brendan Bracken, now head of the Ministry of Information and within it the more sinister Political Warfare Executive from which operated a select band of experts in the arts of deception, subterfuge and psychological combat. He had been a devoted acolyte of the man strolling next to him, Winston Churchill, since Churchill's enforced exile from political power during his *wilderness years* in the 1930's when he stood virtually alone in his opposition to the government's policy of appeasement in the face of increasing German, Italian and Japanese militarism.

Theirs had been a ruthless and successful partnership that had tricked Hitler into thinking he could attain peace with Britain in 1941, ostensibly freeing Germany to attack Russia. This, in turn, would expand the conflict in Europe into a world war and create allies of the Russians and Americans, ensuring Hitler's ultimate ruin though at the cost of 20 million lives in the Russian theatre of war alone.

Sir, nothing has changed in our plan to use German peaceable intent to damage the Reich politically, and we can still take full advantage of the yearnings of many among the leading Nazis to engage in peace negotiations and thus sow mistrust among them that will destabilize the regime and, God willing, end this war post haste.

Whilst Canaris and the like are honorable men, Bracken added, *our information suggests they may be on increasingly thin ice of their own making, I fear. It is not for lack of trying that they have not succeeded in dispatching 'Corporal Schicklgruber,' but it is their collective inertia that imperils them now one and all.*

This drew a chortle from his boss who mumbled, *had his name not been changed, one wonders whether a great and mighty nation would have followed to its ultimate ruin, Adolf Schicklgruber!*

Indeed, sir, Bracken replied. *We still have in the cross hairs the only Nazi, whose duplicity in secret dealings with us could bring down the government. He sees himself possessed of the intellect necessary to take us head on in a negotiation. And he controls the strings of the Nazi security apparatus, which could make an internal imbroglio quite ugly for the regime.*

What do you need from me, Bracken, Churchill growled?

Sir, simply a nod, sir, that we are rowing at the same cadence toward Himmler before we go further.

But what of the group that will seek out the Americans in Zurich on Himmler's behalf, Bracken.

What of them, sir?

It would be well if they never reach Switzerland.

* * * * *

In a setting where humor was by far the last impulse to manifest, the sight of the man-child who had once been her ally brought a smile to her face which nearly spilled over its banks into laughter.

Erika had been sitting in a cell barely six feet long and three wide, one of many along a dingy corridor of the same, a tenement of the doomed. In the dark with scant light from the barred outside window competing with the sickly orange glow from the interior of the cell block, she rose from her cot to meet her visitor at the cell door, solid steel at the bottom, steel bars from the waist up.

She was embarrassed not so much because of the way she looked although she knew she had seen better days, her aspirations to be a fashion model now a distant memory. It was because her quarters in the Charlottenburg Women's Prison smelled of lye, urine and the collective body odor of the many women caged here like herself. This was the last place she would have preferred to greet visitors.

Erika's visitor on that day stood gripping the bars tightly, closely watched by the cell block matron whom he turned to and asked for privacy so that Erika might have the freedom to fully confess her sins.

The matron huffed and, like a huge blob of molasses rolling uphill, sauntered stubbornly toward the other end of the cavernous cell block looking back from time to time at the two of them head-to-head at the cell door.

Erika's visitor wore an ill-fitting black suit and white clerical collar but, as he was tall and lanky, he cut a fine figure, nonetheless. His unruly black mane had been properly slicked back and battened down, perhaps for the first time in his life. It leant an air of maturity and gravitas to his boyish good looks, but it was a mother's instinct that told Erika there stood before her a forlorn child fighting back tears behind a brave face.

She whispered, *what do I call you Leo? Reverend? Father?*

For his part, Leo felt the nearly uncontrollable urge to wretch as Erika words rattled around chaotically in a throbbing skull. He knew that if he let his feelings get the better of him now, his time with Erika would be brought to an abrupt end.

He turned toward the cell block matron who met him with a steely glare and turned back toward the cell proclaiming loudly enough for the matron to hear, *may the blessings of the Lord be yours in abundance on this day.*

Don't look again, Leo, the witch has gone off to torment someone else. What in the world possessed you to come here and good gracious how did you manage it, Erika asked?

I am here thanks to a friend in the prison guard whom I owe doubly now, though I would not have it any other way. In point of fact, Leo and Dietrich had prevailed again on Freddie who had been reassigned to Charlottenburg from his post at Grosse Hamburger Strasse after a summary demotion. Too many *guests* at the way station for Jews on their way to the *Adlon of the Ghettoes* and other points east had managed to slip away from their accommodations, which was just as well with Freddie because he could not deny the kind heart that beat under his brown shirt.

Erika, is there anything I can do for you?

Apart from flying me out of here on a magic carpet? What news is there of Little Otto, she replied?

Erika watched Leo's already cadaverous pallor change to something approaching the iridescent green of the rotting meat they served here each day. She flushed red as tears welled in her eyes to join his own.

Ten years, Erika? I must be able to do something to help you or to help Saskia?

Erika had been sentenced by the *Reichskriegsgericht* to 10 years in a *Zuchthaus* or labor prison. The *Reichskriegsgericht* was the court of last resort for offenses committed by members of the Wehrmacht armed forces as well as for civilians accused of subversion, high treason and espionage.

In Erika's case, she had been convicted of subversion and abetting espionage as a member of a group that the Gestapo had coined, the *Rote Kapelle,* or the Red Orchestra. Indeed, neither Erika nor her fellow conspirators had ever heard the term before their arrests.

Well, that problem has been solved for me, Leo, and just today, as a matter of fact. I don't know whether I should be honored or horrified by the Führer's unwanted attention, but he has personally decreed that I shall be tried again. It is not a well-kept secret, I am told, that I shall inevitably be put to death. That terrible man, Manfred Roeder, will be my prosecuting judge once more.

Those bloody criminals, Leo reacted harshly. *The Nazis are not a political party, just damned criminals.*

Careful, Reverend, remember where you are, she quipped and added, *and as you have demonstrated today, my dear fool, we must make our way but do more than try to survive.* Erika hit Leo with a stare that could melt steel.

Do not turn around, Leo, but the old crone has reached the far end of the block and now returns. So, briefly.

Saskia is with her grandparents in the countryside now and is well taken care of. I need two things. At this she gripped Leo's fingers pulling his grip from the bars. *First, paper and a pencil, so I may write to Saskia. Perhaps, your friend can be of assistance with this.*

And, after that, and this is where I am asking much of you, when that day comes, when I walk through the darkness toward the light, put your suit on again and visit me to bear witness to the fact that nobody should ever say I was crying and trembling. I want to end my life laughing, which after Saskia and Graf, is the thing I love the most.

* * * * *

Marushka had encouraged Leo's visit to Erika and postponed their rendezvous at the *Schwedische Kirche* (Swedish Lutheran Church) in Wilmersdorf. She had bigger fish to fry herself at that moment.

She and her lover Hans were harboring a friend of his, who insisted on leaving the relative safety of their flat in broad daylight because this was the only time he could see the woman with whom he was having an affair. These visits were becoming more and more frequent.

The *Mundfunk* or Jewish *Mouthcast* in Berlin, which were urgently whispered warnings among friends to help keep fugitives one step ahead of the Gestapo, told stories of Jews who had gone for their first walk outdoors after years in hiding to be spotted immediately, often by one of their own, a *Greiferin*. Marushka was going to have none of this man's shenanigans because it would take five minutes for the Gestapo to break him, leading to the destruction of all she had worked to achieve.

Marushka tried to negotiate with the man's lover to keep him during the day, while she and Hans would give him a place to sleep at night. However, the woman was unwilling to take the risk. It was for this reason that Leo's debut with Marushka was postponed several days until she could unceremoniously evict the recalcitrant lothario.

Leo had also put off an anxious Charley in favor of reconnecting with Mehdi. He had overlooked how much Mehdi and *Die Bäckerei* meant to him. It was a safe haven from the storm in more ways than one. Leo basked in the warmth of the baking ovens and his friendship with Mehdi. Leo relished helping Mehdi put out the morning batch of bread that was these days a mere shadow of what it once was thanks to shortages of everything that *buying on the black* could no longer fully ameliorate in this brutally December of 1942 as it gave way to the brutally cold January of 1943.

The happy interlude with Mehdi came to an abrupt end two days later when a black Mercedes pulled up in front of the shop from which the bouncer at Café Alois emerged. He was a formidable man with a barrel chest and head that sat squarely on top of bulging shoulders, distorting the pinstripes of his cheap suit. His name was August, and he was often a very busy man at closing time when the Nazi thugs in the front of the house needed more than mild encouragement to call it a night.

August did little more than stand next to the car looking at the shop window knowing it would not be long before someone got the word to Leo he was being summoned. Sure enough, it was barely 30 minutes before Leo appeared and drove off with the man.

They arrived at Café Alois in the lull between lunch and dinner when there was barely a soul in the place but for a lone, disheveled Obergruppenführer sitting at the bar drowning his sorrows amidst the hustle and bustle of staff preparing for the dinner service.

As usual, Charley sat near the piano with another man and sensed Leo's arrival as he approached. *Thank you for gracing us with your presence, my friend.* Considering the pressure that Himmler was putting on Charley to launch the outreach to the Americans, he was in a decidedly good mood to finally *see* Leo again.

Before he could be introduced, the other man at the table stood, clicked his heels as he bowed his head and introduced himself as Hugo Graf von Reinfeld. He was a tall, handsome man with blonde hair, thick eyebrows, chiseled features and an aquiline nose, who impressed Leo as someone who bore himself more like a young German general than a civilian. Leo guessed that he was probably in his mid-30's.

Over steins of pilsner which an obliging Big Otto brought to the table, Leo learned that Hugo was a Prussian nobleman, who was half-Swedish and half-German and had diplomatic standing with the Swedes. As unlikely as it seemed, he was also an occasional Gestapo operative, who as Leo was about to learn, had been designated by Himmler to serve as his emissary to the Americans.

Charley, why me. Emil just did his damnedest to run me out of Zurich, Leo said once Charley had outlined the plan.

Emil is arranging this meeting on behalf of the Americans, and your involvement is at his insistence. He has never met Hugo and sees you as someone he can trust. Even if this were not the case, our patron has decreed that you will be part of the team, like it or not, Charley replied.

I am told, Leo, that you are a man worth his salt as a comrade in difficult circumstances, Hugo said with a wry smile.

That all depends on whether you survive being around me. Not everyone does, Leo responded.

So, to summarize, it is Hugo's role to impress upon the Americans the sincerity of Himmler's request?

Well said, Leo, Charley, replied. *Today is Wednesday, Gentlemen, and you are scheduled to depart on the train to Zurich on Saturday, the meeting to take place on Sunday. You will return on Monday.*

Leo, if I may suggest, I will meet you in Wedding at Die Bäckerei that afternoon, and we will head to Anhalter Bahnhof from there. I will have our travel papers with me. We will, if challenged, present ourselves as two agents of the Gestapo in search of a fugitive. Is that acceptable to you?

My first Gestapo assignment? I am honored. Yes, Leo replied cheekily.

Then I think we should drink to the success of our mission and to a long life, Charley proclaimed without irony, summoning Big Otto. *Noch drei Pils, bitte!*

* * * * *

As dusk approached, Leo decided to walk the roughly three kilometers from the café to the *Schwedische Kirche* in Wilmersdorf, where he would rendezvous with Marushka and her compatriots but not before one regular stop. Café Alois was barely one-half block from KaDeWe on Wittenbergplatz, and he now routinely left a few counterfeit ration cards and bread from the ovens of Café Alois with Marta at the Épernay counter at KaDeWe.

Today, it was two loaves of *Katenbrot* (barn bread), a traditional bread from the farms of Northern Germany. This dark brown, coarsely textured, strong tasting bread was the perfect complement to Bratwurst. The head chef at Café Alois caustically referred to it as the *Bread of Sorrows* because its baking invariably signaled Himmler's arrival for Bratwurst Night.

These days, the Épernay counter at KaDeWe had lost some of its effervescent luster and featured a bleak sparkling wine from Romania but, if you were in the know, there was always French champagne to be had for a price. Leo enjoyed lingering with the feisty Marta, who was not shy about giving him the lay of the land as she saw it. Marta struck Leo as not shy about anything.

That day, that time when we first met, the only signs of war other than the many uniforms on the street were the constant news reports of the excellent progress we were making, the Fatherland that is, she said. *Heil Hitler,* she added for comic effect as she launched her right arm into the air. A few distracted patrons of KaDeWe heiled back as they walked by the counter.

You are right, Marta, we had no feeling for the war and felt no deprivation. Remember the crowds that swarmed this place. Everyone felt somewhat prosperous, buoyed by a sense of national purpose and resolve.

Don't see it now, Leo, do you. The rumors coming from the East. God help us. And from the West? We have seen what a single bomb can do, and God help us when the dress rehearsal is over, and we look up to see American bombers too. This drew a half-hearted chuckle from Leo, who fought off the sinking feeling of knowing what a single bomb could do to him personally.

Now we wait with the fatalistic stubbornness of all Germans to survive whether you are Nazi or anti-Nazi because the bombs do not choose one over the other, Marta added. *They simply mutilate, suffocate and burn us all —women and children, our dogs and cats and the small things we cherish so dearly that when lost hurt more than death itself.*

His visit concluded, Leo bundled up against the curtains of frost that hung in the air as he left KaDeWe. One of those patrons of KaDeWe who had reflexively returned Marta's Hitler salute followed closely. The Reverend Doctor Martin Sauter who had been in the doghouse with his patron, Goebbels, saw an opportunity to wheedle his way back into the good graces of the Reichsminister of Propaganda because he knew that wherever this subversive boy was going, trouble and perhaps his own salvation would be waiting.

* * * * *

Leo arrived at the *Schwedische Kirche* in a part of Berlin that struck him as another world altogether. The church itself was the extension of a large and elegant villa on an equally elegant avenue flanked right and left by an honor guard of ancient Linden trees. To the rear of the villa, there was a sprawling garden that seemed to extend as far as the eye could see. It was as if, Leo mused, someone had transplanted the Tiergarten in Wilmersdorf.

Marushka greeted him warmly and introduced him to Erik Perwe, the vicar of the church and his wife Martha who offered Leo a bite to eat. Judging from the aroma wafting through the wood paneled vicarate, Martha was a very good cook indeed, and Leo regretted declining the offer the instant he did so.

Leo would soon come to see Perwe for what he was – a man on a heroic mission to save as many human beings as possible. Leo noticed a number of Perwe's *guests,* as he toured the sprawling complex. A few were engaged in the normal routines of church life including clearing the evening meal from the assembly hall. Others seemed content to linger in the shadows.

Our numbers here grow, and we need 100 Marushka's. She has persuaded me that just one of you comes as close to that as humanly possible, Perwe said, as he paused to take the measure of the tobacco in the bowl of his pipe after taking the measure of the boy. Leo was sure he caught a look of worry in Perwe's eyes as he relit his pipe.

Perwe continued with a masterpiece of understatement, *Leo, we have been modestly successful in, how do I say it? Well, I will just say it. We are able at times to purchase Jews from certain members of the Gestapo. I would like to think that their conscience motivates them to do so, but let it be a commercial transaction if it must because the objective is what matters, saving our fellow human beings. I believe that Marushka plans to introduce you this evening to our dear friend, the bona fide genius who dazzles us with this death-defying high wire act with the Gestapo. And those who aren't purchased like a kilo of potatoes now gravitate to us in some numbers encouraged by the Mundfunk or driven by sheer desperation.*

Reverend Perwe, how is it that you are able to get away with having so many of them here, Leo asked.

Our local gendarmerie looks the other way, but there are limits to their forbearance, so thanks to Marushka, we have created a network of safe houses that we use because our flock must stay constantly on the move. We have also been successful in sending a healthy number to Sweden in the guise of Swedish or dual Swedish and German citizens, Perwe replied.

Leo, we have a few immediate problems that could benefit from someone with your skills, Perwe continued. *We believe we are now under close Gestapo surveillance and need someone the authorities in this district do not know. The Gestapo are a fairly provincial lot here in Wilmersdorf and would not know of your exploits elsewhere.*

Next, the numbers we are managing here have become unmanageable, and we must find a bolder strategy to get them out of Germany. And if that were not enough, the remaining challenge is that we have lost the source of the counterfeit identity papers that make this all possible. The wonderfully talented and devout man who produced them fell victim to last month's British air raid in Friedenau.

So, there you have it. Leo, a small number of us meet often, and we hope we can count you as one of us. For now, go forth with Marushka, Leo, and in the name of God almighty, outwit, disrupt, undercut our adversary at every turn. Lives depend on it, Perwe said shaking Leo's hand energetically to end their first meeting.

There was something remarkably familiar about Perwe, and Leo recognized almost immediately that he and Dietrich, both devout men of the cloth, were not about to turn the other cheek in the face of Nazi oppression. It would be exceedingly dangerous work that would make his exploits in the black market look like child's play. Yet he could no longer ignore his natural fellowship with Dietrich, Perwe, Marushka, Erika, Ingrid, Anya and Little Otto. Their world view had won, but so had Leo.

* * * * *

Marushka, you buy Jews from the Gestapo? I can't think of anything more illogical or dangerous, Leo said.

Leo, the maestro who has perfected the art of exchanging goods for lives, is waiting for us in the sacristy. The church has an abundance of cash at hand as well as liquor, believe it or not, and both are the currency of the realm or should I say Reich, Marushka replied. *I am sure the two of you will become fast friends.*

Leo kept his cynical sense of humor in check and followed Marushka through the long and narrow hallways of the vicarate to a small door. Marushka in the lead barreled through the door into the sacristy followed by Leo.

Leo, I want to introduce you to Hugo Graf von Reinfeld, she said.

Hello again, Leo, was all Hugo said with a warm smile.

11. WHEN CHRIST CALLS A MAN, HE BIDS HIM COME AND DIE

Leo and Hugo threw themselves into the work at hand and saved the subject of Hugo's tightrope act for their trip to Zurich two days later. There was much Leo wanted to know. Hugo must have shared their prior connection with Marushka because she did not seem surprised by their familiarity.

Later, Hugo would fill in the blanks, *Leo, I spent two years as a student in Great Britain and later two years with our embassy in London. I developed a voracious appetite for the playwright William Shakespeare who wrote in his play, the Tempest, 'full fathom five thy father lies, of his bones are coral made, those are pearls that were his eyes, nothing of him that doth fade.'*

I was recruited to the Gestapo by my father's friends in the military high command to keep an eye on the Gestapo so as to ensure they were not keeping an eye on those friends. Perverse but true.

My orientation to the work of the Gestapo required a trip East to a Konzentrationslager within sight of the Polish border. Jews, our countrymen, were being gassed to death. Their teeth were then extracted and heated to melt out the gold. Their bones were ground for fertilizer and their fat converted to soap. The factory processing the bodies consumed more than two hundred of them a day, and I was forced to witness this.

Had I wished to return to Berlin with a lampshade made of their skin, they would have been pleased to oblige and were just downright giddy about it. My disgust was so great that I obsessively repeated this verse from Shakespeare to get myself through that visit with some semblance of sanity. The memory of those I saw will never fade.

Little was accomplished their first night together, which ended early the next morning when Leo returned to Oderberger Strasse to help Mehdi put out the morning batch, except for an orientation to the work that Marushka and Hugo were doing in the orbit of the Swedish Lutheran Church in Berlin. It was an impressively large operation frequently involving the Swedish legation in Berlin, which would assist with the *Exportation* of illegals by sending them to the port of Lübeck with false papers in the midst of a group of actual Swedish-German travelers to board a ship to Sweden.

Leo knew that he would need to be at the top of his game if he were to contribute in any meaningful way to this effort. These were not trifling people. In addition, the scope of the effort, however impressive, made mistakes more likely and deadly.

Leo and Hugo rendezvoused at *Die Bäckerei* at the appointed time on Friday in the snowy twilight and decided to walk as far as Hackescher Markt to catch the S-Bahn onward to Anhalter Bahnhof. The frigid air had moved out of Berlin and something wet and warm taken its place launching showers of large snowflakes that looked like feathers and seemed to cleanse the air of the fretfulness that characterized daily life in Nazi Germany.

Leo and Hugo relished the refreshing walk – two characters in a Christmas snow globe shaken once than once more. Hugo was dressed in a camel hair great coat crowned with the customary Gestapo fedora, while Leo reprised his role as a Catholic priest, his clerical garb hidden under an overcoat hastily procured *on the black* by Mehdi. He wore no hat but had again slicked back his unruly mane of hair, which over the course of the walk froze in place.

In the beginning before the Reverend Perwe's small enterprise became the KaDeWe of illegal emigration, things were manageable. He and Marushka were a formidable team. They still are for that matter. Through our connections to each other among the Prussian nobility, Marushka and I met shortly after my return from the camp in Poland and the rest is history, Hugo told Leo as they strolled.

It was a dangerous but relatively simple matter for Perwe to use the baptismal records of individuals born of Swedish parents in Berlin. After checking into whether the family in question was still in Berlin, they would create a past for an illegal with the help of new documents supplied by our now departed printer and endorsed from time to time by the Swedish legation and the sympathetic gendarmes at the local police station.

In the case of the police, that avenue has been largely closed to us now because the Gestapo has placed an agent in their waiting room to observe comings and goings. I fear now for Perwe's safety because this move by the Gestapo suggests he is now a suspect. The church is literally across the street from the station.

What impressed Leo most about Hugo was here was a man with money, poise, intelligence and connections, who did not need to help anyone but yet he did. He was so accomplished and well placed that he was one of the few people that Himmler would turn to for a sensitive mission to the Americans.

The Reichsführer is like a viper, Leo, who will wrap itself around a limb like a pet animal, its venom-injecting fangs folded back in its mouth when not in use. One is lulled into a false sense of security by its caress until in an instant, likely one's last, it strikes, Hugo said. *Let us hope that our success with this mission will charm the viper for just a little longer, so we can remain engaged in Perwe's and Marushka's crusade.*

Leo probed Hugo about their various efforts to create documents for Perwe's *flock. Each police precinct has its own card file of the identities of those living in the precinct, correct?*

Yes, Hugo replied looking ahead toward the elevated train tracks of Hackescher Markt, which had just come into sight.

I assume then that there is some central card file in the event that the card file of a precinct is lost to fire or under present circumstances Allied bombs, Leo asked?

Yes, normally it is kept in an underground vault at the Alex, Berlin's police headquarters.

Know it well, Leo interjected.

However, Hugo continued, *the file was moved at the beginning of 1942 to an undisclosed setting in the countryside. Where is a closely guarded secret and as such it is currently of little real use to us or anyone,* Hugo replied.

What are you thinking, Leo? But before Leo could respond, Hugo added, *let's save that answer for another time when we are alone,* as they climbed the stairs to the S-Bahn platform and melted into the crowd.

In a city where much was going to the dogs, the U-Bahn and S-Bahn systems still ran with remarkable efficiency, and one could still set his watch by the train schedules. Although it would not be long before the Allies would put an end to that.

As they later crossed the small plaza between the U-Bahn station and Anhalter Bahnhof approaching its ornate triple arch and just beyond the outsized zinc doors of the station's main entrance, two men who had been standing in the shadows of the arch approached them from right and left. *Gentlemen, you will please come with us*, one said.

There was something vaguely familiar to Leo about the one who spoke. Hugo began to protest and Leo traced the contours of the Khanjar hooked to his belt, but the man who did the talking opened his coat to reveal a holster cradling an impressively large handgun.

Please, Gentlemen, we do not want to make a scene.

The two promptly escorted Hugo and Leo to a waiting Mercedes sedan near the train station's side entrance and opened the door to the large passenger compartment. Hugo and Leo were instructed to be seated facing the rear of the cab and a single passenger, who struck one at first as a woolly creature of the forest. *He, she, it* was cloaked in an impressive full length fur coat topped by a matching *shapka*, the round Russian fur hat.

Hello Leo, Jani said from somewhere inside the mound of fur.

Before the dumbfounded Leo could answer, Jani turned to Hugo and said, *hello cousin.*

Hugo nodded and replied quizzically, *hello to you as well, cousin.*

* * * * *

It had been an hour since the Reverend Doctor Martin Sauter had been ushered into the presence of the Reichsminister of Propaganda and Gauleiter of Berlin. Goebbels had asked to see him before sending him on to Himmler with his information about the subversive activity centered in the Swedish Lutheran Church.

His meeting with Himmler would not take place for another five hours, and the Reverend Doctor Martin Sauter worried Goebbels, whom he had never seen quite so agitated, was just getting warmed up and would hold him captive until then with his free-wheeling tirade about this, that and the other thing.

Sauter, the Führer has made fewer public appearances and broadcasts as the war has progressed, so I have stepped in to address the bedeviling military setbacks like last year's thousand-bomber raid on Cologne, the Allied victory at the Second Battle of El Alamein and now this catastrophic defeat at the Battle of Stalingrad. These are difficult matters to put before our war weary countrymen. We must work hard to maintain an appropriate level of public morale about the military situation, one that is neither too optimistic nor too grim, by involving them in the war effort on the home front. This challenge, with which I am wrestling at this hour, would crush a man of lesser intellect, Goebbels said.

Sir, our Führer must appreciate your heroic efforts as do we all, Sauter responded slyly sneaking a peek at his watch.

Ah yes, but the people around him. What do I hear yesterday! What!

What, Sir?

The Führer wishes to water down the beer and degrade the quality of cigarettes so that more of each can be produced. That is Göring and Speer talking. My God, cigarettes are of such low quality now, it would be impossible to make them any worse, Goebbels added, taking a short gulp of air and then soldiering on.

Even our measures to energize our countrymen by investing them in the concept of 'total war' have careened off the tracks. My speech at last night's rally aroused the audience to commit to this path. I could see it in their eyes, hear it in their soaring hurrahs. The German people realize that it is the only way to stop the simian Bolshevik.

I remember, sir, the decree of just a few week ago. The Führer's call to total war that is. It was as I recall Wednesday the 13th of January. It was my youngest daughter's birthday. Both events inspired such happiness in me, proclaimed Sauter, at his obsequious best!

Ah, my dear Reverend, our well-conceived proposals to close businesses not essential to the war effort, conscript women into the labor force, and enlist men in previously exempt occupations into the Wehrmacht have been undercut by the weak-kneed. Göring now demands that his favorite restaurants in Berlin should remain open, and that fool Lammers, who has the brains of a movie usher, successfully lobbied Hitler to have women with children exempted from conscription, even if they had childcare available, Goebbels said plaintively, spinning a quarter turn on his good leg like a child throwing a temper tantrum.

God willing, you will prevail, Sauter replied, stopping Goebbels dead in his tracks. Raised a Roman Catholic, Goebbels now believed in neither God nor his conscience. God was a malleable postulation at best for him now to be shaped and reshaped to promote his immediate political objectives. *How do I use the almighty as a bludgeon with my rivals under present circumstance,* Goebbels mused silently?

Herr Reichsminister, your victories are many, your obstacles trifling because you inevitably overcome those mere mortals who stand in your way. If unctuous behavior possessed a high gear, Sauter was by this point in overdrive.

Sir, I await your update on our great leap forward against the Jew and have one of my own. As you requested, I have spoken with the leaders of the Reichskirche and have been assured that one and all will rally to your cause when the action you contemplate begins, Sauter added.

Sauter, over the course of the last year, as you know, we have dealt a heavy blow to the 40,000 insolent, plutocratic Yids still remaining in Berlin, barely one quarter of the city's Jewish population when we took power nearly a decade ago. Through various other means, we believe that we have now reduced the 40,000 still further by a third. Progress, yes. Yet, Judenfrei we are not. Too many remain, many in plain sight.

One is too many, sir.

Well put, Sauter.

I have finally gained the high ground against Speer in the debate as to whether the skilled Jews working in the munitions industry can be replaced with skilled workers from the conquered territories. They of course can, and the Führer is now firmly in my camp. So, the work of organizing February's round-up to render Berlin Judenfrei once and for all moves apace.

He did not call them the children of Abraham but a 'brood of vipers,' sir, Martin Luther's words not my own, Sauter intoned. *Smite them all, sir. It is God's work.*

* * * * *

Sauter arrived at Himmler's office punctually. After several hours with the lugubriously petulant Goebbels, even a meeting with the always prickly mass murderer would be a breath of fresh air.

It was not to be, however, and he was redirected to a conference room where the reliably 100-proof Kaltenbrunner and Sepp Lange were waiting. They introduced him to a third man, one Andre Fuchs, and a fox he was. He was one of Panzinger's most adept predators in the *Sonderkommando Rote Kapelle*, the ruthless Gestapo unit that had effectively rolled up one *Rote Kapelle* group after another in Germany, Belgium, France, the Netherlands, Switzerland and Italy, including Erika and her accomplices.

Fuchs was a squat Alsatian who reminded Sauter of the moles that left little dirt mounds in his back yard replete with a pointed snout, a widow's peak that seemed to start in the middle of his forehead and small beady eyes under a thick unibrow. The good Reverend would come to learn that Fuchs specialized in the disappearance of many of those captured by his unit. The big fish got a show trial; the little fish became fish food.

Sauter found it disconcerting that Fuchs stared at him through those beady eyes for the entire meeting. At intervals of a minute or two, a demonstrable vertical tick would distort the left side of Fuchs' face. It reminded Sauter of repetitive lightning strikes during a heavy thunderstorm.

Sir, where the boy goes, trouble always follows or perhaps was there in the first place, Sauter said addressing Kaltenbrunner.

The pastor there, this Perwe fellow, has come to our attention recently. He seems to be a clever man who covers his tracks well, Kaltenbrunner replied.

At this Fuchs made it a point of making eye contact with Kaltenbrunner but said nothing. Sauter was beginning to wonder if the mole was mute.

Fuchs's meaning was clear, however, and it sent chills down Sauter's spine. *Fuchs you may get your chance here too. I would like nothing better than to make a statement to our Swedish friends in the legation by hanging Perwe from a lamp post, a specialty of yours, I am told,* Kaltenbrunner said. Sepp Lange nodded appreciatively having witnessed Fuchs's handiwork.

They must learn once and for all that they cannot play fast and loose with their alliance to the Reich, Kaltenbrunner continued. *But let us see where all this leads before we exact our just retribution. My hunch is that when we eventually spring our trap, we will catch much more than the boy and a cleric.*

This is good work on the boy, Sauter, Kaltenbrunner added. Kaltenbrunner did not particularly like Sauter, who never struck him as a deeply committed Nazi. Instead, he thought of him rather unkindly as a sniveling opportunist who thrived on licking Goebbels' boots. Yet, Kaltenbrunner was willing to give credit where credit was due if only fleetingly.

And Sauter, what of your efforts with the other matter that you brought to our attention. Frau Solf and her traitorous coffee klatches. Sauter grimaced at the word *traitorous* and Kaltenbrunner seeing this went for the jugular, *Sauter, it was you who brought this to us in the first place. Are you wasting our time? If what you say is true, what else would you call these people?*

Out of the corner of his eye, the good Reverend could see Fuchs smirk. His discomfiture at Kaltenbrunner's probing was ambrosia for the sadistic little rodent, Sauter fumed silently.

Sir, they are a closely knit group and as such have proven nearly impenetrable. However, Elena, my lovely wife and Elisabeth von Thadden, a leader of this group, were contemporaries at Reifenstein school in Baden-Baden although Elena was a year behind von Thadden. Nonetheless, their families were close friends, so there is a bond there to be exploited, Sauter said.

Promising, Kaltenbrunner replied somewhat absent-mindedly. *Sauter, if your wife is able to gain access to von Thadden, there is a young man I would like to have accompany her. He is erudite, well-educated and might be someone capable of insinuating himself into a group of the so-called intelligentsia and provide us with the hard evidence that we require to crush this group once and for all.*

* * * * *

I take it, cousin, you are not in town for the opera?

Good God no, I hate opera, as you know, Hugo.

Jani, as much as I would love to visit, Leo and I have a train to catch and are running late, a mildly peeved Hugo said as he glanced at his wristwatch.

Well, there has been a change of plan. Somewhere inside the station or on the platform or on the train itself there will be people waiting for you who wish you no good. Ironically, it is the 'boys in white hats' who want to stop you as that insufferable American who is in our care would say. That is to say, Hugo, our side, the good guys, or more precisely the British, would like to put an end to your mission by putting an end to you two.

They were made aware of your mission by the same double agent who also warned us of the harm to befall you. Seems the man has a terribly guilty conscience about betraying you in the first place. Ah, Berlin is such a complicated place.

Leo, whose presence was largely overlooked up to that point, finally jumped into the conversation, albeit somewhat feebly, *cousins*?

You ain't seen nuthing yet, as our pet American would like to say, Jani replied, the grin of a Cheshire cat evident once again. Its magnetism left Leo groping for words.

Hugo threw Leo a lifeline, *yes, Leo, we grew up together in Sweden though Jani is a few years younger than I. Her mother and my father are sister and brother. She was the tomboy of the family who liked to fish and hunt with the men and more often than not bested us. She is among other things a crack shot.*

I have noticed, Leo replied.

Jani jumped in, *and Hugo is the scholar of the family and more times than not the conscience, but this is not the time to reminisce, I am afraid. There is work to be done, and I am here to get you to the rendezvous point with the American emissary from Dulles.*

And before you ask, Jani continued, *we are on our way to Teltow and will arrive at the train station there in about an hour. From there we board a train to Munich instead of Zurich and upon arrival there we shall whisk you to the rendezvous about an hour's drive south.*

Questions?

Lovely, Hugo responded, *the Bavarian Alps are magnificent at this time of the year.*

Ah so, Jani replied.

Much of the rest of the trip to Teltow was spent in silence. Hugo seemed uninformed about Leo's prior relationship with Jani, and neither Leo nor Jani was forthcoming about it. The conversation turned to the Americans.

His name is Wayne Lane, and he is either brilliant and acts like a buffoon to disguise this fact or is indeed a buffoon and we overestimate the sincerity of the American side in these discussions. I am agnostic on this point as my assignment this weekend is simply to keep you both alive, Jani said matter of factly. *He is being entertained now by our friends near Munich.*

Why Swiss intelligence? Hugo and Leo asked the same question at the same instant, drawing laughter from Jani. *The American OSS and its representative, Allen Dulles, are stationed in Bern. Dulles is quite the swashbuckling figure much like his boss Donovan and quite entertaining when he wants to be. We collaborate with both against the Nazis and Fascists, particularly across the French and Italian borders,* Jani replied.

If Jani had done it to make him jealous, that is suggest more than a professional relationship with Dulles, it worked, and Leo spent the rest of the ride to Teltow agonizing over the meaning of *entertaining.* It did not help that Jani, who was facing him wrapped her feet around his in the dark well of the spacious passenger compartment, a coquettish smile barely visible in the shadows cast by the voluminous mound of animal fur in which she was buried.

The trip to Teltow and onward to Munich passed without incident. Hugo was preoccupied with his notes for the meeting and Leo with his emotions about the girl who would be his bodyguard for the trip. There was little he could say or do in Hugo's presence that he wanted so badly to say and do with her alone.

They were met immediately when the train pulled into Munich in the wee hours of the morning and ushered through an obscure gate at the end of the train platform to an idling truck. Leo had a difficult time in the darkness deciphering the markings on the side of the large, enclosed truck except for what appeared to be large barrels and smiling faces.

A burly young man wearing clerical garb under a quilted jacket, whispered politely but firmly, *please climb into the cargo hold and go to the far end. We have blankets to keep you warm during the ride ahead.*

The young man introduced himself as Brother Stephen. Leo was intrigued by Brother Stephen's tonsured haircut. The crown of his head was shaven and surrounded by a neatly clipped ring of hair. Leo could not help but notice the layer of frost that had collected on Brother Stephen's bald pate.

Once they had assembled in the back of the truck amidst the blankets with a single kerosene lamp for light, Brother Stephen, addressed them again, *please help yourself, we have bread and cheese and a bit of lingonberry jam. This will tide you over until we arrive at the abbey. Our guests from Zurich await your arrival, at which time we will put out a more complete and convivial meal for you.*

Having expropriated old man Schultheiss's truck for one illicit excursion or another, Leo now recognized his surroundings for what they were. The subtle hint of hops and yeast in the air and the slightly sour smell of the wood from the barrels confirmed that they were in the back of a beer delivery truck. Given the number of barrels and their size, this was more than a casual operation.

Yes, Leo, we are Benedictine monks and have rather large brewing and distilling operations at the abbey, Ettal Abbey that is, Brother Stephen said. *This is not uncommon for our order. I would be most happy to show them to you during your stay with us. We have several varieties of beer and also produce a rather nice herbal liqueur called Kloster Ettal.* As a matter of fact, I have a flask here if you and your companions would like to sample it.

Hugo declined, while Leo and Jani gladly accepted. After a couple of healthy gulps, Leo could no longer feel what had once been his cold feet. Jani's pie-eyed grin evoking their first evening together in Zurich, suggested that the concoction was also working its magic on her.

I know this place, Leo said. *Dietrich, I mean to say my friend, Reverend Dietrich Bonhoeffer, spent time there as the guest of the Abbot. Am I right,* Leo asked?

Yes indeed, Leo, Brother Stephen replied, *it was roughly two years ago. He is an impressive and Godly man, and we saw little difference between his beliefs and ours but for the terminology we each employ to convey these beliefs as obscurely as possible. He is above all a principled man who stands shoulder to shoulder with us in the present struggle. He and Father Rupert, our current Abbot, became fast friends.*

Brother Stephen continued, *the Reverend Bonhoeffer left us with a simple but profound meditation that redounds to this day when my fellow monks and I congregate. He told us that he is haunted by the thought of being judged not by the things he did but by the things he did not do. A challenging idea. A most impressive man, indeed.*

Sounds like Dietrich, a now chemically irreverent Leo said without thinking.

What are we likely to encounter between here and the monastery, Hugo asked Brother Stephen?

Ah yes, the abbey is on the edge of the Garmisch-Partenkirchen valley, an idyllic place surrounded by Germany's highest peaks. There is quite a large military installation there. It is in fact a massive military hospital with a small garrison. The wounded come from everywhere. As to military patrols, as the war drags on, the troop levels at the camp have dwindled as units are reassigned to one war zone or the other. Never say never, but the odds are that we will not encounter a German patrol. This, thank the Lord, gives us a certain amount of tactical flexibility in working with Jani and her colleagues to transport fugitives across the border to Switzerland.

Leo shot Brother Stephen a questioning look. *The passage is not for the faint of heart,* Brother Stephen responded, *but we do what we must in these trying times. It is a 30-hour hike through very rough country to our friends in Rorschach on the Swiss border. We have not lost anyone yet, praise God. Indeed, we have two young gentlemen about to make the trip this evening, but I have said too much.*

Jani added, *we have skilled Alpine rangers meet them halfway. Swiss of course. Tomi and I take over in Rorschach on Lake Constance to conduct the debriefing before sending them on their way. There are two or three teams like ours.*

Brother Stephen used this moment as an opportunity to pop the cork back into the flask of Kloster Ettal, fold his hands and close his eyes either to sleep or meditate.

The Ettal Abbey dating back to 1330 and the village of Ettal sit astride a small plateau at the apex of a series of wooded ridges on the southern spur of the Amergau Alps running North-South from Bavaria to the province of Tirol in Austria. It is one of the largest Benedictine monasteries in Europe.

Leo and Jani managed to convince Brother Stephen to let them ride in the cab for the last thirty minutes of the trip. She sat at the window fingering the mother of pearl handle of the small 38 caliber Walther PPK in her lap, the same gun she had used to dispatch the Gestapo agent before Leo's eyes in Zurich some months before.

As the truck lumbered up the steep dirt track in the predawn, the proverbial time when it is *darkest before the dawn,* they saw the massive hulk of the monastery rise from the dark and what appeared at its center to be a large, bullet shaped church soaring above the sprawling chapterhouse. Lights shone in the inner courtyard of the complex reflecting off the face of the church and the low cloud cover into which its three spires disappeared.

Eventually, the truck reached the level of the monastery and pulled around to the back toward another large building, which turned out to be the brewery, and stopped in a courtyard separating it from the stables. Father Rupert Mayer arrived to greet each of them warmly as they disembarked from the beer truck.

The vigorous Father Rupert shone brightly even in the faint light of the darkened stable yard thanks to his shock of wavy blonde hair whose weightless bangs bounced with each movement, flickering at the top of his head as if they were flames. He did not sport a tonsured coif, Leo would learn later, to preserve some anonymity in his resistance activities. Add to all of this a lantern jaw and Adonis-like physique, and the casual observer might readily consider enlisting in monastic life as a salubrious alternative to taking the waters at Baden-Baden.

The visitors were shown to their rooms, which were little more than monastic cells, and given a few hours to regroup. They were told that the first meeting with the American delegation and a meal would commence shortly after their short rest.

Father Rupert made it a point to intercept Leo as he emerged from his room later having changed from clerical garb to something more familiar, his ever present Khanjar concealed by a light jacket. *I understand that you know Dietrich. How is he,* Father Rupert asked?

He is in it up to his ears, Father. But he would not have it any other way, Leo responded with more angst than he had intended.

When you see him, please convey my regards and my offer, first made when he was here, to provide passage to safer ground. Karl Barth, who writes from Basel, is a brilliant and influential theologian. I could see the same future for Dietrich. We must preserve that intellect of his and his rare ability to penetrate the inscrutability of Christian faith.

Would doing what you offer Dietrich be good enough for you?

Father Rupert recoiled slightly at Leo's cheeky question and cocked his head to one side smirking. Touché.

He took the measure of the young man before him whom he had perhaps underestimated. Slapping Leo on the back, his smirk now an appreciative grin, Father Rupert said, *you and I must speak again before you return to Berlin. But for now, a meal and our American friends await.*

* * * * *

Father Rupert led Leo past a long line of wooden doors beyond which snoring monks lay and downstairs to the darkened refectory where the monks typically broke bread. The refectory was a huge space with whitewashed walls ascending to a high vaulted ceiling held aloft by huge wooden beams that loomed over long tables of the same dark oak. The aromas of food and oiled wood danced in the air and by the time they had reached the door of a smaller room near the head of the refectory, the sound of Leo's growling stomach echoed in the cavernous room.

Father Rupert and Leo were the last to arrive, and as Hugo stepped aside to let them pass, Father Rupert introduced Leo to a hulking man who towered over everyone in the room from across a table set with a veritable feast. *Leo, may I introduce Wayne Lane.*

Leo's hand was engulphed in a paw two or three times the size of his own which the American shook heartily. Lane wore green combat fatigues and a belt with a large metal clasp emblazoned with a golden horseshoe. Tracking Leo's eyes, Lane said, *my lucky horseshoe. It comes in handy these days.*

And let me also introduce you to his associate, Father Rupert continued. *Like Jani, she is a longstanding friend of the Abbey and at least on this visit, represents the Americans. Her name is Mary-Tay and in all the years we have known her, she has never once shared her surname with us. Mysterious, she is indeed!*

A striking young woman with raven hair pulled back from her forehead had been standing inches away from Leo talking to Jani and now turned to acknowledged Father Rupert's humor by skewering him with her dark, piercing eyes and sardonic smile.

She turned to fix her gaze on a dumbfounded Leo.

Hello, cousin, she said.

* * * * *

Jani had been the only person to attend the meeting that momentous night who was aware of Anya's relationship to Leo. Anya deftly redirected the interest of the rest of their companions away from her family history to the sumptuous meal before them.

This did little to satisfy Leo's curiosity about Anya's role in all of this. As they had taken their seats, she took him by the arm and whispered, *I have heard reports here and there about you and want to know more about what has kept you busy since Sweden. We will talk later.*

It had in fact been Anya who had brokered the meeting for the American side through Emil and Charley with Jani serving as the liaison from Swiss intelligence. It was also Charley, a double agent for the British, the fabled Tiresias, who nearly got them killed. Charley had managed to warn Jani at the 11th hour to correct his mistake. Berlin was indeed a complicated place.

Wayne Lane, who had recently been assigned to the field and to Dulles, was a ne'er-do-well with political connections and three years of college German who had been forced on Donovan who, who in turn, forced him on Dulles, who reluctantly put him in the field under Anya's watchful eye.

To his credit, the garrulous Wayne Lane tried his hardest to fit in at dinner and told one American joke after the other in halting German to a polite but largely perplexed audience. Apparently, his language professors at Princeton had not taught him that one culture's sense of irony does not necessarily translate to another's, so most of his humor flew straight over the heads of his counterparts.

At what seemed a preordained moment, Father Rupert and Jani excused themselves to consult with Brother Stephen, who was leaving with the two British flyers. Anya had the table cleared including the beer much to Leo and Wayne Lane's chagrin ready to get down to the real business at hand.

Anya set the ground rules for the discussion – the German delegation would lay out its proposal and Wayne Lane on behalf of Dulles and Donovan would neither reject nor accept any proposal but layout the American view of parameters and possibilities. Leo was intrigued by Anya's central role in the negotiation and the fact that she appeared to work for the Americans. For whom had she been working in Stockholm, he wondered?

Leo was also impressed with Hugo's suave and articulate advocacy for the indefensible position of a mass murderer. He managed to impress Anya and Lane with his sincerity when he pointed to the principle that this was not about Himmler's future but was a unique opportunity for those assembled there to save countless thousands of lives on both sides of the conflict.

As sincere as Hugo's intentions were, the terms he proposed were so hard to swallow they would have choked a python. Himmler sought to convey that he and a select band of men in the SS could and would topple Hitler if the allies would agree to maintaining the frontiers of Germany as they were before Autumn of 1939, which would have preserved the annexation of Austria in 1938 and the remilitarization of the Rhineland in 1936.

For all Wayne Lane's bravado, he listened carefully. Leo was particularly impressed with his poker face. He was nearly as inscrutable as the young woman sitting next to him.

Hugo asked on Himmler's behalf whether the Americans would accept the status quo in Europe and be prepared to make a separate peace shutting out the Russians from any part of the discussion.

Wayne Lane first looked to Anya for the response, but she nodded to indicate he should take the lead. He started by dropping a bombshell.

Just before making the trip here, we were informed that your General Paulus has surrendered a force of over 90,000 souls effectively ending the siege of Stalingrad. Rather than take this bit of news badly, both Hugo and Leo were quietly elated because it brought the end of the conflict closer. Their poker faces were easily the rivals of Wayne Lane's.

Paulus had indeed surrendered despite being forbidden to do so by Hitler. Of more than 280,000 men under Paulus' command, half were already dead or dying, about 35,000 had been evacuated from the front, and the remaining 91,000 were hauled off to Soviet POW camps. The brutality of the Russian winter and the Russians themselves would ensure that barely 5,000 of them would ever return to Germany alive.

I bring up Paulus, Gentlemen, because we are running out of time if your side is to have any leverage to achieve something approaching the end you desire, Wayne Lane said. It impressed Leo that in the heart of this American cowboy beat the desire to achieve something for both sides. Lane was no Dietrich but perhaps there was something to learn here from the American.

Let me convey my boss's thinking on this matter as of two days ago when I was last in his presence, he continued. *My boss, that is to say Dulles, is frankly fed up with listening to outdated politicians, émigrés and prejudiced Jews.* Leo saw Anya wince at this declamation. It was stilted, academic German, but Wayne Lane was coming through loud and clear.

It is his view that if there is to be peace in Europe, it should be equitable this time and there must be no division between victor and vanquished. We are deep in the shit now because nations like Germany should never again be driven by want and injustice to desperate experiments engineered by the criminally insane. Wayne Lane had actually described himself as being *full of shit* rather than the world being *deep in shit* but such were the subtleties of the German language. His audience was, however, getting the gist of it.

My boss is concerned that the German state must continue to exist for the sake of order and progress, which includes preservation of its union with Austria, Lane said wrapping up.

Leo, who was not formally a part of the negotiation, shot from the hip as he often did when it was least helpful. *This is all very interesting but does anyone else agree with you, I mean him?*

Damn boy, my boss is damned influential, but I am not in a position at this moment to make promises and, as I just said, events are moving quickly. And what of our trustworthy friend Himmler? You gonna promise that he can deliver?

Let us just say the window may still be open just a notch, Wayne Lane added settling down, *which is all we can hope for now. It is the general mindset of Dulles, Donovan and their like that the next great war in Europe will be with our allies in the East, so there is tangible value in getting Germany back on the side of the angels.*

I suppose it's time to give that lucky charm of yours a rub, Leo said staring Wayne Lane in the eye as Hugo put his hand on Leo's arm to calm him.

Anya jumped in at this point. *Gentlemen, we have details to work through before we are done here, quite a few of them in fact, Time is of the essence, so let's get started.*

* * * * *

Shortly after the fireworks between Leo and Lane had passed, a gunshot, then another rang out echoing through the narrow valleys surrounding the abbey from some distance away it seemed. Wayne

Lane paused from note taking, while Anya abruptly excused herself and made for the door of the small dining room with Leo close on her heels.

They ran into Jani and Rupert in the foyer of the sprawling chapter house rushing toward the door to the stable yard. Both carried long-barrel, 12 gauge shotguns. Jani's fur coat had been replaced by a waxed hunting jacket and boots along with an ascot cap with ear flaps that freed her blonde braid to rest on the front of her left shoulder. Rupert was decked out in kind.

It is a signal that something has gone wrong with the passage of the British flyers, and we are going to check. Grab guns if you are coming. They are in the mudroom behind the kitchen along with barn coats, Rupert told Anya and Leo.

They have an hour's head start on us, so we have some ground to cover, Rupert added. *Although it is strange, as the shots seemed too close for them to have gone far.*

They emerged into the half-light of a creeping dawn under low, tufted clouds that reminded Leo of biscuits in an infinitely large pan. To the south, a broiling ray of red sun penetrated the clouds igniting the Zugspitze, Germanys highest peak (2962 meters) and its consort, the Alpspitze (2628 meters), like roman candles.

Jani barked with her customary air of command, *Leo and I will follow the road down past the village on the left flank. Rupert, you and Anya can track the riverbed on the right.*

We will rejoin each other on the other side of the first stand of trees on the lower ridge, Rupert replied. *The ground falls off sharply at the next tree line, so I will guide you from there.*

Do you think the SS or Gestapo have found us, Leo asked Jani as she ploughed ahead. *Well technically, Rupert has been under house arrest since 1939, so anything is possible, but my hunch is that this has nothing to do with the American emissary.*

She glanced again toward Leo, eyebrows furrowed, hint of smile, *you are not going to shoot yourself with that thing, are you,* Jani asked? She had noticed how carelessly Leo was handling his shotgun.

She did not get an answer nor expect one. They emerged from the first stand of trees to see Anya and Rupert 50 yards to their right. Both parties ran crouching up and then down a low ridge toward a point in the middle of the next tree line.

Let's go single file until we hit a wide relatively shallow ravine, and then we can fan out to the left and right. No more than 25 yards should separate each of us, Rupert said. *The terrain is dangerous. Stay tight for now.*

They descended into night, the new day no match for the dense cover of the forest. At the shallow ravine, Jani said, *I will be 10 yards to your left, Leo. Do your imitation of a red tail hawk every few minutes so I have a bearing on your location.*

Will do. Be careful, Leo said as Jani disappeared silently into the brush.

Rupert and Anya moved off to the right, and it could not have been more than ten minutes before they found a British flyer seemingly sitting against a tree. He was covered in so much blood that it was impossible at first to assess his wounds.

He's gone, Rupert, Anya said, *I do not see gunshot wounds. It would appear he has been stabbed.*

Then they heard the chicken like cluck of a female owl. Once, and then again once more.

That must be Brother Stephen. They're off to our right, Rupert said.

As a large table like boulder came into view, Brother Stephen hissed, *Rupert, here, I have the other flyer. Be careful, we were attacked by a huge wild boar, which is still nearby. My leg must be broken, and the flyer is out cold although the two of us are otherwise none the worse for wear. The other young man was not so lucky, impaled several times by that beast. That devil must have been stalking us and was upon us before anyone could react. I managed to hit it in the head with the barrel of my gun, which served only to make it angrier. I am sorry, Rupert, that I did not take better care of them.*

At the same moment, barely fifty yards away, where faint light managed to penetrate the canopy of trees overhead, Jani sensed its presence before she heard or saw it. The feral stench of the wild boar hit her seconds before it charged from the brush barely fifty feet away. It was coming from Leo's direction and instead of taking a shot and possibly hitting him instead, Jani skipped out of the way of the wild boar and swung her shotgun at its head to throw it off course. The boar hit the butt of her rifle with the force of a freight train sending the rifle and Jani at its other end into a shallow ravine.

Leo heard the commotion and thrashed through the dense brush to what he thought might be Jani's position and found her in a pile of leaves at the bottom of the ravine cursing everyone and everything, while holding her left ankle.

Leo, get out of here and find Rupert, it is a huge wild boar, easily as tall as I am at the shoulder. Go, please. Now.

But before Leo could absorb how much danger he was in, he heard snorting and turned to see in the faint light of the clearing a burst of steam rising from a large snout at eye level, barely concealed in the carapace of low hanging spruce about 100 feet away. It was grunting in short rhythmic bursts as if it was repeating a war chant to steel itself for the charge.

Leo leveled his shotgun at the beast. The brush rustled, the boar's grunting quickened, and it charged, letting out an awful sound between a screech and growl. Leo pulled the trigger of his shotgun.

But the gun did not fire. Leo had not released the safety, nor had he any clue such a thing was necessary.

Leo threw the gun at the wild boar and pulled the Khanjar from his belt. To run away would have sent him headlong into the ravine or worse seen him impaled in the back. He stood his ground.

The beast rose in the air as if to fling the full weight of its body at Leo who like a bull fighter tried to step out of the way at the last minute. But it was not enough, and the collision that followed sent both of them, victor and vanquished, into the ravine below.

* * * * *

It would not be memorialized in one of the rare, illuminated manuscripts in the monastery's reading room, but *The Legend of the Lower Wood* would endure for decades hence at Ettal Abbey. On that fateful day, the nimble Leo had managed to step aside to avoid being flattened by the massive animal or worse impaled by its five inch tusks.

The clever beast had adjusted course at the last instant but failed to deliver a death blow to its adversary. Both the boar and Leo were carried by the momentum of a glancing blow into the ravine to join Jani where she watched the fracas in horror.

A boar's massive head covers a third of its body and its vital organs are protected by a shield of dense muscle around its rib cage that serves as body armor in battle with another boar. It was pure dumb luck, but Leo managed to thrust the Khanjar upward as they catapulted into the ravine striking the beast in the pit of the right front leg, one of the few places on the boar's body where a knife could penetrate to reach its vital organs.

Both combatants landed feet from a hobbled Jani, who managed to pull a stunned Leo away from the flailing beast as blood spurted from its artery. It was at this moment that Anya arrived on the scene to finish off the animal. Later, the monks estimated the weight of the boar at 300 pounds, a treasure that fed them for over a month.

Eventually everyone made it back to the monastery and a wobbly Leo decided that the best therapy for his near death experience was to devote himself to baking bread for the day. As he did, he could imagine himself living a contemplative life baking bread and brewing beer in these cloistered surroundings.

Brother Stephen hopscotching on crutches had also taken the opportunity when they returned to the monastery to introduce Leo to Brother Andrew, the monastery's herbalist, for a draft of painkiller. Brother Andrew typically prepared the secret herbal blend for the monastery's liqueur, the Kloster Ettal. However, at that moment, Brother Andrew was working on a tonic for the British flyer using dark blue flowers that he had chopped up on a cutting board.

These are called 'Monkshood' fittingly because of the shape of the flower, Leo. It is part of the buttercup family if you can believe it, and they are plentiful here in the mountains, Brother Andrew said in a pleasingly pedantic fashion.

It will aid in the healing process for our guest, but one must be exceedingly careful with Monkshood. Its roots are highly poisonous, and it takes barely four or five milligrams of the dried root to kill a man, and it is a terrible death. One remains conscious and in excruciating pain as paralysis inevitably leads to death.

One hears it called 'Malleus Maleficarum' that is to say the 'Hammer of Witches' because of its use in witchcraft. The ancients also believed that its poison was made from the saliva of Cerberus, the three headed hound that guards the entrance to Hades. The ancients will get no argument from me on that score!

Leo liked Brother Andrew. He liked Monkshood too.

All were to depart the next day. Anya and Jani with Wayne Lane and Leo with Hugo.

Leo and Jani stole away from the group during the lunch hour to the monastery's magnificent basilica with two loaves of potato bread, an urn of gooseberry jam and two large pitchers of the monastery's most potent beer, a varietal the monks called, *The Devil's Due.*

They sat in a pew shoulder to shoulder, beer and bread in hand, amidst the gilded opulence of the baroque church admiring the magnificent fresco of the dome above that seemed to pull them skyward. *One day, Jani,* Leo began as the beer loosened his tongue. Jani immediately squeezed his hand with a vise-like grip until it hurt. Before Leo could complete the thought, she said *mon cher, do not speak of one day or someday. There is just this moment between us and that is enough for me.*

But, Leo said before being cut off again, *but what,* she asked? She did not wait for his answer.

Leo, we are warriors, you and I, and as such we must accept that death for us in this crusade against les Bosch will be just as random in its timing as it is sure to come.

Jani leaned into Leo, her cheeks flushed a crimson red and her body as hot as a branding iron. She lifted her earthenware stein and said, *speaking of this moment and if you are lucky the next few, mon cher, you are falling down on the job. More beer please!*

* * * * *

After Jani and Hugo had turned in for the night, Rupert, Leo and Anya sat around a high oak table with a granite kneading surface in the abbey's cluttered kitchen. Leo had just put the bread for the morning's meal into the open brick oven. The companions basked in its warmth as they indulged in *one more for the road*, a sturdy *hefeweizen*, further reinforcing Leo's notion that he could do worse than a vocation making bread and beer.

Well, I certainly know this of you from past experience, Mary-Tay, but now it is clear after my short time with your young cousin, that I should never expect a dull moment in your presence, and that goes for the two of you, Rupert proclaimed with eloquently raised eyebrows that turned into a wink!

Anya gave no quarter. *Rupert, you would not have it any other way. How you became a Benedictine monk in the first place is beyond me. You are a man of action rather than contemplation and, at least in my experience, it is rare to find both in one man.*

I found it in Dietrich Bonhoeffer, so I am not sure I agree, Leo chimed in out of the clear blue. In the silence that followed Anya studied Leo and reflected that this was no longer the ingenuous boy she had once thrown into the back of a truck in Aleppo.

Both of you make fair points, Rupert replied. *When this is all over, meaning the Austrian pig's knuckle in Berlin has been eradicated, I can envision a time when I am more active in ministry in the real world beyond this idyllic hamlet. I was attracted here because like the Jewish Mundfunk, which is a form of underground communication among our Jewish friends, I saw the prayers here and those in every other abbey, monastery, cloister and what have you, as 'Seelefunk,' a communication of souls, one to the other, one to many, a transmission of emotional and intellectual energy amplified by our congregation to aid our side in the battle between good and evil, which seems to provide the real energy in the universe these days.*

Rupert paused and added raising his stein as if to make a toast, *I firmly believe Seelefunk is real not a fanciful idea borne of a large stein of potent hefeweizen. I can't prove it even though I firmly believe it.*

You have faith, Leo observed.

Leo, I do not know how much time you have actually spent with Dietrich, but it sounds to me like a little bit of him has rubbed off on you, Rupert was quick to respond. *Yes. Faith isn't some arcane church word lurking in our catechisms. Without it, everything we are doing now in this fight would make no sense at all. There is no 'purpose' without faith.*

Dietrich, yes, certainly, and others, Leo responded as he glanced at Anya.

My compliments to all of them, Rupert shot back raising his stein once again in salute.

Mary-Tay, I know that you are probably unable to say much but tell me if you think the Americans can deliver, Rupert asked.

If it were up to Dulles and Donovan, yes. The British who tried to derail our meeting and the Russians are not of the same mind and their objective is to exact full retribution rather than save lives, I am afraid. If they have their way, many more people will die unnecessarily, the good with the bad, Anya replied.

I suspected as much, Rupert said. *I am circumspect about saying this in front of a warrior like yourself*, Rupert said, a serious look passed like a cloud over his handsome face, *but this war feels different. Certainly, the grievances of the German people over land and resources are understandable. Yet Goebbels has taken lying to a level never seen before to mold reality as he sees fit. In doing so, he has pitted brother against brother, Christian against Jew, and torn a nation to shreds. It is not the damage that is being done by the fighting to the material world I fear most, it is the irreparable harm done to the soul of a nation.*

Is this our future I wonder, Rupert added? *A great people who know history, morality, reality only through the lies of their leaders?*

One way or the other, my friends, whatever I do out in the world after all is said and done if I last that long, the time spent here will always provide the compass for my time spent out there. Friends, you are always welcome to join me here for that or for any reason whenever the spirit moves you to do so.

It was an offer that Leo took seriously as he wrestled with the reasons he did.

* * * * *

Alois and Charley, having welcomed their esteemed guest, retreated to the vicinity of the piano. The ever gracious Alois was unflappable in his presence, but Charley could never quite get used to Himmler's appearances for the bratwurst special. Limited eyesight or not, it was always blood-curdling to feel Himmler eyes, looking him up and down, as if he were evaluating his candidacy for Theresienstadt.

On this night, Himmler had Kaltenbrunner in tow. *I take it that we are ready to help our Lohengrin on his hobby horse complete the quest for the Holy Grail*, Himmler asked with a twinkle in his pale blue eyes.

Kaltenbrunner laughed waiving the piece of Weisswurst impaled on the end of his fork as if he were brandishing a sword, *yes, sir, Reichsminister Goebbels seems satisfied with our planned deployment of personnel. Zero hour is 0:400 on the 27th of this month. Code name remains Große Fabrik-Aktion.*

While Himmler often treated Goebbels sarcastically behind his back, they were unified in one thing. Theirs was a shared mania for the extermination of Jews and anyone else lacking an Aryan pedigree.

So, you also have news of our inquiries regarding Abwehr, Himmler then asked?

Yes, but first a quick update. As you know, Shulze-Boysen, Harnack, and Coppi were executed in December in connection with the Rote Kapelle affair. The von Brockdorff woman has now been reconvicted by Röder in the Peoples Court and will be moved to Plötzensee to be guillotined. A date has not been set, Kaltenbrunner reported.

The Führer has taken a personal interest in this case, Kaltenbrunner, so let me talk to him. Frankly, I believe that the executions of the others, especially a military man like Shulze-Boysen, were carried out with undue haste. They did not deserve such mercy. Let von Brockdorff have some time to think about the fate that awaits her. I will arrange it, Himmler replied.

Abwehr, Himmler asked abruptly switching gears?

You will remember our meeting no doubt with Toeppen who heads finance for Abwehr and Herzlieb, head of its legal services group. As you may also remember, there is no love lost between them and Canaris's acolyte, Dohnányi, and for that matter Oster, Kaltenbrunner began.

Well, they have uncovered certain currency irregularities, in particular, exceptionally large currency transfers were made to Switzerland and Italy without undergoing the prescribed reviews and internal approvals. In the case of Switzerland, they were made in connection with the dossiers of 13 Abwehr agents transferred there by Canaris.

And what of it, Himmler challenged Kaltenbrunner? Canaris had in fact briefed Himmler about these agents.

The transfers are well in excess of anything that could be justified by operational requirements. Apart from serious customs and currency violations, there is some reason to believe that these funds are being cached for purposes of a coup d'etat.

You can prove this, Himmler asked as he slathered dark mustard on a piece of bratwurst he had just stabbed with his fork?

We are well on our way to proving it. The Italian currency transfer seems to center around the activities of a fellow call Wilhelm Schmidhuber, a major in the Abwehr. We have already conducted an interview with him about his activities, in general, without tipping our hand on the currency matter, and he struck us as a rather nervous and at times indiscrete individual, who would not stand up to a serious interrogation.

So, the first domino falls, then what, Himmler asked?

At a minimum, sir, Dohnányi, falls next. He is Schmidhuber's superior. However, we can link Schmidhuber's activities to Josef Müller and equally questionable currency transfers to Italy. Müller, as we know, delights in thumbing his nose at us hiding behind his Catholic faith and ties to the Vatican. After Müller, the third domino to fall, someone who is up to his ears in these shenanigans, may well be someone we have had our eye on for quite some time – Bonhoeffer, Dietrich Bonhoeffer.

III. YOU CAN CALL ME MEYER

FEBRUAR 1943

It had been a hellish few hours in an abominable year of a ghastly decade that held Berlin in its grip in the early days of 1943. Trudy closed the door of their apartment with a sigh because she was certain it would be for the very last time.

She and Michael had managed to get by somehow after their segregation along with hundreds of other Jews ostensibly for their own safety in a rundown *Mietskaserne* on Kaiser Strasse, a street of rundown apartment buildings nestled ironically in posh stand of ancient oak and maple trees. Berlin had reached a tipping point in the early days of 1943 from something nearly normal, but for broiling wars to the West and the East, into an all-consuming, to get by day in and day out.

And that was for the typical German. As to their Jewish countrymen, however, having been deemed *sub-human* and unworthy of citizenship, they were forced to climb the mighty Zugspitze each and every day wearing nothing but a gold star.

Trudy and Michael, young, attractive and highly educated, had narrowly escaped the worst of it when in October 1941 the Nazis began to require the Jewish community to supply a specified number of Jews for resettlement in the East. She had been a *Sportlehrer*, a physical education teacher in a secondary school, and Michael, a mechanical engineer, who was deemed essential to the war effort and not subject to immediate deportation. Despite this tiny bit of good fortune, it stuck in Trudy's craw that Michael did the same highly skilled work as before designing and manufacturing precision radio direction finders for Peilfunkers, but now Peilfunkers paid him as a simple laborer.

The day had started normally. Michael had gone to his shift, and Trudy despite the bitter cold of this late February day set off to disappear into the bustling commercial life of a Saturday morning on the upscale Kufurstendamm. As usual, Trudy hid her yellow star as she strolled along the tree-lined avenue to window-shop.

But then the cars and trucks sped past brimming with SS men, who looked like heavily armed schoolboys on a class outing. They were rushing toward sirens blaring in the East.

There was no question, she thought. Something did not feel right. It was time to return to the apartment, also several kilometers to the East, as quickly as possible all the while maintaining her composure. She was a good actress. She had to be. Her anonymity was a life and death matter.

Trudy arrived at their apartment building and her heart stopped. There were Gestapo cars and an SS truck at the main entrance to the sprawling building. Trudy made a calculated guess that it would take them time to reach her apartment to the rear of the city block-sized complex, and she quickly slipped in through the rear service bay.

As he arrived at their tidy apartment, she could hear the commotion somewhere on the floor below and minutes away. She opened the door and made a beeline to their single closet where two innocent looking shopping bags were filled with all their worldly possessions.

What little cash there was had been split between the two of them, hidden in money belts she and Michael wore constantly.

In a world where few options were left to them, Trudy hesitated despite the clanging and banging of approaching Gestapo men, to consider her next move before setting off. She and Michael had planned for just such an occasion and, as much as it galled her as she softly closed the door to their apartment for the very last time, she would stick to the plan.

* * * * *

It could have been worse, Michael thought to himself, grading the morning on a generous curve. As he had approached Peilfunkers, he passed a Jewish colleague heading rapidly in the opposite direction who showed him a notice from the Reich Ministry of Labor for all Jewish workers to congregate in the factory yard for *statistical reasons.*

Michael avoided the main entrance where confused workers, Aryan and non, were milling about and snuck in through a side entrance that would take him directly to the foreman's office. When he arrived, the foreman, an old friend from better times, refused to make eye contact and said, *I did not see you this morning. Get the hell out of here without being seen by anyone else AND do not go home.*

Needing no further encouragement, Michael retraced his tracks and slipped away as Gestapo cars and an SS truck pulled up at the front of the factory, and Gestapo men began barking orders at the assembled workers, singling out Jews. Michael had, at least for the moment, managed to escape Goebbels' anti-Semitic set piece, the lightning round-up of Berlin's remaining Jews by elite units of the Gestapo and SS, code-named *Große Fabrik-Aktion* —Operation Factory. So much for being indispensable to the war effort, Michael thought to himself, as he put some distance between himself and the factory after discretely removing the Star of David from his coat.

Indeed, on the morning of 27 February 1943 across Germany, the SS and the Gestapo would round up Jewish workers, who were then imprisoned pending deportation to concentration and extermination camps. The *Große Fabrik-Aktion* was completed within two days, except in Berlin, where the largest population of Jews lived. Over the course of a week, 8,000 men in Berlin were seized by the Gestapo from their homes or one of the 100 targeted companies.

They were sequestered in six locations – among them a concert hall, two barracks, a synagogue and a Jewish senior center. Those imprisoned in these locations were generally deported to Theresienstadt. Most were later murdered at Auschwitz.

In Berlin, two thousand men, who were married to Aryan women, were imprisoned at the *Jüdischen Gemeinde* or Jewish Community Center on Rosenstrasse. In the days following the *Große Fabrik-Aktion,* their wives and hundreds of relatives, sometimes as many as a thousand people at a time, spontaneously gathered in front of the community center.

These non-violent protests would erupt into raucous chanting and screaming and caused such a stir in Berlin that the Nazis, who oddly enough were quite sensitive at times to public opinion, backed down, releasing the men at Rosenstrasse one by one from the 2nd of March onwards. Twenty-five men who were deported to Auschwitz on the fifth of March were returned two weeks later.

Not long after, Goebbels would write, *I am convinced that purging Berlin of its Jews is the greatest of my political achievements. Whenever I remember the sight of Berlin on my arrival here in 1926 and compare it to its appearance in 1943, after the Jews have been evacu-*

ated, only then can I appreciate the greatness of our achievement in this field. The Reichsminister of Propaganda, no stranger to fibbing, would triumphantly, although prematurely, declare Berlin *Judenfrei* in May of 1943.

As it was for Trudy and so many of his fellow Jews on the day of the round-up, Michael's question was simply – what next? He worked through the possibilities and probabilities systematically as he hid in the doorway of an abandoned shop. If the Gestapo were working with a list, they would raid the workplaces and homes of those Jews they had targeted, most likely simultaneously. The Gestapo was big on lists, so the answer to this question was obvious from the start.

And what of the love of his life, Trudy? She was clever and with even a little notice could slip through their fingers. If she had not, his returning to their apartment would do her no good.

He worried, however, that Trudy would be Trudy and as usual have decided to help others who were being rounded up, not realizing the danger she was in. Since the beginning of mass deportations in 1941, small groups, in some cases entire families, had disappeared on a regular basis from their Kaiser Strasse apartment building. During these roundups, some elderly Jews who were unable to climb into the back of the SS trucks were taken by the arms and the legs and thrown bodily into the truck like sacks of concrete.

Trudy would often intervene and carry the luggage of the unfortunates who had lost the Nazi lotto that day and steady them as they climbed into the waiting trucks. Those were the days when Michael's job afforded a certain air of invincibility. That had changed on this bitterly cold morning in February.

He hoped that she had stuck to the plan if she was able to avoid the Gestapo. He would. There was no other choice for them in a world where good choices were a distant memory.

* * * * *

In the early days of 1943, the Allied bombing of Berlin was sporadic, occasionally deadly and tactically ineffective, a mere wisp of the horror to come by yearend. On the night before *Große Fabrik-Aktion* struck, it had been the Russians, and they seemed to concentrate their efforts on Wedding, which housed several strategically important factories.

Die Bäckerei had taken a glancing blow but despite losing its decrepit exhaust fan to shrapnel would be able to produce the morning batch of bread to bring some comfort to the frazzled inhabitants of the area. The large hole in the wall, where the exhaust fan had once been, would have to provide the necessary ventilation for now.

The bakery was on the edge of a six square block area that included old man Schultheiss's brewery that the Russians had reduced to rubble exposing a forest of piping bent in agonistic poses surrounding massive beer brewing vats that had been dented and, in many cases, turned on their sides in to rest in large pools of pilsner or hefeweizen.

As they surveyed the damage in Wedding, Mehdi and Leo agreed that if the Bolshies wanted to strike a truly strategic blow at the heart of the German populace, beer was the place to start. Madame Schultheiss had disappeared in the wreckage of the Schultheiss villa next to the brewery, while Siegfried and Brünnhilde could be seen running helter-skelter through the district unleashed and apparently bent on terrorizing whomever they encountered on that terrible Saturday morning.

It would be sometime later that day when her body was discovered. Old man Schultheiss, now the grieving widower, returned to claim it after weathering the storm in Fredrichshain wrapped in the warm embrace of his accounting clerk, Hilda.

What a shit in the pants place Berlin has become, Mehdi groaned.

I guess there is no longer any doubt, his name is Meyer, Leo replied, as the two friends shared a laugh.

Leo was echoing a joke circulating among ordinary Germans at the time. Feeling pretty good about himself in 1939, Reichsmarschall Hermann Göring, commander of the German air forces among other things boasted, *no enemy bomber can reach the Ruhr. If one reaches the Ruhr, my name is not Göring. You may call me Meyer.*

The sobriquet, Meyer, as every German understood, was an insult. The Reichsmarschall was basically saying that if bombs fell on the Ruhr, as they had in the early days of 1943, one could call him a dumb ass.

The Gauleiter of Wedding had stopped in for his customary order that Saturday morning and told Mehdi and Leo that the police station was gone, completely reduced to rubble. The police station happened to be the local source of identity papers for the people of Wedding, and one could see if one looked hard enough hundreds of charred and disintegrating identity records drifting in the wind among the scorched detritus of the bombing.

So, what does someone do who has lost his papers and needs to replace them, Mehdi asked? *There will be people who have lost everything but need papers to get food coupons to feed their families.*

We are working through that now, but it is likely that someone in that situation will seek an attestation from me or another official here and register anew with a nearby police station. These new records will be reconciled at a later date with the master archive maintained, who knows where, in the countryside, the Gauleiter replied.

A great idea can come and go like the fleeting scent of a rose. The sweet scent of an opportunity had not escaped Leo's notice, and he knew he urgently needed to speak to Marushka and Hugo.

* * * * *

Marushka beamed like the proud parent of a violin prodigy, while Hugo admired the boy who could always be found at the intersection of seemingly insurmountable problems and their desperate solutions. In this instance, the idea was so deceptively simple that the ever audacious Hugo felt like kicking himself for not thinking of it first. But credit where credit is due, he thought, as Leo laid out his plan in detail in the refectory of the *Schwedische Kirche.*

They had first shared the idea earlier that evening with the supremely taciturn Reverend Eric Perwe, who was so taken with it that he put down his ever-present pipe just long enough to give Leo a bear hug. *Praise the Lord. Brilliant,* was all he said, before the pipe quickly returned to his lips.

Later as the three comrades reviewed the operational plan in detail, Leo said, *I hope that Reverend Perwe does not get his hopes up quite yet. Every plan I have ever been part of generates its own chaos with the good. I think we need to wait until the bread is out of the oven before we get too excited.*

Leo first reviewed the rationale that he had earlier given Perwe. The *Schwedische Kirche* had lost its prized counterfeiter at the end of the prior year in a bombing raid. The bombing in Wedding just the night before had left 1,500 people dead or missing while roughly the same number of people lost their homes and, in many cases, the documents that were so crucial to their survival in Berlin.

These was the obligatory national identity card, the *Kennkarte*, to begin with. Then one needed a residence permit, work permits, a postal card to collect mail and of course cards to buy food and clothing.

Because the central repository for identity records had been moved to an undisclosed location in the countryside, local police stations were now authorized to issue new documents on a temporary basis until they could be reconciled with the central repository. This was true if and only if an applicant whose documents had been destroyed could find someone of good standing in the community to vouch for his or her identity and, better yet, produce a birth certificate.

The word on the street was that, as the tempo of bombings increased along with the human toll, the scrutiny given by authorities to any particular applicant for new papers was increasingly erratic and subject to the vagaries of the Black Market. Therein lay the opportunity for the fugitives in Perwe's flock.

I think we start as before with birth certificates of Swedes with ties to Berlin to create new identities, Marushka said. *That could easily give us a pool of two to three hundred people who would be untraceable if the police were ever to double check. They are so overwhelmed now, I would be surprised if they ever did.*

Although don't rule out the Gestapo, Hugo responded. *And for this reason, we cannot use our friends at the police headquarters across from the church. They are under suspicion and being closely watched by the Gestapo. The Gestapo man continues to linger in the lobby, head buried in a newspaper he never reads.*

Fair enough, Leo said. *We have friends in other areas of the city, who will not be sticklers about procedure. Furthermore, we have identified a few people to accompany an applicant to provide a personal attestation.*

I think that we may have a few good souls of our own who can provide these attestations, an excited Marushka shot back

Then if you agree with the plan, Leo added, *I will involve someone who is a magician in helping our clients disappear and appear on command. Her name is…*

Leo, we don't need her name, Marushka shot back. *If she is good with you, she is good with us.* And at that, the intrepid Hedwig Porschütz became part of the conspiracy.

So how many Jews do you have hidden here or within your network, Leo asked?

Too many, but I would like to focus initially on several who have been fugitives the longest and then whittle the list down from there, Marushka responded.

* * * * *

It was miserably cold, but Liliane was ecstatically happy to be home, a 30 day leave from the Eastern front for meritorious performance under extreme circumstances. Her medical brigade and nearly 1,000 wounded had managed against all odds to evade the pincer movement of the Soviet army in November 1942 that would trap General Paulus and doom nearly 91,000 men in the German retreat from Stalingrad.

She was the equivalent of a lieutenant in the Wehrmacht and the leader of a unit of nurses that worked triage in the field hospitals just behind the front lines. The scars to heart and mind from the brutal conflict seemed to melt away as she fell into the arms of her father when they were reunited upon her return to Berlin.

Her father, Herr Knoebbel, the greengrocer on Granseer Strasse, hated the war and everything it stood for but could barely contain the pride he felt in his 24-year-old daughter who arrived home in full uniform. Liliane had gone to war as a young girl just out of nursing school not as a true believer but as someone who just wanted to be there for the boys when they were most in need.

The greengrocer had reluctantly permitted her to go, although he knew she would have gone without his permission. The vivacious young girl with an electric smile framed by blonde curls and a dimpled chin who went off to war had returned to him as a serious young woman with dark rings around her eyes the color of smoke.

Liliane rose early to prepare the shop for the Saturday rush with a lump in her throat because there was so little to offer their neighbors. Stock in February was never good, but the shortages of just about everything in Berlin had depleted the supply of vegetables still further and today it would be a motley assortment of root vegetables, a few sugar beets, some celery root, and turnips. Her father was away on one of his missions She knew this meant that he was giving away their meagre supplies to the old, the sick and the hunted.

She admired him for that. Liliane had always been apolitical unlike her mother who had become a dyed in the wool Nazi. How could two people so unlike each other marry and produce a child together? What is worse, what did it say about me, Liliane wondered?

Liliane would not see her mother on this trip home and just as well in her book. Frau Knoebbel had risen to the rank of SS Oberaufseherin, or Chief Overseer, at Dachau where she now provided murderous mentorship to young women joining the ranks of concentration camp guards to replace the men in their ranks, who were being hastily called to the front.

Hair pulled up with a mother of pearl hair comb, dressed in green overalls and an oversized brown turtleneck sweater that had been her father's, Liliane spent the better part of the morning greeting her father's longstanding customers who had been like family to her as a young girl. By midday, there was still no sign of her father and most of her stock had been sold, so Liliane had been tempted to close up shop. She decided to take a look outside to gauge the activity on the street and found people scurrying this way and that returning home for lunch or heading to a bierstube for a warm fire and some strong beer. Not a bad idea, the beer, she mused.

Amid the hustle and bustle, she sensed someone staring at her and noticed a young woman with no hat and a threadbare coat standing across the street partially hidden in the doorway of an apartment building. She was holding two large shopping bags. She too was blonde and pretty and could have been Liliane's sister. The young woman looked down when her eyes met Liliane's. It had been the shop she was watching.

Liliane was sure that the young woman was one of her father's *clients*, to use the term loosely, and what that meant. Liliane was her father's daughter after all, and she crossed Granseer Strasse to greet the woman with a warm smile. Liliane took one of the young woman's shopping bags and said, *let me put the kettle on for you, dear. A cup of tea will do us both some good.*

* * * * *

So, you are the daughter he reveres, Trudy said as the warm tea brought the feeling back to her fingers and toes and loosened her tongue. *I have overheard him telling everyone that you are fighting on the Eastern front.*

Fight? Well fighting is something that I don't do as I am not a very good fighter. And if I did, our results in the east would be even worse than they already are if that were humanly possible, Liliane replied with wry laughter. Trudy smiled warmly in response as laughter was harder to come by after the events of the morning.

I am a nurse. My unit fights to save lives. My God, most are just boys. Liliane's voice trailed off as she fought the impulse to relive the indescribable.

War is the worst possible way of cultivating the best type of human being...the best blood is lost, a soft baritone seemed to come from nowhere and the two young women nearly jumped out of their skins. Herr Knoebbel had returned and stood in the doorway.

Scheisse, father, you are getting good at sneaking around.

This is the language they teach you in the army, Liebchen.

This is mild, father. Please don't get me started. We have a guest as you can see who needs our help, Liliane said.

And help it shall be, the greengrocer replied, his heart warm at the prospect of his daughter as an ally in his clandestine activities. A chip off the old block, he thought, as the fleeting image of the other block, now doing God knows what at Dachau, made the hair stand up on the back of his neck.

Liliane, we can for the moment put them in the outbuilding once occupied by Frau Dix, who has joined your mother at Dachau. They were in many ways two crones of the same feather, he said.

Trudy, I have scrubbed and scrubbed again to remove the stench of its former tenant but alas the memories remain. In any event, you should be safe for now if not particularly comfortable in your temporary hideout, the Herr Knoebbel said looking as though the stench of his former tenant still hung in the air.

I am grateful, Herr Knoebbel.

And what of your husband, Trudy, the greengrocer asked?

The downcast expression on Trudy's face said all he needed to know.

* * * * *

The four kilometers from Kaiser Strasse to Granseer Strasse might just as well have been four hundred. The Gestapo meant business, and one could not go a single block with encountering an SS detachment examining identity cards and when the spirit moved, as it frequently did, roughing up their own countrymen.

Michael and his fellow students at the *Technische Hochschule* (later known as the Technical University of Berlin) had wasted countless hours on the new American pinball machines when they took Berlin by storm during the roaring twenties. Flippers would not be invented until 1947, so players would have to bump and tilt the pinball machine to make the ball change direction. This is exactly how Michael felt that day, like a pinball propelled in one direction then abruptly tilted toward another by an oafish and cruel force.

He still had a good kilometer or more to go before he reached the relative safety of the greengrocer's market when someone bellowed his name. He turned ready to flee, blood pounding in his head, knees wobbly to see Constable Klinsmann barreling down the street toward him with a police wagon following close behind.

Klinsmann was a kindly, middle aged policeman with a bushy mustache and a penchant for beer and bratwurst, as his bulging waistline certified. He was an old guard social democrat, who resented the Nazis for their cruelty and unprofessional behavior but was Prussian to the core. Klinsmann patrolled *Kaiser Strasse* on foot and would take every opportunity to flirt harmlessly with Trudy when he could. He also knew that Michael and Trudy were Jewish.

Casually twirling his baton, he approached saying. *Where is your hat young man? Haven't you noticed how damn cold it is out here? Damn bad for your health.*

Before Michael, momentarily rendered mute, could find a word, any word, to say in reply, the police wagon pulled up, and Klinsmann said, *let me give you a lift, young man, up on the side boards here,* as he tapped the side of the police van with his baton. *Then hang on for dear life, boy. These men never did learn how to drive properly.*

Klinsmann turned to the constable on the passenger side of the van and said, *he's with me. Be a good man and take him where he wants to go within reason.*

Thank you, constable, Michael finally blurted out as Klinsmann casually continued on his way down the street. It was then only a matter of minutes before the police van deposited Michael steps away from Granseer Strasse. Michael decided against going directly to the greengrocer's market. He first had to ensure he was not being followed.

It would be the last time he would ever see Klinsmann but not the last time he would thank God for people like him.

* * * * *

Liliane was on pins and needles, which was saying something for someone with nerves of steel, forged in the pandemonium of a German field hospital. In that den of hope and hopelessness, she and her team bore the burden of separating those who might survive from those best served by morphine and a final prayer.

It had been two years since she met the seemingly ubiquitous Hugo Graf von Reinfeld during his first mission to the Eastern front in Poland shortly before Hitler launched Operation Barbarossa, the code name for the German invasion of the Soviet Union. The young aristocrat had gone as an external observer for Reinhard Heydrich to assess the training requirements of the SS counterintelligence operation in Poland.

Since then, they had written to each other once a month like clockwork. His letters had reinforced what she believed in her heart to be true when she first met Hugo that, despite his incongruous involvement with the SS and Gestapo, here was a man of intellect and kindness, someone like herself who loved Germany but hated what it had become.

Hugo had invited her to dinner at the sublimely upscale and sophisticated Borchardt near the Gendarmenmarkt, and it had been a nerve wracking afternoon of trying to find something to wear that Hugo would find equally sublime. Raising the stakes still further, Hugo had been the first and only man she had taken as a lover.

And if the stakes weren't already high enough, she would throw caution to the wind and test her hypothesis about Hugo. Michael and Trudy needed help, and Liliane and her father could not hide them indefinitely. The Gestapo was canvassing door to door with a list of those who had managed to evade capture in the *Große Fabrik-Aktion*. Something in her heart told Liliane that she might find the solution in Hugo.

Hugo, a knight so calm in battle even his armor didn't rattle, could feel the perspiration form behind is thick eyebrows as he greeted Liliane in the foyer of Borschardt. He had played and replayed this moment for over two years and opted for a kiss on each cheek in the French style rather than clicking his heals and giving her outstretched hand a bird-like peck in the Prussian style.

Liliane was as intelligent and sharp witted as he had remembered her, but it became apparent that the harried young girl he first met in Poland had become something altogether different. Hugo prided himself not without justification as being a cool customer under pressure. But he found himself in the presence of a veritable war hero now and a beautiful one at that. He knew he had to measure up.

In a time and place where children informed on their parents, as often did spouse against spouse, her proposal delivered over kaffee and Courvoisier took his breath away. He and Liliane were kindred spirits of that he was sure or almost sure until that point in the evening. But now he was faced with the question of whether her proposal was some elaborate trap by Himmler and his henchmen to test his loyalty.

My father brought me up Catholic, Hugo, but I left the church more or less because I didn't feel like a churchgoer. I could not live with someone telling me I could not do things, Liliane told him. *Ironically, I joined a bible study group that my father found out about only after our group was arrested and detained by the Nazis for two days. There were five of us – three girls and two boys.*

When the Nazis looked at the books we were reading, one of them said, 'I see that you have many books, but you do not have Mein Kampf!' I answered that you look like you have read only Mein Kampf and nothing else! My father and mother were present, and this sent my mother into a rage. My father made doubly sure that he quickly got me out of Berlin to nursing school in Essen where I stayed with my aunt.

What I am asking you to help me do for these two good people is no big moral or religious decision on my part, Hugo. I know it is dangerous and I am sure you think it foolhardy for me to raise it with you tonight. You are the one person in this world I would dare turn to.

I must do this because my Father would say, 'saving one life is as if we have saved the world,' and I am my father's daughter. If I have guessed wrong about you, and you are in thick with those reprobates after all, do what you must to me. But something tells me Hugo, I am not wrong about you.

It was a troubling and reckless move on Liliane's part, but as far as Hugo was concerned, a perfect evening.

* * * * *

April 1943

The Spring of 1943 started inauspiciously for Leo and went rapidly downhill from there. It would be a period in his life he would never be able to wring out of his mind, try as he might.

It started with the freak blizzard on the first day of April, which destroyed the early spring buds in the Tiergarten born of an intoxicatingly warm March. One tried to take a breath but it was knocked away by the snow driven into one's face by the horizontal winds that roared through the urban canyons of Berlin. It was proof positive to Leo that Mother Nature was a Nazi.

The silver lining in the nearly white-out conditions was that it concealed the movement of two small groups, which could be perceived as faintly gray objects in the distance if one looked hard enough. On this day, Michael and Trudy were to apply for their new identity papers at a police station near Hackescher Markt on the banks of the Spree and a few blocks from Otto Weidt's workshop.

Michael had finally been reunited with Trudy arriving at the greengrocer's shortly after he had been deposited by the uniformed Berlin police near Granseer Strasse. Thanks to Hugo's intervention, Hedwig Porschütz was recruited to secret them away to a partially bombed townhouse in Friedrichshain several days after his dinner with Liliane.

Trudy and Michael shared their ramshackle accommodations with another young couple on the run. Trudy recognized them as former classmates at the Jewish school in Berlin, which the four agreed was not just another time in their lives but another world altogether.

To make matters worse, Hedwig had to send a runner to fetch Leo a few days before the planned outing to the police station because she found the two couples readying themselves to slip off into the night. *We have decided that it is better to run the risk of capture than to risk the lives of those trying so hard to save us. As grateful as we are for all you have done, we cannot and will not prioritize our lives over yours,* Michael argued.

This was a tendency among Jews on the run that was sadly all too familiar to Hedwig but less so to Leo. *You are in good hands,* he said. *Those helping you have survived much worse than this and with your documents in hand, there is the real chance we can get you to Lübeck and then to Sweden. You owe this to your children.*

Neither couple had children, but the import of Leo's exhortation hit home. Going for the coup de grace, Leo struck, *and remember this, if you are caught at this juncture, the Gestapo will torture you and when they do, you may last 5 minutes, you may last five hours, but you will most certainly be compelled to identify those of us helping you now. You may identify only one of us who will be tortured until he or she identifies another one of us and so on and so on. So, there is no going back. We are all committed at this point!*

The debate had gone well into the early hours of the morning, and it was decided to delay the excursion to the police constabulary by at least a day. Leo and Hugo at Marushka's urging wanted to give the two couples some time to settle down, an effort to which Marushka devoted some motherly attention.

Two days later, two teams arrived at the police constabulary steps from the Spree River as it was being bombarded by the thunder and lightning imbedded in the blizzard that had swept in the night before. The decision had been made to separate the two couples sending each couple to a different police station and splitting each couple for the processing of new papers with the police. Married couples tended to draw more scrutiny than a random individual here and there.

Mehdi led off with Trudy and they went through the formalities, climbing the mountain of paperwork that the desk sergeant put in front of them. Hugo and Michael waited across the street for their turn huddled in the shelter of a church door, while Leo and Big Otto stood watch at opposite ends of the block.

Mehdi had greased the palms of a friendly desk sergeant who was nowhere to be found that morning. Instead, they got an officious chip off the old Nazi block who seemed to revel in slow-walking Trudy's review.

The officer of the desk who was so puny that the edge of the desk came up to the top of his shoulders, sunk his teeth into the issue of Trudy's heritage. While the neatly doctored birth certificate supplied by the Swedish Lutheran Church was for one Anna Lindberg, the loving daughter of a German father and Swedish mother.

In truth Trudy was the daughter of a mother who was Jewish and a father who was not. In 1933, he was told to divorce his wife or lose his job, but he would not and so lost his job.

This personal history was of course to be avoided in the discussion of new papers and, as they had rehearsed, Anna Lindberg wove a tail that gave the desk sergeant little to work with if he wanted to challenge her identity. Two hours later, the desk sergeant who might have vied for the slowest hunt and peck typist in recorded history was close to having their documents ready.

Just as Mehdi and Trudy were wrapping up, Big Otto saw what appeared to be a large sedan cross a small utility bridge from the direction of Museuminsel coming to a stop across the street from where he was posted and just a block away from the police constabulary. Had one been able to see anything at all in the blizzard, it would have been the perfect vantage point from which to watch the police station.

* * * * *

Don't go in, sir. This is right from Leo, sir, the small boy told Hugo with what sounded like a whistle or was that simply the wind playing tricks on his hearing, Hugo wondered? Big Otto had detected three men in the car by counting the burning ends of three cigarettes.

Big Otto sent a runner to Leo and Leo decided reluctantly to abort the mission and to get word to Mehdi that something was up. Leo's first impulse was to ask himself *how they knew* because he was sure of who they were. But why here? Why now?

Leo had sent the young, red headed boy who was new to the Wedding wolfpack to warn Hugo first. They called the boy Whistling Fritz because he had lost a front tooth in a back-alley brawl and could not help but whistle when he spoke. "W's" were the worst, but that aside, Leo considered him a very clever boy who was good in a tight situation.

Hugo and Michael hesitated but realized that this was no practical joke on Leo's part. There would be another time and place for this Hugo told Michael, arms wrapped around his shoulders, as their forms melted away into the swirling storm.

A few minutes later, Whistling Fritz came flying into the lobby of the police station, *sirs, sirs, I saw a man trying to push a lady in a nice fur coat off the old Pergamon Bridge. Come quickly. He is large and she is small, and it is not a fair fight.*

This was a signal to Mehdi's that something had gone wrong and it was time to leave. Mehdi calmly addressed himself to the desk sergeant, *good gracious you have a trying job. Am I correct that we are done here, sergeant.*

Go, go, the annoyed sergeant said waving his hand as if were swatting a gnat. He was on the phone to the squad room to roust a few uniforms to follow the boy to the scene of the crime.

I will meet them at the bridge, sir, and with that Whistling Fritz was gone. Mehdi taking his cue to head in the opposite direction avoided the main entrance and discretely led Trudy to a side door. They found themselves in an alley that led to the S-Bahn station and to safety, at least for the moment.

* * * * *

The car idling down the block from the police constabulary was not the happiest place in Berlin at the moment Whistling Fritz took flight from the police station. The police would never find Whistling Fritz nor the two antagonists at the Pergamon bridge, who had never existed in the first place.

Big Otto had in fact been wrong and there were four men in the car – Andre Fuchs, the feral Gestapo commissar, two of his men and a beleaguered Reverend Doctor Martin Sauter. Sauter did not smoke and quietly gasped for oxygen in the nicotine laden atmosphere of the sedan. Worse still, he had to work at hiding his disdain for his gruff, working-class companions.

It was as if he were a glass of Dom Perignon amidst threes steins of bock beer. How much more must one endure for the Reich, he fretted to himself.

Sauter, I think we are wasting our time coming here again today. Not a soul approached the police about identity papers yesterday, and we are now to believe they will come in this weather, Fuchs growled, his garlic laden breath fighting for purchase in the nicotine fog.

To his credit, Sauter had done his homework. He had insinuated himself into the life of the *Schwedische Kirche* in Wilmersdorf by spending all of his free time, neglecting his wife and children, to identify an indirect way into the life of the congregation by loitering in the pews day in and day out.

After a time, he noted the regular appearance of the cleaning woman who cared for the altar and sacristy. It was not long before he made his move and complimented her on the stellar appearance of the church, expressing his envy in the quality of her work. He had introduced himself as the pastor of a church in Wedding where he fought the good fight to convert the poor and ignorant to the Gospel.

His quarry was smitten. Sauter would bring sweets, and she would prepare tea in the small apartment she maintained in an annex of the sprawling villa. He casually probed about her role, the pastor, and the work of the church careful not to tip her off to his true intent. All the while, he noted the comings and goings of people who were even less eager to be noticed than he.

It took liters of tea and many kilograms of kuchen before she let it slip. The Reverend Perwe and his friends were helping the unfortunate bombed out of their homes obtain new identity documents and in fact planned to take several of them to the police constabulary near Museuminsel at the end of that very week.

It did not take an enormous amount of imagination for Sauter to divine what was really afoot, and he had made his report to Fuchs. Fuchs needed Sauter more for his progress in infiltrating the subversive discussion group that revolved around Frau Solf than for this, but he gave Sauter the benefit of the doubt and mounted an operation to intercept anyone seeking false identity papers and thus their appearance that snowy morning near Hackescher Markt.

Hopefully, Reverend Sauter, you have a better handle on the Solf group than you did on this. Can I assume that the Solf social gathering is still planned for next week?

You can count on that, Herr Fuchs. My wife made contact with Frau von Thadden and, as we planned, your man just happened to drop by their table when the two of them were together at Café Kranzler. He has worked his way into the Thadden woman's good graces and apparently will attend their next social.

We will be ready, Sauter, but let us not have another false start like the last two days.

Two beams of light that approached the sedan suspended in midair appeared as two uniformed policemen approached the sedan carrying flashlights. *I don't know what this is, but let's move. Our work here is done*, Fuchs growled.

Perhaps, Mother Nature wasn't a Nazi after all.

* * * * *

The second couple had obtained their identity papers without incident despite the brutal weather conditions and were handed over to Hedwig for hiding to await their transport to Lübeck and Sweden. Leo's plan had generally worked like a charm over the prior 30 days, helping Marushka clear her *backlog* of roughly 60 souls.

Michael and Trudy were not so fortunate. Michael had no papers but Trudy had hers, although Leo and Hugo debated whether she could use them given the arrival of the black sedan, the trademark of the Gestapo.

If it were indeed the Gestapo, they would hunt down Anna Lindberg and tie her phony papers to the Swedish Lutheran Church. Marushka joined the debate with Hugo, Leo, Michael and Trudy in their new accommodations at an abandoned storefront around the corner from Marushka's flat.

I can use my Gestapo credentials to determine whether the Gestapo have in fact paid a visit to the police recently to inquire about that day, Hugo said.

Mehdi will look into what happened to his pet police sergeant. In any event, we have to assume the police station will remain under some type of surveillance, Leo replied.

The search continues for those who evaded the Große Fabrik-Aktion. In fact, it seems to have gained intensity with time and, as we know, Trudy's and Michael's names are at the top of the list of those yet to be found. This is simply a fact to be reckoned with, Michael and Trudy, not an invitation to think about stealing away into the night again, Leo said firmly but with a hint of gallows humor.

Addressing himself to Michael and Trudy, Hugo said, *the plan is still to get you both to Lübeck, so Michael and I will take another run at a police constabulary. Marushka?*

It is a dilemma with horns, no doubt. No easy choices. Although we rest now. Something will come to mind. It always does to a rested mind, Marushka replied.

* * * * *

Hugo broke the news to Liliane the following Saturday evening when they met to attend a gathering of Hugo's friends and acquaintances at the home of Hanna Solf, the widow of Doctor Wilhelm Solf, who once served as ambassador to Japan under the Weimar Republic. Like her husband, Frau Solf was a political moderate and anti-Nazi.

She now presided over a circle of anti-Nazi intellectuals in her salon in Berlin, together with her daughter, the Countess So'oa'emalelagi "Lagi" von Ballestrem-Solf, to whom Hugo had been introduced by his mentor Count Helmut von Moltke. Hugo had attended similar social gatherings at Moltke's estate in Kreisau.

The impressive Moltke was a member of the Prussian House of Lords and his father had led German forces at the beginning of WWI. Hugo's own father was regiment commander under the elder Moltke.

Moltke was recruited by Canaris at the beginning of the Poland campaign as an Abwehr agent and he, in turn, had secretly recruited Hugo when by happenstance they encountered each other in Poland when Moltke was there to document human rights abuses on the Eastern front. Hugo would never forget his mentor's admonition about their roles in the atrocities visited on the Poles during their time there, *certainly more than a thousand people are murdered in this way every day, and another thousand German men are habituated to murder. . . What shall I say when I am asked: And what did you do during that time?*

The Solf Circle like Moltke's Kreisau Circle included men and women from a variety of backgrounds, including those of noble descent, devout Protestants and Catholics, socialists and conservatives, who despite their differences found common ground in their opposition to Hitler on both moral and religious grounds. Their discussions would range far and wide but invariably turn to their personal roles in transitioning Germany to a different form of government after the Third Reich was little more than a bitter memory.

For Liliane it was an evening when everything around her seemed to sparkle. She and Hugo were greeted soon after they arrived by Frau Solf with a glass of sherry in exquisite cut crystal glasses while standing next to a priceless Delft epergne on a polished credenza that floated on an equally priceless Persian Isfahan. It was so unlike anything she had ever experienced, and Liliane let herself be swept away by the swirl of polished antiques and people.

Liliane, wearing the same dress she had worn at Borschadt but this time with her grandmother's scarf which made the ensemble something altogether different, was fascinated by Hugo's friends and soon became the center of attention herself because of her work on the Eastern front as a nurse. Hugo, oblivious to what Liliane wore, was on cloud nine simply to be at her arm. Liliane would soon return to the front and the courageous Hugo knew he needed to summon the courage before it was too late to say what he must before she left, that is he hoped for a future together when the war ended.

It was a full house that evening and among the guests was a new face brought to the party by Elizabeth von Thadden, the progressive educator and co-founder of the Solf Circle. He was a handsome Swiss doctor by the name of Paul Reckzeh who said he was practicing at the Charité Hospital in Berlin. Like most Swiss, he expressed anti-Nazi sentiments and was joined in that sentiment by others in attendance that night.

Reckzeh took a particular interest in Liliane's background, too much interest to Hugo's way of thinking. Reckzeh also seemed a bit too eager to share his views on what he called, *these troubled times,* in this reserved and closely knit circle of friends.

He had jet black hair, thick and wavy, and the finely sculpted features of a movie star. When he smiled with a mouthful of brilliant white teeth that seemed more than enough for two mouths, he struck Hugo as a Harlequin, common in medieval passion plays still in vogue in rural Germany, whose qualities as a trickster evoked the devil.

What do you really do, mein Herr, in these troubled times, Hugo wondered?

* * * * *

Leo knew he would be imposing by putting Dietrich's open-door policy to the test on this beautiful Sunday in April, but he needed his help in finding some way, any way to rescue Erika from prison. And besides, he dared not use the telephone.

The memory of the 1st of April blizzard in Berlin was a fading but for an occasional chunk of dirty snow and ice that lurked in darkened gardens and hid under debris by the side of the road. The warm sun shining like a spotlight through gaps in the newly green trees overhead and the hint of wild tarragon on the soft breeze, made it feel like a day of endless possibilities. But, alas, this was Nazi Germany.

He followed a row of stately homes tucked away in a thick forest of spruce, pine and oak trees in upscale Grunewald on his way to the home of Dietrich's father, the esteemed psychiatrist, Karl Bonhoeffer on Marienburger Allee where Dietrich was now staying. As Leo marched down the long stovepipe road toward what appeared to be a *cul de sac*, he wondered whether those inside these houses had lost sons in the war and whether they were Nazis or potential allies if he came knocking at the door. This heavily wooded reach seemed a perfect setting for conspiracy and concealment.

Leo knew that Dietrich would have fresh ideas about how to rescue Erika. He always did. It would not involve Freddie this time because they simply could not go to the well for a third time after his help on Grosse Hamburger Strasse and with the clandestine visit to Erika in prison.

Leo had lost sight of the *cul de sac* behind a bend in the road but heard the voices before he rounded the bend to see the house. He ducked behind an oak tree the size of a flak tower.

Fifty yards ahead, two men were walking Dietrich to a black sedan, the lead car in a procession of three sedans. A large group of Gestapo men were milling about. Dietrich was carrying what looked like a Bible and politely thanked one of the men for opening the car door for him.

Something Dietrich had scribbled on the inside flap of *The Book of Martyrs*, which Leo still had in his possession came immediately to mind, *the tyrant dies, and his rule is over, the martyr dies and his rule begins.*

Gott verdammt! Not you too, Dietrich, not you too, Leo groaned.

Dietrich had been preparing for this day for a long time. He knew it was inevitable. Dietrich had called the Dohnányi's earlier that day by happenstance, and the phone was answered by an unfamiliar man's voice. The man had hung up immediately.

Dietrich then went next door to the home of his sister Ursula and told her about what had had happened and warned her about what was likely to come. Ursula's husband was an Abwehr man as well. Unperturbed, Ursula prepared a large meal for Dietrich after which he returned home to put his papers in order, since the Gestapo would inevitably search his room.

It was about 4:00 pm when two men met Dietrich in his room. One was Judge Advocate Manfred Roeder, Hitler's *Blood Judge*, and

Sepp Lange. Leo recognized him as the leader of the Gestapo group that cornered them in KaDeWe during Harry's escape.

The Gestapo had been gathering information on their rivals in the Abwehr for a long time, wanting nothing more than to bring their rogue cousin to heel. As predicted, Schmidhuber, the Abwehr agent singled out by Toeppen and Herzleib, crumbled like a fresh sugar cookie under interrogation by Panzinger and Lange making it possible for the Gestapo to link Unternehmen 7 to illegal currency transactions and, in turn, to Bonhoeffer, Dohnányi and Oster.

On the day Bonhoeffer was arrested, they also arrested Dohnányi, Joseph Müller and his wife, and Bonhoeffer's sister Christine. Hans Oster would be placed under house arrest. Himmler had expressly ordered Kaltenbrunner to leave Canaris untouched for the moment.

Dietrich was a thorn in the side of the Nazis, yes, Leo thought, as he watched the scene unfold, but he had a hunch that there was more to this story, and it has something to do with Unternehmen 7. He badly needed to get word to Mehdi, Emil, and the others who had played a role in the operation.

* * * * *

On a balmy evening in May 1943, he entered the den of the minotaur, an oppressive zone of fetid air seemingly devoid of oxygen. Drawing a full breath got harder and harder for Leo with each step as he was escorted from the gate of Plötzensee Prison, a massive red brick structure on the outskirts of Berlin, to a small pavilion of the same red brick in a near courtyard of the sprawling complex. It had been a simple work shed at one time but now played an outsized role in the work of the state.

The guard had little interest in joining him and motioned Leo through the wrought iron double doors to the execution chamber.

Once inside, he looked away for an instant from what he knew he must eventually confront to count eight iron hooks fastened to a steel beam running the length of the room. The hooks were used for hangings.

He was not here to witness a hanging, however, and he forced his gaze onto the centerpiece of the chamber, its *Fallbeil,* or *falling axe,* that awaited Erika von Brockdorff. The guillotine was an imposing wooden structure with a blade at its apex, stained, sharp, and poised to kill again. The entire contraption sat on a concrete slab that sloped away at the edges to a drain whose walls were stained the same color as the blade.

The personnel assigned to the shed had taken a break and were now trickling in behind Leo from the outside. They acknowledged him respectfully because he was to all appearances a cleric, who had come to comfort the condemned.

They fell into what must have been their normal routine to replace the small table upon which the condemned prisoner would lay. They also tested a dolly attached to the tabletop that would allow them to slide the condemned back and forth several inches to adjust the position of the neck so it rested squarely under the blade.

Leo had managed to get himself into Plötzensee with the help of Admiral Canaris despite being warned not to go. He was putting himself at risk unnecessarily because there was really very little he could do for Erika now, they told him. If someone in the SS or Gestapo saw through his disguise, it would be the end of him. But a promise was a promise as far as Leo was concerned despite the risks.

The condemned prisoners were kept in a large cell block directly adjacent to the execution chamber. They spent their final hours in shackles in special cells on the ground floor, which the prisoners called the *house of the dead.* Their final steps took them through a small courtyard to the chamber and their fates.

The executioners received an annual salary of 3,000 Reichsmarks and a special bonus of 60 Reichsmarks for each execution, while the families of the executed prisoners had to pay an *invoice of expenses.* The public prosecutor charged 1.50 Reichsmarks for every day of custody in Plötzensee, 300 Reichsmarks for the execution, and 12 Pfennigs to cover the postage for the *invoice of expenses.* Leo had stopped first at the cashier's quarters to settle Erika's debt.

It is strictly forbidden for you to have any contact with the prisoner, but you may witness the execution and say your prayers for her then. I don't know how you managed to get a ringside seat, but you may regret that you did, Johann Reichart, the chief executioner, told Leo as he had approached the doors of the work shed.

She will come in through the side door, Reichart added. *Well, from there it's pretty quick. You can watch a couple to get the idea, or my advice would be you go have a smoke in the yard, and I will have someone fetch you at the right time.*

Leo, fully aware of his limitations, chose the latter. One execution was one more than he was prepared to handle. Twenty minutes passed and at regular intervals of three or four minutes he would hear something akin to a heavy hammer blow on hard wood. Only once did he hear anyone cry out, and it was someone who at the top of his lungs shouted, *everything I did, I did for love of the Fatherland!*

Your turn, Reichart said flippantly as he poked his head out the double doors.

Scheisse, I hope I don't embarrass you, Erika, Leo said to himself as he entered the shed on legs not fully under his control.

And then she was there having just entered through the side door. She blinked several times as her eyes adjusted to the harsh light of the shed. Ericka wore a simple, knee-length gray smock that looked like a potato sack and walked unshackled.

Erika had combed her hair and damned if she didn't wear a small amount of lipstick. Her black eye did not go unnoticed by Leo.

Leo smiled in admiration and stepped forward but was stopped by a guard. The commotion prompted her to look his way. Erika recognized Leo immediately and gave him the hint of a cheeky smile and a whispered thank you.

There was only one person in the room with the stature to bring everything to a halt and that person glared at her captors, raising her voice in defiance, *I pity all of you as I leave the world that I love for a better place, a place you will never see.*

Erika's tone softened, and she added, *I love my country, I love, you, Saskia, and you my dear Graf, and I will bask in the warmth of your eternal love soon*, she said. Her valedictory ended with a throaty laugh as she surveyed her stunned audience. It was the full and genuine laughter Leo remembered from his dinner with Erika at Savigny Platz.

Two guards then took Erika roughly by the arms and lifted her onto the table. She gave no resistance, and Leo hoped that Little Otto was right and that she would be greeted by her loved ones the moment she died. As Little Otto saw it, time no longer mattered in eternity, so Saskia and Graf would be there waiting when she arrived.

The next thing that Leo could recall of that terrible evening was coming to after hitting the pavement on *Schwanenfeld Strasse* hard after being thrown headfirst from the front gate of the prison yard. With scuffed hands and a heavy heart, he picked himself up from the ground for the long walk back to Wedding.

* * * * *

Juni 1943

Leo, Marushka, Hugo and Hedwig had settled into a routine by the time Spring showers gave way to an onslaught of summer thunderstorms and more Allied bombings. The pace of bombing raids had grown steadily, and it was difficult at times to distinguish between the rumble of storms that nourished the city's gardens and those that incinerated them.

In a weak moment lubricated by a bottle of Irish whiskey, which Hedwig had found unopened and unscathed in the ruins of a house in Neukölln, Marushka had confided in her three companions, *this life we live my friends…it has worked itself into an emotional tapestry of one dull dead pattern for me —yesterday is tomorrow, tomorrow we hide someone in Dahlem rather than Zehlendorff and, Oh God, I'm so tired.* The conspirators knew it was the whiskey talking because Marushka would not have had it any other way.

But then there was Marian.

Hedwig had become a master at juggling the demands of her many friends who needed her bravery in keeping Berlin's U-boats submerged and away from those who would sink them. The *Greiferinnen*, (both men and women served as *grabbers*), had been out in force during the early days of summer when their quarry intoxicated by the warm weather would be inclined to carelessly venture outdoors. More than a few were captured and many of those by *Blonde Poison*, the exceedingly clever Stella Goldschlag.

Hedwig had all but perfected the art of hiding people in plain sight, but one was always walking a tight rope even with the full cooperation of those you were trying to help. One of them, a young woman called Marian had thrown caution to the wind putting her life and the lives of those around her at great risk.

Like so many, Marian's comfortable life had been turned upside down by Hitler and the deviants who, to Marian's way of thinking, buzzed around him like flies around excrement. Her mother had once owned a fashionable dress shop steps from the most fashionable avenue in Berlin, the Ku'damm, until she was evicted in the Fall of 1933 soon after the national boycott of Jewish owned businesses in April of the same year.

Marian's father had been a senior official in the Ministry of Justice and an Aryan, who had been sentenced to several months in Sachsenhausen for mingling casually with friends, and friends of friends, who contemplated a time when Germany, whether a monarchy or a democracy, pursued a path freed of Hitler's shackles. That stay in Sachsenhausen had broken him, and his heart failed a few months after his return home.

They had managed to hold on to their small house in Zehlendorff at first because Marian and her mother had lived in a *privileged marriage,* which spared an Aryan husband and his Jewish wife along with their children from the full harshness of the antisemitic and racist Nuremberg Laws of 1935. These laws forbade marriages and extramarital intercourse between Jews and Germans and the employment of German females under 45 in Jewish households.

Its companion, the Reich Citizenship Law, added insult to injury by declaring that only those of German or related blood were eligible to be Reich citizens. The remainder, particularly Jews, were classified as state subjects without any citizenship rights.

Like her fellow U-Boat, Trudy, Marian had been classified as a *Mischling ersten Grades* loosely translated a *first-grade hybrid* as the product of a mixed marriage. Her mother was another story and, unlike Marian, was subject to immediate deportation after her husband's death.

Fortunately, Marian's father had the foresight to apply to have Marian's mother falsely classified as the illegitimate offspring of an Aryan father and Jewish mother cleverly supported by an impressive body of documentation, which he had expropriated from other case files. Her mother's case had been taken up by the *Rassenforschungsamt* (Race Investigation Office) of the Ministry of Justice in 1939 and lingered there still in 1943.

In the wake of the *Große Fabrik-Aktion,* when the Gestapo intensified door to door searches to render Berlin *Judenfrei,* Marian's mother had received a summons to appear for a *routine* interview at the local Gestapo office. Marian and her mother abandoned their home in Zehlendorff straight away fearing the dreaded knock on the door in the middle of the night. A friend of Marian's, one of the Bernstein sisters hidden by Hedwig Porschütz, had given her a slip of paper with Hedwig's name and address before the Bernstein girls disappeared into thin air.

At her first meeting with Hedwig, Marian said, *I must warn you we have limited means and cannot pay you*, to which Hedwig replied, *just as well. I cannot guarantee how long I can keep you alive, so it sounds like we have a fair bargain.*

Hedwig placed them with a Catholic widow by the name of Katharina on a quiet street with a cul de sac lined by lush pin oaks in early bloom. They were introduced to Katharina's neighbors as her sister, *Tante Lisa*, and her sister's daughter, Renate, recent refugees from the Sudetenland. Katharina kept a small apartment in the rear of one of the elegant townhouses on the horseshoe shaped block and, despite the close quarters, she and Marian's mother, who were roughly the same age, hit it off immediately.

The blue-eyed Marian, who wore her blonde hair in a long braid, had even been accepted without question by the two rather nosy sisters who lived together at the end of the cul de sac and shared duties as the block warden. This deflected attention away from Marian's graying mother, and fortunately the Kalbo's paid little attention to her.

Marian and her mother had thus joined the ranks of Berlin's U-Boats with the benefit of newly furnished identity and ration cards, which had once belonged to a mother and daughter who had perished in an artillery duel as the German army invaded Czechoslovakia to free its oppressed Germans. Marian had, however, sewn her real identity card and her mother's into the hem of her prized tweed jacket, one of the few pieces of clothing they could wear or carry on the run. Marian was certain their nightmare would end someday, and they would need them again when that day came.

Even those who resisted Hitler in the war years had to live and work within German society, and Marian struck up a small business doing accounting for the bierstube next door and other local businesses to make ends meet. However, she lived for the activities of the night with a small group of like-mindedly subversive friends from her days in Zehlendorff.

Everything I have done for you and your mother, I do willingly and with great affection, Marian, but your hatred of the Nazis has deprived you of all caution. Think of your mother, please, Hedwig pleaded. Hedwig hoped that she could convince Marian to curb those activities in defiance of the Nazis that imperiled her mother and their benefactor Katharina.

She should heed Hedwig's warning, Marian knew, and be more protective of her mother and their friend. Yet passivity was not an option for Marian, and she felt compelled to do everything in her power to rid Germany of its Nazi pestilence. To whisper, to complain, to hope was simply not enough.

So, it was in the dead of an unusually balmy night in June 1943 whilst a sweet breeze coaxed a melody from the swaying trees, that Marian found herself in an upscale residential neighborhood near the Charité Hospital, dropping leaflets into mailboxes. This time, the leaflets contained a sermon from the brave Graf Galen, Bishop of Munster, which railed against the ungodliness of Hitler's racial policies.

And so it was that Frau Zott returning home from her duties at the Charité saw a small group, perhaps four or five people, scurrying suspiciously about from door to door, shadow to shadow. Frau Zott made a mental note that the one with the crush hat partially concealing a long, blonde braid looked familiar.

* * * * *

The group had assembled for an emergency meeting at Perwe's behest. It was he, Marushka, Leo and this time Mehdi and Big Otto for good measure. Hugo was the last to arrive, and Mehdi took him aside briefly to slip him an envelope that Hugo pocketed without reading it given the urgency of the subject before them.

It was a frenetic time at the *Schwedische Kirche* because Perwe was preparing to send his wife Martha and their children to Sweden. The growing tempo of Allied bombings and harassment by the Gestapo had made her continued presence too dangerous. He would miss her calm and steadying influence and her sense of humor, but he hoped to join her by the end of the year when his replacement had been named.

Perwe was thus not in a particularly good humor. The group's fatigue from constantly racing one step ahead of an increasingly aggressive adversary along with the dolorous atmosphere of life in Berlin in June 1943 combined to make everyone feel like they had been walking in circles through a field of stinging nettles.

The subject before them, sat before them, sobbing uncontrollably. Even the preternaturally compassionate Perwe could summon little sympathy for her.

It was the cleaning lady who had been *spilling the spätzle* to the Reverend Martin Sauter for some weeks now. Her vacuity might have gone undetected had a *guest* of Perwe's not noticed a lapel pin worn by her frequent visitor sporting a red Reich's eagle emblazoned over a gold cross. Sauter had been clever enough to take it off on every visit except one proving perhaps that luck occasionally worked both ways in the Third Reich.

The voluminous discharge of bodily fluids from the snorting and whimpering penitent made her confession slow going. Finally, Marushka offered a hanky more to speed things along than as a display of compassion.

The liaison with Sauter had been spiritual rather than physical, the cleaning lady asserted. This was a fact of little import. What was more telling was that it had lasted over a nearly two month period going back to just before the blizzard in early April.

Having wrung all of the information possible out of her, along with an ample quantity of snivel, they excused her, careful to keep her in the compound under the watchful eye of Big Otto.

She could be useful to us, Leo said. *She has earned Sauter's trust because everything she has given him has come to pass*, Leo said.

Marushka jumped in, *I agree but she is so frazzled that she may not be able to pull it off.*

Finally, Perwe added, *I will have Martha speak with her. They have been close over the years. The rest of us are too angry to make any headway with her, but Martha just might succeed.*

And so, it was decided.

And then the other shoe dropped.

This development does not surprise me, Mehdi chimed in. *I was finally able after nearly two months to find the sergeant I thought I had co-opted for our visit that day to the police station to secure papers for Trudy and Michael. He had taken medical leave and was staying with his mother near Frankfurt an der Oder, the contemptible slug that he is.*

Upon his return to the police station, he was able to ascertain for me that someone was able to obtain a copy of the papers for Anna Lindberg, largely nullifying their value to us. This was about a week after our visit in the snowstorm. That individual was a man of the cloth, who signed for a copy of the documents on behalf of the Gestapo. Does anyone care to venture a guess as to who that might be, Mehdi asked with a sardonic smile?

Marushka replied glancing toward Perwe, *even more reason to give him a taste of his own medicine. I just may have an idea about how.*

She met Perwe's gaze, again. He nodded in agreement before returning to study recent developments in the bowl of his pipe.

And so, a plan was hatched.

* * * * *

Hugo was reeling from the news about the man Sauter. So much so, he had almost forgotten the letter that Mehdi had slipped to him without a word about its source. The handwriting allayed any doubt on that question as did the hint of rose water in the air. He opened the envelope greedily.

Dearest Hugo,

I have asked father to give you this letter after I return to my unit. If you are reading this, then I have indeed left for the Eastern front, which seems to twist and bend and recoil as the Russians prove able to torment us seemingly at will.

I am sorry that I did not readily say yes to your romantic offer as exquisitely tempting as it was. I have seen too many of our boys die with his betrothed's picture in his clenched fists and her name on his lips. One becomes somewhat superstitious in my line of work, so I hope my reaction did not hurt you.

So, please be patient with me.

My father used to take me to ballet performances at the Städtische Oper. I have always loved romantic stories and I was struck by a story in one of those ballets.

It was Orpheus and Eurydice. Do you remember the legend?

Eurydice, the love of Orpheus' life, died on the day of their wedding, bitten by a poisonous snake. Orpheus was shattered but resolved to do the impossible and to journey to the Underworld to confront Hades and bring his bride back to the World of the Living.

In myth, Orpheus is the Father of Music, and his singing before the gods of the Underworld let his immense pain shine through. The gods were so moved that Hades allowed

Orpheus to bring Eurydice back to the World of the Living on one condition. Orpheus was not to turn back to look at Eurydice's face until they had reached the light of the sun.

Orpheus took his love by her hand and started to go upward toward the light. But, on his way, he was overcome with doubt and worried that he had been deceived, that the hand he was holding was not Eurydice's but rather the hand of a creature belonging to the Underworld.

He forgot his promise and so looked back at her and in the instant when their eyes met Eurydice disappeared and Orpheus was powerless to prevent his bride from dying a second time. He understood that this time, death would be eternal, and nothing could be done to save her.

My love, we find ourselves bound to this myth, believe it or not, destined to confront the darkness and to retrieve each other from the confines of Hell. You would be hard pressed to tell me that our current situation isn't Hell, and it is no myth.

Orpheus had no confidence in his deepest intuitions and motivations and did not trust in a higher plan. Dearest, you must. We must.

So, in the humble saga of Hugo and Liliane, we must look only toward what is ahead, for to look back will cause us to lose that which we cherish the most, a future filled with light that knows loss and so cherishes what has been saved.

Your Liliane

IV. MALLEUS MALEFICARUM

—The Witches' Hammer—

September 1943

To say that the fall of 1943 quietly ushered in a dreadful turn of fortune for the people of Berlin would be only half right. There was alas nothing quiet about a 4000-pound bomb when it found its target.

Although not everyone was unhappy. The bolder, more aggressive Allied bombing campaign, which now included the Americans, coupled with rumors of the German defeat at Kursk in July and the Allied landing on the Italian peninsula in September, heartened Berlin's U-Boats who could begin to imagine an end to it all.

Unknown to most Berliners but for a few in military intelligence, the Allies in the early days of 1943 had launched Operation Pointblank, a combined bomber offensive involving both the RAF and US Air Force. Its purpose was the progressive destruction and dislocation of Germany's military, industrial and economic systems with particular attention given to the aircraft industry followed by producers of ball bearings, petroleum, grinding wheels and abrasives. The RAF attacked Germany by night and the Americans took over during the day to destroy objectives not suitable for night attack.

At the same time, the Allies sought to impose heavy losses on the German Luftwaffe and to redirect German fighter strength away from the Russian and Mediterranean theatres of war. This degradation of the German Luftwaffe would also undercut its ability to challenge the Allied landings planned for Northern France.

From Mehdi's perspective, that is from the ground looking up, the increased attention being paid to Berlin by Allied bombers was one thing. However, the well-organized, indiscriminate bombing of large swathes of Berlin, presumably to break the German will to resist, was a diabolical development that he knew would end his days in Berlin one way or the other.

Firestorms had raged in German cities starting in May, starving people of oxygen and burning them alive. On the 24th of July, during the driest month in Germany in ten years, Hamburg was set ablaze leaving 40,000 dead.

The carpet bombing of Berlin had begun in earnest in August raining liquid hell down on the city. Mehdi shuddered at the thought of the small 4-pound magnesium bombs that looked like matchsticks falling by the thousands from a single airplane, erupting in flames on impact.

But this was not the only trick the devil had up his sleeve. There were also the much larger phosphorous incendiaries that were impossible to extinguish with water because of the benzon gel they carried.

Mehdi's preparations to leave the city were almost complete and if the bombs got him first, Emil would handle his considerable wealth, which would be shared with his boys. Leo was another matter. In his relatively short life, Mehdi's young protégé had amassed a fortune well in excess of his own thanks in no small part to a swindle Leo had devised with Emil's help to substitute gemstones of little or no value for a priceless counterpart in the shipment of precious stones Leo brought to Himmler via Charley. Leo's wealth was also invested with Emil to be split between Big Otto and Mehdi should he fall victim to a bomb or follow Erika to the guillotine.

It would be fair to say, Mehdi thought that his job was done in Berlin in one important respect. He had kept his promise to Paladin and Anya. Leo had come to Berlin as a child and an enigma. His time with Dietrich and his singular focus now on helping those in the orbit of the Swedish Lutheran Church had, with a nudge here and there from Mehdi, molded a young man of character.

* * * * *

If they were not bleeding so damn badly his consternation would have boiled over into anger. Marushka's wound was on her left shoulder. She had been grazed but not to worry, she told Hans, these things looked worse than they really are. It was all he could do to keep from screeching about the chances she took. Then he turned his attention to the boy.

Or was he a man? Hans had not quite figured out Leo's age. Was it the light or some chameleon like quality he possessed that changed him or his impression of him from one moment to the next?

The boy's bleeding was worse, and he seemed to be dazed. Hans was back and forth to the kitchen sink as Marushka tried to staunch the bleeding with wet towels.

It appeared to be a head wound. In fact, two bullets had grazed Leo above and below his right ear creating a y-shaped wound. A split second or a different tilt of the head and both bullets would have hit him dead on, dead being the operative word.

Hans felt a combination of worry, anger and jealousy as the two bled profusely, leaving splotches of the stuff throughout the flat that he had cleaned just that day. To make matters worse, Marushka and Leo were now laughing but clearly in pain as they downed one shot of Kloster Ettal after another.

What the hell happened to the two of you, he demanded? It was not Hans who asked but Hugo just arrived from a soiree at Frau Solf's. He was even less sympathetic to their plight than Hans. Hugo was furious because he had never been told of the operation.

It was spur of the moment, Hugo, an exhausted Marushka replied. *We saw an opportunity to move the four we had hidden at Biesenthal by sending them South with the monks. They were in Berlin to deliver a batch of Kloster Ettal to Göring and gave us little warning, although they did give us a nice bottle. Medicinal it is,* she said slurring her words as she held up the flask of Kloster Ettal and laughed again with her young accomplice.

The ever-expanding Göring was a glutton who was especially fond of Kloster Ettal and served it to his hangers-on at parties where he would dress in a Roman toga and sandals. He and this select group of friends, addicted to morphine like himself, would down huge quantities of Kloster Ettal to enhance the effects of the Morphine taken together with a primitive form of LSD, supplied to him on a regular basis by Nazi scientists. LSD was also used by the Nazis as a truth serum.

Marushka and Leo had led the Jewish fugitives to the rendezvous point and made the exchange as planned with Brother Stephen. Minutes later, as they were feeling their way through the heavily wooded area near Dietrich's Biesenthal hut, they were attacked from behind by gunmen.

In fact, it had been the same two Gestapo agents who searched Marushka's flat and unknowingly spared Hans by not firing a shot into her sofa. They had been put up to the caper by Kaltenbrunner at the encouragement of the Reverend Doctor Martin Sauter, who prophesied that no good would come from the woman and boy going anywhere together.

Indeed, Marushka and Leo might well have ended up lying dead in the densely forested hills near Biesenthal thanks to Sauter but for a fatal mistake by one of their pursuers. The two Gestapo agents were having the same difficulty with the thickly wooded terrain as their prey, and the younger of the two agents, tripping over a log, inadvertently shot his colleague in the back as they clumsily pursued Marushka and Leo.

The older agent gurgling blood from a lung pierced by the younger agent's bullet died unhappily under the glare of his companion's flashlight. Even in death, he seemed to stare in disgust at his inept companion.

So, Hugo, is it just us or is your dark mood attributable to something else, Marushka asked shakily?

I have just come from another session at Frau Solf's, Hugo replied, *and I ran into that infernal physician who says he is posted at the Charité and, in point of fact, he does seem to be, but the origins of his appointment are a mystery to my friends on the medical staff. I have no evidence that he is Gestapo, but I shared my concerns with Moltke and von Thadden. She seems smitten with the man, so I was overruled. As I was leaving, Reckzeh was collecting letters from some of the guests to share with anti-Nazi brethren in Switzerland. I shudder to think what they put in those letters.*

And he knows you, Leo asked, emerging from his herbal fog momentarily.

Liliane and I, yes, unfortunately, Hugo replied. *Don't think the implications of this have not crossed my mind.*

Apart from this, there is some bad news and good news, Hugo added.

Such is our lot, the bad news that is, Marushka said absentmindedly as she helped Leo wobble to his feet.

So, I shall give you that first, Hugo shot back.

I spoke with Erik just before going to the Solf gathering, and he informed me that he had been called in earlier today for an interview by the Gestapo. Hugo was referring to the ringleader of their small group, the Reverend Erik Perwe.

The meeting was in the tombs of Prinz Albrecht Strasse and lasted four hours, a not particularly subtle escalation of their interest in our activities and worse yet, in Erik. In circumstances like this, it might not be long before the other shoe drops and there will be no returning from that vile place, he added.

Martha has already left for Sweden, and we need to convince Erik that it is time for him to follow, Marushka responded, as Leo followed the conversation from the echo chamber of his rattled brain.

He is halfway there, Marushka. While Erik is a courageous man, he is no fool. A few encouraging words from you might solidify his thinking, Hugo said.

So be it, she replied. *And the good news?*

As Erik had envisaged, Stockholm has given the order for the evacuation of Swedish consular officials here, as well as in Köln and Munich. Those evacuations move apace as we speak, Hugo said.

Erik has also been made aware by your friends with the railroad that the furniture and possessions of our countrymen will pass just North of Berlin on their way to Lübeck for shipment to Sweden in just under three weeks from now.

Marushka shot up from her chair but caught herself before she could scream in delight, instead growling, *yes, yes, we are in business.*

A jubilant Hugo replied, *indeed we are.*

* * * * *

Both men were in a foul mood, but Ernst Kaltenbrunner knew that when Himmler was in this state, he should tread lightly. At times like this, everyone was at risk of being consumed by the flames of Himmler's rage, even those who were nominally in his inner circle.

Himmler was meeting with his battle commanders in the East and had just returned from an inspection of Theresienstadt, the hybrid concentration camp and ghetto established by the SS during World War II in the fortress town of Terezín in German-occupied Czechoslovakia. Theresienstadt was simultaneously a waystation to the extermination camps for train loads of Jews and a *model retirement settlement* for the elderly and prominent among them to mislead the Jewish community about the true nature of Final Solution.

Its *guests* were allowed more privileges, including postal correspondence and the right to receive food parcels. Even though the conditions were deliberately engineered to hasten the death of its prisoners, Theresienstadt served an essential propaganda role, and therein lay the problem at the moment.

The International Red Cross was demanding an inspection and the Führer along with Goebbels was apoplectic about what the Red Cross might find in the current circumstances thanks in large part to the weak management of the sprawling camp. In late August of that year, 1,200 Jewish children from the Białystok Ghetto in Poland arrived at Theresienstadt. They refused to be disinfected out of fear that the showers were gas chambers. It was now coming on four weeks since their arrival, and the children were being held in strict isolation. It was one more sore on an already putrefied wound.

The people running this camp possess the collective intellect of a sack of potatoes, Himmler growled. Not interested in Kaltenbrunner's response, he added, *your report please.*

Sir, the Solf group has met again, and the Reverend's intuition has borne fruit.

You mean that insufferable man Sauter, Himmler responded.

Yes, sir. Reckzeh has been successful in gaining the trust of this group and gathered about a dozen letters from various members ostensibly to be sent to their anti-Nazi allies in Switzerland. They are quite revealing and indicate a broader network exists than previously known.

Recommendation, Himmler shot back.

Sir, I have already put together an operational plan for a round-up of the bunch of them beginning with Frau Solf and her daughter. Your aide de camp has been given the details and will review them with you on your trip back to Berlin.

Good, Himmler said. *What else?*

One of those in attendance, in fact it was the second meeting in which Reckzeh encountered him, was young Count von Reinfeld. He seems quite ingrained in the group although one can only infer his sentiments toward the Reich from his attendance. We did not collect a letter from him. By the way, he is also seen often with the pastor of the Schwedische Kirche in Wilmersdorf, so one plus one?

He acquitted himself well in Switzerland on my behalf with the Americans, so much so, there is a follow-up meeting set, Himmler interrupted. *Max Hohenlohe, whom you know, will represent us this time. Might be time to bring him in for an interview. Go easy though. Make it look routine so that he doesn't begin to cover his tracks.*

And, Himmler added?

Two disturbing items, sir. First, we had an agent killed two nights ago by terrorists in the forest near Biesenthal. This too stems from a lead provided by Reverend Sauter and may involve people in the orbit of the Schwedische Kirche in Wilmersdorf.

Von Reinfeld, Himmler asked?

No, sir, he was with the Solf people that same evening, Kaltenbrunner replied.

Again, Kaltenbrunner, go easy on this for now. We are in negotiations with the Swedes to expand access to their heavy industry as ours is currently under some stress. In this case, I am less concerned about finding the actual people, particularly if they are closely connected with the Swedes, than finding someone whom we can make an example of if my meaning is clear?

Yes, sir, it is.

And, Himmler demanded?

Equally troubling, sir. Five of our agents were assassinated in Brandenburg yesterday. They were Obersturmbannführer Panzinger's men from the Sonderkommando Rote Kapelle. This very group of men is responsible for the arrests of the Harnack-Schulze Boysen network and more recently the Swiss and French agents near Brussels.

An exasperated Himmler asked, *how did it happen?*

We have few clues, Kaltenbrunner responded, *except for an eyewitness who swears he saw two whores lead them into a deserted villa on the outskirts of the town. The burned corpses of our men were found the next morning on the villa's grounds. It looks like revenge for the work they did near Brussels. They were forced to disrobe and were injected with Phenol and then, paralyzed but fully conscious, witnessed themselves burned alive – an exact replica of what they did to the enemy's spies.*

Turnabout is…well, I wish these ruthless people worked for us. In any event, this receives top priority. Hunt them down, Kaltenbrunner. We cannot be embarrassed in this way. Are we clear?

Quite, sir.

So, the next time we meet, I want answers, results, man, Himmler said walking out of the meeting.

An angry Himmler upon leaving the meeting ordered the 1,200 irksome children deported to Auschwitz and an investigation into the malfeasance of the camp's leadership, who would soon follow the children to Auschwitz. None would survive the end of the year.

* * * * *

The fall breeze brought music to the pin oaks on the quiet cul de sac where the sisters Kalbo were up to no good as was their custom. The rustling trees displayed their fall colors of yellow and red, while the Kalbo's displayed their true colors.

The Frau Kalbo who was by temperament *sweet and kind* to animals was heard to utter, *do we really need to bother those nice men with the Gestapo about these people until we have proof? The resemblance to the girl with those miscreants distributing those awful pamphlets is there, but I do think further investigation is required. Blonde girls are as common as the sniffles. Sister, is it really worth drawing attention away from our work on the winter relief fund?*

The Frau Kalbo whose emotional life revolved around the stuffed animals on Museuminsel responded as she took a bit of schnaps with her afternoon tea by saying, *dear one, a Jew is a Jew, a traitor a traitor. We have a duty to the Reich, and I resent one of our own on this very street giving comfort to those animals if that is indeed the case. I grant you that we need proof and proof there shall be.*

What if we summoned the Goldschlag woman to do what she does best. It is only fitting that a Jew bring another Jew to the knife, the sweet Frau Kalbo suggested.

I am told by reliable sources, her sister responded conspiratorially, *that her parents have just been deported to Theresienstadt. How rich,* she said with a double measure of sarcasm that brought both to laughter.

Well, I can't imagine that Goldschlag will be of much help to us now, the sweet Frau Kalbo said as their laughter faded away.

Well, here is one idea, the other Frau Kalbo replied. *We are doyennes of the BDM-Werk Glaube und Schönheit (the League of German Girls Belief and Beauty Society). Perhaps we could invite Katharina and her guests for tea ostensibly to recruit them for the group and catch them off guard. We are clever that way, you know.*

There is merit in what you say, the sweet Frau Kalbo replied, *the young one with the long blonde braid, whom we suspect, is rather ill-tempered and, as they say, one does catch more flies with honey. Were she to know our real intent, she would never come, and then we would truly need to intrude on the good work of the Gestapo.*

* * * * *

The blood was pounding in Leo's ears like the rhythmic motion of a locomotive at full throttle. Were Hugo and Marushka brilliant, insane or a little bit of both, he wondered, as he waited for their plan to unfold in the pitch black of a pine forest thirty kilometers Northeast of Berlin.

The stars shone brightly like the sparkling cut glass he would substitute on occasion for one of the precious stones he smuggled for Himmler. His eyes kept coming back to one sparkling constellation that Marushka called *Cygnus*, the Swan, which was crowned by one of the brightest stars in the Northern sky.

Try as he might, Leo could not make out a swan nor any other living thing in the jumble of light above him. However, to make their escape when the mission was accomplished, Marushka had instructed Leo to take his boys and follow the crooked right branch of Cygnus, which to the untrained eye looked like a cross fallen on its side. This branch would lead them back to the juncture of two service roads where Mehdi would be waiting with the Schultheiss brewery truck.

This was not the first time Marushka and Hugo had smuggled people out of Germany using a system they called *Schwedenmöbel* (Swedish furniture). In the past it had been one or two here and there as they seized a timely opportunity to substitute a refugee for a crate-ful of furniture being shipped to Sweden through the port of Lübeck.

This time, it would be twenty of them, increasing the complexity of the operation 200-fold in Leo's view. Marushka had never promised that working with her would be easy, but this was insane, especially when one considered that the area where their plan would unfold on that dark and tense night was cheek by jowl with two Nazi forced labor camps.

The group of refugees, some political dissidents but most Jews, now huddled together in the woods included Michael, Trudy's husband. They had managed to get Trudy out of Germany on a flight from Tempelhof gambling that Anna Lindberg's identity papers had not been compromised. Jani had escorted Trudy to the door of the airplane just to be sure using her own Swedish diplomatic papers.

Rather than pine away during his separation from Trudy, Michael had become a valuable member of Marushka's *gang* putting his life on the line more than once to help his countrymen escape the Gestapo. Selfishly, Leo hated to see him go.

The group that night also included Arnold Huber, Marta's brother, whom Leo had first encountered in a culvert in the Tiergarten. Huber was having an increasingly hard time avoiding the Gestapo because of his unrelenting commitment to subversive political activities. Marta had finally convinced her brother that he could do more good by writing his subversive pamphlets from Sweden.

And then there was the late addition to the group at the urging of Hedwig Porschütz, two sweet, elderly women. One called herself Katharina and the other her *Tante Lisa.* Katharina had gotten the word to Hedwig just the day before, frantic that Tante Lisa's daughter, Marian, had finally gone too far. Word had arrived the day before that their block wardens, the Kalbo sisters, were interested in talking to the three of them, which could only mean one thing.

This was the last straw for the hot-headed Marian. *Enough is enough*, she growled! Hedwig pleaded once again with Marian when she and Big Otto arrived at their flat on the lovely street nestled under lush pin oaks to put her mother and Katharina's well-being before her hatred of the Nazis.

Marian had decided to march into the Kalbo's flat unannounced and confront them. Hedwig begged for a 24-hour head start to move Katharina and her mother to another location, and Marian relented.

It would be bad enough were a U-Boat to be discovered. There would be hell to pay, however, for a gentile harboring a Jew.

Leo took another look toward the cockeyed looking cross above him as he waited for the latest edition of *Schwedenmöbel* to unfold. It brought the image of Mary-Tay to mind. Anya's story of the beautiful, raven-haired girl crucified in Cilicia had captivated his imagination as a boy. *Mary-Tay, if you are looking down on us tonight, be kind,* Leo pleaded.

* * * * *

If fortuitously Mary-Tay was looking down on Leo from the foot of Cygnus, so too was Marushka from her vantage point on the opposite side of the tracks at the top of a densely wooded hill. She had escorted the twenty refugees from their collection point to the edge of the steep hill overlooking a clearing with the train tracks and a small shed next to a service road intersecting the tracks. Leo would be waiting in a stand of trees just behind the shed with a handful of boys from the wolfpack including Whistling Fritz, who would serve as the courier between the elements of the resistance working the plan that night.

You will hide in the woods on the other side of the tracks about 25 meters behind the shack, Marushka had instructed her charges. *Our people will be there to help you. When the train comes, stay hidden until they fetch you. You will be told what to do then. Now move out one at a time, and God be with you,* she said.

From his vantage point near the shed, Leo saw them skitter or slide down the hill, one by one, then run several yards to the train tracks, crouch looking up and down the tracks and sprint as best they could the last 25 meters to the cover of the woods. There his boys would silently take them in hand and hide them in prickly bramble behind a waist-high hedge of wild blackberries that ran parallel to the tree line.

Marushka wanted to remain at the edge of the clearing to ensure that everyone made it to cover safely, but her work was not yet finished. It was her job now to retrace her tracks to make sure that no one had followed them.

There was the crackle of gunfire up the tracks in the direction from which the train was expected. Everyone near the clearing froze. There was a forced labor camp less than five kilometers up the line from which laborers routinely tried to escape. If there were gunshots, then eventually there would be dogs, and their group would surely be discovered. Someone or something had just raised the stakes in their perilous race against time.

While they waited, afraid even to breath, amidst unseen creatures skittering through the brush around them, they first heard the droning of Allied bombers coming from the North en route to Berlin. They could also hear the beginning of bomb blasts to the South, which could only mean that another wave of bombers approaching from that direction was already pummeling the city.

On balance, Leo was pleased with this turn of events, which he had expected given the perfect weather in the area. This would occupy the attention of those who might hinder their efforts. Although, rail lines like the one before him running North to Lübeck were always vulnerable to attack. However, there could be no turning back now.

A few minutes ticked away, and they felt it before they heard it. There was a rush of warm air being pushed down the tracks in their direction by a massive unseen force. This was followed by a squealing sound as the approaching train took a sharp curve and then the clickety-clack of the train's wheels on the joints of the old steel rails.

Leo left his hiding place to stand in the middle of the track ready to signal the engineer with a yellow flag illuminated by a kerosene lantern. Big Otto stood 20 meters to his rear with a kerosene lantern and a red flag. As the massive locomotive came into view, it flashed its lights to acknowledge the yellow flag. It then turned its running lights off, becoming as it did a massive hulk that appeared darker than the night. The train slowed as it approached Leo's position and followed the tracks as far as Big Otto coming to a complete stop at the red flag.

More gun shots up the line. No dogs. Not yet.

The instant the train came to a stop, a group of men led by Hugo and Big Otto emerged from the woods and opened one of the box cars. The men working quickly started breaking the official customs seals on a number of large crates carefully prying the crates open. The crates contained furniture which quickly began to pile up on the side of the tracks.

The mass exodus of Swedish consular officials and their families in Berlin, Cologne and Munich along with all of their worldly possessions was in full swing. Alas, some of their furniture would never make it to Sweden with them.

Hugo had been able to work his magic, bribing the engineer and conductor to stop at the appointed place and time. They knew little about the plan and for that matter could not have cared less about it. They were not like the younger train men, all pig-headed Nazis, who had gladly marched off to war. Those who were left behind tended to be elderly and happy to accept the food, coffee, cigarettes and money offered by Hugo.

In a matter of minutes, on Leo's signal, two refugees at a time ran from the woods and were hoisted into the boxcar to be placed inside one of the now empty crates. Each would receive food, water and a pot for their waste. The latter had been an innovation of Marushka's in a prior operation when she said, *a crate that is supposed to contain a piano does not leak. Let's get a pot under our guest's behind so that the piano does not leak!*

It seemed like hours to Leo but in fact all refugees were placed in crates in less than 45 minutes by Hugo's men working with ferocious energy. There were more gunshots and this time the distant baying of hounds, but the resistance men did not skip a beat. They finished nailing the last crate shut and replacing the original customs seals with counterfeits.

Finally, the train lurched forward picking up steam as it moved Northward, and Leo collected his group for the hike back to Mehdi's truck. They would rendezvous later with Hugo's men, who were now destroying the furniture, to cart away what they could.

Leo to whom superstition and religion were indistinguishable, raised his eyes to Mary-Tay with a whispered prayer of thanks as he and his boys set off following the crooked right branch of Cygnus despite the staccato flashes of white light from bomb blasts that would momentarily erase the stars from the sky.

The train would arrive in Lübeck the following morning where the crates would be loaded onto a freighter. By the end of the next day, one and all would safely reach Stockholm, where Trudy and Michael would be reunited.

* * * * *

It was a living nightmare, Hugo thought to himself as he, Leo and Mehdi along with a couple of the boys crept through the Northern reaches of Berlin in the battered and bruised Schultheiss beer truck loaded with furniture. Their destination was *Die Bäckerei* in Wedding several kilometers to the Southwest.

They had been forced to take one detour after another, zigging and zagging to avoid the bombing. Theirs was a city engulphed in flames as far as the eye could see. Hugo imagined a massive, apocalyptic battle being waged above among the giants, Valkyries and demons with little thought of the mortals being terrorized below.

There were the demonic, lumbering bombers overhead raining thunder and lightning with unrestrained ferocity on the innocent and the guilty, lightning that spread as it hit the ground. The dry weather spawned firestorms that propelled smoke columns thousands of feet into the air, adding further chaos to the battle waged above.

Speedier Valkyries and their equally agile adversaries ran circles around the bombers spitting fire at each other. And for their part, earthbound giants challenged the invaders overhead by hurling flaming boulders thousands of feet into the air.

A direct hit on the road ahead produced a fireball that surged skyward to join the fray forcing the compatriots to veer off on a badly paved road toward a portentous stone archway which led to little more than a complex of run-down industrial buildings. The complex had once been the major sugar beet refinery in Berlin and now churned out grease and ball bearings for the Fatherland.

Across a narrow canal about 50 meters away, they saw a six-story building and the silhouettes of those inside take a direct hit. The phosphorous bomb burst open upon contact and sent a river of glowing green goop down the sides of what remained of the building incinerating everything in its path.

The shimmering green fire monster was at the same time beautiful and terrifying. As the companions painstakingly tried to avoid being hit themselves on their slow trek back to the relative safety of *Die*

Bäckerei, assuming it was still there, large swaths of Berlin seemed to be inundated by these rivers of unquenchable flame.

It was close to dawn when they arrived home to find *Die Bäckerei* and the sprawling Mietskaserne on Oderberger Strasse that housed it largely intact. The green flames that engulfed much of the city were losing some of their gruesome luster as the rising sun fought to break through clouds darkened by the cinders that once were people and places.

Indeed, Oderberger Strasse was an oasis of calm in an increasingly chaotic city, although the Wedding district had not escaped entirely. Just a few blocks away from Oderberger Strasse , the raised tracks of the Eberswalder Strasse U-Bahn station, which had recently been rebuilt after a prior bombing, had melted to the ground after taking a direct hit from a phosphorous bomb.

The boys whom they had left at *Die Bäckerei* to stand guard reported that there was no sign of Marushka who was to meet them there but that two unexpected visitors were waiting for them in the storeroom. The lead boy gave Leo a subtle nod to signify that whoever they were, they posed no threat.

In the rear of the cool, cavernous warehouse they found their guests. Both appeared to have seen better days. There was a petite blonde with what had once been a pert nose, which had recently been rearranged by someone's fist. She was wearing a bandage on her right hand. The taller of the two, an equally young woman, sported a swollen black eye that made Leo wince when he saw it.

Hello, Leo, they both said in perfect harmony ignoring the others with him.

Good, God, Jani, Tomi what happened to you two, he replied?

She burned herself cooking, Tomi said as Jani raised her bandaged hand smirking.

And you, he said looking at the wounds on their faces?

Jani cut him off, *a story best left for another time, mon cher.*

And what have you boys been up to, Jani added coyly. *We have just come from Reverend Perwe who told us that you both had a train to catch*, Jani added smirking.

A story best left for another time, cousin, Hugo responded.

Well then, enough of these pleasantries, we have news from Reverend Perwe, Jani said.

How have they fared tonight, Hugo asked clearly concerned.

Two houses are burning nearby, but the church and rectory along with the other buildings on the grounds are intact even though they have lost quite a few windows. No one has been injured, Jani replied.

Thank God, Hugo responded.

Has Marushka been seen there tonight, Leo asked also concerned about their missing comrade.

Certainly not while we were there nor immediately before, Jani replied.

And your news, Cousin, Hugo asked?

There are two problematic developments, Jani said as if giving an after-action report to her superiors. *Firstly, Reverend Perwe received a visit from the Gestapo, one of their lead men, a Sepp Lange just today. The interview last two hours. There was no search of the church grounds and no real outcome to the interview, so apart from this unwanted visit, the Gestapo seems to be playing its cards close to the vest.*

He is one of Kaltenbrunner's acolytes and dangerous, Hugo replied. *And this is Erik's second interview. It is now imperative that he join his wife and family in Sweden. It was only a matter of time before the Gestapo started to turn the screws and, search or no search, we all know the trajectory this situation will now take,* Hugo added.

And the second development, Leo asked?

No better than the first, Jani said. *The good Reverend asked us to tell you that Lange asked about your whereabouts, Hugo, and left this. I took the liberty of reading it. You have been summoned for an interview at Prinz Albrecht Strasse,* she added.

Hugo shut his eyes and exhaled through pursed lips.

The timing, cousin, may not be coincidental, Jani said. *Someone by the name of Otto Kiep who described himself as a friend of yours visited Reverend Perwe. Apparently, Kiep knew of your association with the church. He asked Reverend Perwe to tell you that your worst fears about the physician from Charité were well placed and anyone associated with Frau Solf's circle of friends is at great risk. He said to tell you that Moltke had enlisted his help in warning Frau Solf's guests.*

It had been Hugo's mentor von Moltke who had learned of the betrayal of the Solf Circle, particularly those who attended her gathering on the 10th of September, through a friend in the Air Ministry who had tapped a number of telephone conversations between Reckzeh and the Gestapo. Moltke and Otto Kiep, a high official of the foreign office, rushed to inform anyone associated with the Solf Circle. Many tried to flee for their lives, but Himmler had his evidence, and the Gestapo would round up most of the group by January 1944.

The news hit Hugo like a 4000-pound bomb, and he had to sit on a nearby crate lest his legs give way from under him. Head in hands he cursed himself for not doing more to convince von Thadden of the danger she and the group faced. He worried out loud that Liliane had been implicated after their chance encounter with Reckzeh at an earlier Solf gathering.

It was at that moment that Marushka finally joined the party.

* * * * *

No one spoke. No one could. Even the unflappable Jani was flapped.

The understated elegance that was Marushka's calling card had disappeared and in its place, there before them stood a whirlwind of competing sensations much like one of the crazy abstract expressionist paintings of the day.

Her hair was matted as if she had been swimming and her clothes smelled of rancid water and smoke. Those standing nearest to her picked up the scent of cow manure.

Now that you have all had a chance to gawk at my appearance, shall I tell you what happened, Marushka said to the sound of a popping cork? Big Otto had just arrived with glasses and two bottles of Dom Perignon, a pre-planned celebration of their successful escapade that night. Big Otto proudly announced that it was taken from Himmler's private stash at Café Alois, as Marushka waited impatiently for the group's attention.

It had been a very close call, and those assembled heard a stream of consciousness accounting of a pursuit by armed men and dogs, bright lights that attempted to cut off her escape route, a roll in a pile of cow manure and a dip in a small stream to confuse the pursuing bloodhounds. That still may not have been enough had she not happened on a factory that had just been bombed. She threw herself into the task of helping to fight the fire along with other volunteers, and it was a note from the fire brigade commander that finally secured her safe passage back to Berlin.

When she had finished, Hugo proposed a toast to the intrepid Marushka, to sanity and to better days to come for themselves and the 20 souls that were now on their way to Sweden. All raised a glass and downed their champagne.

It was at that moment that Marushka passed out, glass held firmly in hand.

* * * * *

The compatriots managed a few hours of fitful sleep. Two of the wolfpack had taken over many of Mehdi's and Leo's responsibilities in the bakery in recent months and later that morning served the group warm Vollkornbrot. Mehdi and Leo had been good mentors and the lusciously dense bread along with ersatz coffee revived the group.

I think that we need to be realistic about Erik's position, Hugo said. *He must be convinced that it is time to rejoin his family in Sweden. There is a limit to everything, and it is time for this brave man to think about himself and his family rather than others.*

Marushka and Leo agreed without hesitation. *I think that we can get the exit papers that are required for a flight out of Tempelhof, although there are no guarantees the Gestapo won't intervene*, Marushka said.

I may be able to help you there, as the good reverend's traveling companion, Jani chimed in. *Thanks to my father, as you know by now, I still have diplomatic papers and arguably the immunity that goes with it, although in this hell hole, one can't be sure of anything. A few days in Stockholm might do me some good. A telegram from Bishop Björkquist's in Stockholm officially recalling Reverend Perwe would also help with appearances.*

You are an agent of Swiss intelligence, Jani. What if the Gestapo agents who were on that train are there and recognize you, Leo asked? Leo was referring to his escape to Switzerland with Ingrid and their rescue by Jani and Tomi.

Can't worry about every 'what if, mon cher. If I did, I would have curled up and started sucking my thumb a long time ago.

This drew laughter from the group and agreement that this was the best way to get Reverend Perwe out of Germany in a timely way.

I will talk to him today, Hugo said. It was an offer that was met with total silence.

Leo took the lead, *look around you and tell me if you find anyone sitting here who thinks that this is a good idea, Hugo. Think about it. The Gestapo will have the church under surveillance and would like nothing more than to have you drop by.*

Marushka said nothing weighing for the moment the pro's and cons of Hugo's idea. Jani was not so hesitant, *cousin, you are really no better off than Reverend Perwe at this point. Your summons to another interview by the Gestapo makes that plain. And if you have this other matter with the Solf people hanging over your head, your days in Berlin are also numbered.*

Hugo did not answer Jani but started to think out loud, *I know these people and can handle myself in an interview. Himmler will vouch for me. Although, if I go underground, I could still help with our cause?*

A clear-eyed Marushka finally put in her two cents, *after Erik, Hugo, I have never worked with anyone as brave and resourceful as you. Never. Scheisse, but both of your ideas are bad. First, we have friends, too many friends, who had far less skullduggery hanging over their heads than you, who never returned from Prinz Albrecht Strasse. Also, while we would hate to lose your steady hand, you are no longer anonymous but someone that the Gestapo has squarely in its crosshairs. If they aim at you, they are liable to hit one of us and there goes all we have built.*

Hugo, your fight against the Nazis does not end here. It moves elsewhere now, Leo added. *I think that Father Rupert could use a man like you to support his work at the border.*

Jani let go with a sonorous, *Bravo, Leo, Bravo. Rupert is a good idea,* having regained some of her effervescence now that she was operating on a full stomach.

So, one problem solved but....How do we get Hugo out of Berlin and then to Ettal, Leo asked of no one in particular?

Silence. Tomi moved from her perch on one crate in the Mietskaserne's warehouse toward Jani who was perched on another and whispered in her ear.

Roger will not care as long as we have the names, Jani announced to the group. Jani was talking about Roger Masson, their boss and the head of Swiss Military Intelligence. *In fact, I think he would like the idea,* Jani added.

Jani brought her compatriots up to speed on the plan, *we have come by five sets of identity papers of Gestapo operatives. Don't ask how. Let's say, we were simply returning a favor, Tomi and I. They belong to a group called Sondercommando Rote Kapelle, a relatively new but lethal group of agents who pose a threat to our own agents in the field.*

Let us pick two that Leo and Hugo can use to run the gauntlet to Ettal. I think we must make the assumption that despite having neutralized these agents, no word of their demise will have yet reached checkpoints or border crossings. The Gestapo will want to play this one very close to the vest.

Tomi obligingly grabbed a handful of paper from a nearby leather satchel and threw it on the warehouse floor for the group to examine.

One set of papers was charred and useless. Another bore the picture of an agent who looked remarkably like Hugo. They were the same height and weight and could have been brothers. This was one problem solved.

The other papers were less than an ideal match for Leo, but the group zeroed in on the best of the bunch. They would have to remove the seal using the customary hardboiled egg and replace the original agent's picture with one of Leo, but this was a skill that Mehdi and the wolfpack had nearly perfected.

Once that was accomplished, agents Mateus Hummels and Bernd Klose would be reborn to fight another day.

* * * * *

Jani pulled Leo aside as everyone prepared to go their separate ways, and they simply held each other, forehead to forehead, Jani lost for words for the second time that night. Nature abhors a vacuum, so Leo jumped in, *you know how much I.....*

Jani held a smile in check with visible effort. With a serious expression that seems to Leo entirely foreign to her personality, Jani put two fingers to Leo's lips and said, *I know how you feel. It radiates from you and warms me whenever we are together. Leo, you are brave, handsome and clever, all qualities that I admire. There is also an innocence about you that I envy. You will become something, someone important, someday.*

I love and admire Anya for the same reasons, Jani added, *although she is much farther along than both of us in sorting it all out.* Leo raised his eyebrows at the word *love* and Jani was quick to respond, *not in that way, mon cher, but I would not refuse were it to be offered.*

Jani added, *somehow, I managed to grow from a silly little girl to one who is resolute in her desire to rid the world of evil, to destroy the Nazis. But I have blood on my hands and fear that I have come to love it too much and for that reason am no better than our adversaries. My quest, I suppose, will be to find redemption someday when this insanity is behind us for good.*

Liebling, they were interrupted by Tomi at that point, *Liebling, we must go*, she said to Jani.

After a long kiss that replaced her usual playfulness with craving, a tearful Jani was gone.

* * * * *

When the dust had settled and the flames were quelled from the previous night's horrendous pounding, they found Marian and the Zott sisters in the charred rubble of the *cul de sac* under scorched pin oaks. As far as anyone was concerned, the three of them had officially died as victims of the Allied terror, so each of their coffins would be draped with the Nazi flag. The city of Berlin would also pay for their funerals. In a final gesture that might have ranked as the eighth dirty trick of the perverse Max and Moritz, the three would be buried together.

* * * * *

Leo was never one to take comfort in a good omen because it reaffirmed that there was such a thing as a bad omen, but Leo and Big Otto had heard a cricket chirping in the warehouse, which according to Mehdi brought good luck to those within earshot. And so, it was preordained, or so they thought, that the trip to Ettal would be largely uneventful at a time and in a world when the only constant was chaos.

They set off in mid-October in the long-suffering Schultheiss beer truck. They stopped first at Tempelhof airport to let Leo see Jani before she boarded a flight to Stockholm with Erik Perwe. His companions were Hugo riding shotgun in the passenger seat and Big Otto along with Tomi in the jump seat of the truck's spacious cab, who were made to look like prisoners being returned to stand trial in Munich by Gestapo agents Matteus Hummels and Bernd Klose.

Despite appearing to be in shackles, Tomi sat behind Leo the entire time with her right hand in the pocket of her leather jacket resting gently against the trigger of a 9mm Walther PPK loaded with hollow point parabellum bullets. Anyone standing in their way would come to an unhappy and painful end.

There was an intense encounter near Munich at a Waffen SS checkpoint where one could continue southward toward Ettal or west toward Dachau. Leo and Hugo, that is Matteus and Bernd, were put to the test by the Waffen SS sentries and forced to wait over 30 minutes while the SS tried to reach Berlin. Fortunately for the four traveling companions, the telephone lines to Berlin were down and Hugo was highly effective as the aggrieved senior Gestapo man in a hurry. Walther PPK or not, they would have been heavily outgunned had the cricket not come through.

Tomi eventually took her leave of the group just south of Munich at a non-descript railroad crossing where a hay wagon drawn by a colossal shire horse was waiting. The three remaining companions set off again for Ettal, another two hours to the South.

* * * * *

Mehdi, a child of the Levantine, would revel in the stories his mother told him about the ancients. The most violent among them would terrify Mehdi and his brothers giving them nightmares. Among those was the story of how the fearsome Persians murdered the Roman emperor Valerian by pouring molten gold into his mouth.

He shuddered imagining his boys suffering a similar fate. He had just left ration coupons, money and his condolences with two families who lived in the slums of Kreuzberg. They had lost their boys, his boys, the night before in an Allied air raid. They were good boys whose instinctive nobility rose above the squalor of their surroundings.

One was a distant cousin, a light skinned Egyptian whose family had escaped detection for nearly a decade. He and his companion had volunteered as *Luftschützen*, (air wardens) and, as the Allied bombers ploughed through Berlin, led roughly eighty of their neighbors, young and old, Nazi and not, to shelter in a deep cellar.

Several phosphorus bombs hit the area near their bomb shelter and one emptied its detestable green goop onto the street where a glowing rivulet seeped down the cellar stairs into their bomb shelter, sealing its exit. Those who did not succumb to direct contact with the incandescent particles that burned at nearly 3000 degrees Celsius would most certainly have perished from inhaling the hot, dense white smoke of the bomb.

Phosphorus particles continue to burn until they are completely consumed or deprived of oxygen. Mehdi could do little more than watch in sorrow and disgust as rescuers worked into the next evening to put out the blaze and recover those entombed in the bomb shelter.

Goebbels exhorted the population of Berlin that same day to resist this horrible new turn toward Allied carpet bombing with supreme irony, *this unconscionable behavior of the air pirates is at one and the same time impersonal, indiscriminate and inhumane and must be resisted. The glory of the Fatherland shines brightest in its darkest moments.*

From where Mehdi stood watching the valiant but futile rescue efforts, there was nothing *impersonal* about the bombing. *Nothing of military value in Kreuzberg, just good people, Allah yel'ena'k, Allah damn you, Churchill,* Mehdi growled to no one in particular!

To make matters worse if that were humanly possible, Hedwig Porschütz had found him to deliver news from Marushka. The flight carrying Erik Perwe and Jani had disappeared over the Baltic Sea. Authorities were searching for survivors but had yet to find them or any sign of wreckage.

Mehdi had no doubts about who was responsible for that disaster. *I must break the news to Leo,* he told himself, tears worse than any firebomb burning in his eyes.

Allah yel'ena'k – Allah damn you, you Nazi pigs!

* * * * *

It fell to Father Rupert to tell Leo about Jani's fate. It took nearly two days to get word to Ettal. Mehdi was able to prevail upon his friends at the Wedding police constabulary to get word to their counterparts in Ettal by means of a *teletypewriter,* which at that time was the chief means of communication between police departments in cities throughout Germany.

Leo and Hugo's visit to Ettal had started well enough because as they finally pulled up to the sprawling Abbey at dusk, they saw a military truck with a red cross on its side. A young woman in unform was saying goodbye to Rupert.

Mein Gott, the eminently self-contained Hugo shouted as he launched himself toward the door of the cab. Hugo would have been out of the truck in a split second had Leo not grabbed him by the collar.

Hold on, hold on, what is it? What is so important, Leo asked?

I believe that is Liliane, a bewildered Hugo croaked.

Before we do anything, let's talk to Rupert. There are Germans carrying guns standing next to the truck and we are fugitives. Remember? Let's not draw attention to ourselves.

Yes, I'm sorry. Thank you, Leo, Hugo said as he took a halting breath.

It seemed like an eternity before the truck left and judging from Hugo's facial expressions, Liliane's presence during that time seemed both to beguile and torture him. When they could finally see Rupert, he explained that indeed it was Liliane, a captain now in the Wehrmacht medical corps, who would come to pick him up to minister to the needs of her patients at the huge German medical complex at Garmisch-Partenkirchen in the valley below.

She is a lovely girl, Rupert said. *So bright, so caring.*

The usually self-assured Hugo was barely able to put a full sentence together and struggled to explain his connection to Liliane. Noting his discomfiture, Rupert mercifully added with a sly grin, *she comes again in two days to take me to the camp. Perhaps, we can arrange a medical consultation!*

But now we must turn our attention to one more thing, Rupert said gravely.

* * * * *

Both men took the news hard. Their stoic silence belied the depths of their sorrow and despair. A lively young woman, a fearless and fearsome compatriot gone from their lives. Leo for whom religion was superstition and superstition religion hoped that if Jani died with the Reverend Perwe that her proximity to the good man would smooth the way for her welcome into the next life.

Hugo thanked Rupert for his kindness in breaking the bad news to them, and both Hugo and Leo left Rupert's presence without saying another word. They went their separate ways. Brother Stephen reported that he had seen Rupert walking toward a meadow farther up the ridge line, head and shoulders slumped over.

Rupert found Leo in the ornate baroque chapel of the abbey later. The impenetrably dark dome of the basilica seemed to absorb virtually all remaining light in the chapel except for one bright oasis where Leo's silhouette was outlined against a large wrought iron stand of flickering votive candles.

Leo looked like he had been crucified. He was slumped in the wooden pew, his long arms extended outward along the top edge of the pew. His head had fallen back over it so that his tears ran up his face rather than down.

Rupert sat next to Leo and bumped him on the shoulder, arousing Leo from his reverie, eyes fluttering open, confusion racking his handsome, wet face.

Here, take a swallow. I think that we both need this, Rupert said as he handed Leo a flask of Kloster Ettal.

You know, Leo, my chosen vocation is to light the path of redemption for those searching for it, but I fear we Germans will be stained for a thousand lifetimes by what we didn't do, that is to stop the madman before he could perpetrate the horrors that have shaped the history of this time. Our best hope for redemption lies in reluctant heroes like Dietrich and Erika, Perwe and Jani whose example will lead us out of this darkness, Rupert said.

Leo reached for the Kloster Ettal and took a prolonged guzzle. *A friend of mine believes, believed, that there is no such thing as time in eternity and, after we die, we are immediately reunited with those we love, who will already be there to greet us when we arrive. Or maybe it is just that we all get there at the same time somehow,* Leo said.

There are mystics who believe much the same thing although they would describe it differently. Some might describe it as a final dream, the instant we die full of such vivid anticipation of all that will come after that it is the equal of all that will come after. Others might portray it as returning to the one true state of reality once our present dream state passes, Rupert replied.

My tradition paints a romantic picture of the afterlife in our catechisms. Yet the true nature of what we are talking about is unknown and a matter of faith for each of us, Rupert added.

I think it must be earned, Leo replied, swerving between his own train of thought and Rupert's. *Otherwise, Himmler and Hitler would be treated no differently. They would die with their hopes and dreams intact.*

Your time with Dietrich has been well spent, Leo. What news do you have of him, Rupert asked?

We came very close to getting him out of Tegel prison with the help of his friend Corporal Knoblauch, a prison guard. Thanks to him and the bravery of Dietrich's sister and brother-in-law, they obtained a mechanic's uniform for Dietrich to use in his escape while Mehdi and I supplied papers, coupons and money. Turning to face Rupert for the first time, Leo added, *but I suspect you know something of this, Rupert, because Emil would have been our ticket out of Germany.*

I did. The contours of the plan rather than details, Rupert replied. *We were to be a stop on Dietrich's way out of Germany if needed.*

Knoblauch had paved the way for Dietrich to simply walk out of Tegel with him in his mechanics uniform at the end of a guard's shift, Leo continued. *But then the Gestapo turned the plan upside down by arresting Dietrich's sister and brother-in-law for unrelated reasons, which meant that several members of the Bonhoeffer clan had now been imprisoned,* Leo replied.

It was at that point that Dietrich refused to go through with the plan. He realized that if he did, he would make matters much worse for his family, especially his parents. I was confused and a little angry at first. But then I remembered Dietrich's reaction a long time ago when I told him that the martyrs portrayed in his Book of Martyrs should not have resigned themselves to their fates and should have been cleverer because there is always a play, always a way to slip the noose.

Leo, nearly everyone working for Canaris has now been arrested and those who have not are only free because Hitler thinks he can gather more information by waiting, Rupert responded. *It sounds like you had a perfect plan that suffered from terrible timing. What would you have done if you were in Dietrich's shoes,* Rupert asked?

I don't know for sure, Rupert. But it is pretty clear to me that like the martyrs, Dietrich knew that in the end there is no escape if you believe, and like the martyrs, Dietrich's immortality will be well earned.

So, when you see Jani, what will you say to her, Rupert asked? Leo paused to study Rupert's expression to make sure he was serious.

That I was never as clever in battle as she, Leo responded without hesitation, *but that I fought and succeeded all the same. And for that reason, Rupert, I need to see Brother Andrew before I return to Berlin and learn more about this thing he calls, Malleus Maleficarum.*

* * * * *

NOVEMBER 1943

It was at twilight the night before Leo's return to Berlin that Rupert found him doing what he seemed to love most – baking in the capacious abbey kitchen. Rupert chose to avoid the subject of Leo's recent conversation with Brother Andrew. It worried him but who was he to second guess his comrade's armamentarium.

Leo, our monks rejoice in your visits because they know they will eat exceedingly well thanks to your genius. Indeed, the baked goods spread on the large oak table before him and the aroma of those still in the domed wood-burning oven were as intoxicating as a dozen flasks of Kloster Ettal.

The Bread of Life, a breathless Rupert said to no one in particular.

A reflective furrowing of the brow. The hint of a smile. Leo replied, *thank you, Rupert, because like Dietrich you always seem to find the loftiest of meanings in the smallest of things. I fear that I am like a meadow lark flying in place against the wind when it comes to the insight that seems to come so naturally to the two of you,* Leo added with a snort.

Rupert cut a huge hunk of warm Vollkornbrot and pulled it apart, relishing each bite as if it were a host. He reflected on the nobility of the boy and despite his protestations to the contrary, he sensed in Leo a rare consciousness of the vanity of all achievements and of the suffering of all life, not merely of one's own.

Leo, I have never met anyone with the capacity to use that meaning quite as successfully as you. If one day, you would like to learn why, you are always welcome here, Rupert responded.

* * * * *

Frost glazed the earth. Red cheeks and runny noses abounded.

At first light the next day, Leo and Big Otto readied their departure. Rupert had supplied barrels of beer and official papers to establish that the boys were making a delivery on behalf of the Abbey. As was customary, an ample supply of Kloster Ettal was stockpiled to facilitate safe passage if a little bribery was needed. The Schultheiss truck had even been blessed during its stay with a full tune up and idled so smoothly that the spirits of the monks soared as if they were listening to a well sung Ave Maria.

Hugo, who was not returning to Berlin urgently sought out Leo and took him by the arm into the stables *for a word*.

I hope this is good news, a bemused Leo said.

It is if today goes as I hope it will, Hugo replied. Hugo had been reticent to share his plans with Leo because of the loss of Jani but could not wait any longer because he felt that he would be cheating his friend.

I plan to ask Liliane to marry me when I see her today, Leo. Rupert has agreed to officiate. This has all happened for a purpose. Imagine, despite all the chaos that swirls around us, Liliane and I are somehow reunited here.

Or perhaps it is because of that chaos that you are here in the first place, Leo replied.

Hugo tried desperately to restrain his jubilation for Leo's sake and nodded as if Leo has a point, *perhaps, but in any event, I want you to be my best man. Marushka shall be the maid of honor. In your places, I will ask Brother Stephen and Brother Andrew to stand in and bear witness for you. It will be you nonetheless who will be named as my best man if you will honor me so.*

Of course, I will, Leo said. *Brother Stephen is a better man than I, so you made a good choice of stand ins.*

Hugo gave Leo a bear hug, *God speed, Leo. Until we meet again.*

Goodbye, Hugo, Leo said with an air of finality.

* * * * *

Götterdämmerung descended on Berlin in November 1943 with relentless carpet bombing of a scale and tempo never seen before, making the sum total of all previous bombing raids seem like a summer fireworks display at the Brandenburger Tor. When Leo and Big Otto returned to Berlin, they found a city that was almost unrecognizable. One city block might appear largely intact, while the next had been reduced to dirt, filth and destruction.

It might be the celestial intervention of Mary-Tay, whom Leo imagined had now been joined by Jani, or a trap set for him by the perverse Max and Moritz, but the opportunity Leo sought, his raison d'etre for returning to Berlin, all but dropped into his lap upon his arrival.

Charley would urgently like to see you, Leo. There is something he needs you to do for him within the month and he has been apoplectic about your absence, Mehdi told Leo. Leo and Big Otto had finally been emancipated from day-to-day servitude to Alois and Charley, but Big Otto still worked as a barkeep and assistant to the maître d.'

This must involve Himmler somehow, Leo told himself.

The Mietskaserne in which *Die Bäckerei* snuggled was a beehive of activity, and it appeared to Leo that Mehdi was preparing to close the shop and liquidate the contraband in the warehouse. Just as well, Leo thought as long as the boys were taken care of. He would certainly have no need of anything soon.

As he arrived at Café Alois, tucked a half block beyond KaDeWe in Wittenbergplatz, the square struck him as an oasis in the wasteland of rubble that was steadily consuming the once proud city. For a split second, he imagined returning to the glory years of 1941, when a pristine Berlin seemed immune to the havoc it was wreaking elsewhere in Europe.

He found a frenetic *spit and polish* drill underway at Café Alois. This was a meticulous top to bottom, all hands-on-deck, exercise ordered from time to time by Alois, to put the café into white glove condition for special occasions. Floors were being scrubbed then waxed, beer steins and tchotchkes in every nook and cranny were being polished. In his prime, Alois would circulate the entire time chanting the same thing over and over again, *make it glow*!

I trust you are well and not at this moment on the run from anyone or anything, Charley said with equal parts sarcasm and affection before giving Leo a bear hug.

Are you well, Charley? How is Alois? Why did you need to see me so badly, Leo asked, ignoring Charley's question because he would not have liked the answer.

Where do I begin, Charley replied, huffing and puffing as he was wont to do when he was upset.

Yes, at the beginning, Charley mumbled pensively. *I was forced to take Alois to his house in the country last week. His nerves have gotten the better of him, and he is now prone to blinding headaches and fainting spells. Berlin's ebullience about going to war has been turned on its ear by these bombings to the detriment of his health. He is better off there.*

Who wouldn't be, Leo replied. *What is going on today and for that matter, where is everyone*, Leo asked?

We are barely at half strength because of these bombings, Leo. One or two of our kitchen workers have been killed by bombs, we believe. There are several others tending to families that have been forced to take up residence on the curb outside where their houses once stood.

So, what does this have to do with me, Charley?

On the night of the 23rd of November, two weeks from today, we have been asked to host a rather extravagant party that is being thrown by Himmler himself. It is to honor those Gestapo agents who have made recent, meritorious contributions to the war effort. We are being told that Goebbels and Hitler will attend.

Ok. And my role, Leo asked, his interest piqued.

Our baker is one of those missing. I need you to handle that part of the evening and to be on call to assist the chef. His nerves are also a little rattled. Whose isn't but if he falls apart, I have no one to fill the gap. You will be paid handsomely.

Charley braced himself for a fight. He desperately needed his bull-headed friend's help but putting food on the table for Nazi warlords and their minions was he feared going to be a hard sell to Leo.

Leo hesitated. He continued hesitating and said at last, *I have one condition, and it is non-negotiable.*

Let me hear it, Charley, surprised that he was making any progress at all, said hesitantly.

It is that you join Alois in the countryside that night. He needs you there more than we need you here. You can count on Big Otto and me to make it a night to remember.

Charley hesitated. He continued hesitating, feeling an odd combination of relief and suspicion that left him unsettled.

Non-negotiable, Leo repeated.

Done, Charley said. But I shall be very much involved in the planning leading up to that night.

I would expect nothing less, Leo said obligingly. He said a silent prayer of thanks to May-Tay and Jani as the vile Max and Moritz looked on sniggering.

* * * * *

The Reverend Doctor Martin Sauter along with his wife and girls strutted gayly around their home like characters in *Die Meistersinger von Nürnberg* which was now playing at full volume on the family gramophone. In his heart, the *Meistersinger's* sublime vocal solos and stirring ensembles evoked the soaring arc of his career and the good fortune it now brought to him and his family.

The Sauter family readied its wardrobe for a celebration one week hence that would recognize their father's successful, one might even say triumphant, because of course it was, service to the Reich and hence to the Gestapo as one of its most valued members. The Reverend Doctor Martin Sauter was to be honored by the Führer himself at a chic celebration for the Nazi elites at Café Alois.

What Sauter did not know is that this star-studded event was a contrivance of his mentor Goebbels to rally the flagging morale of the Nazi aristocracy or at least those who had not already fled to homes in the countryside. Nevertheless, Sauter and Sepp Lange would be among a select group of Gestapo men who would be feted for their success in crushing the *Rote Kapelle* and the rapidly disintegrating network of the once redoubtable Wilhelm Canaris. There would also be mention of the blow struck more recently against agents of the Swedish Lutheran Church of Berlin to send a message to the Swedes that there would be further lethal consequences if the patience of the Reich were again tested.

Sauter had gradually abandoned his ministry to spend more time as an undercover operative of the Gestapo. *Our redemption lies in the Reich*, he told himself and his wife. *One day, we will take our proper place for all time in the Pantheon of heroes from whose purity of purpose the sinew of the infant Reich was formed.*

Goebbels and his protégé, Sauter, had become the Ying and Yang of Nazi propaganda as the Reich struggled with an increasingly difficult adolescence. Goebbels could count the score and his growing cynicism about the eventual outcome of the game it had foisted on the world brought a certain muted quality now to his instinctively hyperbolic lying. Delightfully detached from reality, Sauter blithely produced fulsome quantities of drivel that he sent to Goebbels by the barrel load which in turn found its way into the various propaganda outlets of the Reich.

And if his cup did not *overfloweth* enough, word had come from his source at Café Alois that the boy they had been seeking, the vile imp who escaped his clutches at Sigtuna and who was thick as thieves with the subversives at the Swedish Lutheran Church, was working again at Café Alois. Sauter had not mentioned this to anyone hoping to spring the trap himself. What a triumph it would be!

Voices soared from the family gramophone in exaltation of the good Reverend, *Morgen ich leuchte in rosigem Schein, Tomorrow I shine in the rosy glow.*

* * * * *

Leo kneaded the mound of thick, gooey dough that resembled a large white dog lying on its side. It would be a trial run absent the main ingredient. Charley had enthusiastically embraced Leo's proposal to do a new savory roll with an inner pocket that held a surprise which would burst open in one's mouth when eaten unleashing a sensual combination of herbs and meat. From Leo's point of view, it would be both the grand debut of this new delicacy at Café Alois and its farewell performance.

As he wrestled with the dough, his meditation turned to the night in Zurich not that long ago when he lay wedged between a snoring

Tomi and a pensive Jani, who wanted to talk, *there was once a girl, mon cher, who thought going to war would be quite exciting, even fun. There would be handsome young men in fine uniforms marching off to battle with the pomp and circumstance befitting their gallantry.*

I happened to live then with Hugo's parents on a fine Pomeranian estate. Father was a diplomat in Sweden at the time and as always Mother was at his side.

Then the Nazis came. They were gruff hoodlums by and large who descended on the village that served our estate. There was a wonderful man who trained our horses. I used to play with his daughter who wrote poems and played the piano elegantly. I looked up to her because she was such a refined young woman, something I was not.

One day, there was a commotion in the village, and we found the Jews living there lined up by the Nazis to be marched off to a railroad junction several miles away. There was my friend, tears welling in her eyes, but when she saw me, she caught herself and gave me a reassuring smile before she and her parents and two younger brothers trudged away, each carrying one bag with their all of their worldly possessions.

That shallow girl, the one who celebrated the pomp and circumstance of war, was I, and she died that day. A year later, my father introduced me to a Swiss diplomat by the name of Roger Masson and to an exotic young woman who would train me for the work I do now.

Some months later at the rendezvous with the American at Ettal Abbey, Jani would tell Leo that the exotic young woman was none other than Anya. *She was such a mysterious figure even to those who worked closely with her, and she seemed to move from one dangerous assignment to another, between one intelligence agency and another, with the ease of a swan gliding over a still pond. What I have always admired about her is that she had an unshakeable sense of purpose. Don't get me wrong. I am good at what I do but seeking vengeance against the Nazis for what they did to my friend does not feed the soul, and I would like to think that I have a soul that hungers to know a higher purpose.*

Large, salty tears fall, ran down his face to dot the dough he was now cutting. He knew he could destroy 200 Nazis in one blow, but he was the son of Hayk and Mina and in a strange way Dietrich too, who devoted their own lives to saving others.

This was the hell that Jani lamented. Leo knew he must win the battle at hand before he let God take him. His anger and blood lust would be satisfied, yet there would be no redemption.

* * * * *

Come fastht, Leo. Mehdi neeths, you.

A breathless Whistling Fritz arrived at Café Alois the evening of November 22, 1943, the day before the grand Nazi soirée, face red as a beet to match a shock of flaming red hair.

Big Otto, get Fritz a bite to eat and keep an eye on things here. I will go and see Mehdi. Also, see to it that those who are staying here tonight go to the storage cellar. The bombing gets worse by the day. And keep anyone who remains away from the icebox containing my dough and herb mix, Leo said with an air of command.

Got it, boss, Big Otto replied.

Charley had left that morning to join Alois in the countryside just as the Allied bombing started for the day. The *air pirates* now bombed day and night giving the increasingly war-weary inhabitants of Berlin little respite from the very same misery to which the Reich had subjected its European neighbors.

Wittenbergplatz was still relatively unscathed from the storms that raged around it. As Leo crossed a bridge over the Spree, the thunder grew louder and the lightning more terrifying. It reminded him of the horrible storm his last day in Aleppo that pummeled the old city with fish, eels and snakes from the Euphrates, which drew birds of prey and the city's rats by the thousands to slaughter the defenseless creatures flopping on the flagstones of the old city. On this day in Berlin, however, the storm rained fire and metal.

Leo ploughed into a visible debris cloud that blew toward him from the direction of Wedding to the north. The grit and grime that fell from it reeked of oil, cinders, vaporized stone from buildings that stood no more and the vile perfume of those who perished in them.

The fleeting thought of what a 4000-pound bomb could do to him came and went. He prayed to Mary-Tay and Jani to give him one more night before he joined them at the foot of Cygnus.

His eyes burned as he held his sweater over his nose to breath, maneuvering his way through the chaos to Wedding. As he approached Prenzlauer Berg passing near Otto Weidt's workshop, he saw figures in the haze kicking another figure that lay limbs akimbo on the sidewalk. It turned out to be a British airman whose parachute had apparently failed when his airplane was shot down.

Leo and the group kicking the flyer's corpse hit the deck when an Allied airplane crashed a block away in a park between Hackescher Markt and the Spree sending a huge ball of flame into the night sky and funneling its heat straight down a narrow street toward them. They heard the screams of those consumed by the flames near the crash. Leo struggled onward, hair and eyebrows singed.

Dazed, eyes watering, ears ringing, Leo finally reached the foot of Oderberger Strasse where the grand Neoclassical building that housed the waterworks and bathhouse had lost two of its three ornate gables and much of its red slate roof but was otherwise intact. He made a wide berth of the building's debris and then saw it dead ahead.

The Mietskaserne at Oderberger Strasse 15 just two blocks away burned like a roman candle. Towering flames roared skyward from the roof of the massive five story building illuminating Wedding with a horrible red glow a far as the eye could see.

He picked up his pace and found Mehdi working with fire crews in a futile effort to control the blaze. As he pulled Mehdi away, the top two floors of the building caved in on the floors below crashing through the roof of the vaulted warehouse space that had been the wolfpack's base of operations for as long as he could remember.

It was clear that *Die Bäckerei* would be unsalvageable and that Mehdi's decision days before to empty the warehouse of their contraband had been prescient. Leo shouted in Mehdi's ear, *the boys, did we get everyone out?*

We did, but only Allah knows what happened to them after that, Mehdi shouted in reply.

Leo took Mehdi by the arm and moved him across the street to Oderberger Strasse 61 directly opposite *Die Bäckerei*, which had once served at Dietrich's retreat. It had been spared for the moment from the fire that raged across the street. Leo encouraged Mehdi to rest because he could do very little to help the situation now.

As they sat on the building's stoop catching their breath, an elegantly dressed man, hands in the deep pockets of a black wool coat, silver hair shimmering under a black Homburg, casually walked up to them. It was as if he were simply out for an evening constitutional and was asking for directions.

It was difficult at first to make out his face in the wildly contorted light shed by the fire, but it was not so difficult to see that there were two heavily armed men in uniform following him, who were alert to the wellbeing of the man in the Homburg. The deeply resonant voice proved all too familiar.

I am sorry to see you both again under such terrible circumstances, Admiral Wilhelm Canaris intoned.

Sir, what in God's name are you doing here, Mehdi said, as he nervously glanced at Canaris's bodyguards.

Gentlemen, I have been asked for a favor, which involves the two of you. Your benefactor is a very persuasive young woman, and I owe her at least this much. I also owe both of you more than I could ever repay for your able service to me. At the same time, I would like to think that I will also be repaying a debt to our mutual friend, Dietrich Bonhoeffer, Canaris said.

Mehdi and Leo were aware that the Admiral's allies were dropping like flies. The balance of power had shifted toward Himmler. Dietrich was in prison as was Hans von Dohnányi and General Hans Oster.

Who is this woman and why would she want to do us a favor, Mehdi asked, and then almost immediately cuffed himself on the head with the heal of his hand when he realized who she was.

Let's say this, I owe this exotic creature my life. Hitler is not the only one that would like to see the last of me and, in my case, it was the Italians. I apparently did not make a very good impression on Mussolini. In her ability to move phantasmically from one intelligence agency to another, she thwarted the Italians. I have used her talents in my cause and, had we 100 of her, our struggle would have achieved a far different outcome by now.

One of his last conversations with Jani came immediately to mind. The identity of their benefactor was no mystery to Leo as well.

Sir, we thank you for the favor but perhaps you should think about your own future, Leo said.

Thank you, son, but my future is Germany, good or bad. At this Canaris turned straight away to the business at hand.

Tomorrow night a Junker leaves from our base in Dahlem. Leo, you know the place and the aircraft. There is room for you both on the flight, which will get you to a place of relative safety, I promise you. Your destination will be revealed when you are en route.

There will be a Kubelwagon attended by the sharp looking marines standing behind me that will be waiting just north of here at midnight tomorrow. It will be stationed at the southwest corner of Schönholzer Heide, the point in the park with the cultivated mulberry grove. My men will wait ten minutes before leaving.

Sir, Mehdi interrupted, breaking Canaris's train of thought and immediately regretted his disrespect.

Canaris parried briskly before Mehdi could take his next breath, *gentlemen, I must go. Godspeed, to you both. The new Germany will need men like you.*

* * * * *

The little mongrel in Wedding the night we picked up the Rote Kapelle people squirmed at the end of the rope for longer than I had expected, gunshot wounds and all. These are the best kind. Of executions that is. Their prolonged agony is most satisfying. I do give the boy credit, though. He fought for longer than most men we have put to the noose!

This declamation had just been given by a mole-like man dressed in his best SS livery, one Andre Fuchs who entertained the group assembled at his table still further by grabbing his neck and making a prolonged gagging sound. Such was the erudite repartee as the merriment unfolded on the evening of November 23, 1943, the monumental night at Café Alois when those assembled, nearly 200 at this point, celebrated their cruelty and themselves as the alcohol and vituperation flowed in abundance.

The performance by Fuchs had not been lost on young Gerda who had just delivered steins of bock beer to his table. Gerda was very young, very pregnant, and very much in love with Big Otto. She had been the mysterious girl in Charlottenburg that Big Otto was seeing when Little Otto spilled the beans in the Tiergarten.

The handsome and dapper Big Otto was serving as the maître d'hôtel that night in Charley's absence and cut a fine figure in one of Alois' best suits. He was a natural and moved smoothly among the Nazi elites who mingled with the mangy livestock that did their bidding.

Gerda made a beeline to Big Otto. If he didn't do something about this rat man, she would take matters into her own hands.

* * * * *

The full moon had given way to a Waning Gibbous that shed just enough light through the low clouds so that a snow-covered Wittenbergplatz looked like a shimmering pearl set in a black onyx ring. The full moon had been no friend to Berlin and the enemy's bombers took full advantage of it to drop their bombs wherever it pleased them.

Every business, every apartment surrounding the square hid behind thick blackout curtains. The looming hulk of KaDeWe, which would normally be incandescent with Christmas lights at this time of the year, intensified the gloom.

Apart from a few patrons leaving the department store, the square was relatively quiet. Dark figures, disembodied voices, scurried toward the U-Bahn station in the center of the square, which served as a bomb shelter for local residents. Much of Berlin would have fled to bomb shelters by this time of night hoping against hope that the Allies would take a night off.

However, at Wittenbergplatz 3, the gloaming calm was broken by the roiling dissonance of idling trucks, automobiles and military men barking orders and taking them. The area in front of Café Alois was teeming with activity. Many loud party goers had spilled into the street and scores of serious young men with fingers on triggers maintained a perimeter around their merrymaking.

Storms soon arrived from two directions. To the distant west, came the drone of aircraft that one could feel as well as hear. The hair stood up on the back of one's neck at the rumble of waves of bombers that reminded one of the continuous beating of a thousand bass drums. The thunder was punctuated by the whining of bombs in freefall, random flashes of hellish light and the odd popping sound the bombs made as they sucked the oxygen from the air around them upon impact. Windows rattled across the square.

Then from the east, a motorcade sped into the square. The headlights of the vehicles had been angled downward and were covered by three horizontal slits of dark cloth. White lines were painted along the middle of the road to help drivers as were curb edges and car bumpers. The speed limit for night driving was officially 20 mph, but the motorcade drove at a speed that would have been dangerous even in daylight.

The military men on guard at the perimeter facing Café Alois jumped-to, aware of the importance of the motorcade. When the motorcade came to an abrupt halt in front of Café Alois, men were called to attention as from the lead car emerged Himmler himself in full dress uniform followed by Kaltenbrunner and Panzinger.

From the car just behind Himmler's emerged the Reverend Doctor Martin Sauter without his family. Goebbels had telephoned him to warn that events such as the night's festivities often turned into a debauched carnival and suggested that his family would best enjoy the evening if he regaled them with an account afterwards relying on his proven talent for gross exaggeration. Himmler and entourage entered Café Alois without a thought to one of their honorees, Sauter, who hurriedly brought up the rear.

* * * * *

One of them is here, a breathless Gerda shouted as she rushed through the door to the kitchen.

One of them, Leo asked? *Which one of them?*

Gerda was by nature superstitious, and she was afraid that if she said Himmler's name, it would bring the Devil's wrath down upon her.

Big Otto says to come now, Leo. He, him, one of them, wants to talk to you, Gerda said, nerves bubbling over. *Leo,* she added in the same labored breath, *we need to get the meal out soon. If we give them another round of drinks and no food, they will tear the place apart.*

And then Gerda disappeared as the sound of chaos in the front came and went with her passage back through the swinging kitchen door.

Leo was dressed in the livery of a head chef by necessity as the head chef himself was in a drunken coma in the storage cellar. The pressure had finally gotten to him – a home with a hole in the wall, a wife by his own telling with a hole in her head, the prospect of more bombing and now a likely visit from the Nazi triumvirate – Hitler, Himmler and Goebbels.

Bratwurst night with Himmler had already been an ordeal for the jittery chef. Now there would be three of them!

Just as well, Leo thought. He had deliberately kept only a skeleton crew on that night because of the danger from the bombing and from the evening's menu.

In a few minutes, when the savory rolls are out of the oven, serve the meal. And no one, I mean no one working tonight touches the savory rolls. You will regret it if you do, Leo said to the sous chef. The kitchen staff had come to trust Leo as a straight shooter who had their best interests at heart. And thus, the savory rolls remained sacrosanct.

At that moment, Leo felt as a soldier must feel before going over the top to leave his foxhole. He was queasily anxious and impatient to join the battle, come what may, as waiting seemed worse than death itself.

Leo saw Big Otto's head above a scrum of helmets and crush caps. Big Otto turned toward Leo to acknowledge his arrival, as the circle around him opened to reveal that *he, him* was in fact Heinrich Himmler waiting to have a word with him. *One down*, Leo thought to himself.

Sir, I hope that you and your men are enjoying our hospitality tonight on this grand occasion. Will we also be joined soon by the Führer and Reichsminister Goebbels, Leo asked expectantly?

Himmler looked into Leo's eyes with the same combination of interest and murderous lust that a panther would show another animal before sinking its teeth into its victim's neck.

Tell me, young man, I was unaware that Charley would not be present.

Herr Reichsmarshall, he is tending to Alois who is seriously ill. Nevertheless, he has been deeply involved in the planning for tonight. May I speak for those of us present. We will take very good care of you tonight.

It was said of Leo by his admirers and detractors alike that he was *doubly sly*. The quick witted Himmler, whose own cunning knew no bounds, hesitated in responding as his eyes locked onto Leo's. The hint of *double entendre* in Leo's greeting had not been lost on him.

Our men are getting a bit restless. When will dinner be served, Himmler asked, brushing his suspicions aside.

Sir, we have given them a round on the house and some small Vorspeisens (hors d'oeuvres) to tide them over in the hope that you and the other dignitaries would arrive to share in the dinner service.

I would not count on the Führer or Reichsminister Goebbels tonight. In view of last night's hideous bombing, they are, I am sure, huddled in a bunker somewhere not to emerge until the dawn. I would suggest you proceed.

Sir, of course. Your presence is more than one could hope for, Leo responded. *Please excuse me and I will see to the dinner service. I assume that awards and recognitions will come after?*

There was no answer from Himmler as his attention was drawn toward a commotion at the front door of the café. Two men in jackboots and black helmets that displayed the Totenkopf, the skull and cross bones that identified them as SS, approached Himmler.

Sir, the Waffen SS Administrative College and barracks have been hit tonight. There are heavy casualties and damage.

Himmler immediately turned to his adjutant. *Ready the convoy. I must go to inspect the situation. We can't all cower in a hole tonight.*

He turned back to Leo and Big Otto with a perfunctory nod and was gone. In passing Kaltenbrunner, Himmler said, *you come with me and leave Panzinger here. Order Panzinger to pick up the boy, Leo, when all of this is done. We shall see if there is anything we can wring from him that we do not already know. As for the big one, the maître d,' let's close the file on him. A simple bullet in the head will do.*

* * * * *

Marty McSorley, an Irish kid from the Corktown section of Philadelphia, had been pretty lucky thus far and had hoped his luck would continue this night. Marty and his co-pilot Thomas ("Don't call me Tom") Dollar who hailed from Greenville, Delaware had managed through some miracle to return without a nick from the *Black Thursday* bombing of the Schweinfurt ball bearing factory just a month before. Of the 291 Eighth Airforce bombers on that mission, 60 were shot down with 600 airmen lost. Another 17 bombers crashed in England and 121 needed extensive repairs.

There was heavy flak that night back in October and that was to be expected. After friendly fighters turned back at the German border because they did not have the range to go deeper into Germany, the bomber formations fought a running battle alone with Luftwaffe fighters.

Tonight, he was piloting the *Liberty Belle* again, call sign *niner-niner-charlie-baker*. She was a B-17, the magnificent *Flying Fortress* and part of the first Eighth Air Force squadron to join the Brits in the Battle of Berlin. She was a beauty – a heavy bomber 74 feet long with a wingspan as long as a ten story building is high. The *Belle* had been modified for nighttime bombing raids and to carry a payload that included a 4,000 pound bomb.

Marty was 23, his co-pilot Thomas 22; both were lieutenants. They left base earlier in the day with ten crewmen, but now only four remained. Flak had taken their belly and tail gunners as it had their bombardier and navigator who were stationed in the clear nose compartment below the cockpit where they were operating the *cheek and chin* guns at the time. That same flak had set fire to the number three engine precariously close to the cockpit.

Worse still, they had lost the better part of their rudder. While the rudder cables were intact, they offered little control of the aircraft, so the imperturbable Marty and Thomas were forced to steer with the throttles.

Thomas having returned from the fuselage of the *Belle* reported, *we have a hole in the fuselage you could drive a jeep through. Our flight engineer and radio operator are OK but that's about it.*

I inspected the bay and the drop mechanism was jammed by shrapnel. The bay door is actually fused in place now, so we can't drop the 4000-pounder. Hell, Marty, for all practical purposes, the Belle is now the 4000-pound bomb.

Thomas, do we have radio contact?

Negative.

What are the odds of our limping back to base?

One in 100, Marty.

And the odds of dislodging the 4000-pounder?

Worth a try, but not good, Thomas replied.

Give it a try. Visibility is shit, but it looks like our first wave is dropping its payload at twelve and one o'clock on the horizon. Given our time in route, I estimate we are already in the western reaches of Berlin.

Thomas, bring the men up, please. I want to complete this mission rather than get shot in the ass running away like a coward, but I want our guys in on it. They need to know what that means.

* * * * *

Malleus Maleficarum, the Witches Hammer, struck the unsuspecting Sepp Lange as he devoured copious quantities of *Choucroute Garnie* along with the stack of Leo's savory rolls served alongside it. The Choucroute, a German inspired Alsatian dish, was served on huge platters heaped with sauerkraut and covered by every sort of pork *delicacy* imaginable including bacon, Bratwurst, Kielbasa and pigs knuckle.

After round upon round of strong beer, the guests of Café Alois ate with abandon. The effect of Leo's savory rolls took hold well before the inebriated Lange and his fellow Gestapo and SS revelers knew what hit them. Leo, Big Otto and Gerda looked on expectantly from the swinging kitchen door as the *Witches Hammer* lowered the boom.

Brother Andrew had prepared a powdered compound for Leo of *Monkshood*, which he combined with a rare herbal poison from Asia called *Heartbreak Grass*. During his botanical tutorial at Ettal Abbey, Leo was warned by Brother Andrew to wear a mask over his mouth and nose along with industrial rubber gloves when using the powder, as Leo had done when he shooed everyone away from the backroom of the kitchen to mix this lethal compound with the meat and herbs, which formed the center of the savory rolls.

Monkshood, an ornamental purple flower of the buttercup family, contains three poisons – Aconitine, Mesaconitine, and Hypaconitine, which are potent neuro- and cardiotoxins. The Latin name for Monkshood, *Aconite,* comes from the Greek word for *without dust* or *without struggle*. It was used as a poison for arrow heads when hunting wolves, hence its popular name *Wolfsbane*, and is so fast acting that a wolf hit by a poison arrow would be dead before it hit the ground.

Lange and those at his table first felt severe stomach pain and several of his companions immediately lost control of their bowels. He noticed that other tables were suffering much the same fate and it was then that confusion and paranoia set in as the *Monkshood* went to work on his brain. He started wailing when he thought he was warning his compatriots of the danger they were in. Lange stumbled to the bar in search of a glass of water and on his way tripped over Andre Fuchs who was crawling in full uniform to the kitchen with his gun drawn.

Soon the *Witches Hammer* struck again when the *Heartbreak Grass* went to work. Its active toxin, a substance called Gelsemium, is a poison that had been used for eons to quickly dispatch its victims but not before subjecting them to punishing pain. Lange caromed off the bar suffering from a combination of dizziness, nausea, and blurred vision, and tried to steady himself before his knees gelatinized and he crumpled to the floor.

The impulse to vomit was overpowering, but the Gelsemium had already worked its terrible magic on his spinal cord, and Lange's stomach and other vital organs started shutting down. It was then that the convulsions hit him with full force. Under the crippling blow of the *Witches Hammer*, Lange and his fellow revelers were relegated to watching themselves asphyxiate to death in a state of paralysis and extreme pain.

The image of Stella's naked corpse swaddled in bed sheets staring up at him in mocking rigor flashed before Lange as his mind was progressively starved of oxygen. Then came the image of his father years before cuffing him hard on the side of his face, his transgression unspoken. He turned away to evade the next blow and fled to the edge of a deep pit in which he saw the humbled flag of the Nazi Reich in tatters. Lange tried desperately to turn and flee once more because he knew his next step toward the pit would take him to Hell.

Café Alois had become a slaughterhouse of baying, moaning animals, wallowing in their own waste. Ironically, it was the kind of grisly ending to which they would have thoroughly enjoyed subjecting others.

* * * * *

The Reverend Doctor Martin Sauter sat at a table next to Charley's piano and across from the empty semi-circular dais where honors were to have been dispensed that night. He was ploughing through a second bottle of fine champagne and the more he sipped, the more he sulked.

He was now alone in the darkened amphitheater of Café Alois reserved for fine dining. Two aristocratic Nazi couples who had also been waiting at tables in the amphitheater had surrendered to the idea that there would be no awards ceremony that night and left. Even the substitute piano player whose repertoire seemed to consist solely of a romanticized version of the Nazi anthem, which he played over and over again, had abandoned him.

The evening had gone to the dogs, the Reverend Doctor Martin Sauter thought to himself huffing petulantly. There would be no Führer, no Goebbels, no Himmler and no adulation for his many achievements in behalf of the Fatherland.

He would find some way to break it to his wife and daughters in a way that would serve to burnish his image with them still further. Perhaps, a raid or an arrest of a dangerous fugitive in which he took part. No, took the lead!

A Jew preferably!

In the depths of his brooding, he had lost sight of his second objective that night and that was to arrest that smug young fiend, Leo. How the wretched boy had looked at Himmler earlier that evening. Disgraceful! Eye to eye, chin to chin, as if he were the equal of one of the greatest heroes of the Reich. A travesty that.

The aggrieved warrior took one last sip from his tulip shaped champagne glass as he absent-mindedly buffed the toes of his injured Crocker and Jones brogues on the back of his pant legs. He poured another glass of champagne to steal himself for battle and downed it in one gulp.

It was then that the horrible sounds in the front of the house finally penetrated his senses. His mind, which had mastered with demented virtuosity the use of glib metaphors in the service of the Reich, likened it to the same horrible sound that must have issued from the fallen angels as they were cast to hell forever for following Lucifer, the *Morning Star*, in disobedience of the almighty.

* * * * *

SS-Obersturmbannführer Friedrich Panzinger was a cop at heart, a studious detective who delighted in the thrill of the hunt. As such, he had no interest in the debauched spectacle that would unfold at Café Alois.

He had left men at the front and back doors of Café Alois with instructions to take the boy Leo alive if he attempted to escape before his return. Panzinger and his number two man had made their escape after the encounter with Kaltenbrunner to have a meal at a bierstube on the other side of the platz that remained open despite the bombing.

He had demurred about receiving an award that night, but Kaltenbrunner had insisted. Just as well that the awards ceremony had fallen apart, he mused.

Panzinger had never been political. Cops shouldn't be in his book. It was a job required of him by the Fatherland and he was before all a good German.

It was a job that had also cost him his marriage. His wife, a devout Catholic, had left him ashamed of what he had become. He had pleaded with her over and over again to see both sides. He didn't hate Jews. He didn't hate anyone, but when called to duty, he must answer.

So, as it was on so many nights now, it was bratwurst and beer. A strong Pilsner went well with bratwurst and loneliness.

Panzinger was finishing his meal and making ready to go when one of his men ran into the bierstube shouting.

Come, sir, it is hellish, hellish!

* * * * *

Sauter recoiled upon entering the front of the establishment and instantly put his arm over his nose. He fumbled for a handkerchief with his free arm and was finally able to replace the arm with a handkerchief.

The raucous merrymaking of murderers had been replaced with a scene worthy of the river Phlegethon on the seventh level of Hell with its boiling blood and the strong odor of clotted blood. He instantly made the sign of the cross. This was not an act of faith for any faith that his heart had once nurtured had also clotted.

It might have been an act of compassion for the suffering of the poor souls he saw arrayed before him. But it was not. Sauter was capable of compassion only if he was its object. Once the initial shock had passed, the scene before him simply made him impatient.

Remember the objective, he told himself. This had always been Goebbels' admonition to him when he had become a jumble of nerves letting his emotional side overcome the rational.

He noticed Sepp Lange sitting on the floor spread eagle, back against the bar. His face was contorted with agony, and his eyes were glazed and seemingly lifeless. Sauter had to step over several bodies in a similar state that seemed to float on the surface of their own indescribable pools of effluvium.

One poor soul, whom he recognized as the mole-like Fuchs, was still trying to crawl toward the kitchen gun drawn, groaning but determined, unable to move an inch. Fuchs had left behind a brown trail that reminded Sauter of the mucous trail left by a snail when it moved.

He made it to Lange and stood between his spread legs, opening Lange's suit jacket to find his holstered gun. *He won't need this anymore*, Sauter told himself.

His next impulse was one he would regret. He kicked one of Lange's legs to see if he was still alive. A brown stain suddenly expanded on the motionless Lange's trousers, splattering his urine onto Sauter's brogues.

Scheisse, I will kill that boy for this, Sauter screeched as he stepped out of the expanding puddle and made his way post haste to the kitchen.

* * * * *

Is everyone out, Leo asked Big Otto, as they stood near the stairs to the basement storage room, which served more and more these days as a bomb shelter.

Yes, Big Otto reported.

It was also an escape route. Alois, years before when his status with the National Socialist Party was still unclear and a quick exit was potentially useful, had created a narrow tunnel roughly eight feet long from the far end of the storage room to a series of subterranean U-Bahn utility tunnels that crisscrossed Wittenbergplatz. The tunnels had made it possible for Leo's crew to elude the heavy guard posted outside.

Otto, where is Gerda? It is time for you both to go as well. There is no time to waste if you are to meet Mehdi in time to make the rendezvous with Canaris's men.

A chagrined Big Otto did not know where his bride-to-be had gone. He had last seen her heading back through the swinging kitchen door to the bar.

Leo, you must come too. There is nothing left for you here, Big Otto replied.

Perhaps, but there is Marushka. I cannot abandon her.

You will do her more harm than good, Leo. You must know that. After tonight you will be Berlin's most wanted terrorist.

And for that reason alone, my friend, I cannot put your escape in jeopardy by coming with you, Leo replied. *Trust me. I will be fine*. Leo was at peace when he spoke these words, a true peace that came from a place in his heart inhabited by Dietrich and Erika and his own desire to make his final break to the foot of Cygnus.

Otto, one could not have asked for a better friend than you, but you have a child to consider now, Leo added. *I will help you find Gerda and then you go.*

As they turned toward the swinging kitchen door, Sauter, a man inflamed by love of country and his place in its pantheon of heroes, barreled through it from the other side.

Halt!

Sauter held a gun pointed directly at Leo's forehead. He flicked it toward Big Otto and then back to Leo. He had not given much thought to what he would do next. Should he shoot them now or march them outside to receive the adulation of the waiting SS?

He shifted his feet nervously back and forth as he tried to divine his next move. Leo and Big Otto noticed a strange squeaking sound and terrible odor emanating from his shoes as he did.

In the meantime, Gerda had returned from the bar via a utility room where the dishes were washed and stored. She could see and hear Sauter through the partially opened door that separated this room from the kitchen.

She had been circulating through Café Alois as a good host would naturally do, putting her heal to the neck of the maggots responsible for Little Otto's lynching. She had never been so heartsick as when she had held Big Otto in her arms as he quivered and cried over the loss of Little Otto. Revenge felt good, really good.

She was slightly to Sauter's rear just behind his right shoulder as he was looking the other way, pointing his gun at the boys. She heard him order Leo and Big Otto to turn and put their hands on the wall.

The baby gave her a hard kick, which Gerda took as a signal to act.

Gerda surveyed the utility room for a weapon and found amidst the other items that lay unwashed on the counter Leo's Khanjar, the large, curved knife with an ivory hilt in the shape of a lion's head. She grabbed it, gauged its weight and balance, tightening her grip on its handle.

Leo said something to Sauter, and she heard Sauter cock the trigger. Was he pointing his gun at Leo or Big Otto, Gerda wondered. Did it really matter? Then, inexplicably, Sauter set the heavy revolver down on the countertop to his right, his finger still on the trigger.

Scheisse, girl, what are you waiting for, Gerda said to herself, and she charged through the door to the kitchen, Khanjar held high, screaming like a banshee. Before Sauter knew what had hit him, the Khanjar had come down on the gun hand with such force that she took it off cleanly at the wrist with one stroke.

Sauter looked at his hand as it lay on the counter now, his right arm gushing blood. Then, he looked at Gerda and back to a startled Leo and Big Otto Leo with a mixture of fear and anger. He tried to scream, his indignant rage issuing as little more than a squeak. Sauter charged Leo swinging his dismembered arm, performed an awkward pirouette on the tips of his toes, and fell at Leo's feet to join Lange in Hell.

The habitually equable Leo and Big Otto just looked at each other in total amazement. *Boys*, Gerda, said, prying Sauter's revolver from his dismembered hand, *we have one piece of unfinished business before we go.*

Leo and Big Otto reluctant to disobey the murderous Gerda followed her through the swinging kitchen doors to the bar area where they found the snail-like creature, Andre Fuchs, barely alive and aware of his pitiable circumstances. He grunted and groaned as he looked up at them, incomprehensibly begging for help.

Remember what you said about *the little runt,* Gerda said addressing herself to the prone Fuchs, a frothy white fluid spotted red flowing now from his mouth. She handed the gun to Big Otto and said, *it was he who hung Little Otto and shot him in the hands and feet. He deserves the same.*

Big Otto hesitated as did Leo. They had just murdered roughly 200 people, but the idea of shooting the helpless creature at their feet stopped them dead in their tracks.

Scheisse, men, useless, Gerda growled!

Gerda then retrieved the gun from Big Otto and proceeded to deliver a Nazi stigmata shooting Fuchs in both hands. Fuchs shuddered once and shuddered twice but refused to die. Gerda then moved to his feet and took two shots, one into the sole of each booted foot. Fuchs still refused to die.

Scheisse, she uttered again. Gerda came around to point the gun at Fuchs's head, just as men crashed through the front door of Café Alois, Panzinger in the lead. They, like Sauter before them, recoiled in horror at the mayhem that greeted them.

Gerda dropped the gun, hesitated a split second considering her next move, glanced at Big Otto, and lunged toward Leo putting him in a bear hug before he could react. Pressed to Gerda's ample and growing bosom, Leo was powerless to escape as the two lovers and their passenger hurried through the swinging kitchen door before Panzinger could get his bearings.

A moment later, there came the roar of a thousand freight trains followed by a shock wave that seemed to lift the buildings framing Wittenbergplatz off their foundations. The pandemonium propelled brick, steel and fire through the front window of Café Alois shredding everything in its path.

* * * * *

The raids of the 22nd and 23rd of November 1943 ushered in the Battle of Berlin, a massive bombing campaign that caused immense devastation and loss of life in Berlin. On the 22nd of November, raids killed 2,000 and rendered 175,000 homeless. The following night another 2,000 were killed and over 100,000 were again made homeless. Over 10,000 would be injured.

This intense carpet bombing campaign would last until March 1945. By then, half the homes in Berlin would be damaged and an estimated 20,000-50,000 civilians would be killed.

However, history would overlook the hideously painful death of nearly 200 Gestapo and SS men on the night of the 23rd of November. That story would be erased from memory, incinerated by flames from the blast of a 4000-pound bomb.

On the morning of the 24th of November, as the German home guard sifted through the rubble in Wittenbergplatz, they found near the ruins of the yellow brick U-Bahn station the tail section and rudder belonging to an American bomber that had crashed the night before into the roof of KaDeWe, nearly burning it to the ground. Though badly mangled, the aircraft's tail number was still visible *—niner-niner-charlie-baker.*

MANNA

I. JUEVES SANTO

Johanna Spechalova marveled at how far she had come since her days growing up in Pittsfield, Massachusetts, the daughter of a Czech immigrants, whose father had worked as a precision machinist at the GE plant in town. Fortunately, Andrej and Jara had seen the handwriting on the wall before the plant shut down and the family scrimped and saved enough to buy the old Howard hardware store at 1st at Fenn. Johanna and her sister worked at the store in their spare time although Andrej secretly preferred Johanna to her sister because she could lift more.

Johanna, her friends and colleagues called her Jo, wades through the dense 105-degree heat and 100% humidity toward the sanctuary of the surprisingly large church that dominates the tiny village of La Concordia just North of Mexico's border with Guatemala. The mangy dogs along with the small and largely naked children scampering through the filthy gutters of this rundown outpost prompt a silent prayer of thanks that she had grown up amidst the bucolic surroundings of the Berkshire mountains in Western Massachusetts.

Jo had seen a lot in the last two years, but the uphill battle fought here by so many good but destitute people just took the cake. La Concordia drove home that the embarrassment of wearing hand me downs from her big sister in high school paled in comparison to the challenges these children would face as would the countless Central American immigrants massing at the border, all aspiring Americans, who saw this border crossing as the gateway to a better life. These folks realized what many of her fellow Americans had forgotten that America's greatness rested on being the only country in human history built on an idea — the idea of human liberty.

Jo was a star athlete in high school as a scholarship student at the Darrow School in Pittsfield, tall, wiry, and strong. Instead of college, she had decided to enter the Massachusetts State Police Academy where she graduated at the top of her class, a harbinger of important things to come. Andrej and Jara wanted Jo to follow her sister to college at UMass Amherst, but there would be time for that later, Jo thought. She wanted to give something back to the country that had given her family so much.

The turning point in her young life, she was 24 at the time, was the active shooter incident at the Eastfield Mall. Jo was in the second car to arrive. One officer was already down. Instinctively, she pursued the sound of gunshots into the J.C. Penney's where they seemed to be centered.

She had not gone much farther than the front door when a bullet grazed a middle-aged woman directly in front of her whose husband was on the floor bleeding profusely. She moved toward them to shield the two and, as soon as she did, was herself grazed by a bullet that ripped her shirt as it skittered along the bullet proof vest underneath from left to right.

And then the shooter appeared from behind a clothes rack to her left. A kid, not more than 16 or 17, with an assault rifle. He was looking the other way now triangulating the movement of his prey on the far side of the store, lining up his kill shot. Jo lunged, catching him before he could pull the trigger, knocking the gun from his hands and him to the floor.

It was a rookie's luck, she knew. The bullet that left a groove in her body armor could just as easily have left a hole in her left temple. The margin of error was a matter of seconds and centimeters. Her police colleagues liked to tell her she had *stepped in shit*, their way of congratulating her on her good luck.

Jo was OK with that good-natured ribbing, and she would gladly step in the same shit over and over again because her bravery at the Eastfield Mall had caught the attention of the U.S. Secret Service. After a flurry of interviews, a lengthy security check, and a rigorous boot camp, she was assigned to the security detail of the First Lady of the United States. Andrej and Jara never mentioned college again.

She was in La Concordia with the President's entourage, no first Lady this time, because her Spanish language skills put her in line for the assignment with POTUS. The President's trips were always a circus but this one was going to be a real doozy. The Office of Refugee Resettlement (ORR) had opened a new "Welcome Center," center on the border to streamline the processing of Central American migrants, and POTUS had come for a photo-op in his bid for the Nobel Prize.

The summit with the Mexican and Guatemalan presidents was an inconvenient afterthought by his Secretary of State. Between this, the swarming reporters, massing refugees at the border and townspeople preoccupied with the rituals of *Semana Santa*, *Holy Week*, the Secret Service had its hands full with security for *El Hefe*, the code name assigned to POTUS, who would arrive in 48 hours.

She had the afternoon off and sought to take sanctuary from the oppressive heat in La Concordia's church whose worn stone steps now lay dead ahead. It would also be one of the great moments in her young life because *He* was hearing confessions. By this she meant the former Papal Nuncio to the United States, who had abandoned it all to return to his ministry with stateless refugees, the work that had brought him to World prominence in the first place.

He was a legend. Some even said a saint in the making. Here they called him *El Panadero* because he brought sustenance to their bodies and their souls by baking and distributing bread to the refugees on the border.

Jo needed the latter more than the former now. All was not right with this trip, and the import of it gripped her with a subdued throbbing like that of an oncoming migraine headache.

* * * * *

Jo loved old churches. They all seemed to smell the same – the faint aroma of incense absorbed by the pews over the many years, the acrid smoke from the votive candle she had just lit, and the smell of something like Murphy's oil coming from the main altar, which was fashioned entirely of deep, reddish-brown mahogany. It was the most valuable possession in the village.

She knew it was weird, but she opened a hymnal and buried her nose in it to inhale deeply the sweet and sour bouquet of the porous paper and cheap newsprint. It was not hygienic but to someone who carried a Sig Sauer P-229 handgun at her hip, there was more in life to worry about than a few germs. At moments like this, she would recall the pastor at St. Mark's Church in Pittsfield, where Andrej and Jara drug two sleepy daughters every Sunday morning, quoting Thomas Merton from the *Seven Story Mountain* that it is the fragrance of the Lord from the tabernacle that drew many to seek Him after simply entering a Catholic Church.

The moment was at one and the same time all too short and exquisitely timeless for Jo, whose reverie was broken by a tap on her shoulder from the kind CNN reporter who held her place in line while she paid her respects to the master of the house. Now she was nervous, and she was not predisposed to nerves. In her line of business, it could be fatal.

He was not Mother Theresa, but he was the closest she would ever come to a living saint. Even the President she protected, the leader of the world, who was little more than a rude, overweight man in an expensive suit, desperately wanted to bask in the unfamiliar glow of virtue and gravitas by meeting with *El Panadero* on Easter Monday as the emotional climax of his trip. They would break bread together, the very same bread that the sainted man baked for the poor in the region in his own ovens at his own expense.

The baking of bread for displaced refugees had become *El Panadero*'s brand, although he never thought of it this way. It was a singular talent he had acquired from his parents and a form of artistic expression since he was a boy. In later years, it had also become a deeply mystical meditation for him on the mystery of life and death because during its life cycle, a grain of wheat dies and is reborn months later in the form of a spike capable of providing sustenance to countless human beings.

CNN cheekily coined his work, *the* ***Man****na from Heaven*. Fox called it a Venezuelan propaganda stunt.

The Service had profiled *El Panadero* in anticipation of his meeting with the President and was able to find surprisingly little about his background, particularly his early years. Rumors abounded that he had actually been ordained in the Swedish Lutheran Church and had saved the Papacy by bankrolling it from massive offshore accounts under his control. Tucker Carlson had even found someone who claimed that *El Panadero* had worked for Nazi military intelligence during the 2nd World War.

Controversy had swirled around his association long ago with Frantz Fanon, the French West Indian psychiatrist and political philosopher, who was a key figure in Algeria's war of Independence from France. The two had become fast friends while Fanon was recovering in Rome from wounds suffered in that conflict and *El Panadero* was a young cleric posted to the Vatican.

As the story goes, much of it unconfirmed, the man who would one day become Papal Nuncio to the United States had joined Fanon in Algeria where his interest in working with refugees took root. He is said to have contributed to Fanon's most famous work, *Les Damnés de la terre (The Wretched of the Earth)*, in which Fanon delineated the forces leading to the national independence movements that engulfed much of the world after World War II. In defense of the use of violence by colonized peoples, Fanon argued that human beings who are not considered as such by their colonizers, are not bound by principles that apply to humanity in their attitudes toward the colonizer.

Later in life as Papal Nuncio to the United States, *El Panadero* had generally flown under the radar, at least for a time. He was the consummate diplomat, a deft negotiator and had earned a reputation for picking the pockets of the moneyed elites when it came to supporting refugee causes.

He had rocketed to international notoriety when during a sermon to an ecumenical gathering of dignitaries from around the globe at the National Cathedral in Washington, D.C., he spoke about two of his greatest heroes, Dietrich Bonhoeffer and Frantz Fanon and speculated about what a conversation between the two might sound like. The newspapers glossed over the subtleties of his allegory to dwell on one of Fanon's more notorious quotes, which the Papal Nuncio shared with his audience:

> *The unpreparedness of the educated classes, the lack of practical links between them and the mass of the people, their laziness, and, let it be said, their cowardice at the decisive moment of the struggle will give rise to tragic mishaps... When we (the mass of people) revolt it's not for a particular culture. We revolt simply because, for many reasons, we can no longer breathe.*

This of course scandalized those predisposed to this state and entertained those whose ministries were closer to the heartbeat of their third world flocks. When word of this sermon arrived at the Vatican, the Pope said a mirthful prayer of thanks for the man he loved like a brother. The Pope, himself no stranger to risking life and limb to revolt against the evil of the Third Reich, had taken great satisfaction in elevating a comrade in the same fight, his rabble-rousing priest, to the status of bishop before sending him to the capitol of the first world to rattle a few cages.

In the end, *El Hefe's* top advisor on immigration, the cadaverous Steven Gorman, who invariably sneered when he meant to smile, had approved the photo op between *El Hefe* and *El Panadero*. They would break bread together, Gorman commanded, despite the peculiarities of *El Panadero's* background because he was an old man who drank beer and baked bread, so what harm could he possibly do.

Jo took a deep breath to steel herself before entering the confessional through a musty curtain to wedge herself into a triangular sliver of pew that seem to creak loudly every time she fidgeted. She slid on to the equally small *prie dieu* just as the sliding wooden door behind the confessional screen opened abruptly.

Sit friend, let us get to know one another better, El Panadero intoned. Jo could see the profile of the great man through the screen. Between his sharp silhouette and the depth of his voice, he seemed much younger than they said he was.

Not knowing what to do really, Jo sat upon command. Each time one of them would shift position, the entire structure of the rickety confessional seemed to sway and groan in agony.

Bless me father for I have sinned. It has been a month since my last confession. I am guilty of impatience with my colleagues, and I have neglected my parents by not communicating with them as I should have.

Jo paused momentarily expecting *El Panadero*'s perfunctory admonition to do better and got, *that's it? You will be my easiest penitent today!*

El Panadero, followed up quickly by saying, *you are American are you not?*

Yes father, I am U.S. Secret Service preparing for the visit of the President, she replied. Jo knew that she had said too much but her defenses had abandoned her in the timeless comfort of the confessional. She was a child of God now in the presence of the Lord, no more and no less.

There was an awkward silence broken by *El Panadero, I take it that this is not an official visit on your part to confirm that I am or am not the crackpot they say I am?* Jo could not help but laugh, *no your Eminence, this visit with you is one of the high points in my life in many ways. And it is something I so very much needed.*

First, 'Father' will do, he said. *'Eminence' gives me too much credit. Second, you needed to unburden yourself about being unkind to co-workers?*

Jo hesitated a moment before responding but then jumped in with both feet. She was fully committed now.

No, Father, I am from a family of immigrants and what I have found here is unsettling. First and foremost, these families are treated like dogs, but they are living breathing human beings. Worried she had insulted her confessor, Jo added quickly, *Father, I am not talking about your work of course. I did not mean to give you that impression.*

No offense taken, the man on the other side of the grill replied with a hint of humor.

An awkward silence ensued, and the man on the other side of the grill said, *And?*

I am a civil servant and trained to be apolitical in my job. However, I cannot overlook, my conscience will not allow me to overlook, that there is a more sinister angle to this so-called welcome center we have established at the border, Jo said.

You mean to say that your President will not be greeting these families with open arms. But the Nobel Prize awaits, he declaimed!

Father! She gasped with a hint of genuine exasperation.

I am sorry, friend, that was unfair, he replied. *So, what is it you find to be sinister?*

Jo's heart began to pound, and it was not without some effort that she was able to bring it under control. Usually, a cool customer, this reaction surprised her.

Father, this is all second hand, but I would appreciate your guidance. Unfortunately, family separations are nothing new. I can taste the gall in my mouth every time I use this term.

Please continue, was all he said as he looked ahead not turning toward the grill.

There is a group in our government, its radio code is 'Red Eagle,' that appears to work closely with the ORR, I'm sorry, that is Office of Refugee Resettlement.

Yes, I know about the ORR, thank you, he said. *Most are good people doing a thankless job, who alas do not make policy.*

Exactly, Father, Jo gushed emphatically!

This group appears to select children who have special medical needs and, rather than address them there in the clinic at the welcome center, they are taken up into the hills near a place called La Tigrilla. There is a good deal of scuttlebutt floating around our advance team that this activity is strictly off limits to us, which serves only to raise my suspicions.

I have seen the ambulances and vans that pick up the children, Jo continued. *They appear to be associated with another group called La clínica de Rafael Arcángel. I looked them up online and found little more than a reference to Raphael as the patron saint of healing. This made me worry all the more.*

I also have an ORR contact there, a social worker, who told me that once they are gone, some children are taken off their rolls completely.

Ah, the road to La Tigrilla. Have we not been down this road before, Jo's confessor said softly, which gave her the impression he was talking more to himself than to her.

Before Jo could respond, the man behind the confessional screen said, *for today's penance, friend, I would like you to do an online search for a group called the Charitable Society for Transportation of Sick Persons. And can you come by at this same time tomorrow,* he asked?

From Jo's point of view, this was the strangest penance she had ever been given and that was by a long shot. And why did she need to return? Would the penance be incomplete if she did not, she wondered?

Is that not possible, he asked?

Jo was flattered, but why would a living legend, a saint in the making, want to spend more time with her. She checked her watch. She had now been there for nearly 30 minutes, easily the longest stint in a confessional in her life.

Well, Father, I suppose that I could. I have this same period off tomorrow and could come by again. Just to be clear, that is what you are asking is it not?

It is, indeed, he said gently.

Then tomorrow it is, Jo replied.

Go in peace, friend, and return with your penance completed, was the last thing he said before the wooden door behind the grill slid shut.

* * * * *

The small boy and larger than life figure in *El Panadero*'s past blushed scarlet at the good-natured ribbing. She had indeed been the boy's first and only love.

You will see, Leo, that everyone is there when you arrive. Everyone, including you, was there when I arrived. Erika, he said, her treasured memory swathed in a deep breath. *All of you – Saskia, Mehdi, Big Otto too, you were there to greet me because there is no such thing as time there. Nothing is relative anymore. It just is*, Little Otto said.

El Panadero took another sip of beer, a Mexican beer called Victoria, a Vienna style lager, into which he had dropped a small green cutting from the garden. The sprig's hallucinogenic properties were well known in the region and among other things turned the beer's flavors of orange, honey, apple butter and star fruit into vivid, moving imagery, each singing an anthem extolling its own flavor.

You have always dealt with situations like this well, Leo. We always skated on thin ice, especially Erika and her friends who sacrificed so much, along with those of us you tried to protect. It was not because we wanted to skate on thin ice. It was because we knew we must under the circumstances, and you set the example for us, Little Otto added.

You give a feckless black marketeer too much credit, I am afraid. Erika and those like her were a cut above. Leo responded.

I will grant you that. None of us in the wolfpack knew enough to put the difference between right and wrong into words, but we always knew the right way to do things, whether it was a deal, a swindle or helping someone like Erika fight her fight. It was by watching you, Little Otto said.

If I am that insightful, then why am I in such a quandary about what to do here, Leo asked?

You know what you are going to do. I am sure of it. You just want me to talk you out of it, Little Otto responded.

This is what skating on thin ice means, Leo. Erika was not afraid to face the facts, nor could she rely on someone else for the strength to do what she knew must be done even if her countrymen might vilify her as a consequence.

Remember the joke they used to tell in Berlin. It is the one about the good fairy who came to give Hitler three good wishes at his birth. The first wish for him was that every German should be honest, the second that every German should be intelligent, and the third that every German should be a National Socialist. But then came the bad fairy, and she decreed that every German could only possess two of these attributes. So, the Führer then was left with intelligent Nazis who were not honest, honest Nazis who had no brains, and intelligent, honest citizens who were not Nazis.

Sounds familiar, does it not, Little Otto asked? *These three types did indeed live and work side by side oddly enough in our Germany. Yet there was another group, Erika and those like her, with the gumption to act on their beliefs by resisting tyranny however great the risk and backlash.*

I am not afraid to act on my beliefs, Leo replied more abruptly than he knew he should have done. *I may well go down in history as a total crackpot, and so be it. But there is a man's life at stake here. If my precious time with Dietrich and then with Rupert at the abbey in the final years of the war have taught me anything, it is fight with vigor but respect the sanctity of each and every human being, however good or bad,* Leo replied.

Leo, you and Big Otto and Mehdi are the three people I have loved most in life, but you have your head up your...well let's say in the wrong place, Little Otto pressed Leo. *Aktion T4 rears its ugly head, again, Leo! Is he a soul— a life — that is redeemable, this American president? What of the innocent lives at stake,* Little Otto pressed harder?

The Leo that I knew in Berlin did not struggle with this decision.

11. VIERNES SANTOS

Once the solemn procession commemorating Good Friday in La Concordia had ended, the worshippers evaporated into narrow streets of ramshackle homes like the steam rising from the wet ground under a broiling sun. For the better part of the morning, the townspeople had snaked through the small village, some bearing large crosses on their shoulders. Harassed by thunderstorms all the while, they followed the 12 Stations of the Cross to reenact the journey of Jesus carrying the cross to his place of crucifixion.

As Jo made her way again to the church in La Concordia for her rendezvous with *El Panadero*, all she saw at midday were the few remaining stragglers rushing home to join their families in quiet contemplation. Here, as in much of Mexico, quiet would fall over the village from 12-3 pm to signify respectful mourning because these are the hours when Jesus is believed to have been dying on the cross.

Andrej and Jara were devout Catholics, who had faithfully observed the Holy Week traditions of the church, so Jo knew the drill. Jo and her sister had been willing to withdraw into solemn contemplation on Good Friday afternoons, no TV, no phone calls, no soda pop because they knew when midnight on Saturday came, proclaiming Easter morning, they would feast in their pajamas on Jara's Easter bread and her fresh ham roasted in a Czech tradition that had been passed down from her grandparents and theirs before them.

Jo knew this place in spirit and felt at home here. It was an authentic celebration of life embraced by people who were dirt poor and savored a celebration all the more.

In her case, a fresh ham surrounded by vegetables in a thick Czech gravy after a penitential 40 days of bologna sandwiches and Rice-A-Roni was a rapturous experience when she was a young girl. Jo said a silent prayer of thanks for her parents and their part in making sure that she only had small sacrifices to make in her life although, truth be told, she did love Rice-A-Roni.

A lot was rattling around in her *noggin* as she caught sight of the church dead ahead. It was gruesome and sad to contemplate all she had learned in fulfilling her assigned penance. She would have much preferred three *Hail Mary*'s and one *Our Father*.

Yet the analytical Jo, ever the police officer, knew that *El Panadero's* assignment had not been a frivolous exercise, so she was eager to find out why. How did it relate to her mention of *La Tigrilla*, which had apparently prompted the choice of penance in the first place?

Jo was steps away from the church when a young boy in khaki shorts and a Brooks Brothers sport shirt that seemed totally out of place here in La Concordia made eye contact with her and said in surprisingly good English, *are you here to see El Panadero?*

Yes, I am, Jo replied. *Is he waiting inside,* Jo asked as she came to a stop towering over the boy? *Hopefully, I have not kept him waiting long*?

He is waiting, yes, but not inside. I am here to take you to him if you would come with me, the boy said politely.

This was very *007* of *El Panadero*, but what choice did she have, Jo thought. *Thank you. I will,* she said. *Are we going far? And your name is?* The instinctive tone of a police officer's interrogation was tempered by her willingness to embrace the mystery that lay ahead.

Omar, the boy replied. *And he is staying at my father's – a 10-minute walk into the hills above town,* as he pointed to a small cluster of relatively upscale homes that sat just above the village.

Jo attempted a conversation, but all that she learned was that *El Panadero* and Omar's father *went way back and were good friends.* After a short walk up the hill and through an area of comfortable, middle-class homes they reached the pinnacle of the hill and a dwelling that looked very much like a large Hobbit's house. Most of the structure was built into a large rock outcropping, although Jo could see a stone wall to the left shielding a lush garden that must have been connected with the house.

They entered the house, and Jo saw a smidgeon of the garden shining brightly at the far end of a dark and cavernous room. It was remarkably cool in the room, a rounded space that seemed to extend on one level in all directions. The cool stone provided a natural respite from the pulsating heat and humidity, which Jo and the boy had just escaped.

Omar deposited Jo in the garden and excused himself indicating that *El Panadero* would join her shortly. Jo's heart raced in anticipation of actually meeting the great man. To relieve the tension, she distracted herself by studying the riot of colorful plants in all sizes and shapes that dominated the tiled patio until he appeared from the house.

Jo resisted the impulse to do a double take because the man who appeared was not the man she had envisaged. He was tall and lanky with unruly salt and pepper hair and prodigious sideburns, who moved fluidly like a much younger man than his dossier claimed.

The only clue that *El Panadero* had been a young man during the years of the Second World War were the laugh lines, deep creases around his eyes and mouth. As per the agency's dossier, she noted the two obvious scars. The long scar on his left forehead dating back to that war had faded with time and could be mistaken for a laugh line in the right light. The other, on his right cheek, was just as long and faintly scarlet. He had been grazed by a bullet while tending to the wounded during anti-government protests in Aleppo in 2011 during his assignment to the Apostolic Vicarate of Aleppo.

El Panadero incongruously wore a wrinkled black shirt over faded blue jeans. The shirt seemed to be powdered with something white. Jo caught herself staring but not before *El Panadero* had done the same. *I am baking,* he said. *An experiment with a new recipe. Such things keep me going.*

May I offer you a beer, he asked politely with the hint of a German accent. *I have poured one for myself.* A beer with a future saint, could this really be happening, she wondered?! Did Francis of Assisi or Theresa of Avilla occasionally knock one back with their amigos?

He was an attractive man, Jo thought, and if his legendary love for beer and bread had anything to do with his youthfulness, then she would happily follow suit. *Well, I am off duty technically, she said, so yes. Thank you. What are we drinking?*

El Panadero chuckled smiling broadly. *Well, we are having whatever our host has to offer, which will not disappoint you,* he said.

Once they had two cold beers in hand, delivered promptly by Miriam, whom *El Panadero* introduced as the mistress of the Hacienda, they clinked glasses and *El Panadero* toasted her crisply with *Prost.*

Tell me a little about yourself, he said, which she proceeded to do.

He followed by proposing a garden tour, which Jo gladly accepted, and they stopped in front of an impressive, shrub-like mound of brilliant yellow flowers whose tentacles had wrapped themselves around two flanking palm trees. Clippings had been taken from the shrub and sat on a low retaining wall in front of the plant next to an impressive, curved knife whose ivory handle ended in a lion's head.

It's beautiful, Jo said, pointing to the shrub.

Ah yes, the beautiful and deadly Allamanda, he replied. *Just touching it can make you sick. Eating it, well, you will need someone with my skills to help get you ready for your first meeting with our creator.* Then, what were the clippings for, the highly trained police officer in Jo wondered, but before she could ask, *El Panadero* moved on, inviting her to sit at an elegant wrought iron table in a partially shaded corner of the tiled courtyard.

As they relaxed at the table, at least *El Panadero* was relaxed, he asked, *may we speak as friends?*

Good Lord, I'm sorry to be so abrupt, friends, with you? Good Lord. I almost called you, 'Your Majesty.' I'm flattered, but are you serious? Me? The self-disciplined and taciturn Jo had fallen victim to the unusual circumstances, cold beer and broiling sunshine.

Her host laughed heartily, apologizing in the same breath. *I apologize, Jo, I forget on occasion that some at the Vatican have already carved my wax mask,* he said with a warm smile that reminded her of Redford or Newman. Jo thought to herself, I have never had a friend, a good male friend, really, but I would like a friend like this.

El Panadero, for his part, finally realizing how unfair his informality might have been, asked in a more serious tone, *were you successful in completing your penance*? *Yes, Father*, Jo replied. *It wasn't a pleasant assignment, but I guess that is what penance is all about.*

Well said, came his deadpan reply.

Needing no further prompting, Jo gave her report, a police officer giving a situation report.

The 'Charitable Society for Transportation of Sick Persons,' was part of a program called 'Aktion T4' that collected hundreds of thousands of mentally and physically disabled Germans in marked buses and ambulances, removing them from hospitals and care homes from 1939-1945 to be evaluated and if necessary, I use this term advisedly, to be administered a 'Gnadentod,' did I pronounce that correctly? At which El Panadero nodded reassuringly.

As you know it means a 'merciful death,' Jo continued. *Apparently, this organization was a front for an organized effort by the Nazis to involuntary euthanize mentally and physically disabled Germans. It was mass murder pure and simple. Many of these people became the subjects of gruesome medical experimentation and most were murdered outright.* Jo took a deep breath and a sip of beer, shivering in the nearly 100-degree heat.

When all was said and done, roughly 200,000 Germans were killed this way along with another 100,000 in the occupied countries, El Panadero said picking up the thread. *It was a pet project of the Führer himself and his personal physician Karl Brandt, and I am ashamed to say that about half of those killed were taken from church-run asylums, often with the approval of the Protestant or Catholic authorities of those institutions. This is a prime example of how the corrupt actions of a leader can make the unthinkable seem mainstream.*

Finally, the Holy See announced in December 1940 that the policy was contrary to divine law and that 'the direct killing of an innocent person because of mental or physical defects is not allowed,' but the declaration was not upheld by some Catholic authorities in Germany. In the summer of 1941, protests were led in Germany by the preternaturally brave Bishop Clemens von Galen, the Lion of Münster they called him, whose intervention led to the strongest and most widespread protest movement against any policy since the beginning of the Third Reich.

Jo sat mesmerized. It was not so much that *El Panadero* was especially eloquent or handsome although he was both. It was that he sat gazing at her from across the table talking about horrors he knew firsthand. It gave her chills.

Thank God, there will always be good people to stand up to something like this, Jo said. *Indeed,* he replied, now looking at her as if to size her up.

So, Father, Aktion T4 and La Tigrilla, Jo said. *I assume, perhaps wrongly, you see a connection between the two. Clearly, the ambulances and buses collecting children from the welcome center is an unfortunate parallel. No Führer, however.*

Let's come back to your last point in a few minutes, he said. *I would like you to meet someone. Please excuse me for a moment.*

Several minutes later, *El Panadero* returned with two fresh glasses of cold beer and two boys carrying bottles of Coca Cola. The small bottles, the old kind that you could only find south of the border now.

One she knew, Omar. The other was a younger boy, who looked at Jo suspiciously, *Emilio, por favor sientate, El Panadero* said with a gentle air of command pointing to a chair.

I have asked Omar to join us. Emilio is Honduran, and Omar has somewhat better command of the dialect than yours truly.

Story? Jo smiled at Emilio, who gave her a wan smile back and looked at *El Panadero,* who said gently, *puedes contar tu historia, (please tell your story)*. Emilio started hesitantly, not knowing whether to look at Jo, Omar or El Panadero. He finally settled on Omar, his translator.

We arrived at the border 10 days ago, my father, mother and two sisters. I am 10 and my sisters are six and two. My father and mother signed all sorts of papers at the nice place where they welcomed us.

I had a sore throat and a nice lady who noticed it asked if she could take me to the clinic. It was nearby just down a long hallway. My parents were grateful for this kindness.

I could not understand anything they were telling me at the clinic or saying to each other except that they both agreed on something that had to do with me. They gave me a shot and then went to talk to my parents. They came back with the nice lady who had taken me there in the first place, and she told me that the shot they gave me would help my throat, and they were taking me to another building where I would get more care. They told me that my parents were happy to let me go there and that we would all be together again soon.

So, they took me there in an ambulance. It was more than one building behind a high chain link fence. There were other boys and girls. They separated us so that boys and girls didn't mix. I got clean clothes after they made me take a shower. The food was good.

The day after I arrived, they took me to a room and put something in the back of my shoulder. Emilio pivoted quickly to pull back his LeBron James t-shirt to show a scar where apparently the object had been inserted. *El Panadero* looked at Jo and said, *let us come back to this too in a few minutes.*

It hurt, but the food was good, so I didn't care. I had only eaten a couple of plantains in the three days before we arrived at the border. So well, anyways, Emilio said shrugging.

The next day I was taken to another building that was in the same compound but behind another taller, chain link fence. It was guarded. I went with several of my friends from the same dormitory.

There we received shots. The first day they didn't make us feel better, and we all wondered why we were getting the shots.

We were brought back to the same place the next day and given shots again. I began to feel queasy almost right away. My friend, who called himself Vato, became extremely ill and vomited. All this time, the people around us who looked like doctors and nurses were typing on small computers.

They made us lie down for 30 minutes and gave us Gatorade, the lemon flavor, then returned us to our dormitory. None of us wanted to eat dinner that night. That afternoon was the last time I saw Vato, who never returned from the other building.

The next morning, everyone – staff, boys, girls, guards were sick. There was diarrhea everywhere. Someone said that the dinner the night before had been contaminated and got everyone sick, except me and a few of my friends, who had not wanted to eat because we were already sick.

They take the garbage out to trucks every day and have to open the gate to let the trucks in. The guards were sick too. Three of us saw our chance and ran. Everyone else, well they were holding their stomachs, throwing up, moaning. We ran like hell, and then someone found me and brought me here.

Bien hecho (well done), Emilio, El Panadero proclaimed enthusiastically! *Omar, please take Emilio to the kitchen and get him situated with Miriam for lunch. Join us again in about 15 minutes. Thank you.*

A dumbfounded Jo, said, *Gracias Emilio,* in her best academic Spanish, and she waited along with *El Panadero* for the boys to leave.

You are not suggesting are you that.... She pulled up short when *El Panadero* pulled a microchip out of his shirt pocket and put it on the table. *Suggesting what, Jo, that they are microchipping migrant children like your family dog or experimenting with the idea? It would make it much easier for ICE to find illegals in the future. No?*

First and foremost, Jo said, *where is Emilio's family?*

I am afraid that we don't know the answer to that question, Jo. We have feelers out, but they seem to have disappeared. Unfortunately, Emilio's surname is the Honduran equivalent of 'Smith,' so our progress has been slow.

Jo persisted. *So how did he find his way here?*

Omar's father and I go way back. He is the grandson of an old friend in Zurich. They are Sephardic Jews, and your host Emil, no relation to Emilio, is a rather successful businessman in Latin America. At one time, he was a gunrunner to leftist freedom movements in Latin America until he became disillusioned with the results. In the final analysis, all he did was arm the emerging drug cartels and gangs. Rather than free the masses from their oppressive regimes, he had shackled them to others.

El Panadero could see that Jo was becoming increasingly uncomfortable with where this all was headed but pushed on, *some time ago, we were able to persuade him to turn his attention to the Coyotes, who smuggle migrants into Mexico and the U.S. A rare few purveyors of this service are honest people, honest used in the most charitable sense of the word, but the vast majority of them are what you hear they are in the news media – predators. Emil and his men are cleaning that up.*

But…, Jo said before *El Panadero* stopped her. *He has the tacit approval of your CIA, who keep their distance from the project but provide occasional intelligence. These aren't tour guides Emil is targeting; human trafficking of slave labor is involved.*

It was Emil's men who fittingly found little Emilio. As chance would have it, they had the camp at La Tigrilla under surveillance because the hoteliers who run that four-star B&B seem to have cut a deal with one of the most reprehensible networks of Coyotes for direct delivery of young guests. Apparently, the welcome center your President established ostensibly to build his case for sainthood is not supplying children in sufficient numbers for the experiments that we think may be taking place at the camp.

Hold on a moment, please. This is a U.S. Government facility working with the Coyotes, an exasperated Jo asked?

Jo, I realize this is a tumble through the looking glass for you. It is for me as well in the truest sense in which this phrase was intended. La Tigrilla is no illusion; it is no dream. It is a memory returned to haunt us, El Panadero said.

Ok, Jo said, hesitantly, trying as best she could to get her arms around the literary reference and the problem at hand.

Her face showing the strain of the moment, *can't you take this business about the Coyotes to the Mexican authorities,* Jo asked?

Jo...Coyotes...the Mexican Police...it is a distinction without a difference, I am afraid, El Panadero replied.

But what about this business with the shots, she asked?

The picture that Emilio painted for us is reminiscent to those of us old enough to remember such things of the Tuskegee Syphilis Experiment, which was a clinical study conducted between 1932 and 1972 by the United States Public Health Service (PHS) and the Centers for Disease Control and Prevention (CDC) that observed the natural history of untreated syphilis. African American men with the disease or infected as part of the study were told they were receiving free health care from the federal government of the United States.

Of the 600 impoverished African American sharecroppers enrolled in the experiment starting in 1932, only 74 were still alive when the experiment ended in 1972. Of the original 399 men, 28 died of syphilis itself and 100 died of related complications. Forty of their wives had been infected, and 19 of their children were born with congenital syphilis.

That is inhuman, Jo reacted with indignation.

I have been around long enough to know that to be inhuman is quite human to those for whom the ends justify the means, he replied.

So, if the perpetrators of what is going on inside La Tigrilla are authorized under our immigration policies, which are micromanaged at the highest levels in the chain of command, then...

Then we have a very special problem, El Panadero completed Jo's sentence. *This is where Omar comes in. Ah, here he is right on cue.* Omar returned to the table with a laptop computer which he opened and a small felt pouch.

We need incontrovertible evidence of what is happening there and to get it to the FBI, where we think we can find an impartial audience. This is where we need your help, Jo, he said.

El Panadero continued, *Jo you may not be aware of this, but this brilliant young man sitting next to us leaves Monday for Boston. He enters MIT next fall and is about to embark on several months of remedial English and calculus to be ready for a grueling first semester. Omar, please tell Jo what we have in mind.*

Well, I have tried to hack the network in the compound, which would give us access to their internal email traffic, Omar said. *We expect to find what we need there. However, I cannot get a strong enough signal from their encrypted network. In fact, they are using bafflers, a virtual chain link fence, to prevent external hacking of their network.*

However, if we could get a signal booster inside that I control, we should have no difficulty getting into their system. At this, Omar pulled from the felt pouch a small metal ball like a silver jingle bell sitting on a tripod. The whole thing was about three inches high.

All we need to do is get inside and hide this somewhere —a storeroom or bathroom or something like that, and we can steal the signal and the network traffic.

This is where *El Panadero* picked up the thread, *Jo if we were asking you to help us do this in a military facility or someplace else where we could do some real harm to American security interests, then you would have every reason to put us in handcuffs and haul us away. I know that we are on thin ice here asking this of an officer of the law like yourself, but what they are doing to those children is the crime, not what we are trying to do to get to the bottom of it.*

Jo stared at them both, on thin ice herself in more ways than one. Her silence seemed to go on forever, and *El Panadero* was beginning to wonder if he had misread Jo, mistaking her for a potential ally.

I don't know, I don't know, but I must go now, she abruptly announced to no one in particular. *I can find my way out.*

I will attend morning mass tomorrow, 8:00 a.m. Confession before. We will talk then, Jo said on the way out.

* * * * *

Cock sure of yourself weren't you. Like our first meeting at Café Alois, his guest said.

Leo had to admit to himself that he had taken a big chance with Jo. If his plan was ultimately to make sense to a world in shock from all they would see in the next few days, the facts needed to come out.

Leo took another sip of beer as he sat in the darkened study of the stone hacienda. *Had it been within our power to cut off the head of the monster we knew then as the Third Reich before it…he…could do any real harm, would we not have used it? What would Germany be like today if thousands, no millions, of our countrymen had never been subject to the madman's calamitous regime,* Leo asked?

I prefer 'murderous,' she said in response. *Are you struggling with whether the bread you will share with that man is baked with a healthy, perhaps that is not the right word, let's say robust dose of Allamanda, or whether you are putting a damsel in distress by putting her in the middle of all of this,* Erika asked from a chair bathed in moonlight at the window where they sat together?

Leo did not respond. It was both in fact. The wisdom for which he had gained international fame over the years had escaped him at the moment when it was needed most, and he sought the comfort of an old friend.

You men are such romantics, she continued in a decidedly uncomforting way, not waiting for his response. *Harro Shulze-Boysen once told us, that is told Libertas his wife, along with the Harnacks and me at the height of our resistance to the Reich, 'even if we should die, we know this: the seed bears fruit. If heads roll, then it is the spirit that nevertheless forces the state to change. Believe with me in the just time that lets everything ripen.'*

I adored him, Libertas and the Harnacks for their bravery and humanity, Erika continued, *but men like Harro go to battle singing anthems like this at the top of their lungs, hearts soaring, as they walk in tight formation toward blazing enemy guns. Women like Libertas, Mildred and I prepare for the worst. Just as women resign themselves to the knowledge that their men may not return from battle, we were under no illusions then that our time in the struggle would end well for us, and we prepared for that moment. Mildred's call to warn me, Panzinger's arrival soon after on my last day, indeed in my last minute of freedom, were anticipated,* Erika added.

But when we knew each other in Berlin, you appeared to be more of an optimist than that, Leo challenged Erika.

Certainly, for Saskia's sake. I dreamt of a better world for her, and my greatest fear was not for my personal safety but that she would never remember me as anything more than a traitor to the Fatherland for trying to realize that dream.

What does the God you now serve so conspicuously say, Erika asked repressing a hint of sarcasm? *'Unless a kernel of wheat falls to the ground and dies, it remains only a single seed. But if it dies, it produces many seeds.' It sounds to me like Harro was saying much the same thing.*

Leo, you and I have seen monsters lurking in the darkness baffle and seduce some who would gladly be seduced and others powerless to resist. And by the time these monsters emerge from the cesspit in which they were bred, and their plan comes into full view, it is too late to turn back the clock.

It is alas this fundamental battle between good and evil that provides the real energy in the universe, and we are its reluctant foot soldiers. The malevolent buffoon you would send back to his own cesspit is not the first of his kind nor will he be the last.

You are a leader, Leo, and have proven it with Dietrich and Mehdi, the Otto's and the wolfpack, Fanon, and no less with me. Your presence at Plötzensee said all that needed to be said about your character.

So, lead, damn it, and the girl will make the right decision. It is her future and her fight as much as it is yours. Make that clear to her.

III. SABADO DE GLORIA

Jo returned to the Secret Service base camp from her early morning run into the hills as the indigo night that swallowed her when she set out turned into a blue-gray canvas, painted here and there with copper-colored clouds. The southern horizon shimmered, reflecting the campfires and undiminished hopes of thousands of migrants camped along the border.

She had taken a muddy dirt track to a road barely more than that, which led up a steep hill into the tangled subtropical forest. She knew *La Tigrilla* was up in this general direction and wanted to get a fix on its exact location.

It was already 80 degrees when she first set out and as temperate as it would be that day. Jo was in top shape, but the humidity and pitch of the hill gave her all she could handle.

After roughly four miles, she started to notice discreetly placed intrusion sensors about six feet in from the road on both sides of the track. This was no trivial encampment, but why did they need this level of security for children?

In another quarter mile, she saw a gravel roadway off to the right again flanked by sensors. She thought better of proceeding further. The sign in English and Spanish read, *Danger. US Government Property. Intruders May be Shot.*

Shot, she thought. Really?!

Just as she turned back, high beams flashed off the cloud cover above her as a jeep ground up the hill in her direction. Jo sought cover behind a mango tree at the side of the road slipping and sliding on the rotting fruit at her feet, hoping if the sensors picked her up, it would be written off as the random movement of an animal.

The jeep bore a symbol, like the North Star hovering over the planet earth. She knew immediately who the four heavily armed men in the jeep were – private contractors from one of the most secretive and, some said, brutal security firms on earth, Polestar. Its CEO, a well-known evangelical Christian, was one of the President's top political contributors.

As the jeep turned on to the gravel roadway, Jo broke cover and hoofed it back in the direction of her base camp, working through the permutations of what might be going on at *La Tigrilla*. What was there to hide of such importance that the government, her government, would threaten people with bodily harm? Why were they using contractors who had earned a reputation as a brutal, Black Ops guns-for-hire?

She had slept fitfully and had hoped the run would do what her attempt at sleeping had not – calm her and sharpen her focus on the problem. Jo was repulsed by the idea of a camp, a concentration camp for God's sake, run by her own government to imprison migrant children.

What was wrong with this world? She abhorred the idea of the camp. It offended everything Andrej and Jara had taught her about living in a free country, but there were Americans at *La Tigrilla*, presumably good Americans, whose mission was to protect and maintain this place. Where was the disconnect?

Was she simply being hysterical about this or was *El Panadero* right to raise the alarm? Did this mean that she was in conflict with the government she had sworn to serve? What now?

Then she realized that everything Andrej and Jara had taught her about living in America told her now that, while she might have a beef with her government, she was not in conflict with her country. She knew then she had no choice.

* * * * *

El Panadero saw Jo and her two companions as they entered the church at 8:00 the next morning. Jo looked like she had not slept and her two hefty companions, presumably Secret Service agents themselves, eyed everyone and everything with suspicion.

His eyes met her's long enough for Jo to communicate that she needed time with him in the confessional. He managed to placate those who were already in line by explaining Jo's role in the visit to their village of the President of the United States.

Holy Saturday was an especially important day for confessions and, given the line down one side of the nave, El Panadero had his work cut out for him. Two younger priests would have to carry the load.

The morning mass would be a routine affair, although the special mass that night signifying the Easter vigil would be quite long due to Easter's lengthy reading. In addition, a large number of adult baptisms would be performed.

Bless me father... she said as the grate opened.

We can dispense with formalities, Jo, he said. *Were you about to confess that you and your stern looking colleagues are about to put me under arrest?*

God no, Father, Jo said emphatically. *My friends are devout Catholics but as longstanding Secret Service agents, there is nothing that they can do about the expressions on their faces, which have been indelibly imprinted over years of service. Although, they were taken aback by the President's effigy in the set-up for the bonfire in front of the church.*

El Panadero laughed and Jo could not help joining him. *I am sorry, Jo, but there is nothing I can do about it. One of the most unique traditions of Holy Week in Mexico is the preoccupation with the apostle Judas, who as you know betrayed Jesus and accepted payment to betray him to the people who would crucify him. Therefore, he is much despised by the faithful for his failed loyalty.*

So, cardboard and paper are decorated to resemble Judas. He is made very ugly on purpose, sometimes even resembling a devil or modern celebrities, and thus is the village's commentary on your President, I suppose. These figures will be burned at a rather raucous gathering this evening that will stretch well into the night.

Father, I will be brief, Jo said.

Thank you, Jo, it will be much appreciated by our friends in line outside.

Jo quickly recapped her early morning adventure and added, *I have managed to get myself assigned to Steven Gorman's trip to La Tigrilla today. This is the good news. The bad news is that it directly connects our President to whatever is happening there.*

Gorman doesn't sneeze without his authority, Jo added, *and for that matter the President is highly dependent on Gorman, who functions at times as his left brain. That is to say, the President rarely makes a policy move without a nod from Gorman.*

Trust me, this is not so much what I think as what I have heard the First Lady tell her confidants. She doesn't trust Gorman, Jo added.

Goebbels, Göring, Gorman, El Panadero replied softly.

I am sorry, Father, what was that, she asked?

Nothing...nothing, Jo, I apologize for the ramblings of an old man.

Father, do you have the signal booster with you? I will find a way to hide it in La Tigrilla.

Not here but stay for mass and when I call you and your colleagues to the altar, play along. Got that?

You bet, Jo replied.

* * * * *

Jo watched her partner in crime, a rather serious Federal crime, say mass. At one point during the blessing of the host, *El Panadero* lingered, deep in thought, for such a long time that a wave of concerned whispering washed up one aisle and down another.

After what seemed like an eternity, *El Panadero* placed a piece of the host in the chalice before raising it for the congregation to venerate, moving on from there with the liturgy at a normal pace. Jo who had not realized she was holding her breath during the uncomfortable interlude with the blessing of the host exhaled audibly prompting one of her partners to look at her quizzically.

As promised, immediately after the final blessing *El Panadero* made a point of asking, *our friends from the United States,* to come forward to the altar for a special blessing. The three Secret Service agents plus the ubiquitous CNN camera crew knelt in front of the altar and *El Panadero*, assisted by an altar boy who just happened to be Omar, gave each of them a box with an ornate cross that he blessed for them on the spot.

Jo's companions were thrilled. Unbeknownst to them, Jo's cross sat in a box that was deeper and heavier than theirs. Her eyes met Omar's for an instant as he handed her the gift.

Game on, she said to herself.

* * * * *

The scuttlebutt was that the sullen and cadaverous Gorman was an unpleasant man who treated his security detail like personal servants, and the trip to *La Tigrilla* did nothing to allay those rumors. Jo and her companions on the security detail shared a silent commiseration, *we got it, he's an asshole*, when Gorman singled out Jo by commanding her to *fetch* his brief case and bring it to the Hummer before departing on the trip.

The road to *La Tigrilla* was no more appealing in the daylight than it was at the break of dawn. It was a narrow muddy track surrounded by subtropical growth twisted in agonistic poses. It looked to Jo as if the sprawling compound had been hastily hacked out of the jungle with a machete.

Barely 100 yards after turning off the road onto the gravel roadway, they arrived at the main gate of the camp. There was barbed wire attached to workhorses that demarcated the outside perimeter, which the guards accompanied by very large Belgian Malinois dogs pulled back to let them through to the main compound 50 yards beyond. The compound itself was patrolled by heavily armed men with dogs walking the perimeter.

What the hell kind of clinic is this, Jo wondered? They proceeded through Emilio's chain link fence to what looked like the main administrative building in the middle of a patchwork quilt of Quonset huts.

The group passed through a metal detector at the entrance to the main Quonset hut. Jo having anticipated this, had slipped the signal booster into an ammunition pouch on her gun belt.

She and the two members of the Secret Service detail that accompanied her were told by Gorman to stay put as he was ushered to the back of the building by a man and woman in white medical coats. Jo knew it was now or never.

They stood near the front desk manned by a Polestar guard, and Jo approached him to ask for the restroom. He hesitated but Jo responded by saying, *look man, the food in this godforsaken part of the world is awful and, I need a minute in the 'lav' if you know what I mean.*

The guard smirked and pointed down the hallway behind him with his thumb. *Girls room is third down on the left.*

Jo nonchalantly walked toward the bathroom and upon entering it began looking for her spot. The sink wouldn't work. Stalls. Nope. They would find it in a heartbeat.

Then she zeroed in on a good, old fashioned gray locker that stored paper towels and cleaning supplies, and she quickly pulled the signal booster out of her holster and reached behind the supply of paper towels on the upper shelf. She stood the little silver ball on its tripod behind two rows of unopened Clorox bleach containers.

What are you doing in here, someone shouted!

It took all the self-control she could muster to nonchalantly turn toward the source of the shouting with a pack of paper towels in her hand. A young girl no more than 14 had run into the bathroom followed by a female orderly who continued to shout at the frightened child. Jo started to wash her hands and the female orderly ignored her lunging for the now shrieking girl whom she dragged from the lady's room.

Jo bent over the sink, eyes closed, chest heaving, trying to catch her breath. *What the fuck is happening here*, she said to herself as she returned to her comrades at the front of the Quonset hut.

* * * * *

Am I simply a crackpot like the deranged man who sets fire to a mosque or trains an AK47 on unsuspecting worshippers at a Sunday service? Rather than gaining wisdom with age is everything I have learned…I believe, crumbling in decay?

Is that what bothers you, Leo, that people will think of you as a crackpot if you go ahead and do what you are planning.

Leo and Dietrich sat in the garden sipping beer. The full moon had not yet arrived on the warm and muggy night, so the two old friends studied each other in the faint glow of a candle flickering in the middle of the elegant garden table.

Well, Dietrich, I have never cared about what people think of me, as you know better than most. On one hand, I do fear how it may reflect on the work I have done over the years and the people who have rallied to my cause, Leo replied.

On the other hand, I cannot, will not, follow the perverse example of the high-minded Prussian aristocrats who dominated the German officer corps all those years ago – as you would not – those who let their so-called code of honor get in the way of slaying the beast that ran rough shod over our country and for that matter the world.

Leo, you did not know my former student, Werner von Haeften. As aide-de-camp to Claus von Stauffenberg, Werner was one of those who were involved with Stauffenberg in the abortive July 20th, 1944, attempt on Hitler's life. He was also one of those who were summarily executed with Stauffenberg that night, shot in the courtyard of the Army High

Command in the Bendlerstrasse. His brother told me later that he faced death calmly and bravely.

We were together, the brothers von Haeften and I, at some point in the winter of 1942. I believe I was visiting his brother Hans, and Werner prodded me about whether it was permissible to kill Hitler. It was at a gathering of the Kreisau Circle, so all of us knew that he was part of the group within the military high command planning the removal of Hitler from power by any means.

'Shall I shoot,' he asked? 'I can get inside the Führer's headquarters with my revolver. I know where and when the conferences take place.' Despite our foreknowledge of his role in the conspiracy, these words stunned all of us who witnessed the moment.

You will appreciate this, Leo, but of course I gave one of my frightfully elliptical answers because there was no straightforward answer to be given. I told him that the shooting by itself meant nothing. Something had to be gained by it, a change of circumstances, a change of the government. The liquidation of Hitler in itself would be of no use; things might even become worse.

Dietrich, isn't that too much to ask of anyone? To rid the world of a monster, the resistance must first have carefully planned its aftermath, Leo, the skeptical disciple, asked?

Young von Haeften, who came from an old and respected family of military officers was a gentle type, enthusiastic, idealistic, and before all a man of Christian convictions who believed in inherited traditions. In the face of my Delphic answer, he suddenly reacted with enormous energy making it clear he was not content with 'theoretical' reflections. Sounds a little bit like present company, Dietrich said laughing softly as the comrades paused to take another draft of their beer.

Digging deeper, Werner's questions became more direct, 'As a Christian man bound to a military code of honor if I see my chance, shouldn't I take it?'

I finally said that I could not decide this for him. The risk had to be taken by him and him alone. If he felt remorse in not making use of a chance such as this, there was certainly as much guilt in the light-hearted treatment of an act as grave as bringing down the leader of a government.

I knew that we were on the knife's edge at that moment, a pensive Dietrich pushed on. *I told him that to live in fear and guilt was to be 'religious' in the worst possible sense of the word. I knew, and I made this view known to him then, that to act freely could mean inadvertently doing wrong and incurring guilt. In fact, living freely meant that it was impossible to avoid incurring guilt, but if one wished to live fully and responsibly, one should be willing to do so.*

I believe Hans von Dohnányi spoke of this when you two were together in Zurich. He recalled my last legally sanctioned sermon in Berlin in 1932 when I said, 'the blood of martyrs might once again be demanded, but this blood, if we really have the courage and loyalty to shed it, will not be innocent, shining like that of the first witnesses for the faith. This blood will lay heavy with guilt, the guilt of the unprofitable servant who is cast into outer darkness.'

Leo, despite our different styles, yours, and mine, Dietrich said, his eyes locking on to his companion's, *I have never known anyone who so deftly displayed such courage and loyalty when it was demanded of him. You and von Haeften are kindred spirits, and you too will make the right choice, of that, I am sure.*

IV. DOMINGO DE PASCUA

On a brilliantly sunny Easter morning, La Concordia broiled in the lead-up to morning mass. The heat and humidity smothered the village at such an early hour that even the village's operatic roosters made little more than a half-hearted attempt to herald the new day.

In contrast to many other countries, the day of *Domingo de Pascua* is fairly reserved affair in Mexico, and in La Concordia, it was no different. After attending mass, families would head directly home to share a festive Easter meal taking the better part of the afternoon. There would be fireworks and dancing that evening in the square before the church where, the night before, villagers had set fire to the effigies of Judas in his various incarnations.

Jo's day started with soggy cheerios in powdered milk after a cold shower in the mobile 'lav' of the Secret Service encampment. It was not the best start to a day, but it was a benign problem to have compared to the suffering of those on the border who had been demonized by her government. How could anyone endanger a great nation, who struggles to find barely enough food to survive one more day, she asked herself?

El Hefe had decided to skip the Easter Sunday service in favor of a second trip to the Welcome Center where he waved to the confused immigrant crowds kept at a safe distance from his motorcade by heavily armed Mexican troops. After some consideration, it had been decided that the photo-op with *El Panadero* should be moved to the Welcome Center from the church in La Concordia where, *El Hefe* groused, he might be upstaged by *the damned priest.*

Word had gotten back to the *chief*, the head of the Secret Service detail, that Jo was a devout Catholic who had been acknowledged by *El Panadero* at the end of the Saturday mass, so she had been assigned to prep *El Panadero* for his meeting on Easter Monday morning with *El Hefe*. Jo would also pick him up and escort him to the meeting, which was fast becoming an international media event.

It was a lucky break to be sure because it would give her an easy opportunity to debrief *El Panadero* on what if anything he had found in the email traffic at *La Tigrilla*. She would simply need to finesse getting some time alone and away from the Secret Service colleague, who would accompany her to brief *El Panadero*.

They met *El Panadero* at Emil's home in the hills shortly after the Easter service and were greeted with cold beer and a plate of delicious Easter bread, something of special significance to *El Panadero* from his distant past, they were told. He called it *Choreg*. It was the same bread he would share with her boss the next morning.

It was 100 degrees and nearly 100 percent humidity and, were that not enough to justify a cold beer, Jo had come to the conclusion that you never turn down a saint. Rob, her partner, also needed no arm twisting. Jo first joined Miriam in the kitchen to help transport plates and silverware to the garden table.

She noticed a large mixing bowl that looked like it had been made from stone on a back counter near the door to a utility shed. Miriam called it a *Molcajete,* an ancient cooking tool stretching back several thousand years to the time of the Aztecs and Mayans.

Traditionally carved out of a single block of vesicular basalt, *Molcajetes* are typically round in shape and supported by three short legs. They are used to crush and grind spices and other ingredients. The rough surface of the basalt stone creates a superb grinding surface that maintains itself over time as tiny bubbles in the basalt are ground down, replenishing the textured surface. A large pestle of the same material sat in the bowl. Both were coated with a bright yellow paste.

Molcajetes are frequently decorated with the carved head of an animal on the outside edge of the bowl, giving it the appearance of a short, stout, three-legged animal. In this case, it was a pig.

Apparently, someone had been grinding the yellow substance, which Miriam explained was often the case when *El Panadero* was baking something exotic. *He enjoys adding this and that to the recipe*, Miriam told Jo with a possessive sort of pride in her house guest, as she excused herself abruptly and took the *Molcajete* with her to the utility shed still wearing dish gloves. It occurred to Jo as she returned to the garden courtyard table with the dishes that the bright yellow in the bowl resembled the yellow clippings taken from the *Amandulla* the day before.

El Panadero was in good form, and he explained the family origins of the *Choreg*, the Armenian Easter bread he planned to share with the President when they met the next day. He would, he said, be preparing the *Choreg* dough for baking that afternoon. Jo and her colleague Rob then walked him through a carefully choreographed agenda for his tightly scheduled visit with the President the next day, and arrangements were made for Jo and Rob to transport *El Panadero* from Emil's house to the big event.

El Panadero deftly signaled the end of the meeting by uncustomarily failing to offer his guests a second beer and by asking Jo whether she wished confession one last time. He offered the same to Jo's companion who expressed his gratitude for the offer but decline with wry laughter saying it would do him little good because he was Jewish, although he wholeheartedly accepted *El Panadero's* parting blessing. Jo accepted the invitation to confession as her colleague excused himself to take a walk around the area.

Jo and *El Panadero* joined Omar in the study in front of Omar's laptop. *We should keep this brief*, she said. *Understood, El Panadero* replied. *At 'Red Eagle," so to speak, Jo, there seems to be both a 'Red Team' and 'Blue Team.' Please bring the first Red Team email up on the screen, Omar.*

> Twixt and between is the way I see it. The best chip is in the nodule with problematic biodegradability. The substrata component breakdown causes inflammation at the insertion site, sometimes severe with the occasional onset of sepsis. And to make matters worse, our best nodule in resisting degradability contains a chip that has proven unreliable. Tracking is impaired in areas near large electric grids and microwave towers. A "cluster" to be sure!

We will get to Blue Team's email traffic in a minute, but here is one more for good measure from Red Team. Next please, Omar.

> I have communicated to Osiris that you have made excellent progress against monumental technical challenges and that despite this he and I believe a new day dawns when magnanimity (or the appearance thereof!) is one of our

most effective counter weapons against the illegals. ICE enforcement shall never be the same once we can track individuals by name to their exact locations.

Jo, here now is something from Blue Team. Same facility but it would appear to be a different project. This too is from yesterday, probably written soon after your visit.

Please do not refer to our visitor in future emails by his surname. **Osiris** was impressed with our progress during his visit and wants to see acceleration to Phase 2. A report is to be provided within a week of his return stateside.

Jo, this must refer to Gorman. Look at the time stamp. It suggests that he is the man in charge. And I suspect he is not freelancing, El Panadero said. *Omar, Blue Team email number two, please.*

While I realize Phase 1 testing with animals to determine basic safety of the experimental molecules was truncated, we need better screening of subjects or more effective intervention in the event of adverse reactions. A handful of subjects will not be missed, but we must do better going forward. Remember, these foundational vaccine variants will arm us with the building blocks for a quick response in the future to Disease X and related threats to our countrymen.

Jo, look, the response to this email reads as follows, El Panadero said.

Two Polestar contractors have asked too many questions about their role in disposal operations and seem a bit squeamish. They will be reassigned. We can keep a lid on this for now, but there is no way to pretty up a *bb*. Should we consider other modalities?

There are many more like this, Jo. So, what do we have here?

On one hand, Team Red seems to be working on the kind of tracking device we pulled out of Emilio's shoulder, El Panadero continued. *I have seen another 'new day dawn,' and God help us if this one is anything like the last one.*

Then, not to be outdone, we also have Team Blue to consider.

El Panadero could see that Jo, who was sitting now, forehead cupped in one hand, staring at the laptop, was white as a sheet. For her part, she knew the slang they were using from her police days, and she had broken into a cold sweat as the realization swept over her.

Jo, this clinic to use the term loosely also appears to be an experimental site for vaccines, where people, should I say children, Vato among them I fear, have been harmed? You know, don't you to what the letters 'bb' refer?

Body bags, she croaked.

What the hell was she going to do now, Jo thought. In police work, you meet people who range from the sociopathic to the chronically prone to bad decision-making and everything in between. Rarely, did one encounter evil in the purest sense of the word. But here it was now, staring her in the face, and its source was undoubtedly the man she was sworn to protect.

Do we, you, have a plan, she asked? *If so, I'm in.*

I can't say that we, I, do, El Panadero replied. *Let us sleep on it or if you are prone, as am I, not to sleep at moments like this, then don't sleep on it. You must rejoin your friend now, Jo. Tomorrow is another day.*

* * * * *

There is not a day that I do not think about them – Ahmed, the brave, Al-Bari, the strong and kind, and of course Baba, the wise. You and I both have been fortunate to have people like this in our lives, Leo. Their memories sweep over me now like a warm and gentle wave as does the potent Raki you have chosen for our libation this evening. When I think of them, I am always joined in spirit by your parents —Hayk, my companion on those visits to the Bektashi and his beloved Mina whose Choreg, intended on that terrible day to nourish the Bektashi, set our life stories in motion, yours and mine, she said.

I came by the Raki thanks to a close friend, Leo responded, *a Turk and a Franciscan brother, as a parting gift on my last night in Moria on the Isle of Lesbos, where we were trying to sort out the futures of several hundred unaccompanied children among the thousands of stateless refugees there,* Leo said in reply. *Brother Isaiah delighted in telling me that your old nemesis, Atatürk, would indulge in late-night Rakı-sofrasi sessions where he and his closest friends and advisors debated issues of state late into the night, which no doubt included the extermination of Armenian Christians.*

Brother Isaiah knew nothing about my background and of course nothing about you, Leo continued. *I did not have the heart to tell him that Atatürk was so fond of the stuff that he drank up to a half-litre of Raki a day and died from cirrhosis of the liver. Atatürk was hardly a good advertisement for Raki as 'aslan sütü,' lion's milk, 'the milk of the strong,' and for its ability to sustain those who seek wisdom.*

Here's to cirrhotic livers, Anya replied, raising her small glass of opalescent liquid. *It could not have happened to a more deserving person than Atatürk. I hope it was painful,* she replied as she kept Leo company in the garden courtyard as the last minutes of Easter Sunday slipped away.

They were alone but for a tiny whiskered screech owl whose luminescent yellow eyes kept watch on them from atop a large mango tree. It would occasionally make its presence known to its companions at the garden table with a series of eight regularly spaced "boo" notes, the pitch slightly higher in the middle, slightly lower at each end of the refrain.

Leo noticed that Anya no longer sought to conceal her Bedouin tattoos as she had during the war years. He admired the cross in the customary Bedouin position on the chin as well as the Sufi symbol of a heart held aloft by wings on the back of her right hand. And at the hairline on the nape of her neck, he had earlier seen the jar afloat on waves, a symbol whose meaning had shaped the life of its bearer.

Her visit felt rich and reassuring to Leo, a hidden treasure newly rediscovered.

Their traditions, the Bektashi that is, are not well documented and each Bektashi clan tends to improvise a little, but they all have one thing in common, Leo. It is the belief that each of us is on a journey, and it is to find the good in our collective experience not to nullify it.

The friends we left behind in Germany many years ago gave their lives for essentially this same principle in their struggle to end the Third Reich. It is one thing to look back on that time and wax eloquent about their bravery over a glass of Raki. It is an entirely different thing to have lived in that harsh and terrifying moment, guided day in and day out simply by one's basic humanity and faith in the future. Yet they did and they saved the soul of the German nation from extinction.

The same faith animated Hayk and Mina and so many of our Armenian countrymen, who got up and brushed the dirt off their clothes every time they were kicked to the ground by Atatürk and his henchmen, Anya added without taking a breath. *And there were many such times.*

Faith was superstition and superstition faith to Leo still to this day. He found it not in absolutes like a good Christian might but in the exotic young woman who sat across from him, just as he had in the compassionate Dietrich and his irrepressible friend Fanon.

As with you, a brave young girl at the foot of Golgotha, Leo acknowledged respectfully.

Not skipping a beat, Anya continued, *you are nothing if not clever, Leo, so let me ask. Your end game is to break bread with this demon that the Americans have brought to power and to die instantly together in the sweet embrace of your yellow flower? Then what?*

Not waiting for an answer, Anya added, *The girl may escape blame, barely, but is this how we treat a comrade,* she asked? *The Bektashi would simply ask 'do two evils – La Tigrilla and your plan – create a good?'*

So, given the opportunity, Anya, if you had the shot, had the opportunity to eliminate the Führer at any point before or during the war years, what would you have done, Leo countered?

Leo, let me come back to that question. First, do you remember when we met in Berlin just before 'der Mauerfall?' It was November 9, 1989, to be exact, she said.

Yes, I remember celebrating with you as the Berlin wall came down and then your being taken away in handcuffs early the next morning. It was also the last time I saw Big Otto who ran his uncle's bistro on Savigny

Platz and Gerda, whose stubbornness and strong back are the reasons I am alive today. I envied their simple, joyful life full of children and grandchildren, which I finally stopped counting at some point along the way, Leo said warmly.

I suppose as people like to say today, you and I, Leo, were not 'wired' for a simple and joyful life. Yes, I was taken away because I was a Stasi agent working for the German Democratic Republic, in fact, I was top of the heap. It was my last assignment from Wild Bill Donovan because he suspected something like the wall coming from the Russians, and it did indeed in 1961. My assignment was what they called in the trade 'deep cover,' and I loathed every waking minute of it.

It was for me one part revenge for Harry's death. As you know, I led the team that rescued him and nearly 200 POW's in 1945 from Gusen, a satellite of the grotesque Mauthausen concentration camp, but the damned fool felt he had to take a few men back to make sure that everyone had escaped the camp in the confusion of the firefight with the Waffen SS garrison there. The SS got the worst of it because Harry was one hell of a warrior, but only one man on Harry's team managed to make it back to our position, and it was not Harry.

Leo, sensing the emotion in Anya's voice said, *I know how much he meant to you and you to him, Anya.*

War is a perverse matchmaker, Leo. By then Paladin and my faithful Pushpa were gone and, well, you knew Harry and can appreciate my affection for him better than most, she said.

Many in the GDR security apparatus ran those camps even though it was swept under the carpet. But apart from the vengeance I could exact on some of them, my fight, your fight, as I told you many years ago in Aleppo, is to ensure that with every generation of hardship, displacement and repression, the people we champion will grow stronger as those who despise them, those who turn a blind eye to their suffering, or wield their power and wealth to torment them, grow weaker.

My time in the Stasi made it possible for me to dismantle their capabilities plank by plank so by 1989 they were a ship adrift and unable to strike, unable to resist. We were by then a government of two minds. The younger leaders of the GDR were torn between political orthodoxy and envy of the opulence of the West. As such, they were reliably unreliable and putty in my hands. The gerontocracy that survived the war, of which I was considered one, provided what little backbone was left in the body politic of the GDR.

And to answer your original question, Leo, yes, I would have taken the shot. But what separates me from a crackpot in a downward spiral toward his own nullification through the nullification of others is the knowledge that nothing is resolved with a single shot.

The audacious men and women like Dietrich and Erika, most just everyday people who populated the German resistance, knew that. They were animated by the desire to find a principled and incorruptible True North in the tempest of the Third Reich, a journey that in many cases would lead them to the foot of a guillotine at Plötzensee Prison like Erika or a hangman's noose of piano wire at Flossenbürg like Dietrich and Wilhelm Canaris. Hans Dohnányi and Oster fared no better.

Many will say that in the overall scheme of things, against a regime whose evil left over 50 million dead in its wake, their successes were small. Although tell that to the many children and grandchildren of those they saved.

It is their legacy that matters now. Just as the Manna you so skillfully bake in your ovens nourishes your flock and brings hope to them, the memory of our friends, our 'aslan sütü,' our milk of the strong, guides the German nation and those of us still in the resistance unrelentingly to True North.

These are no idle platitudes, Leo, because the same forces that brought the Nazis to power then lurk today in the shadows in Germany just as they do here on the Mexican border. Today, like our friends many years ago, you are forced to confront the moral corrosion that made Atatürk, Hitler and this American president possible because it did not begin with them, nor will it end with them.

Cousin, my capable comrade in arms, you never forgot the example your family set for you, Anya said with a hint of pride in her voice. *Whatever it is you decide to do tomorrow, know you will have friends waiting for you.*

V. INGEMISCO

Through the dying thief forgiven
Thou to me a hope has given

—GIUSEPPE VERDI

La Concordia was submerged in a roiling sea of media people and their broadcast trucks, security personnel of various nationalities, and even a contingent of *El Hefe's* golfing buddies who were eager to get a selfie with one of the quaint locals as a souvenir of their expedition into the third world. The morning procession from the small Catholic school in the village to morning mass on this balmy Easter Monday was delayed by the collision of a BBC broadcast truck with one from France 24 and the ensuing fist fight between the drivers in the square facing the church.

Much of the Secret Service detail had been dispatched to the Welcome Center to ensure *El Hefe's* security at a breakfast hosted for his wealthy donors. At the same time, Jo and her team prepared the setting for *El Panadero's* meeting with her boss, which was to the North of the Welcome Center on a hilltop separating it from La Concordia.

Gorman, the propagandist who never missed a beat, saw the hill and the natural bowl below it as reminiscent of the hill upon which

Christ multiplied the loaves and fishes. He had seen it in the movies, *the Greatest Story Ever Told*, or some such movie, he said.

He was sure it would bring some added verve to the occasion and thrill the evangelicals in *El Hefe's* party. Guests were being carefully screened for admittance to the bowl hours in advance of the big event – donors to the front with porta-potties and a champagne bar and locals to the rear with a single open water spigot that had once fed the weed-bound animal trough next to it.

At the top of the hill sat something that looked oddly like an altar although there were no plans for anything more than *El Panadero* blessing the President before breaking bread with him. The faux altar, freshly planted for the occasion, stood between a low hedge of brilliant yellow flowers to the front outlining the crest of the hill and *El Panadero's* mobile bread ovens arrayed in a semicircle behind it.

Jo had dispatched her Secret Service colleague, Rob, to pick up the bread, which had been baked by *El Panadero* the evening before. The Styrofoam container, the size of a large beer cooler, had been taped shut for security reasons after the bread had been loaded into it and would be reopened by *El Panadero* when he arrived at his rendezvous with *El Hefe*.

Jo was uneasy. It was not about the logistics of the event. She could handle this and more.

It was instead about the confluence of all that was happening at *La Tigrilla* and *El Panadero's* imminent encounter with the man who had sanctioned it. She had taken it for granted that all would go smoothly until now. She had a better sense of the man behind the legend, and she could not envisage a scenario in which *El Panadero* would not act.

Would it be an impromptu address to the crowd as *El Hefe* nibbled on his bread, *hell*, she thought to herself, an impromptu address to the world! Would that come with a physical confrontation between the two men?

She had been trained that loose ends could not be tolerated in an operation like this, and what would play out on the top of that hill a few hours hence was rife with loose ends. She would be there to assist *El Panadero* and have the perfect vantage point to intervene if it became necessary.

Jo had also be dispatched to pick him up, which would give her a chance to discuss *El Panadero's* plan on their way to the event. She had not shared any information with her superiors about the circumstances at *La Tigrilla* and the implications for *El Hefe* and found herself in a strange place where following her conscience meant violating the oath she had taken when she became a Secret Service agent.

The implications of this decision for Andrej and Jara, especially if it blew up in her face, also weighed heavily on Jo. She reminded herself that betraying her boss was not the same as betraying her country, but this did little to make her feel better.

For now, Jo the cop would operate on a cop's instinct. *La Tigrilla* was not only wrong it was criminal. She was committed, but what was she committed to? She needed to talk to *El Panadero* about the next move.

* * * * *

Rob, I am heading out now to retrieve his eminence. No need for you to make the trip again. In fact, if you would keep an eye on the container of bread while I am gone, it would be much appreciated. It should stay sealed until I return, Jo said.

Roger that, he replied.

Jo had parked her jeep next to the faux altar and, as she pulled away winding down the hill on a dirt track along the perimeter of the bowl, she looked in the rearview mirror to see the hustle and bustle surrounding the scene partially obscured now by the hedge of yellow flowers.

She would have to go into the village to reach the small road to *El Panadero's* house, and it was slow going. The pace of the trip relaxed her as she methodically dodged one bottleneck after another. The yellow hedge on the hill came to mind again along with the image of a large and unruly plant in a walled garden with the same yellow flowers, one image joining the other like the pieces of a jigsaw puzzle. She could feel the hair on the back of her neck bristle.

A third and final piece of the puzzle came into focus as if a spotlight had just been cast on it. It was a *Molcajete* with yellow residue and Miriam's pronouncement that *El Panadero* enjoyed using exotic ingredients in his baking.

Holy shit, she growled!

Was this it? Was the man she admired so much planning to poison the man she was sworn to protect? Was *El Panadero* also planning to consume the poisonous bread himself in one final act of resistance?

Fuck, fuck, fuck, she said loud enough to startle the people near her jeep! She had to confront him. She could not let this happen!

Jo landed on the horn and hit the gas hard sending the milling crowd running for cover from the charging jeep.

* * * * *

The balance of the short trip seemed to take an eternity and Jo hurtled out of the jeep toward the front door when she pulled up to the house. It was unlocked, and she did not bother to knock before entering. She called first for Miriam, then Omar and finally for *El Panadero*. There was no response.

The cavernous house was empty as was the garden patio. Jo eventually came to the study and opened the door to find an envelope taped to the TV screen and book with a threadbare leather cover propped up on the screen under it. The note in the envelope read as follows:

> *Jo:*
>
> *Please accept this book as a small token of my esteem. It was given to me by one of the greatest men that I have ever known, and it was poorly understood by me at first.*
>
> *It is the Book of the Martyrs, and my friend's name was Dietrich Bonhoeffer. Read about him.*
>
> *I used to scoff at the men and women depicted in the pages of this book much to Dietrich's consternation. I could not understand why they could not or would not find a clever way to circumvent the martyrdom that the book treated as inevitable.*
>
> *He and so many of our mutual friends understood what I did not in my callow youth —that principle is the flag we carry into battle and some battles cannot be avoided.*
>
> *Such is the case with La Tigrilla. Omar and Miriam have taken transcripts of the emails to Washington to be shared*

with the FBI. Contained herein are instructions on how to find them there.

Please accept my apologies for the abrupt change in plan and my blessing for the battle ahead. I know that you are up to the challenge.

—Leo

The note made it clear that *El Panadero* was not in the house nor likely to return, and Jo immediately called Rob on the satellite phone clipped to her belt.

Rob, our guest is not here. Is the container of bread secure?

Well in a manner of speaking, yes, Jo. I have eyes on it, but Gorman who has been acting like a real Nazi this morning, opened it and took a huge slice, he said.

Little did Rob know how close he had come to a true description of Gorman, Jo thought to herself.

Can you see him?

Roger that. He is directly in my line of sight about 25 feet away ordering people around.

And the bread, she asked?

I have eyes on what's left. What's up, Jo? What's going on?

Secure the rest of the bread and keep an eye on Gorman. And if El Panadero arrives under his own steam, ping me. I am going to take another look around here and then return to base.

What should I say to the chief and to Gorman, Rob asked?

Nothing at the moment, I will call you just before I get on the road.

Roger that.

It was clear to Jo as she surveyed the scene that Miriam and Omar had packed and gone. She opened the door to *El Panadero's* room, which was tidy but for a fine white layer of baking flour that seemed to dance in the sunlight from the window and coat every piece of furniture. His clothes and personal belongings suggested a man with a Spartan lifestyle.

Perhaps, he was not gone for good, she thought. She was angry with him but desperately wanted to see him again.

What are you doing, Father? Where are you, Jo said aloud?

Her satellite phone beeped, and Rob said presciently, *we may have found our missing person. Is there a TV nearby*?

* * * * *

Jo returned to the TV in the study and switched it on first to a Telenovela with two scantily clad lovers rolling around in the high sea grass of a windswept sand dune. She scanned the channels and quickly arrived at CNN International. It took her a minute to understand what she was watching. There was a crowd but oddly no crowd noise.

The CNN reporter on scene, the one who had tapped her on the shoulder the day she first met El Panadero, said, *we are told, he will speak any minute now.*

Her gut told her who "He" would be. As the camera panned, it looked like the entire village of La Concordia was standing in the clearing in front of the compound at *La Tigrilla*. The sawhorses and barbed wire that had once formed the outer security perimeter were nowhere to be seen. The security guards and their dogs were also gone.

Then the CNN camera panned unsteadily toward the front of the crowd to settle on two or three rows of women who starting chanting,

Libera a nuestros hijos, Libera a nuestras hijas. They were chanting "free our boys and girls."

Jo, come in. Are you seeing what I'm seeing?

Roger that, Rob.

How's Gorman, she asked?

Apeshit would not be too strong a term to describe it. Look now, Jo!

Apeshit, she didn't care about. Jo said a silent prayer, however, that he would survive *El Panadero*'s *Choreg* if indeed it had been laced with Amandulla.

The CNN camera crew had managed to work its way to the front of the crowd and there a stood a sole figure. It was *El Panadero* in a flowing white Alb over which he also wore a long white and gold stole, the same liturgical garments he had worn on Easter Sunday. His Alb was sashed at the waist and tucked into that sash was a curved sheath that concealed all but the ornate handle of a large dagger, a curved Bedouin Khanjar, capped by an ivory hilt in the shape of a lion's head.

* * * * *

They had assembled as the Easter celebration in the town square wound down the night before. Leo circulated quietly via his lay deacons, the nuns at the small parochial grade school and the Catholic Youth Organization with a call to march on *La Tigrilla* to end the wrong there. The nature of the problem had incensed the women of the village, who took control of organizing the march and, as Easter Sunday tilted into Easter Monday, there were few in the village who were not setting off on the 10-kilometer trek to *La Tigrilla*.

Most of the interlopers who had swarmed the village during Holy Week were fast asleep but for a CNN camera crew and one from France 24. They had been briefed on the objective and the danger posed by the security forces at *La Tigrilla*, which made the spectacle even more intriguing to them.

To mitigate the risks to his flock, Leo had arranged for some of Emil's men to neutralize the security guards at the outer perimeter, which in this context meant quietly catching them off guard and marching them and their dogs at gunpoint away to a nearby ravine where they would be detained. As dawn broke, Emil's men also cut the power grid disabling the intrusion sensors and allowing the procession to proceed undetected along the dirt track and up the gravel road to the complex of Quonset huts in the American camp at *La Tigrilla*. The overnight security detailed logged the outage as another episode of animals chewing through the remote power lines.

Leo knew he was playing with fire, but he hoped that the presence of camera crews and the sheer number of people would forestall an overreaction from the well-armed security detail in the encampment. And so, it was in the early morning hours, as Jo was heading to retrieve him from the house, *El Panadero* and hundreds of villagers emerged from the mist of a heavy marine layer that had blown in from *Tres Picos* on the Pacific Coast, to stand before the encampment as startled guards took to the rooftops and the chain link fence on the outer perimeter of the camp.

The villagers of La Concordia would celebrate morning mass with *El Panadero* in the clearing before the camp, surrounded on the other three sides by the bramble and brush of the subtropical forest. The significance of Easter Monday was primal to Leo, and he prayed for the children imprisoned there as he did for the thousands on the Cilician plain who fled their homes so many years before. He also did not forget the handful of friends who once congregated in a hot bakery at Oderberger Strasse 15 one Easter Monday past, who molded a boy into a man.

* * * * *

As *El Panadero* gave the final blessing at the end of mass, Jo dropped to both knees as if she were there kneeling in the crowd. The tears in her eyes that she was now unable to contain washed over her face because the saint in waiting, her irksome hero had indeed chosen a different path. No Amandulla, no poison, instead a parry that was courageous in the face of the fire power she knew the camp could rain down on him.

Rob, come in.

I'm here, Jo.

Where is Gorman?

He has gone to the Welcome Center to collect the President, Jo.

Does he know what's going on.

Damn straight and that is why he sped out of here like a bat out of hell.

Rob, tell the chief, we need to get a team up to La Tigrilla. Now! The priest and those with him are in extreme danger.

With press cameras in *El Panadero's* face, he began. Jo thought that the camera took decades off his age and she could easily imagine the boy to whom he now referred.

When I was young and, fortunately, I am not so old as to have lost sight of those days, a majority of my countrymen allowed a tyrant to succeed by not daring to protest, and in this they were no different from human beings under any dictatorship. That tyrant was Adolf Hitler.

Here we are today to protest something that is uncomfortably close in so many respects to the evil that darkened those days. Simply put my friends, this complex before which we stand is an American concentration camp that conducts vile experimentation on the helpless children of immigrants who want nothing more than to raise their children in a land where hard work can bring them a good life.

As we will show with documented evidence, the shame attached to this place rises to the top of the American government. We have shared copies with you in the press and with the FBI in Washington, D.C.

Today, we dare to raise our voices in protest against the tyrant who sanctioned this vile place and to free our children from this criminal enterprise.

* * * * *

Jo, come in, Rob said through the satellite phone, now sitting next to the TV.

Jo here, she said as she picked up the satellite phone, her eyes still glued to the TV.

Jo, I convinced the chief to send a tactical detail and it is on its way. The chief is pissed and wants to know what the hell is going on with you.

Rob, I will explain when I return.

One more update, Jo. El Hefe and Gorman are on the move. Looks like they want nothing to do with this. Marine One lands in five minutes.

A roar of shock and terror rose on both ends of the satellite phone at the sound of gunfire, as Jo and Rob watched.

* * * * *

It is said that if one has the misfortune to be killed by a sniper one never hears the sound of the shot because the bullet arrives first. In the aftermath of that momentous day, many claimed to have seen a single puff of smoke on the roof of a Quonset hut. Others say they heard a sharp crack.

Was this eternity that lay before him, a place he could see, feel and touch, or his surging brain chemistry from which sprung an illusion of the eternal that would remain fixed for all time? Doubt gave way with the last beat of his heart to fulfillment because Leo now understood that Little Otto had been right all along.

Everyone was there. Little Otto with *I told you so* written on his small face, Big Otto and Gerda on either side of Mehdi, his mentors Dietrich and Erika standing with Hugo and the indomitable Marushka. And standing apart from the group was the enchanting Jani who greeted him with a playful smile.

All were waiting and smiling, and he knew then they had carried the day at *La Tigrilla* ending the scourge of the monster who had created it. There would be ample time to celebrate with his friends, he told himself, when a hand warm to the touch took him by the arm. It was Anya. She locked her arm in his as they moved as one toward the outstretched arms of Mina and Hayk.

EPILOGUE

If you are reading this Epilogue, I hope that it means you liked the book. I started writing this story with a singular focus on the German resistance to Hitler and its main protagonists. However, as you know by now, the arc of the story extends beyond the period of the Second World War to include the Armenian Genocide on the front end and the ongoing tragedy at our Southern borders on the backend.

Sometimes a story takes on a life of its own.

I was inspired to write this book by two of my heroes in the German Resistance to Hitler. The first is Dietrich Bonhoeffer, the brilliant theologian, whose somewhat complex theology of resistance made acting to confront tyranny a matter of Christian faith, a conclusion he did not come to easily. However, to give the seeker of truth a lot more to chew on, Dietrich also believed that taking such action was not always guiltless.

This brave young man was executed by hanging at dawn on the 9th of April 1945, age thirty-nine, at Flossenbürg concentration camp in Bavaria exactly two weeks before the camp was liberated by American troops. Bonhoeffer was stripped of his clothing and led naked into the execution yard where he was hung with piano wire along with six others who populate this novel including Admiral Wilhelm Canaris and General Hans Oster, Canaris' deputy. Hans Dohnányi, Dietrich's brother in law, was murdered that same day at Sachsenhausen concentration camp just outside of Berlin.

Less renowned perhaps but no less courageous is Erika von Brockdorff, the second inspiration for this book. I knew nothing about her story before I started researching this book but, fortuitously, I was introduced to her daughter by an organization called ZeitZeugen-Börse (www.zeitzeugenboerse.de), which is dedicated to preserving and disseminating an oral history of Berlin.

I spent a delightful two hours with Saskia von Brockdorff, who had just turned 84, and her friend Frau Roloff, who was then 94, at Saskia's flat in the bucolic suburbs of Berlin, where they mesmerized me with stories of wartime Berlin over *Tee und Kuchen*. They were also kind enough to give me a quick German lesson on how correctly to pronounce the title of my book —*Die Bäckerei.*

More importantly, Saskia's story about her mother Erika was riveting and galvanized my desire to write *Die Bäckerei*. Erika's story is largely as it is told in the book although Little Otto's role in aiding her is entirely fictional.

There are two important facets to Erika's story that I would like to highlight. First, Erika was just an everyday person like you and I. She had a young daughter to raise, held down a job and dreamed of a day when her husband would return from the war to his wife and daughter to live happily ever after. The fact that the German resistance to Hitler was populated by ordinary people like Erika whose principled lives set them at odds with the overwhelming majority of their countrymen, is one of her story's most incongruous and in my view compelling aspects.

More compelling still, is that Erika was able to smuggle a letter written to her then four year old daughter, Saskia, out of Plötzensee

Prison where she would soon be guillotined at age 32. Saskia was a young woman in her twenties before she ever saw that letter, which had been withheld from her by her father, perhaps out of embarrassment that he had survived the war and Erika had not. Growing up, Saskia believed that she had been abandoned by her mother during the war.

A transcript of the letter, given to me by Saskia, follows this Epilogue.

Let me take a minute to fill you in on a few other biographical details. Wilhelm Canaris, the spymaster of the German war machine, was a complex and heroic figure who kept an open line of communication to British intelligence and was a key figure in efforts at the highest levels in Germany both to assassinate Hitler and to negotiate an end to the war with the British, albeit on equal terms, which would prove to be unacceptable to the British. He also saved countless Jews and was the architect of *Unternehmen Sieben* featured with a fictitious spin in the book.

Hitler and Himmler also took separate paths in unsuccessful overtures to end the war in the period of 1939-1944. In addition, Dietrich's outreach to George Bell, the renowned British Bishop, and Bell's efforts on his behalf with the British government, are well documented although the scene at Sigtuna Monastery in Sweden is a work of fiction.

The audacious Reverend Erik Perwe and Countess Maria von Maltzan did indeed work under the auspices of the Swedish Lutheran Church in Berlin to save hundreds of Jews including those secreted out of Berlin in furniture crates as depicted in the book. Both are fascinating people, but von Maltzan, that is to say, Marushka, who survived the war has a biography worth savoring. Her exploits were portrayed by Jacqueline Bisset in the 1984 film, *Forbidden*, and she was granted the *Righteous Among the Nations* designation from the Israeli Government for those exploits.

So too was the Reverend Erik Perwe for his remarkable work. Perwe did indeed die in a suspicious plane crash over the Baltic Sea on the Berlin - Malmö route in November 1944. I moved this event up to November 1943 in service of the plot. However, the enchanting and fictitious Jani did not die heroically with him.

The daring and lovesick Hugo Graf von Reinfeld is fictional and based on a young Swede by the name of Eric Wesslen, who rounded out the heroic triumvirate of Perwe and Marushka starting in 1942. He had originally come to Berlin to study landscape architecture and developed an informal relationship with the *Schwedische Kirche* in Wilmersdorf as a parish worker.

Wesslen was *up to his ears*, however, in much of the clandestine work of the Swedish Lutheran Church, and his special talent was indeed to free Jews and political prisoners from the SS by buying them back. It is said he had a highly placed contact in the SS, but he had also formed a network of guards and policemen who would let arrested Jews and political prisoners disappear in exchange for money, coffee, liquor and chocolates. Working with Marushka and Perwe, he would hide these fugitives until they could eventually be *exported*.

On a personal note, the aforementioned and enchanting Jani is the second character in two successive novels, who is modeled to some degree on my wife Jane. Both the character Jane in my novel *Bocage* and Jani in this book die, albeit heroically. My Jane has protested the treatment of these characters, and I have assured her that it is nothing personal.

It is also worth noting here that the *Righteous Among the Nations* honor is bestowed by Yad Vashem, the Shoah Martyrs' and Heroes'

Remembrance Authority, established in 1953 by the Knesset of Israel. The *Righteous* were defined as non-Jews who risked their lives to save Jews during the Holocaust. In total, 27,712 men and women from 51 countries have been recognized as of January 2020, accounting for more than 10,000 authenticated rescue stories.

One of the most fascinating stories among them is Hedwig Porschütz, who is portrayed in the book. From 1940, Porschütz worked in Otto Weidt's workshop for the blind as a stockroom worker and later as a typist and stenographer. She worked closely with Weidt to protect his employees by hiding Jewish women in her home and illegally trading for supplies on the black market to ensure their survival.

Although it should be said that her activities pilfering a blue *Schliersee* jacket from KaDeWe to help Leo smuggle Ingrid out of Berlin were not among her many actual accomplishments.

After the war, Hedwig's requests to be compensated for political persecution and to be titled an *Unsung Heroine* were rejected by West Berlin authorities in 1959. At that time, the authorities did not consider helping Jews an act of resistance!

Due to her prior work as a prostitute during the depression, Hedwig was also regarded as an immoral and dishonorable person. She died penniless in 1977.

It took until November 2010 for Hedwig to be honored by the city of Berlin with a memorial plaque, which was placed at her former address, *Feurigstraße 43*. Yad Vashem recognized her as *Righteous Among the Nations* in 2012 and a street in Berlin Mitte, *Hedwig-Porschütz-Straße*, was named in her honor in 2018.

On a less uplifting note, Stella Goldschlag, the Greiferin who betrayed her fellow Jews who had gone underground, plied her trade for the Gestapo until the end of the war. Estimates of the number of

U-Boats captured through *Blonde Poison's* efforts vary from 600 to 3,000.

She was arrested by the Soviets soon after the war and served ten years of hard labor. She then returned to West Berlin and was tried again and sentenced to another ten years imprisonment, a sentence that was suspended because she had already served time in the Soviet Union.

Stella agreed to become a Greiferin for the Gestapo in large part to avoid deportation with her parents after they were arrested and tortured by the Nazis in 1943. Her employers would eventually break their promise to Stella by deporting her parents to Theresienstadt concentration camp and from there to Auschwitz where they were murdered.

Stella is said to have died by suicide in 1994.

Finally, an American bomber did in fact crash into the roof of KaDeWe during the bombing on the night of November 23, 1943, the fateful night of Leo's calamitous soiree at Café Alois, which is entirely fictional, although the existence of the café on Wittenbergplatz run by Hitler's half-brother is not. However, the *Liberty Belle* and the call sign, *niner-niner-charlie-baker* are fictional.

To wrap up *Die Bäckerei* after 150,000 words, it has been suggested by my readers that I add several questions about my subject for you to ponder as is the custom these days with books like this. Before I turn you loose on them, a final word.

I have used, arguably, overused words like heroic, brave, audacious, etc., in describing my subject matter – the everyday people of the German resistance to Hitler. However, I can think of no better way to describe them.

At the level of the political elites, the dithering German Generals failed to remove from power the man they helped put there. Their on-again, off-again efforts were beset by a conflux of ambivalence, hubris, bad timing, and bad luck, the heroic efforts of Wilhelm Canaris, Hans Oster, Hans Dohnányi and Claus von Stauffenberg (author of the ill-fated July 20th assassination plot) notwithstanding.

At the street level, the resistance of everyday Germans consisted of individuals and small, isolated groups, operating largely in a vacuum, that were unable to mobilize widespread political opposition. I have chosen to focus on some resistance groups at the expense of others, e.g., White Rose, Uncle Emil, etc., with no slight intended to any.

One could argue that they failed —one and all. Although tell that to the thousands of descendants of those they managed to keep one step ahead of the Gestapo, which brings me to the title of the book, *Die Bäckerei*.

Bread as a source of physical and spiritual sustenance figures prominently in the plot as does the biblical reference (John 12:24), *unless a kernel of wheat falls to the ground and dies, it remains only a single seed. But if it dies, it produces many seeds.* On one level, the writer is talking about the mystery inherent in bringing a loaf of bread to life, so to speak. A stalk of wheat from which flour is made cannot grow unless the seed first dies. On another level, he is talking about the mystery of Faith, a Faith that compelled Dietrich, Erika and others like them to sacrifice their lives to save the soul of the German nation.

I have a few people to acknowledge and thank. First, there are my "test readers," whose opinions about plot and character were extremely helpful. Then there is my wife Jane and her sister Susan whose commitment to rigorous quality control helped me produce a much better story. Finally, I would like to thank Martin Sauter. M.A., Ph.D. (yes, for whom one of the story's arch villains is named), whose keen editorial eye and deep knowledge of German history and culture were invaluable. By the way, Martin is also one of Berlin's most sought after private tour guides.

In closing, I was drawn to the everyday people of the German resistance because I potentially see my own unfinished story in theirs. Would I know what to do and have the guts to do it if I found myself in similar circumstances, as Jo did in *La Concordia*? This hypothetical has become especially trenchant with the ascendance of fascism from the Yangtze to the Dnieper (Ukraine) to the Rio Grande and with the all too real conundrum that has emerged in our political discourse over of whether and when political violence is a permissible form of resistance.

As Anya, or the spirit of Anya, tells Leo on her nocturnal visit when he is struggling to formulate his next move with El Hefe, *it is their legacy (the Resistance) that matters now because their example will guide us to a moral 'True North.' Like our friends many years ago, we will inevitably be forced to confront the moral corrosion that made Atatürk, Hitler and El Hefe possible because it did not begin with them, nor will it end with them.*

READER QUESTIONS

1. What are your attitudes about the German people who lived during World War II?

2. Were you aware that there was a German resistance to Hitler? How would you characterize what you knew?

3. Do you know the story of the July 20, 1944, assassination plot led by Claus von Stauffenberg? What other efforts were there to remove Hitler from power?

4. Compare and contrast the societal forces that led to the Armenian Genocide and the Holocaust.

5. What set the Armenian genocide apart in its treatment of women?

6. Could a tyrant like Hitler emerge again in a modern democracy?

7. Describe the development of Leo and the pivotal moments that led to his commitment to save others?

8. Who was your favorite character and why? Do you see yourself in any of the characters?

9. What did the Bedouin symbols, when first mentioned, signify to you personally?

10. Is a hero made or born?

11. What distinguishes a resistance fighter with a gun from a terrorist with a gun?

12. Which method of resistance would you pursue —quiet and behind the scenes or louder and upfront, and why?

13. Do you think that the carpet bombing of Berlin that killed thousands of innocent civilians was justified?

14. Has this book influenced your own view of the world in any way and how?

15. Is there a moral equivalency between Leo's mass murder of Gestapo and SS functionaries at Café Alois and the reasons that drove Americans to storm the US capitol building on January 6, 2021?

Letter from Erika von Brockdorff to Saskia von Brockdorff in the last days of Erika's life.

Ein Kassiber Erika von Brockdorffs.
(Abschiedsbrief an ihre Tochter Saskia, mit Bleistift auf beiden Seiten eines 7cm mal 7cm grossen Zettels geschrieben)

Meine liebe Saskia. Ich hoffe, dass Dich diese Zeilen einmal erreichen werden. Dann werde ich lange nicht mehr sein. Aber ich wollte Dir mit diesen Zeilen sagen, dass ich in meiner Zel[illegible] sehr oft, ja am meisten nur an Dich gedacht habe. Du bist jetz[illegible] erst 5 Jahr alt und noch bei meinen Eltern. Sie werden Dich über den Schmerz trösten, dass Du nun keine Mutter mehr hast. Mein liebes, liebes Kind, ich wünsche Dir für Dein Leben alles nur erdenkliche Gute. Mögest Du ein offener, ehrlicher, gerade[illegible] Mensch werden. Du warst mir alles, ausser Deinem Vater, den ic[illegible] über alles geliebt habe. Es ist ein Trost für mich, dass wenigstens Dir der Vater erhalten bleibt, wenn ich auch heute noch nicht wissen kann, wie dieser unselige Krieg ausgeht, ob er noch einmal zu den Soldaten geht, und er Soldatenglück hat. Abe[illegible] so hart kann das Schicksal ja nicht mit Dir verfahren, dass es Dir auch noch den Vater raubt. Auch wenn ich nicht mehr bei Euch sein kann, werde ich um Euch sein. Wenn Du heute auch noch sehr klein bist, eine kleine Erinnerung wirst Du doch an mich bewahren. Das wird mich auf meinem letzten Gang trösten. Weisst Du noch, wenn ich sagte, mich liebt wohl keiner, und Du kamst gesprungen, legtest mir Deine kleinen Arme um den Hals und sagtest, doch, Mama, ich liebe Dich so sehr? In diesen 4 Monaten habe ich noch einmal die ganze Zeit von dem Tag an durchlebt, da ich Dich in der Klinik zum erstenmal in meinen Armen hielt. Man kann mir viel vorwerfen, aber eines nicht, dass ich keine gute Mutter gewesen.- Ich habe das Beste gewollt, daran sollst Du Dich immer halten, wenn man mich klein machen will in Deinen Augen. Ich habe den festen Glauben, dass mal eine Zeit kommt, wo man anders über mich und die vielen andern denkt. Ich hätte sie auch noch gern erlebt. Nun bin ich aber auch nicht traurig, dass es anders ist. In mir ist so eine wundervolle Ruhe und Klarheit. Sei 1000 mal gegrüsst und geküsst von

Deiner Mutter

Ein Kassiber Erika von Brockdorffs.
(Ein letzter Wunsch und Gruss, mit Bleistift auf beiden Seiten eines 4 cm mal 4 cm grossen Zettelchens geschrieben)

Erika Gräfin von Brockdorff
Alex 14.1.1942.
Ich möchte gern, dass meine Tochter Saskia v. Brockdorff meine Puderdose als persönliches Andenken an ihre Mutter erhält. Sie hat mich diese vier Monate hier im Gefängnis begleitet. Sollte dies nicht möglich sein, möge man ihr aber doch wenigstens den letzten Gruss übermitteln.
Saskia v. Brockdorff b. Schönfeld, Dramburg Pom. Nordmarkstr.5.
Ich grüsse meine Eltern, meine Schwester und meinen Bruder und alle andern Verwandten. Erika

Secret message by Erika von Brockdorff
(farewell letter to her daughter Saskia, written with pencil on both sides of a 7cm x 7cm slip of paper)

My dear Saskia,

I hope these lines will reach you some day. At that point, I will have long since ceased to exist. But with these lines, I wanted to tell you that, in my cell, I have often -- yes, mostly -- thought of you. You are only five years old now, and still with my parents. They'll help you find solace for the pain of not having a mother any longer. My dear, dear child, for your life I wish you everything good imaginable. May you become an open, honest and straight person. You were everything to me, except for your father, whom I loved more than anything. It is a comfort for me that at least your father remains for you, though I can't know today how this disastrous war will end, whether he will return to the front and have a soldier's luck. But fate can't be that hard on you that it robs you of your father, too. Even if I can't be there with you, I will be around you. Even though today you are very little, you will keep a small memory of me. That will give me solace on my final path. Do you remember when I said that maybe nobody loves me, and you came running up to me and put your little arms around my neck and said: Yes, Mama, I love you so much? Over these four months I have re-lived once more the entire time since the day when I held you in my arms for the first time in the clinic. They can accuse me of a lot, but not of one thing -- that I wasn't a good mother. I wanted the best for you, and you should always remember that when they want to belittle me in your eyes. I have the firm belief that some day, a time will come when they will think differently about me and the many others. I would have liked to have lived to see that. Yet, now I am not sad that it is different. Within me is such a wonderful peace and clarity. Be greeted and kissed a thousand times by your mother.

Secret message by Erika von Brockdorff
(A last wish and greeting, written with pencil on both sides of a 4cm x 4cm slip of paper)

Erika Countess of Brockdorff
Alex 1. 14th 1942
I would like for my daughter Saskia von Brockdorff to receive my face powder box as a personal memento of her mother. She has accompanied me during these four months here in prison. Should that not be possible, may at least my last greeting be conveyed to her.
Saskia von Brockdorff c/o Schönfeld, Dramburg Pom. Nordmarkstr. 5
I greet my parents, my sister and my brother and all other relatives. Erika